DO YOU BELIEVE IN MAGIC?

ANN MACELA

Medallion Press, Inc.
Printed in USA

DO YOU BELIEVE IN MAGIC?

ANN MACELA

DEDICATION:

To my critique group: Mary Jane, Rita, Victoria, Laura, Sherry, Noirin, and Jan. This book would not have been as good as it is without your generous help, astute critique, and unflagging support.

Published 2007 by Medallion Press, Inc.

The MEDALLION PRESS LOGO
is a registered tradmark of Medallion Press, Inc.

Typeset in Adobe Garamond Pro
Printed in the United States of America
10-digit ISBN: 1-9338361-6-4
13-digit ISBN: 978-1933836-16-4

10 9 8 7 6 5 4 3 2 1
First Edition

ACKNOWLEDGEMENTS:

Many thanks to my critique group; to Paula and Helen, good friends and great readers; to sisters-in-law Connie, Laraine, Elaine, and Barb and nieces Megan and Caryn for their reading at the "beta" level. Thanks also to Windy City RWA, RWA Online, and especially to JoAnn Ross and her group, for their encouragement and support.

And, as usual, to my very own "Blue Mage" and computer wizard, Paul, without whom I couldn't have produced a word and who is always ready to be my "research assistant" and helper in spellcasting.

PROLOGUE

Floating along on a bed of rainbow colors, he'd never felt so pleased or comfortable or happy or smug in his life. In a few minutes, his soul mate would be there, and they'd come together in their First Mating.

He was ready. More than ready, his body told him.

Where was she? Why wasn't she there yet?

He stood up and began to pace. The colors of his bed swirled and coalesced into the walls, floor, and ceiling of a room. A door appeared on the far side. It opened.

Through the door walked his dream woman. Tall, blond, gorgeous, built.

Oh, yes, built.

But clothed. More than merely clothed. Dressed in what appeared to be a suit of armor right out of the Middle Ages. Complete with some sort of round helmet in her hand. It looked like a basketball.

What the hell was going on? She was supposed to mate with him, not fight. She was supposed to be naked like he was. How could they mate with that metal between them?

"Why are you wearing that ridiculous getup?" he asked.

She looked at him like he was crazy—or like she was totally surprised to see him there at all. Maybe she hadn't heard him. She turned, as if to leave.

He shouted, "Where are you going?" His voice seemed to come out in a whisper.

She glared at him, ran her eyes up and down his body. That only served to excite him more, and his erection grew to painful proportions and throbbed to match his increasing heartbeat.

He reached for her, but she retreated a step. Held up her hand like a traffic cop. "Stop!"

He couldn't move. He'd run into an invisible wall.

"No," she said. She put the helmet contraption on her head, lowered the visor, turned, and stalked out the door, slamming it behind her.

"No!" he yelled.

"Noooo!" he groaned as he realized his soul mate—the only woman in the world for him—had left, abandoned him, denied their connection.

"Noooooo," he whimpered as the enormity of her action hit him in his magic center, and he doubled over in pain. Without a soul mate, he was doomed to live alone and lonely forever.

"No," he snarled as he thrashed in his bed, finally

waking himself enough to come to his senses.

He sat up, panting and sweating like he'd just played a fast quarter on the court. His chest ached as if somebody had punched him. And he felt horribly, totally sad and abandoned.

He concentrated on breathing until his body was back to normal.

What a nightmare. Where had it come from? He never had bad dreams, much less anything like that . . . disaster.

He must have been spending too much time around his sister and her new husband. All their soul-mate togetherness must have rubbed off on him. Reminded him he might meet his mate soon.

Not that he wanted to. He was only thirty-four and wasn't ready to settle down. He had at least a couple more years of glorious bachelorhood. The dream was just a manifestation of his wanting to get his latest job going and over with.

Why, then, did he feel so wasted? So alone? So lost?

Like a bad hangover, the feeling of utter devastation followed him into the shower, and he had to concentrate on programming spells before it went away.

CHAPTER ONE

"Are you accusing me of hacking into our system, Herb?" Francie Stevens looked her boss straight in the eye while dismay warred with outrage in her mind. How could he think such a thing about her, that she would be a party to such an act? And against the company she worked for?

She grasped the edge of the conference table between them, ready either to push back from it or to propel herself across it at her accuser, but she wasn't sure which.

"Not at all, Francie." Herb Greenwood, vice president for information technology at Brazos Chemical, made placating gestures with his hands. "Don't jump to any conclusions. Just calm down and we'll explain. Bear with us, okay?"

Francie struggled to control herself. This news was the last thing she expected. She told herself to follow Herb's advice and calm down, but to listen very, very carefully to what was being said. She wasn't going to be a fall guy or a scapegoat for anybody. She pushed her glasses up on her nose and nodded stiffly, but didn't relax her posture. "Okay."

Herb waved a hand at the man sitting on Francie's right. "As I was saying, thanks to Clay Morgan here, we've discovered someone's been invading our computer system for a couple of weeks. Clay installed a program that tracked the guy back to his computer. That computer turned out to be your desktop at home. We know you're not the one doing the hacking."

"But how?" she asked. "How can someone be using it without my knowing? Nobody's broken in. I'd certainly notice something like that." She glanced at the two flanking her on each side, Morgan to her right and Daria Benthausen, Clay's sister and fellow consultant, on her left, then looked back at Herb. "How do I prove I'm innocent?"

"We already know you are. You don't have to prove anything." Her boss ran a hand through his thinning brown hair and turned his bright blue eyes on Morgan. "You explain, Clay. You were running the operation."

Francie concentrated on the consultant. Herb had hustled them all into seats at the table after she came into his office, and she had not really studied the man when they were introduced.

So this was the famous Clay Morgan. She had heard of him, but never met him: the man reputed to work magic on computers. Francie didn't know about his effect on computers, but he certainly had one on women.

Even she, immune though she was to good-looking, charming men and armored behind her clothes and her glasses, could feel the potency of his masculinity. No wonder Laura, the system administrator, had practically swooned over him when she relayed the tale of how quickly he had fixed the network and one of the servers after an electrical disaster last year. No wonder rumors swirled of his reputation with women—which included his never dating one for very long.

Tall, dark, and handsome, indeed, with coal-black hair and an action-movie hero's firm chin and jaw, although the small hook in his nose saved him from being beautiful. Six foot five if he was an inch—one of the rare men to whom she would literally have to raise her eyes.

She reminded herself again of her immunity to such men. Not that he was trying to be charming; at the moment he appeared positively grim, but with an overlay of confidence . . . and perhaps arrogance. She'd always liked self-confidence in a person, male or female, but arrogance was a turnoff. Especially arrogance based on good looks coming from genetics, not hard work. She wondered if he really lived up to his "computer wizard" fame.

If she had to be honest—as she tried to be to herself, at least—there was something about him that called to her, stirred up her insides. She'd probably been listening too much to Tamara and her pronouncements about Francie's need for a fling and some romance. But she couldn't stop from fidgeting under the intent gaze from his pale gray—no, silver—eyes. She shivered and shifted in her chair. His gaze as sharp and hard as a sterling-silver blade, he was staring at her as though he could see into her soul.

"We've had you under surveillance, Francie. Herb was certain you were *not* the hacker, but *I* thought it better to put someone on a watch first to discover what was really going on."

His words cut through her anguish and anger, and she looked at him with a feeling somewhere between horror and fury. "You actually had someone following me?" The fact that she had never noticed added a layer of dread to the mixture of reactions scrambling in her brain.

"Yes. It's a good thing we did, because it cleared you of any suspicion," Clay answered, his tone cool and certain—as if he had all the answers to her questions.

Francie clenched her fists on the table to keep them from shaking. She took a deep breath and forced herself to focus on the words, "cleared of any suspicion." Relief and curiosity pushed her anger aside—but only slightly. She couldn't help sniping at the man who lounged in his chair with such total self-assurance. "Well, I'm very happy to hear my innocence has been proven to your satisfaction, Mr. Morgan." She turned to Herb. "Look, I need some straight answers. What is going on? Did you suspect me, too?"

"No, I swear to God, Francie . . ." Herb began.

"Francie." From Francie's other side, Daria interrupted and put her hand on top of Francie's clenched one. "It's okay," she said calmly.

Francie turned her gaze to the consultant and knew immediately Daria was going to help with this strange situation. The small woman with dark curly hair and bright green eyes was on her side. A light flicker from somewhere caused her to blink for a second, but then the men seemed to fade into the background as Francie focused on Daria's next words.

"Herb believed in you all along," Daria said. "We used surveillance to see if there was anyone who might have access to your computer when you weren't home. Last Wednesday night when you went to your party . . .?"

"My book club." Francie nodded.

Daria nodded also. "While you were there, someone entered your apartment and used your computer to access our system. He ran right into Clay's trap. When the operators reported the hacker's attempt to log in, Clay sent the investigator following you back to your place. Through the window, the investigator saw a man sitting at your computer. He followed the man when he left. We know who he is. We know you didn't have anything to do with the hacking."

A real wave of relief washed over Francie, and she closed her eyes for a moment to take a deep breath. She opened them again and asked, "Who was it?"

"Kevin Brenner, Tamara Lewis's boyfriend," Daria replied.

"Kevin? Kevin!" Disgust surged through Francie at the revelation. She pushed her chair back and almost rose before accepting the statement as the truth and falling back into the seat. "Oh, *ick*, to even imagine Kevin in my apartment, going through my things."

Just saying the words left an awful taste in her mouth, and she scraped her tongue over her teeth as if she could remove both it and the idea. Then several impressions clicked in her brain. "He looks at me sometimes with a weird expression, as if he knows all my secrets and has a big one of his own." She shuddered in revulsion and hugged herself. Kevin had broken into her home, but . . . "How on earth did he get in?"

"Francie, he had a key," Daria said softly. "How could he have gotten it?"

"Tamara's my best friend and lives across the court-yard. She has my key and I have hers so we can water each other's plants and bring in the mail if one of us is traveling. He must have stolen it from her."

Francie thought about her friend a few moments, then swung her gaze around the table, settling on Herb. "Look, I can't believe Tamara is mixed up in this. We've been friends for a long time, ever since we were room-mates at UT. We're like sisters, and I can guarantee her computer skills consist of word processing, spreadsheets, and accounting applications. She doesn't have a dishonest bone in her body. There's no way, no way at all, she could be hacking or be an accomplice to Kevin."

That statement raised another problem in her mind, and she couldn't help blurting out, "I have to tell her. Oh, my God, she's going to be devastated to find this out about Kevin. What if she's really serious about him? She hasn't said so, but . . ."

"Francie, we can't tell her," Daria said. "Not yet."

"Why not?"

"Because we have a plan to find out what Brenner is after, and we'd like you to help us with it," Herb said. "We don't know if he's working on his own, or if he's doing it for his employer. He works for NatChem, did you know that?"

"Our competitor? No, he never told me, and I didn't ask. Tamara just said he was in sales, a manager, I think, but he never discussed business with me." She clenched and unclenched her fists to lessen her seething tension. All she could think was, *That putrid son of a* . . .

"Will you help us, Francie?" Herb asked.

Francie blinked at Herb's question, then sat back in her chair and crossed her arms. She frowned at him for a moment while she contemplated his question. You bet she'd help. She'd do whatever it took to get back at the slimeball. She'd like to punch him in the nose. She'd like to see him roast in hell. She'd like to . . . *Stop*, she commanded herself. Throwing a hissy fit in front of her boss would not help the situation. With an effort, she grabbed hold of her roller-coasting emotions and couched her answer in calmer tones. "Certainly. What do you want me to do?"

Clay watched Francie calm herself down. She'd looked for a minute like she wanted to beat Brenner up. He raised his eyebrows at Daria, who nodded affirmatively, their prearranged signal that her spells had worked and Francie was telling the truth.

He'd been studying her while Herb and then Daria explained. Francie was quite the mousey little computer nerd. Well, maybe not so little. Only about five or six inches shorter than he was. He couldn't tell much about her body in her bulky sweater. For once, he regretted the tendency in Houston, even in September, to keep buildings chilly to combat the outside heat, thus forcing women to wear jackets and sweaters indoors. He didn't think much of her clothing choices, either—definitely bland, to go with the pulled-back blond hair and horn-rimmed glasses.

But then he noticed how fine and almost luminescent her skin was, how the streaks in her hair ranged from pale yellow to gold to almost amber, and how large her brown eyes were behind the glasses. They were sort of a smoky brown, not unlike his favorite single-malt Scotch, and the sharp and wary look in them as she reacted to his earlier statement lived up to Herb's assessment of her intelligence. Clay speculated briefly that there might be more to her than his first impression of "computer nerd, female variety."

Then she shifted in the chair and the sweater pulled

tight across her chest. *Oh, my.* It appeared Ms. Mouse was by no means flat chested. In fact, the evidence indicated she was quite the opposite—in a word, *built*. He felt his body stir slightly, but he ignored it. Right now, he had a job to do.

From the corner of his eye, he observed the spell aura around his sister flare as she boosted the enchantments she had already cast on herself. Francie jumped just the smallest bit as the spells' power increased. Like a small percentage of the nonpractitioner population, the woman wasn't oblivious to magic. She didn't appear alarmed, however, since she settled herself in her chair, her attention on her boss. She probably hadn't even noticed anything. Good. Daria's magic would work as it was supposed to.

Then he spoke, drawing Francie's gaze directly to his. "We want to get close to Brenner, find out what he's after, if his company is behind him or if this is simply a freelance effort on his part. He's a lousy, inept hacker. He wanders around the system haphazardly. We can't tell what he's looking for, or if he's even after any particular piece of information. We thought we'd frustrate his invasion attempts, then supply him with a real expert and see if he will take the bait of using someone who's a better hacker than he is, who might be looking for easy money, and whose ethics match his." Clay paused and drawled, "I'm to be that someone."

He could almost see her mind working behind those

big brown eyes. She appeared at first to be somewhat confused, but she seemed to pull herself together quickly after breaking eye contact with him.

She nodded slowly. "It might work. Kevin does seem to be ambitious. I've always thought there was something shady or untrustworthy about him. Something not quite right. How do you expect to get close to him?"

"By becoming your boyfriend."

He had meant to say "posing as" instead of "becoming," but once the words were out of his mouth, Clay realized he liked the idea very much. Despite her drab clothing, he was attracted to this woman. There was just something about her. He couldn't quite decide what it was, but he felt its presence. He shrugged mentally; real attraction would make his playacting all the more convincing. He couldn't help grinning at her reaction.

"Wh-what? M-m-my boyfriend?" Francie stared at him. What was he talking about? She almost reeled physically from the idea but managed just barely to keep her wits about her. She didn't want or need a boyfriend. Certainly not him. Especially not him. His grin, however, was devastating—and challenging. On top of the confidence and arrogance, he was definitely a charmer, and he knew it.

She shook her head and attempted to marshal her arguments. Who would believe someone like Clay was interested in her? How would they possibly convince

Kevin, and especially Tamara? What about her determination to keep away from men like him? She tried to put absolute conviction into her next words. "I really don't believe your plan will work, Mr. Morgan."

He waved his hand dismissively, and a mischievous glint sparkled in his eyes. "Nonsense. And under the circumstances, you'd better call me Clay."

"I'm hardly your type." She was beginning to get a little angry at his presumption and drew herself up primly. She welcomed the emotion. Anger might pull her out of this confused state. Didn't the man have eyes in his head to see she was not interested in doing such a thing? There must be another way.

Evidently not, because he stated with more than a whiff of conceit, "This plan will work. An introduction through you is our best chance to find out what he's up to. Remember, it's your computer he's using to hack. Until we know more from him, he can always claim you let him use it."

He had a point there, she conceded, but only to herself. To him, she said, "How are we supposed to have met? Tamara knows my comings and goings and most of my friends. Won't she be suspicious when you suddenly pop into my life?"

"We'll say we met at the computer workshop Herb sent you to last month. Two computer geeks with a common interest." He smiled, then sobered. "Oh, I just thought of something. Is there any other man in your life at the moment, Francie?"

"No," and a shake of her head were all she felt capable of for an answer. Common interest, indeed. His smile seemed to bind them together. A shiver went down her spine as she had the sudden feeling he could see straight through all her defenses. Her breastbone began to itch severely, and she put a hand on her rib cage, pressing with her thumb to alleviate the torment in as ladylike a manner as she could.

"That's fine," Clay said. "We won't have to worry about another player then. If I'm your boyfriend, you can introduce me to Brenner, and we can spend time with him and Tamara as a couple with no one the wiser about our underlying purpose."

"Oh, God, Tamara," Francie groaned and shook her head. "I really don't like the idea of deceiving her."

"I understand your feelings," Daria said, in a woman-to-woman tone. "But if she were to break up with him, we'd lose our entrée. How good of a liar is she? If you tell her, could she pretend to still like Brenner, stay as his girlfriend? Or if they're sleeping together, could she continue that level of intimacy without alerting him?"

"Probably not. She's not a very good liar. Everything shows on her face." Francie sighed. "She already knows I'm not particularly fond of Kevin. I've made no secret of the fact I think she's too good for him."

Francie felt some of her anxiety lift as she analyzed her friend's situation further. "On the other hand, Tamara doesn't usually stay with one man for long. Now that I think of it, I'm surprised she took the time for Kevin at all and that they've lasted as long as they have. She's been channeling most of her energy into her business. She owns a boutique in the Galleria area, but I guess you know that. We don't talk about their relationship much."

"How long have they been seeing each other?" Clay asked.

"About three months. They met at a club."

"We'll have to see if he knew of her connection to you when he met her," he said. "If so, he's been using her from the beginning. In the normal run of things, how long would you expect them to continue as a couple?"

"Another month or so, if Tamara is true to form. Oh, Lord, I hope she's not in love with him. I could lose a very good friend over this if she thinks I've betrayed her." She felt her stomach lurch as her sense of loyalty to the company, her own integrity, and her anger toward Kevin warred with her loyalty to and love for Tamara. How could she keep such a secret from her friend?

"Place the blame on me when the time comes," Herb stated. "Tell her I threatened your job if you didn't help us."

"Oh, Herb, I can't do that, but thanks. I almost wish you hadn't told me about Kevin."

"We considered it," Herb replied, "but I couldn't do that to you. I knew you'd want to be a part of stopping this screwball. The good thing is, we found him before he managed to frame you for his hacking. You know how important it is that we get to the bottom of this, Francie. Can we count on your help?"

"I guess I'm in," Francie acknowledged wearily, finally leaning back again in her chair. What else could she do? She had a responsibility to Brazos Chemical and to Herb especially. He'd been the one who hired her. But she also had to protect Tamara somehow, and if it took pretending to be Clay's girlfriend, so be it. "I don't seem to have a choice. What do I do first?"

"I'll pick you up at seven for dinner tonight," Clay said.

"Tonight?" Francie exclaimed. So soon? She'd hoped for more time to get used to the idea of it all. She'd assumed all she'd have to do was introduce him at one encounter with the other couple. Now they were going to *date*?

Clay studied her for a moment, gazing into those smoky eyes, wondering how they would look with the fire of desire in them. He discarded the thought before it really registered and, leaning toward her over the table, stated, "It's Friday, a perfect date night. We need to establish our relationship quickly, so I'm going to sweep you off your feet."

He'd had a revelation of sorts while watching her react to the scheme. She was an intelligent woman and fiercely loyal to her friends. And courageous and ethical as well. She was really a golden lioness, not a brown mouse. Despite obvious misgivings—mostly, it appeared, directed against him—she was going ahead with his plan.

The more he observed her, the more he'd bet the money for his next computer upgrade that her dress and those glasses were camouflage. He could tell from the lack of refraction the lenses were plain glass. Why she wore them, he didn't know, but he'd really like to find out what she looked like without them—and without her god-awful sweater. His body stirred again, more forcefully this time, and he idly rubbed at a small itch on his chest under his tie.

Out of the corner of his eye, he noted his sister looking back and forth between him and Francie. Daria had a particularly intent expression on her face as she studied them. He'd have to remember to ask her about it later. Right now, he concentrated on the tall blond next to him.

Francie stared into his eyes for a moment, mesmerized by the combination of male confidence, attraction, and something else she couldn't quite put her finger on. Then her common sense and determination kicked in.

She'd be damned if she'd let this, this . . . consultant, attractive or not, get the better of her. She'd help them put a stop to Kevin, but she'd keep her feet planted firmly on the ground, thank you very much. "Well, if that's all we have to talk about at the moment, I need to prepare for my meeting this afternoon." She looked at Herb and raised her eyebrows.

"Why don't we get together on Monday, say at ten, and discuss our next moves? That will give you, Francie and Clay, the chance to think through the situation and discuss the best approach to Brenner," Herb said. When the two nodded, he leaned back and rubbed his hands together with a smug expression on his face. "We're going to teach this idiot a real lesson. Go to your meeting, Francie. If you need anything, let me know. Thanks for all your help."

"Seven o'clock," Clay reiterated as she opened the office door. "We'll go someplace nice."

CHAPTER TWO

Francie arrived at her apartment out past the Galleria shopping district about six, showered, put on her make-up, did her hair into a French twist, and then stood in front of her open closet. She alternated between dithering about what to wear and fuming about the arrogance of the man who was taking her out "someplace nice."

Why couldn't she have invented a previous engagement? Not that it would have helped, she snorted as she took a dress out and held it to her in front of the mirror. He would have ordered her to break it. Overbearing man. He was probably stubborn, too.

She stared at herself in the mirror and sighed, then gave herself a little shake. She was in this conspiracy now, and she might as well make the best of it, be civil to the man. They both had a job to do. And who knew, she might learn some useful computer tricks from this hotshot consultant.

When the doorbell rang, she tightened the sash on

her robe and hurried to the door, praying Clay had not decided to come early. She peeked through the peephole and saw only Tamara's red hair.

"Hi!" her friend said when Francie opened the door.

"Oh, thank goodness." Francie leaned against the door in relief.

"What's the matter? Are you sick?" Tamara stepped in, and Francie closed the door.

"No. I have a date. He's coming at seven."

"A date?" Tamara's face lit up with delight. "A real date? Tonight? Who with? How did this happen? Did you finally give up your self-imposed idiocy to have nothing to do with men?" Her eyes clearly stating that Francie needed help, she looked her up and down. "At seven? We don't have much time. Tell me everything while we get you dressed," she ordered as she dragged Francie into the bedroom.

Tamara started rummaging in the walk-in closet, scrutinizing and rejecting clothing items. She stopped long enough to stick her head out and command, "Talk to me, Francie. Where are you going?"

"Dinner. Someplace nice, he said." Francie sat on the bed, totally exhausted all of a sudden. How in the world did she get into this situation? And she had to keep the truth from her best friend.

"Okay, I get the picture." Tamara pulled out one of the dresses she had forced Francie to purchase last year about this time. "This will be fine. It's more a Sunday-go-to-meeting dress than a 'date' dress, but the orange and brown pattern fits the fall season. It has sleeves, so you won't need a jacket in the restaurant, and it's still in the high seventies outside. Don't you just love Houston in September? Anyway, the colors will play off your brown eyes and blond hair. And glory be, it shows off your fabulous figure. Who's the man?"

Francie struggled to remember the story as she took the dress from Tamara. "Uh, his name is Clay Morgan. We met at the computer workshop I went to last month."

Tamara rolled her eyes as she turned to Francie's lingerie drawer. "Just what you need, another computer type. I can see him already: scrawny, thick glasses, bad haircut, pale with a computer pallor from being inside all the time, and the usual pocket protector. He probably thinks 'someplace nice' would be one of the upscale burger joints. Well, I'll do what I can to help you. A date is a date, and it gets you out of the house. So, what happened? Did he just call you out of the blue?"

"Uh, no. He's a consultant. We ran into each other in the lobby of my office building." Francie wasn't about to correct Tamara's assumption of Clay's description. That would raise too many more questions, and she didn't have the time or the strength to answer them now. After she put on the underwear and hose Tamara pulled out of the drawer, she looked down at her peach lace-and-satin bra and panties set. "Isn't this a little too much? It's just a date."

"I've always approved of your lingerie, you know, and no, it's just right. I'm glad you didn't give up nice underwear when you went drab." She held up another set, this one a light lavender. "Boy, howdy. If the guy could only get a glimpse of this, he'd probably keel over on the spot. No chance of that, unfortunately," she ended with a sigh.

"Tamara," Francie said, injecting a warning note in her voice to leave the subject alone. She shivered. She didn't want to even consider Clay seeing her in her underwear. She stepped into the dress and put her hands through the sleeves.

"Okay, I'll be quiet." Tamara came behind her and zipped up the dress, then dug around in Francie's jewelry box. "Here, put on this necklace and these earrings with it. And hold still while I punch up your makeup. Do you have to wear those glasses?" She nodded at the spectacles resting on the chest of drawers.

"Yes." Francie shoved them back on her nose when Tamara was finished with the eye shadow and blusher. She needed some sort of defense against Clay, and in this dress, her glasses would be all she had.

"You don't need this hairdo, either," Tamara ordered, taking down the twist and fluffing her mass of blond hair so it fell over Francie's shoulders. "There. That looks nicer."

The doorbell rang. "Finish dressing," Tamara said.

"I'll let him in."

"But . . ." She was too late. Tamara was out the bedroom door and closing it before Francie could stop her. All she could do now was put on her shoes, change purses, and hope Tamara wouldn't grill Clay about their meeting.

Tamara whirled back into the bedroom within a couple of minutes, closed the door, and leaned back against it panting, her hand on her upper chest.

"Tamara, what?"

"Francie, that is no computer nerd out there. That is an absolutely gorgeous MAN, in capital letters, in a navy suit I know for a fact cost big bucks, and he's got a smile that would tempt a saint."

"Oh, please." Francie rolled her eyes.

"And with a deep voice that slides over you, and a backside that cries to be touched, well . . ." She grabbed Francie by the shoulders, gave her a little shake, and whispered fiercely, "Francie, you listen to me. Don't you dare go into your don't-touch-me act with this one. He's definitely *not* Walt. I don't care what his brain is like or if he just wants your body. Let yourself go! It's about time you had some fun with a man, and if ever there was a man to have fun with, it's this one!"

She stopped to take a breath. "My goodness! I'll never think of computer nerds the same way again. And if he has a brother, or a cousin, or even a friend like him, promise me you'll introduce me." Tamara increased her shaking of Francie until they were both vibrating.

"Tamara!" Francie whispered back, just as strongly. "Get hold of yourself. This is only our first date."

Tamara stepped back, gave Francie a once-over, straightened her necklace, opened the door, and whispered, "Go get him, tiger."

Clay had grinned to himself as he watched a flustered Tamara disappear down the hall. He was obviously not what she had been expecting, but then other women had had similar responses to him before. False modesty aside, he knew what he looked like, and after all, females had been drawn to him ever since puberty. It made for a certain amount of self-confidence even his two sisters had not been able to bedevil out of him. He wondered what Francie's reaction to him would be when they were alone. She had certainly run through a gamut of emotions during their meeting that morning.

He knew what his reaction had been to her. Attraction, pure and simple. Daria had even noticed. Worse, she had teased him when he took her home after the meeting, suggesting Francie might even be his soul mate.

Yeah, right. Just because she had found hers among nonpractitioners, she was on the lookout for his with every woman she met. She was correct about one thing and one thing only: Francie wasn't a practitioner. They had both looked her up in the Registry before the meeting.

Lightning in the form of another nonpractitioner soul mate wouldn't strike the Morgan family twice, Clay calculated. Since warlocks could be the lovers of non-witch women without incurring the soul-mate bond, he had clear sailing where Francie Stevens was concerned. And he intended to be her lover before this hacker mess was over. He put out of his mind Daria's malicious little-sister grin and her taunt—"Just you wait, big brother, your soul mate will knock you right off your high horse."

He looked around and idly rubbed the end of his itching breastbone as he waited for his date. Her apartment, full of light, color, and plants, displayed the real Francie, he decided. The pictures and paintings on her walls were brightly impressionistic, and their hues were picked up in the throw pillows on the pale green couch. An overstuffed dark green chair had a book on its seat, and a Tiffany-style lamp sat on the end table next to it. An oak coffee table contained some larger books and a vase with golden mums. No dull, drab colors here. No petite, spindly furniture, either, but that wouldn't fit her size—or his. He immediately felt comfortable.

Francie walked into the room, and he turned to greet her.

He almost gasped. He'd been correct, those clothes *were* camouflage, he thought as his eyes roamed over her. This was more like it, with a dress outlining her body. And what a body, he realized, feeling his own responding to her high full breasts, trim waist, flaring hips, and long, long legs. Lord, have mercy, she was gorgeous.

"You look very nice, Francie. Shall we go?" he managed to get past his vocal cords as his eyes came up to meet hers, and he noticed hers grow smokier.

Francie felt tension crackle like lightning between them. His eyes had flared silver and darkened when she appeared. He had affected her senses in Herb's office, but it was nothing compared to seeing him in her own living room. Suddenly the room was much smaller, and the pull toward him, the urge to touch, much greater.

Just looking at him made her blood course faster through her veins, heated her all the way through, scrambled her brain. She repeated to herself her vow to keep her feet on the ground around this dangerous man. And *dangerous* was the correct word, she decided—dangerous to her equilibrium, dangerous to her friendship with Tamara, dangerous to her determination not to let a man hurt her again. She had to swallow to say, "I'm ready."

Tamara preceded them out the door. "Bye, y'all have fun," the redhead said at the bottom of the stairs, as she turned the other way toward her apartment.

"Thanks, we will," Clay answered, ushering Francie toward the parking spaces at the front of the building. "So, that was Tamara," he commented as they stepped out of the gate guarding the apartment complex.

"Yes. I told her we ran into each other in the lobby of my building and you asked me out. I hope it was all right. I didn't want her to think you were in the Brazos offices because she might tell Kevin."

"Perfect. I thought we'd go to a restaurant in the Montrose-Westheimer area, if it's okay."

"Fine," she replied.

He helped her into his silver Jeep Grand Cherokee, and they were quickly on their way. Traffic was heavy and took much of Clay's attention, so they didn't talk much, just made inconsequential comments about the weather and the idiocy of some drivers.

Lack of conversation gave her the chance to think, to remind herself of her decision to make the best of the situation. Clay was stuck with her as much as she was with him. For all she knew, he could be unhappy with having to play her boyfriend. She resolved to be pleasant company; not only would the time go faster that way, but she'd show him she wasn't intimidated, either. She had to do a good job for Herb and Brazos Chemical.

It was all strictly business.

They made good time, and soon were seated at a candlelit table in a cozy corner. After they ordered, Francie looked around the restaurant. The décor was a mixture of old and new, with antique-looking chairs at the tables and contemporary art on the walls. The styles somehow melded into an elegant, welcoming atmosphere. "I've always wanted to come here," she confided. "Several people at work have recommended it highly."

"I've always liked the place," Clay replied with a smile. "It was originally an old house the owners renovated and added several rooms for the restaurant. They serve a great brunch on Sundays."

His smile caused a tiny shiver to run down Francie's back. Damn, the man looked good by candlelight. His silver eyes practically gleamed, and she wondered at the spell of attraction he seemed to be casting on her. But, no matter. She'd ask questions to keep him talking. "I enjoyed meeting your sister. What exactly is her specialty? I've never heard her name connected with computers."

"She's a human-relations and management-organization consultant. She studies a company's management system and people and recommends changes for efficiency, competence, and teamwork." Clay stopped talking, leaned forward, and stared at her intensely.

"What?" she asked, sitting stiffly upright. She felt his scrutiny all the way to her toes.

He reached across the table, removed her glasses, and put them in his coat pocket. "The candlelight reflects off your glasses, and it hides your eyes. You don't have to hide from me, Francie," he said gently.

Maybe not, but they certainly helped her maintain the fiction of invulnerability. "I need those. Give them back, please." She sounded prim and proper and scared, even to herself. She held out her hand for the glasses.

"No, you don't," Clay said. He took her hand, brought it to his lips, and kissed the back of her fingers, his eyes never leaving hers.

Francie snatched her hand back. It tingled as electricity raced all the way up her arm and scattered across her body. "What are you doing?" she whispered while the additional question rattled around in her brain: *And why do you suddenly look like you want to eat me up?*

His gaze may have been hot enough to melt steel, but his voice was as bland as bread pudding when he answered. "Francie, we're supposed to appear to the outside world as lovers. We need to get used to each other's touch." He suited his action to his words and ran his hand down her arm. She shivered. "If we don't, when we touch in Tamara and Kevin's presence—and we have to touch to be convincing, you know—*they* will know something's wrong between us."

"All right," she acquiesced glumly, but she moved her arm away from his hand. "I get the point. Just don't push it, okay?" Maintaining equilibrium was going to be harder than she thought. His caress had sent a bolt of heat following his fingertips, and her fingers still tingled from his kiss. She took a sip of her ice water to cool off. It didn't help.

Clay just grinned as he watched her efforts to distance herself. The waiter's arrival with the wine and the appetizer interrupted the need to reply to her request. Which he had no intention of honoring. He had been in a state of semi-arousal since she walked into the living room in her apartment. Now he felt himself responding even more as her eyelids lowered and her eyes grew smoky again. Playing out this charade with her was going to be a combination of pleasure and pain, he could tell already.

It's no charade, he heard a voice in his head say with utter conviction. The certainty of the statement stamped-ed through his body and settled in his bones, causing him to catch his breath. Where had the notion come from? No matter, he dismissed the thought to study the way the candlelight showed her luminous skin to great advantage, and he smiled again in appreciation. Yes, there was definitely more to this "mouse" than met the eye.

As he gazed at her, he wondered what had happened in the past to turn her off men. To make her hide under those awful outfits and glasses. It had to have been something like a bad relationship to cause such a beautiful woman to disguise herself as she did. He did not doubt he would discover the reasons, even without his sister's witchy abilities to draw the truth out of anyone.

But now it was time to settle down and get to know Francie. They had to work together amicably if they were going to catch Brenner. She seemed to be trying to be pleasant. He would be the same. After the waiter left, he asked typical get-to-know-you questions about her family.

She answered readily enough and relaxed as they munched on the fried calamari. "I'm an only child. My parents were older, in their late thirties when I was born. Daddy's a middle manager in accounting for a company in Dallas, and Mother is a secretary for a lawyer. What about yours? Besides Daria, I mean."

"Dad's also an accounting type, a consultant. I don't know how we ended up with three consultants in the family. Maybe it's in the genes, because none of us likes taking orders or being in a managerial structure. My younger sister Gloriana's a botany prof at UT. She and Mother own a plant nursery and herb farm not far from Austin. They're in the midst of planning a restaurant and cooking school on the property. I'll have to take you up there sometime."

She didn't seem to notice the implications of his last statement, but asked instead, "How did you get involved with computers?"

That led them into a discussion of their mutual interest, stories of disasters, comical encounters with programmers, complaints about department heads who expected miracles from their computers, the Internet, and the computer industry in general.

By dessert, Francie was astonished to realize she was totally beguiled, thoroughly relaxed, and enjoying herself immensely. Clay had surprised her, by listening to and commenting carefully on what she said, by having many of the same interests as she—classical and country music, beaches, science fiction, and more—and by demonstrating a self-deprecating and slightly off-balance sense of humor similar to her own. The man was simply downright fun to talk to.

Furthermore, and most important, his appeal was not forced or phony. She'd become an expert of sorts over the past few years and could spot phoniness across the proverbial crowded room. Even Tamara agreed about Francie's ability, although it had not stopped the redhead from hooking up with underhanded, two-faced Kevin, something Francie still could not understand.

She shrugged to herself. One way or another, Kevin wouldn't be around much longer. As for Clay, if this dinner was any indication, they could work together. And it never hurt to have around a little eye candy, because he certainly was nice to look at. Maybe taking part in this deception wouldn't be as difficult as she feared.

Clay took a sip of his coffee while he watched her daintily demolish dessert, a fudgy cake with chocolate mousse icing and raspberry sauce. Thank goodness she didn't eat like some of those women who barely touched their food and didn't enjoy what they did swallow. She'd never get along with his family if she had.

His last thought drifted out of his head as he watched the play of candlelight picking out the golden highlights of her hair, the lick of her lips capturing the last little bit of cake, and her hands cradling the coffee cup. He could easily imagine that hair spread out on his pillow, her tongue tangling with his, her hands on him. Stifling a sigh, he tried with only minimal success to control his body. Think of her intelligence, their common interests, the job they had to do, he told himself.

Then it was time to leave. They made the drive back to her apartment in a companionable silence, listening to country-and-western on the radio.

As they walked up to her stairs, Clay could feel Francie becoming tense again, wary of him, probably because he had tucked her arm in his. To distract her, he said, "Don't be obvious about looking, but I think we're being watched."

"What? Who, where?" She jumped, but he wouldn't let her get away from him.

"Tamara. I just saw the curtains move in her apartment."

"Oh, good grief. I know she means well, but really!" She dug in her purse for her keys.

"Invite me in, Francie," Clay said as he took the keys from her and opened the door. When she looked up at him wide-eyed, he continued with a matter-of-fact tone, "I need to see your computer and show you how to tell if Kevin has been on it."

She made a jerky nod and led the way into the apartment. Clay followed, took off his coat, and laid it on a chair.

Francie put down her purse on a side table and turned to face him. "I really enjoyed myself tonight, Clay. Thank you for dinner."

She was nervous, and he almost smiled. It was so nice to know he was having an effect. But when her eyes fell on his lips and her own opened as if waiting for his kiss, the effect was on him, and he had to tell his muscles to relax. Then she clamped her lips back together and defiantly raised her eyes to his. She was certainly not going to let him kiss her.

Or at least not yet. He only said mildly, "You're welcome," and raised his eyebrows. "Your computer?"

"Oh. This way." She quickly led the way to the apartment's second bedroom, which she had converted into a home office.

"Very nice. Good computer," Clay said, loosening his tie and glancing around at the filled bookshelves, the comfortable easy chair with ottoman by one window, and the desktop computer by the other. Not as good as his own setup, of course, but certainly adequate.

Francie sat down at the computer and turned it on. Clay pulled up the extra chair from against the far wall to sit at her side and slightly behind her. His placement put him close enough to catch her scent, a light peachy fragrance, and he felt his nostrils flare. To pull his attention back to the computer took more effort than he wanted to admit, even to himself.

"The last time Kevin dialed in to Brazos, a program uploaded to this machine." He showed her how to find and start the little application. The screen immediately filled with characters and symbols.

"Why, these are the keystrokes and mouse clicks he used, aren't they?" Francie exclaimed after reading the code for a moment. "This shows exactly how he went about logging on and where he tried to go. Oh, I see what you mean," she said, scrolling the display down. "He really doesn't seem to know what he's doing, does he?"

"Not that we can tell. Do you see anything to help us?" He sat back to better enjoy her enthusiasm. Finally, someone who understood and appreciated his work.

"Give me a minute here. There's something in his keystrokes . . ." She leaned closer to the screen and studied the displayed data.

"You know," she said with a hint of victory in her voice, "I'll bet he's trying to find sales and order information. Look here and here." She pointed at three lines on the screen, scrolled it down, and pointed at two more. "If he's working for Brazos's competitor and could learn what we charged our customers, he could undercut our prices and steal them right out from under us. I think he hasn't found the right database or application yet, although he's come close."

"Damn," Clay said. "Herb and I didn't talk to someone like you who knows the applications from the user's point of view. Are you sure?"

"Yes, one of my areas is Order Entry. See, here and here," she pointed at the screen again. "It looks like he's trying to open the sales-order program. If you know how to display orders, you can see exactly what sort of deals the salespeople have made with each customer—volume discounts, rush orders, special shipping, all the rest."

"If I remember correctly from a conversation with one of their IT people at a conference, NatChem uses a different software package from Brazos. It's obvious

Brenner doesn't know how to navigate in yours or where the data resides. Let's go over this with Herb on Monday. There should be a way to set a trap for our hacker. Scroll back to the beginning."

He pointed to the display. "Each time Brenner tries to access Brazos, the program will create another file and put it in this folder. See, here's the name, number, and date of the file. All you have to do is come to the file and open it to see what he's been up to. Here's the time of his access. If you'll send me a copy by e-mail, I'll study it for trapping possibilities."

"I'll do it right now. How do you think he gained entry into our system?" she asked as she called up her e-mail program.

"Offhand, it looks like he used a hacking program he found on the Internet. God knows they're out there. Herb is going to upgrade his security and firewall as soon as we're done." He gave her his e-mail address, then rose and looked over her library while she sent the message.

"About tomorrow," he began, but stopped as he spied a title he knew.

"Yes?" She turned to him.

"Do you like this guy?" he asked, pointing to one of her favorite sci-fi authors. "So do I."

For some reason pleased by his approval, she watched him peruse her shelves for a minute before she shut down the computer. She was surprised to realize that he seemed to fit here in her office, as though it was a natural place for him to be. "Tomorrow? What about it?"

"Yes, it's Saturday." He shot a glance her way. "Do you have any plans for the evening?"

"Uh, no, I don't think so." She managed to keep her tone even, but she couldn't help dropping her eyes. Her seemingly nonchalant answer didn't fool him one bit, she knew, because of the way he smiled. He could probably read her like one of those books, see the emotions she was trying to hide: consternation that she had answered him truthfully and wariness about what he would say next. She tried to project a distant coolness to portray disinterest, but deep down lay an underlying excitement she couldn't deny.

"The musical *Wicked* is playing downtown. Let's see it and have a late dinner afterward."

"I don't know," Francie said, sounding even to herself like a wimpy coward.

"I'm supposed to be sweeping you off your feet, remember? We have to make our relationship look good. What will Tamara think if I don't follow up on tonight?"

"Oh, heavens, Tamara." Francie's shoulders slumped. Every time she turned around, she ran into the problem of deceiving her best friend. She knew exactly what Tamara would think: Francie had driven away the perfect man. She cast about for a valid reason to refuse him, but could come up with nothing. She had agreed to this scheme, after all. She gave a great sigh and took a step back. "All right, we'll go to the play."

"Good, I'll pick you up at seven."

They went back into the living room, where Clay shrugged into his coat and turned to her. He pulled one of his business cards out of his jacket pocket and laid it on the table by her purse. "Here's my address and phone numbers if you need them."

"You must show me how you managed the upload and the programming on your capture application," she said, trying to think of anything but the man in front of her, trying not to stand too close, but attracted to him just the same.

As he looked into her eyes, Clay suddenly wanted to tell her everything—exactly how he had used his spells to create those programs and place them on the computers, how wizardry was an integral part of him, how he could show her the great magic between the two of them.

Wait a minute. Great magic? Explain himself? What was going on in his head? He certainly never told anyone about practitioners or their talents. No practitioner did. So, he gave her an honest, if misleading, answer.

"Magic," he murmured as he put his hands on her shoulders and drew her closer. He dipped his head and kissed her.

He meant it to be a small, first-date kind of kiss, but her eyes closed just as he glimpsed a flame in the smoky brown. Then her mouth opened, and he was lost. She tasted of chocolate and herself as he explored her mouth, delving deeper. He couldn't help it, his kiss became possessive, and he claimed her as gently as he could, while his body demanded full satisfaction, the relief to be found inside her. It was all he could do to keep his hands on her shoulders and not wrap his arms around her and pull her closer.

Magic, indeed, echoed in Francie's mind before desire took over and the heat from his lips shot through her body. She had the distinct impression multicolored lights were sparkling on the backs of her eyelids.

Where had her resistance to him gone? She hadn't meant to let this kiss happen, had forgotten the possibility in the computer demonstration and talk of their next date. But once his mouth touched hers, all her intentions, all her resolve, flew from her body. She raised a hand to his face and felt him shudder when she touched him. When he thrust deep, tasting all of her, she dueled with his tongue and heard him groan.

He kissed like the man he was—confident, expert, decisive, and at the same time charming, seductive, spellbinding. A kiss had never been like this before; she had never even *imagined* a kiss like this, one that caused her breasts to swell, her womb to ache, her whole being to demand more. It was . . . truly magical.

No, the last vestiges of her rational mind asserted themselves. It couldn't be magical; it shouldn't be this arousing. She shouldn't be here like this. She couldn't be succumbing again to the charms of a handsome man.

From deep in her mind she grasped for the power to resist. Forcing her body to go along wasn't easy, but she managed to pull her hand from his face to his chest and push, a slight nudge, hardly any pressure, but all she could bring to bear.

He raised his mouth from hers immediately but kept his hands on her shoulders until she took a deep breath and stepped back. Separation helped her gain control again. When she looked him in the face, he seemed more stunned than angry or frustrated at her action.

"This isn't part of the deal, Clay," she said, shaking her head from side to side. "We're only pretending to be involved. There's enough deception and complication in this scheme as it is. Please don't do that again."

He took his own deep breath before nodding. "I'll make you a deal, Francie."

"What kind of deal?" she asked, telling herself to be ready for anything.

He drew her glasses from his coat pocket and held them out to her. As she took them, he looked her straight in the eyes. His voice was low and slightly hoarse. "When we're alone together, no glasses, no camouflage, no artificial barriers. Only the truth. Deal?"

"What do I get in return?"

"The same, no camouflage, the truth."

The glasses she didn't care about, the camouflage must mean her usual clothing, but the truth? Yes, that was important. He had to understand she was not interested in anything except catching Kevin and protecting Tamara—and certainly not in a relationship with him. "Honesty is what I'm after, too. Deal."

She would have said more, clarified the agreement, but before she could open her mouth, he said, "I'll see you tomorrow. About seven? Francie, I really had a good time, too."

And he let himself out, giving her a wave as he walked down the stairs.

She shut the door, leaned against it for a minute until she was sure her suddenly wobbly legs would hold her, and, turning off the lights, stumbled into her bedroom. She went through her nighttime routine and fell into bed, exhausted.

What was the matter with her? Why had she let him kiss her? Why had she returned his kiss?

Replaying the kiss, she mumbled, "Magic, it's got to be magic," but she felt the anticipation—no, the *yearning* to see him again. The need—no, the *craving* to experience one of those kisses again.

She wondered where her resistance to him had gone, for it had vanished in his embrace as swiftly as a rabbit disappeared in a magician's top hat.

She'd had to pull the determination to protest—even so feebly—from deep in her brain. To simply push on his chest, she'd had to do battle with an interior force she didn't even know was in her.

What was the matter with her? She almost felt as if

that force had taken control of her brain and her body.

Business, she kept repeating to herself, until her resolve was firmly back in place. It was strictly business. Clay was too much like Walt, too good-looking, too experienced, too charming. She was not going to be hurt by a man like that again, no matter how enchanting he was. She would not allow him to repeat that kiss. No more caresses, either. She had to be strong.

She was strong. She was twenty-eight-years-old strong, not nineteen. She had to think of him as an opponent on the basketball court. Play the game, watch out for the other guy's sneaky moves, come out the victor, no matter what the score. She could, she *would* do that.

They had an agreement of sorts, which needed clarification, but they'd have the chance for that tomorrow night. Then she realized that he hadn't agreed with her first statement about only pretending they were in a relationship and not kissing her again. She'd have to bring that up also.

Definitely the part about no more kisses.

All that stuff about magic? Sheer piffle. It simply did not compute.

She rubbed the itching spot beneath her breasts again—it had developed a slight prickle—and her last thought before she slipped into sleep was wondering what had bit her.

"Magic," Clay said to himself as he lay in bed after the cold shower hadn't worked worth a damn. "What's between a man and a woman. That's the true magic. All the rest is just dabbling."

And the attraction between him and Francie was strong, stronger than he'd experienced with any other woman. The voice in his head at the restaurant had been right; this was no charade. He would be Francie's lover.

The kiss had rocked him to his foundation, and he thought she had been likewise affected. But then she'd shaken her head at him and asked him not to do it again. He'd never had a woman respond like that, even after a kiss only half so potent. What was going on?

She was more wary than he'd expected. That was all right; it only made the challenge to have her greater. More fun. He just needed to take things slower. Damn, he'd like to get his hands on the bastard who drove her into those formless clothes, caused her to deny her beauty, made her distrust all other men. That had to be the explanation. She was no shrinking violet.

Mercy, what a body.

Holy hell, what a woman.

His thoughts totally negated the slight effect of the shower. Damn, how was he going to get to sleep? But he did, almost, until he remembered the way her eyes shone with intelligence and humor when they had talked so long over the meal, until he saw again the delight of her smile, the golden highlights in her hair, and heard the sound of her laughter. Oh, man, did he want to feel her body against his. No camouflage, no barriers.

The promise they had made each other, especially about telling each other the truth, stopped his fantasies for a moment. Tell her the truth? About being a practitioner? He'd thought about it just before their lips met.

Where did that idea come from? Practitioners never told nonpractitioners about their abilities to do magic. He'd never told any of his other lovers. Why should he tell this one?

But he hadn't agreed not to kiss her, and his emotions and desire weren't pretense, but true and real. Convincing her would be fun. He grinned into the darkness.

He turned over, punched the pillow, and tried to concentrate on the dullest computer motherboard diagrams he could think of. Eventually, he, too, slept, but the next morning his sternum was itching like mad.

CHAPTER THREE

A loud banging on her door pulled Francie out of a deep dream in which she and Clay were definitely alone, with no eyeglasses, no camouflage, and absolutely no artificial barriers between them. She fought with the sheet as she struggled to determine what the noise was all about and why Clay had vanished from her arms. Groaning, she opened her eyes and glanced over at the alarm clock.

Seven o'clock.

In the morning.

Saturday morning. Who on earth . . .?

Tamara. Of course, coming to check up on her date with Clay.

Francie hauled herself out of bed, threw on a robe, and staggered barefoot into the hall. "I'm coming," she muttered as her tormentor beat on the door and also poked the doorbell to add the ding-dong to the din. At the front door, she peeked blearily out the peephole. Yep,

Tamara.

With her eyes barely open, she opened the door and slumped against the frame. "What, Tamara?"

"Good morning!" The petite redhead bounced in, holding up a delicious-smelling bag she waved under Francie's nose. "I brought you some croissants and a piece of the apple torte you like so much. Close the door and let's put on the coffee, and you can tell me all about your date." She headed for the kitchen without waiting for a response.

Mumbling under her breath imprecations against people who woke up both early and horrendously cheerful, Francie stumbled in pursuit. She sagged against the kitchen door and watched her friend bustle around, fixing coffee and setting the small round table in the window nook. "Do you know what time it is?" she asked around a yawn.

"Sure, but I wanted to talk to you before I had to go to the shop. I knew you wouldn't let him stay the night, not on the first date, even if he is the best-looking man I've seen in a long time. Now sit down, and spill it. How was the date? Where did you go? What time did he leave?"

"Tamara, please." Francie sat, put her head in her hands, and massaged her scalp to wake herself up. She hoped vaguely she was wiping those disturbing dreams out of her mind at the same time. "You know I can't talk until I've had some coffee."

"All right, Miss Non-Morning-Person. You have until the coffee's ready and you've had three swallows."

Tamara blessedly kept her mouth shut while the coffee dripped, and true to her promise, until Francie had the promised three swallows. She didn't even say anything when Francie finally looked up from contemplating the rich brown brew as though it could foretell the future. She didn't have to; her raised red brows made her point eloquently.

"All right," Francie said after a fourth sip. "I think I'm beginning to wake up." She took a bite of the apple torte and another sip. "We went to that restaurant on lower Westheimer you and I always talked about going to. It was very nice. The calamari was cooked just right, and he ordered a California chardonnay that went wonderfully with the meal. We both had fish, but I had grilled red snapper and he had sea bass sautéed in butter and wine. I had a scrumptious chocolate cake for dessert, but he didn't have any, just a bite of mine. We both had coffee. We came home. End of evening." She recited the events in what she hoped was a calm, thoughtful manner.

"Frrrannnncie! You know I don't care what y'all ate, for crying out loud. C'mon. The juicy stuff."

"Tamara, there was no 'juicy stuff.' We just talked about our families and computers."

"Families and computers! Well, of course, computers. What else is there?" Tamara waved her hand in the air dismissively and leaned across the table intently. "So, what's he really like? Does his mind live up to his great bod? The man must be successful. He had to have his gorgeous suit custom hand-tailored. Do you have any idea how much that outfit he had on last night cost?"

Francie took another bite and another sip as she tried to decide how much to say. Tamara had always shared tales of her own dates; it was only to be expected she would want Francie to do the same. But Francie couldn't tell her everything, especially about Clay's little tracking program or Kevin's treachery. Hoping her thoughts didn't show on her face, she hid behind her cup. Oh, why did she agree to do this?

"Well," she finally said, thinking furiously. "He's very nice, despite his looks."

"Yesss! A breakthrough! You've never said that about a date before," Tamara interrupted, pumping her fists in the air. "Keep going."

"He has two sisters, one's a management consultant and the other does something with plants, owns a plant nursery with their mother, I think. His father's a consultant, too."

"What else did you talk about? You couldn't have spent all dinner on those subjects alone." Tamara had a look on her face that told Francie the redhead wouldn't give up until she knew more.

"We talked about computers, of course, and books, and movies. It turned out we like lots of the same things. He has an offbeat sense of humor, and we laughed a lot."

"What about when he brought you home?"

"He wanted to see what kind of computer I had," Francie said, just to be on the safe side in case Tamara had seen the two of them in her home office when she was peeking out her window.

Tamara just shook her head and rolled her eyes. "No matter what he looks like, a computer jock is always a computer jock, I guess. But that's not what I want to know. Do you like him? Are you seeing him again? Did he give you a good-night kiss?"

"Oh, for heaven's sake, Tamara. Can't I have a little privacy?"

"No."

"All right. Yes, I like him. Yes, I'm seeing him again."

"When?"

"Tonight. He's taking me to *Wicked* and dinner."

"Great! What are you going to wear?"

"I don't know. Probably my brown dress with the jacket."

"Ugh! That awful thing?" Tamara made a face clearly indicating her displeasure with Francie's choice. "No, you're not. Get dressed. We're going over to the shop right now and find you something. A nice little blue outfit just came in. It will look wonderful on you, and it's perfect for a theater date. And don't tell me you can't afford it," she continued as Francie opened her mouth to object. "You make good money, and you might as well enjoy it."

"Do you bully all your customers this way?"

"Only the ones I care about." Tamara turned serious and put a hand on Francie's. "I can't tell you how happy I am you had a good time last night, and you're seeing him again. It's past time for you to forget Walt. Just because he was a sleazeball doesn't mean all men are." She put up a hand as Francie started to reply. "I know, you don't like to talk about it, so we won't. You just go get dressed."

Francie sighed. It would be easier to surrender to Tamara's demands than to argue. It made a good diversion also. With any luck, Tamara would forget her third question. Francie had no intention of mentioning Clay's kiss, or her determination to resist him, or those dreams—especially those dreams. "All right," she said, rising to pour herself another cup of coffee. "I'll be ready in a few minutes."

"Good. That blue dress will knock his socks off. You'll have him eating out of your hands in no time."

Francie escaped to her bedroom with the idea of Clay without his socks—and other items of clothing—insinuating itself into her head. *You idiot!* she told herself. She would have liked to sit down and analyze what was happening, work out a more coherent approach to Clay and the effects he had on her. She couldn't do that, however, with Tamara around.

So she put thoughts of her problems aside. Instead, she focused on the here and now and concentrated on the tasks she had to accomplish before going out tonight. Putting on her bra, she looked carefully at the end of her sternum, but could see no indication as to why it was itching so much.

✳✳✳✳✳

That night, Francie studied her reflection in the mirror. Tamara had been correct: the outfit looked great. The deep blue dress clung in the right places and made her hair look blonder. The collarless, buttonless jacket hung to just the right length. Her upswept hair in its neat twist, her pearl necklace and earrings, gave her an air of sophistication—she hoped. The makeup she had applied, again following Tamara's instructions, worked to enhance her eyes—with or without her glasses. Somewhat self-consciously, remembering Clay's admonition against them, she put on the eyeglasses and took them off again. She couldn't help feeling vulnerable without the comforting frames.

She looked over at her open closet, hanger after hanger full of drab browns and dull greens and dingy rusts and faded yellows, not to mention the beiges and grays. Funny, she hadn't realized until this moment how much she missed wearing brighter colors. Or dressing to look good. Look good for herself, she amended. Certainly not for a man. Certainly not to attract a man. Certainly not for Clay Morgan. *You're not going to let yourself get hurt or be made a fool of again*, she silently reminded her reflection. Resolutely she closed the closet doors.

She glanced at the clock. Only a quarter to seven. She hoped he would be on time. What could she do for fifteen minutes? Her apartment was tidy, the plants were watered, and she had read the newspaper. Her eyes fell on the book on her bedside table. It would have to do as a distraction from fidgeting; she needed to get started on it anyway for the discussion group. As she reached for the book, however, the doorbell rang. She automatically put on her glasses and picked up her purse before heading for the front door.

A smiling Clay, resplendent in a gray pinstripe suit, greeted her as she opened the door.

"Hi, I hope you don't mind, I'm a little early." The truth was, he had been driving around for half an hour until he finally said to hell with it and just went to her. What was this woman doing to him? He knew he was always relentlessly prompt, and he didn't like to rush his dates in their preparations, but he couldn't wait to see Francie, ready or not. Now that he was standing in her entryway, he decided he had done exactly the right thing.

"You look wonderful," he told her, sliding his gaze down and up the long length of her. When his eyes reached her face, however, he frowned. "Uh-uh," he stated, shaking his head.

Francie blinked, and her face went from a welcoming smile to a look of puzzlement and wariness at his disapproval. "What's the matter?"

"These," Clay stated, reaching up to remove her glasses. "Did you forget our deal?"

"Oh. No, actually, I didn't. I had them in my hand when you rang the bell and just put them on out of habit, I guess."

"Well, okay, I'll let you get away with it this time." He handed the glasses back with a small bow and an expression of mock censure, and she turned to place them on a nearby table.

Clay looked at the wisps of hair just tickling the nape of her neck and contemplated kissing that spot and around to her delicate earlobe and . . . Giving himself an enormous mental shake, he dragged his mind back to the business at hand. "Do you think Tamara's watching us?"

"No. She's probably still at the shop. She said something about Kevin picking her up there for their date tonight. I guess that means he won't be on my computer this evening."

"Probably not," he answered. "We'll have to give him a shot at it soon, however, if for no other reason than to frustrate him more with his inability to crack the Brazos system and to soften him up for me. We can discuss the possibilities on the way. Shall we?" He ushered her out, waited for her to lock the door, and let her precede him down the stairs.

Once in the Jeep and headed for downtown, he

brought up the subject again. "I've been thinking about how to get to Brenner. What are your plans over the next week for being away from home during the evening?"

"None really. I have something to do after work on Tuesday, but I'll be home by eight, eight thirty at the latest. Nothing at work is critical, so I wasn't planning on working late this next week."

"What about Tamara? Is she away during the evenings, besides out with Brenner? As I understand the situation, he uses your computer only when both you and Tamara are out because she can see in the window by your desktop from her apartment."

"Well, she keeps the shop open later on Thursday, till nine. She usually gets home about ten, after tallying up her sales and dropping by the night-deposit box at the bank."

"Can you find out if she's following her usual schedule and at the same time let it slip that you have to work late on Thursday? In time so Kevin will know the computer's free then?"

She sighed as she said, "I guess so. I don't know if she'll tell Kevin, though."

"That's okay. It's been a while since he had access to your machine, so he might be looking for a chance to use it." He heard her sigh again. Flicking a glance at her, he put a hand on the fingers she had clasped together on top of her purse in her lap. "I know how hard this is for you, Francie. You feel like you're betraying your friend. But I honestly don't know any other way to catch Brenner."

"I keep hoping she will get tired of him sooner rather than later, or have a fight and break up. I hate duplicity of any kind, and just the *thought* of lying to her . . ."

Clay gave her hands a reassuring squeeze before releasing them. "Don't think of it as lying. In fact, you're not lying to her at all. You're just not telling her all of the truth about her boyfriend, that's all."

"Well, I'm lying to her about you, aren't I?" she said, turning toward him.

"In what way?" he asked, eyebrows raised, but he didn't take his eyes off the road.

"The idea you and I are dating, becoming a couple, that you're sweeping me off my feet."

He grinned and shot a look from the traffic to her face and back again. "I thought I was doing a pretty good job. Is there something else I need to do?"

"You are. I mean, no, . . . that is . . ." Francie's voice petered out as she realized what she had been about to admit—despite her resolve, she was becoming more and more attracted to him. This whole reaction was so unlike her. How could what she was feeling have happened so fast? Only her distress and anxiety had kept her from shivering under his touch on her hands.

"You know as well as I do, Clay, this is all just business. I meant what I said yesterday. It's all pretend." She made her tone as brisk and as positive as she could. She couldn't let him get away with his arrogant statement.

"Is it?"

"Yes, of course." She nodded sharply to emphasize her opinion.

"Let's take it easy here, Francie, and see how it goes, okay? Let's simply go to the theater and have a good time," he suggested calmly.

His request wasn't exactly an agreement with her assessment, and she almost opened her mouth to push for one, but she couldn't bring herself to do it. He was right. They had to get through this evening, and at least one other evening as well. At some point she had to introduce him to Kevin. She had to keep control of herself, guard her heart, and not succumb to a handsome man's charms.

"I've read a couple of good reviews for this show," she said to change the subject. She certainly didn't want to continue this one.

Clay gave her a quick glance. This relationship didn't have to be and wouldn't be purely business. Not if he had anything to say about it. Damn. He didn't want to have a conversation about this attraction between them in a moving vehicle, when he couldn't look her in the eyes or touch her or concentrate totally on what her body and eyes were really telling him. For now, she had accepted his suggestion to keep things light, so he followed her lead for something else to talk about. "Daria and her husband saw it and recommended it."

They discussed the musical for the remainder of the

trip. At the show, by mutual—if unspoken—agreement, they made only inconsequential conversation, mostly about books they had read as children.

For dinner after the show, he took her to a French bistro on Montrose Boulevard, not far from the Museum of Fine Arts. Both of them still avoided any mention of what had brought them together. Instead they went off on a sports kick and found a mutual interest in basketball.

"I played point guard on my high-school team, but not college," Clay said. "Didn't have the interest or the drive it took to compete at an almost semi-pro level. Didn't want to spend the time on it, either, I guess. I was happiest in the computer lab. How about you?" He didn't say he'd been team captain or the team had won the state championship. It seemed too much like bragging. So did mentioning his winning team at the Downtown YMCA. Little disgusted him more than guys who relived their teenaged athletic careers as though it made them special. They often hadn't done a thing to be proud of since.

"Where'd you go to college?" Francie asked.

"MIT. How about you?"

"Texas at Austin. I had the height for center on the women's team, but didn't play after high school, either, except on some intramural teams," she answered. "I had academic scholarships, so I concentrated on my studies." She didn't mention she'd been on the All-State Girls' Team or that her high school had been state champions.

She also didn't mention her university intramural team had been champions in their league or that she continued to play in the women's league at the Downtown YMCA. It seemed too much like bragging. Besides, she didn't like being seen as only a jock who couldn't possibly have a brain in her head. Or worse, a body to be lusted after with no thought as to the woman who inhabited it. Clay wouldn't treat her like either one of those. She knew that deep down, somewhere in her middle, but she didn't have time to dwell on the revelation as he asked another question and led her thoughts elsewhere.

They went on to discuss basketball, the NBA and the Houston Rockets, the WNBA and the Houston Comets. Francie maintained the women played a "purer" form of ball, running plays, cooperating as a team, instead of "hot-dogging" like the men did. Clay, because he discovered he liked arguing with her, defended the men's style vigorously, extolling the speed, the play above the rim, and the magic of the superstars. They finally agreed to disagree.

As they rose from the table, Clay asked, "Would you like to go to a Rockets or Comets game some time? The NBA season will be starting soon, and I have a friend who can get us good tickets."

"That sounds like fun," she replied. "I've never seen the pros play in person."

"I'll see what I can do."

He didn't mention the implication they'd be seeing

each other after the hacker mess was over. Neither did she.

It was just past midnight when Clay drove up to Francie's apartment. The witching hour, he thought. Apropos because he was already under her spell, and she wasn't even a practitioner. He had never been able to talk with a date, practitioner or not, the way he had with Francie. They had covered so many topics. She had interesting viewpoints and cogent reasons for her opinions.

And to find out, of all things, that under her hard shell of god-awful clothes and computer earnestness lurked a basketball player. He'd have to get her out on a court sometime and see what kind of moves she had. As he rounded the car to open her door, he almost groaned at the thought of their bodies touching, bumping, sliding when one of them went around the other's guard for a basket.

But now he had to say good night. His hardening body let him know exactly how it wanted to end the evening. His mind—or something—told him to take it easy. Francie wasn't ready for it yet, and they still had to concentrate on the hacker problem. Despite her protestations, however, he couldn't see why he couldn't have a good-night kiss. After all, he hadn't agreed to her request. As if in agreement, his magic center vibrated.

As they walked up the stairs, he glanced across the courtyard at the dark windows of Tamara's apartment and asked, "Do you think our observer is at home?"

Francie stuck her key in the lock and opened her

door. "I doubt it," she answered. "She and Kevin usually stay out much later than this." She stepped inside and turned around toward him, clearly nervous again, clearly debating with herself if she should ask him in.

He took the decision out of her hands by moving forward, closing the door behind him. She backed up automatically into the dimly lit apartment. He put his hands on her waist and drew her forward. "Time to practice," he murmured.

"Practice what?" she asked as her hands went to his biceps.

"Sweeping you off your feet," he answered, lowering his head, his gaze fixed on her lips.

She opened her mouth to protest, but his mouth stopped any utterance and his tongue took advantage of the opening to tease and coax and explore.

She stiffened at first, but relaxed as he kept the kiss light, tasting, nibbling, sipping. When her arms wound around his neck to draw him closer, he rejoiced. Wary though she might be, she couldn't resist their attraction any more than he could. Then he deepened the kiss, taking her mouth as he wanted to take her body. The heat between them escalated to a flash point, and Clay felt her take fire in his arms.

She returned his kiss with one of her own, one that demanded as well as offered, gave as much as took. He answered by wrapping one arm around her waist, pressing them together from thighs to shoulders, while his other hand slid up her back to entangle itself in her hair and send hairpins scattering to the floor.

She gave a little growling purr, and the sound vibrated through him, reverberating in his very bones. Her scent, a combination of peachy tones and pure Francie, enveloped him, making him so light-headed he would have staggered if not for her support. Her hips pushed against his, a subtle brush that instantly overwhelmed all his senses.

Clay suddenly felt as if he were swimming in the Gulf on the edge of a whirlpool of desire, fighting the roaring current straining to pull him in while colored lights flickered in the distance. He was no stranger to lovemaking; he'd been in these waters before. But here in Francie's arms, they were incredibly deeper and more turbulent than he expected, he realized somewhere in the back of his mind, as his body hardened to the point of pain. How easy it would be to dive in, be swallowed up in the rush of need and want, surrender to the maelstrom of passion in her embrace.

He knew what it was to want a woman, but the strength of this yearning, this craving for her that burned in his body surprised him. He knew what it was to kiss a woman, to hold her in his arms, to make love with her until they were both exhausted. But never before had anything felt like this kiss, so all-consuming, so all-encompassing, so demanding of . . . *more*.

It wasn't enough, he would never be able to get

enough of her. Again his mind's eye conjured up the whirlpool beckoning him deeper, he felt the vortex sucking at him, and his arms tightened even more around her, his siren and lifeline all in one.

Only some primitive feeling of self-preservation, or maybe hereditary caution, or a practitioner's innate intuition, or, hell, he didn't know what, made him pull himself back from the abyss. He ended the kiss but held her close to his chest for a long moment, struggling to sort out his feelings and control his body.

When she took a shaky breath, he realized how tightly he was holding her and loosened his arms. He drew back so that he could see her eyes, and she blinked at him in a dazed fashion. "Did I hurt you?" he asked in a hoarse whisper, all he could manage from tortured lungs.

She shook her head slowly, but said nothing, her eyes still on his. The smoky brown of her irises was almost obscured by her dilated pupils, and she looked as stunned as he felt.

He put trembling hands on her shoulders to brace them both and stepped back. His body protested the separation, but he ignored it. "I think we've got this backward, Francie," he said in a low, grating tone.

"Wh-what?" She took a deep breath and swallowed. She looked at his mouth and frowned slightly, as if he were speaking a foreign language and she was trying to understand him.

"About who's sweeping who off whose feet."

She licked her kiss-swollen lips, and he almost groaned at the sight. He had to get out of her apartment before he took advantage, too much advantage of her. It wasn't yet time to take her to bed. Not that he didn't want to, and not that she was in any state to deny him. But somehow he knew it was too soon, and the last thing he wanted was for her to regret their lovemaking.

"I'll call you tomorrow night," he said, as he released her shoulders.

She swayed, but steadied. "Tomorrow," she repeated in a husky voice.

The need to kiss her again flashed through him so strongly he could have howled, but he summoned the strength from somewhere and opened the door. "Tomorrow night," he confirmed. He walked out and closed the door behind him. After one deep, deep inhalation of much-needed air, he forced himself to keep going down the steps and to his car.

Once inside the vehicle, Clay sat for several minutes, waiting for his body to relax enough so he could drive home safely. "Holy hell, where did all *that* come from?" he muttered later as he lay in bed, slowly rubbing the itch that seemed to emanate from under his breastbone. Exhausted, he slept.

✶❀✴✴✶❀

After Clay left her apartment, Francie staggered to

the couch and collapsed on it. Several minutes passed before her bones solidified again and she was able to sit upright. She ran her hands through her hair, and a few remaining hairpins fell into her lap. She held her head tightly and forced her mind to focus.

"Good Lord, what was *that*?" she breathed out loud.

Her mind had no answer. Her body, however, relived every moment from the first light touch of his lips on hers. The small, insignificant brush of his mouth had flung her mind into turmoil and her body to his. His deeper kiss had obliterated thought, leaving only the certainty she was in a hurricane, then swallowed up in a tornado. She could have sworn colored lights flickered and whirled all around them. She'd become giddy, dizzy with desire. She couldn't get close enough to him, not enough to cool the heat or halt the lightning zinging through her body.

She'd had no control whatever, neither mental nor physical. He could have done anything to her, anything in the world. Ravished her on the floor. Torn her clothes off and taken her against the wall. Carried her into the bedroom and . . .

"No!" she cried aloud. *Yes*, her body reveled at the idea.

But he hadn't done any of it. In fact, he'd calmly ended that devastating kiss and walked out the door. Cool, composed, unmoved. *He'd just walked out the damn door.*

How dare he?

How dare he leave her in this . . . state, or . . . condition, or . . . whatever it was? How dare he reject her?

How dare he not give her a chance to remind him of their agreement? To tell him she wouldn't kiss him again? To reject him first?

"Whatever it was" transformed itself into anger—hot, seething anger—and she beat her fists on her knees in frustration.

Didn't the arrogant bastard feel anything at all? After reducing her to a pile of storm debris, how did the man have the gall to leave, saying only he'd call her tomorrow night?

Wait a minute. What was she thinking?

"Oh, God! Oh, damn, damn, damn." As her brain finally clicked into its analytical gear, she realized how she was reacting. She wasn't thinking straight. She hadn't meant for another kiss to happen at all.

What was she angry about? Had he, in fact, rejected her? Why should it matter to her? She should be angry not at him, but at herself, for cooperating in that kiss. She hadn't secured his actual, verbal agreement to her no-kisses rule, and the SOB had ignored her demand. And she'd given in.

What had happened to her willpower? Was she falling for another handsome, charming man? Was this going to be Walt all over again?

The last question galvanized her, stood her on her

feet, and propelled her toward the bedroom. She told herself, "No," several times down the hall, and she fussed and fumed while she removed her clothes, put on her nightgown, and washed her face.

Rubbed her breastbone, which was now aching, not itching. Aching, with little sharp pinpricks of pain every so often. Just what she needed, another problem.

"Damn, damn, damn," she muttered again through the toothpaste foam as she brushed her teeth and her mind traveled right back to Clay. She'd had such fun this night, enjoyed his company so much. And the things they'd talked about. She hadn't had a chance to talk basketball with anybody in a long time. Her computer buddies didn't care much about sports, and Tamara liked to watch the men, not the game.

But she and Clay together as a couple couldn't go on, wouldn't after they caught Kevin.

She couldn't take many more kisses like the one tonight. Not and remain sane. Not and remain her own woman. Not and keep Clay where he firmly belonged, in the business side of her life. She had to end this confusion between her mind and body.

She could not let him touch her again when they were alone. Not let him kiss her. She would arrange the double date with Tamara and Kevin so Clay could meet the smarmy bastard. After that, she wouldn't need to have anything to do with him. She'd tell Tamara they'd broken up.

That would do it, she told herself in the bathroom mirror. She looked at her image and realized she was rubbing that spot right between her breasts again. She had to stop; she was only making it more sore. She busied her hands putting the toothpaste away.

Once in bed with the light out, however, her body reminded her again of its pleasure at being in Clay's arms, of its certainty of being exactly where it was supposed to be, of its longing to be there again.

And her memory conjured up his words, "I think we've got this backward. About who's sweeping who off whose feet." And the look on his face, silver eyes so intent on hers; and his muscular body, so hard against her soft one; and the strength of his desire, so evident pressed against her aching sex. He had been as breathless and aroused as she was.

Good. Let him stew for a while. The pleasure that idea brought made her smile in the darkness. It even seemed to lessen the discomfort in her chest.

Maybe she was mistaken in her original conclusions. Maybe he had been affected. She was an analyst; she could look at the evidence, plot the sequence of events, map the procedure. He'd been breathing hard also. His voice had sounded like he had trouble getting the words out. And she remembered the way his hands had trembled on her shoulders. Separating their bodies had been as hard on him as it was on her.

Maybe his honor and integrity had stopped him

from . . . from what? Pushing her over the edge? Taking her where she had implied she didn't want to go? She'd been the one who wanted to keep it all businesslike, and she'd told him so.

But he'd been the one with willpower. How had he known to stop? Why had he? Thank goodness he had. She wasn't ready for more. Wasn't she? Would she ever be?

Her body told her it was ready *now*. Her mind just wallowed around in confusion, as if it had been possessed by aliens. And the pain in her solar plexus seemed to come and go on its own schedule. At this rate she'd be a candidate for the loony bin in no time.

Francie snorted at herself and punched the pillow into a more comfortable position. For a woman who'd always prided herself on her ability to think and act clearly, she certainly wasn't doing any of that now. She'd come in a complete circle, from frustration to rage to frustration of another sort.

What was she going to do about Clay Morgan?

Put a stop to his kisses, somehow. Keep her distance. Live through this debacle.

Survive.

Hoping daylight would bring respite from her problems, she closed her eyes and snuggled into the pillow. Her last memory of the effect the kiss had on Clay caused a small smile of satisfaction to cross her face before sleep overtook her.

CHAPTER FOUR

Sunday afternoon, Francie was about to turn on her computer to check her e-mail when the doorbell rang. She was almost afraid it was Clay at her door and she still hadn't decided what to do about or with him. It was Tamara, thank goodness.

"Hey," the redhead said when Francie let her in. "How was the date?"

"What, no 'Good afternoon,' or 'How are you?'" Francie teased.

"You know me, I cut right to the chase," Tamara grinned back.

"Well, come on in. You want something to drink? I was going to make some tea."

"That sounds good." Tamara followed her into the kitchen and plunked herself down at the table. "So, give."

"The show was great," Francie said as she filled the kettle and put it on the stove. She described what they had seen and where they had eaten dinner. "We had a great time talking about basketball. He played on his high-school teams just like I did, and we had a lot of fun arguing about the NBA versus the WNBA."

Tamara rolled her eyes. "You two must be made for each other. Computers and now basketball. I don't know any other woman who would have argued with her date about sports. Are you going to see him again?"

Francie prepared the teapot and placed cups on the table as she answered, "We didn't make any firm plans. I'm sure we both have plenty of work to do. I was assigned to a special project last week, and I'll have to work late at least one night this week, most likely Thursday. I hope it won't be Tuesday, because my basketball league plays at the Y then." There, she'd told Tamara about Thursday, so her mission was accomplished. A wave of remorse about deceiving her friend struck her, and she turned back to the stove to hide her feelings.

"You know, I may just come to watch y'all play sometime."

"You keep saying that, but you never do." Francie poured the hot water into the teapot and carried it to the table. As the tea steeped, she asked, "How's Kevin? How was your date?"

"It was okay," Tamara replied, spooning honey into her cup. "We went to the new club over by the Galleria. Kevin was feeling really good. He hinted about some 'big plans at work,'"—she waggled her fingers in quote marks—"but he wouldn't tell me what they are exactly."

"Oh?" Francie tried to say nonchalantly, but thought the word came out in a croak. She coughed to cover her reaction and poured the tea.

"Yeah, it's probably some sales promotion. You know how these sales types are, always looking to the next big score, the next big client."

"How's the shop?" Francie asked to change the subject, and they talked about Tamara's business for the rest of her visit.

After the redhead left, Francie sat at her computer, staring blankly at the screen. What was she going to do about Tamara? She felt like she was betraying her closest friend. She had to be able to do something to protect Tamara from Kevin, no matter what. But she knew neither she nor Tamara made very good liars, Tamara least of all. Clay and Herb had to stop Kevin from whatever he was attempting to find in the Brazos computer, so she herself couldn't say anything to spoil the project. Therefore, all she could do for Tamara was what she was doing—keeping her mouth shut. God, she hated deception.

Morosely she booted up the computer and stared out the window for several minutes after the familiar display appeared. When no answer appeared out of computer heaven, she sighed and clicked the button to check her e-mail.

⁕✻✻✻⁕

Sunday afternoon Clay went over to Daria's. Their sister, Gloriana, was in town, but wanted to go back to the plant and herb farm that evening, so they were eating early. Moving up the dinner hour fit in with his plans to call Francie later, and he didn't often have the chance to see Glori these days, so he was happy to accept the invitation.

Being with his family would also take his mind off Francie for a little while. He still hadn't come to terms with his reaction the previous evening. Maybe not thinking about it would allow the situation to percolate in his brain cells. Let his subconscious handle the puzzle. He had often used the method to solve problems in the past. Besides, to deal with Glori's usual teasing, he had to pay attention or she'd get the best of him. As her older brother, he couldn't allow that.

He pulled up to Daria's home off Sunset Boulevard by Rice University and saw Gloriana's dark green Mercedes convertible sitting in front. His younger sister drove like a bat out of hell, and Clay shook his head as he got out of his car, remembering the last time he had been so foolish as to let her drive him somewhere. Talk about a white-knuckle trip.

It was almost the end of September, but the temperatures remained high, and in Daria's garden, the lush plantings still bloomed. Clay surveyed the grounds with a practiced eye as he approached the front porch. From the state of the plants, he had at least another month before Daria would be wheedling him to help Bent clean out the annuals.

"Hello, Zorro, Lolita," he greeted the two cats sitting by the front steps.

"Mmrow," answered Zorro, his large black body lounging insolently, the tip of his tail flicking. Lolita came to twine around Clay's legs as he rang the doorbell. He reached down to pet her while he waited. "Yaaah," the dainty Abyssinian said, arching her back to take full advantage of his caress.

John "Bent" Benthausen opened the door with a big smile for his brother-in-law. "Come on in. We're back here." The tall, auburn-haired man led the way to the kitchen.

"Hi!" Two green-eyed women greeted Clay as he walked in. They put down the cooking implements they had been using, and both gave him a hug at the same time.

"Hi, yourselves," Clay said as he returned the hug. He leaned back and surveyed his two sisters. They looked so much alike, so like their mother, he thought again as he always did when seeing them together after the passage of time between visits. The only major differences were that Gloriana was a little taller and her dark hair much longer, past her shoulder blades, in fact, while Daria's short curls danced whenever she shook her head.

"Something smells good," Clay said, sniffing the air as he released them.

"Roast chicken," Daria stated as the timer dinged. "And it's time to baste." She put on oven mitts and, opening the oven, pulled out the pot. First she poured sherry over the browning bird, then used a baster to suck up the drippings and squirt them over the chicken. "I'm trying a new recipe for stuffing," she told Clay, "with apples and pecans and raisins. No bread."

"But lots of sherry," Bent interjected. "She soaked the raisins in the stuff."

"Does Mother know about this?" Clay asked as he stole a piece of the tomato Gloriana was cutting for salad.

"She will as soon as I get home," Gloriana said. "We concocted the recipe yesterday."

"Sounds good." Clay smiled a thank-you at Bent's handing him a glass of wine. "So, how have you been, Glori? How're the plants and your classes and all?"

"Fine. The farm's doing well, the university is its usual self, and my botany classes are full," Gloriana replied, as she scraped the tomatoes off the cutting board into the salad bowl. "I have a couple of very promising graduate students this year."

"Didn't I see your name in W^2? Some sort of letter to the editor about how to cast spells?"

"Oh, that was in response to an article by a theoretical mathematician who wants to reduce spell-casting to a strict formula. He claims casting never emerged from the Middle Ages. Shows how much he knows, stuck in his ivory tower. I attempted to set him right."

"If anybody can do it, it's you," Clay laughed.

"I'm sure he's one of those with no respect for our

history or knowledge of practical conjuring. You know how these theory guys have their heads in the sky," Gloriana stated as she put the salad in the refrigerator.

Daria interrupted. "Let's take this discussion into the family room. The chicken needs to cook about a half an hour longer." She picked up a tray of munchies and led the way.

The conversation over hors d'oeuvres and dinner covered Gloriana's writings and other articles in *W²*, *The Witches and Warlocks Journal*; Bent's reorganization of his finance department, sans criminals; Daria's latest consulting work; and finally, Clay's hacker investigation.

Daria brought up the latter subject as they finished dessert and coffee. "How's Francie and the big sting?" she asked.

Clay noted the expression of conspiracy and glee on her face but couldn't fathom what was behind it. Why such a look when talking about a hacker? "She's fine. She's being a big help. She's still bothered about her friend, but she's going ahead with the plan. The sting is progressing."

"What are you talking about?" Gloriana interjected.

Clay told her the story of the hacker and the plan for catching him.

"And you're pretending to date this Francie to get close to the hacker?" Gloriana asked.

"Sort of," Clay answered, thinking that pretense was rapidly becoming reality.

"You ought to see her, Glori," Daria said to her sister.

"She's about six feet tall, blond, and gorgeous. I'm sure it's a real hardship for Clay."

"Oh, really!" Glori grinned. "A real bombshell? Built like a proverbial brick . . . ?" She waved her hands in the classic hourglass shape.

"Yeah," Daria smirked.

"All right, you two," Clay grumbled as the two women laughed. God save him from little sisters.

"So, how are y'all getting along?" Daria persisted.

Her nonchalance could have floated a boat, it was so strong. Clay had seen her play the game before. It usually boded ill for him, and he raised his eyebrows as he asked pointedly, "Fine. Why?"

Daria laughed, more of a snicker really, and exclaimed, "He's clueless!" She rested her forearms on the table, leaning toward her puzzled brother. "When you're with her, does your blood seem to run faster and hotter? Can you feel yourself drowning in her eyes? Do you have the constant need to touch her? Do you think about her when you're not with her? When you kiss her—and I'm sure you've kissed her by now—is it all you can do not to take it further, or at least as close as the nearest bed? Does she reciprocate your feelings?"

"Daria! Whatever is or is not between Francie and me is none of your business!" He never discussed any woman he was interested in with his sisters, and he wasn't about to start now, even if Daria did hit every nail right on the head.

"Oh, Clay, you idiot. I was right. I told you after we met her. I'll bet she's your soul mate!" she retorted, still laughing.

"What?!? My s-, s- . . ." He couldn't say the word. A cold zip of panic raced up his spine as his thought processes stalled. His magic center grew warmer, however.

"Soul mate. S-O-U-L M-A-T-E. The good old soul-mate imperative is at it again. I just know it," she crowed.

Clay sat back in his chair and rubbed his hands over his face, partly to hide his expression from Daria and partly to jiggle his brain back to action. Was she right? Memories of the night before flooded his mind. Walking away from Francie was one of the hardest things he had ever done.

No, she couldn't be, he denied to himself. He wasn't ready to meet the woman who would become the love of his life. He did know he had to give his sister an answer and decided the best defense was offense.

"How did you arrive at this conclusion? You've only seen the woman once. This doesn't make any sense, Daria. You've had soul mates on the brain ever since you and Bent got together. Just because you found yours in a nonpractitioner doesn't mean that I will, too." He tried to make his voice as stern and disbelieving as possible, but he could see it didn't affect her. He ignored the itch behind his breastbone.

"I observed the two of you together at our meeting, remember? All of a sudden, you were both looking at each other so intently I'm surprised sparks didn't shoot between you. She was nervous, and it wasn't because of the subject of the discussion or because she'd done something wrong. She was definitely reacting to *you*. Furthermore, she's not impervious to magic. She jumped when I kicked the spells up a notch. I know you saw that."

"So what? A lot of nonpractitioners react that way," he retaliated.

"You know," Gloriana put in with an innocent tone matching Daria's, "just the other day, Mother and Daddy were wondering when you and I were going to find our mates now that Daria's found Bent."

"I don't need such nonsense from you, too," Clay complained, pointing his finger at her. "Bent, give me some help here." He extended his hand toward his brother-in-law.

"Hey, I'm just telling you what they were saying." Gloriana carefully folded her napkin and shrugged at him, but her face displayed a gleeful smile.

Bent looked from one woman to the other. "Daria, give your brother a break. You know what it's like, finding your soul mate and then getting used to the idea. That damned imperative can make it downright painful." He rubbed his chest as if it still hurt.

Clay recalled the story of the imperative's "persuasive" techniques it used on Bent and winced in sympathy.

"Clay teased both of us enough. You remember."

Daria assumed a smart-alecky voice. "How many soul mates does it take to screw in a lightbulb? Two and no-body cares about the lightbulb." She went back to her normal tone while Gloriana laughed. "It's time he got some of his own back," Daria told her husband. "Well?" she asked Clay.

"No, I don't think so," he answered, but a sharp pain hit his solar plexus, as if he had been stabbed with a hot ice pick. He hid his grimace behind taking a drink of water.

Her eyebrows raised, Daria just sat there, looking at him.

"It could be," he admitted, as memories of the kiss flooded his mind. His chest grew pleasantly warm.

He slumped in his chair. "Hell, I don't know." The ice pick jabbed him again. What the hell was going on with his stomach? Well, worry about that later, he told himself. This business Daria was talking about was much more serious.

He waved his hand in surrender. "Yeah, all right, it might be." The pain ceased, and the warmth returned, accompanied by a tingle. It felt like his magic center was grinning.

He replayed the memories of last night and the night before. Those kisses, those leave-you-weak-and-hurting kisses, those can't-get-enough-of-her kisses. If Francie was his mate, then no wonder she'd affected him the way she did, more than any other woman. No wonder he had so much trouble sleeping. All he could think of was her.

"God, if this is what you went through, I apologize for all the teasing."

Bent chuckled. "And it only gets better—or worse, before it gets better."

"Thanks a lot," Clay muttered. "You're a big help."

"Now comes the real question." Daria sobered and looked him straight in the eye. "When are you going to tell her about us, what we are?"

The deal he had made with Francie came back to him: *No camouflage, no artificial barriers. Only the truth.* Now he knew the source of the idea and his notion last night of telling her about his wizardry—the imperative's handiwork. "You're right. I owe it to her to tell her all about practitioners and soul mates before . . ."

"Before you're irrevocably bonded," Daria finished for him.

Clay nodded. "She has to know what she's getting into, doesn't she? I need to do the same thing you did with Bent, don't I? Lay it all out for Francie."

"I concur," Bent said as Daria nodded. "If you're feeling the way about Francie like I was about Daria, with your control hanging by a thread, the sooner the better."

"Thanks for the advice, I guess." Clay rubbed his hand over his face. "I need to think about this before I do anything. I'm still not totally convinced she's the one. We've only been out twice. I hardly know the woman." He thought his last sentence sounded hollow, even to himself. His center gave a flutter, as if it was laughing at him.

"Let us know what happens," Daria said. "But first, let's clear the table. Glori, shouldn't you be hitting the road if you want to get home by nine o'clock?"

"As much as I hate to leave just when the discussion's getting good, you're right," Gloriana said. "But y'all have to keep me posted. Shall I mention any of this to our parents?"

"Glori, if you have any regard for me at all, please don't say anything to Mother or Dad," Clay pleaded. "I don't need *them* on my back."

"Okay, but it will cost you, and I'm not making any promises, either. You know how Mother seems to pull secrets out of us as easily as she makes up healing potions."

"Only too well," Clay said with a grimace.

There was a flurry of activity as the foursome cleared the table, said good-bye to Gloriana, and watched her drive away. Clay and Bent helped with the dishes and talked sports. Daria did not bring up Francie or soul mates again.

"I've got to be going," Clay said when the chores were finished. "Thanks for dinner."

"Good luck with Francie," Daria told him as she hugged him.

"If we can lend moral support or Daria can turn us into dragon illusions or anything as a demonstration, let us know," Bent said as he walked Clay to the front gate and out of Daria's hearing. "You know, I don't envy you.

I wanted Daria so badly, I didn't care what she was or if some relative who didn't like me would turn me into a toad. But I don't have the slightest idea how it will be for a woman on the other side of the equation. Women take things so differently from men. God knows, Daria agonized over the whole situation for days."

"Yeah, I remember what both of you told me about the experience. But, damn, the pressure's incredible, isn't it? And the whole concept of some ancient whatever-it-is pushing you together, not to mention the consequences, takes some getting used to." Clay rubbed the back of his neck where the muscles had not relaxed since Daria's interrogation.

"There you were, carefree bachelor, then *wham*?" Bent said with a grin, hitting one fist into the other palm for emphasis.

"*Wham* is right."

"But you already know she's worth it, don't you? Speaking from experience, you're going to be vacillating between frustration and euphoria. Are you going to accept the inevitable or fight?"

"I don't know. Part of me is asking if Francie really is the one. I mean, I've dated nonpractitioners before, and the practitioner rules for women don't apply to them. I can make love to them and not get caught in this irrevocable bond. Is she just another one of them, and the chemistry is stronger than usual?

"But part of me is feeling like something very important just happened, and it's going to take some getting used to. This is the trapped feeling Daria talked about, isn't it?" At the same time, however, he felt wonderful, if frustrated. Would Francie feel trapped by the phenomenon—the soul-mate *imperative*? The annoyance in his chest returned.

"I think Daria felt ambushed before the attraction kicked in," Bent said. "She kept talking about free will and making up her own mind, not merely accepting such a medieval concept, not being forced, being in control, that sort of thing. When she finally accepted the idea for herself, then she worried *I* would feel trapped or bamboozled."

He ran a hand through his hair and shook his head. "I have to tell you, the idea of being soul mates, committed for life and all the rest, scared the hell out of me at first, and that's putting it mildly. I fought it for a while, and the damn thing almost killed me. The imperative won in the end, but it wasn't easy on either of us."

"Just what I wanted to hear," Clay said with a sarcastic grimace. The damn irritation increased, and he rubbed it again.

Bent's eyebrows shot up as he saw what Clay was doing and he grinned. "Got an itch?"

"Yeah, something bit me, I think."

"Clay, ol' buddy, I hate to tell you this, but this bite wasn't from a bug, not the six-legged variety, anyway."

"What are you talking about?" He looked down at his chest, as if he could see through his shirt.

"Daria and I both had the same sort of itch. It went into a pain for me, and I thought I was getting an ulcer. It's right over the center of your magic, isn't it?"

"So what?" Clay asked as he scratched. Then it hit him like a blow to the solar plexus, and he flattened his hand over the spot. "Oh, no."

"Oh, yes." Bent started laughing again.

"But you're not a practitioner. How could you itch?"

"Hell if I know. Francie probably itches, too. It's a sure sign, or so your father told me after the fact."

"I'm doomed." Clay could only shake his head.

"And remember, being soul mates just gets better all the time." Bent had a smug grin on his face.

"Yeah, assuming I survive the notification process." Clay clapped him on the shoulder and left before Bent told him something else, anything else he didn't want to know.

CHAPTER FIVE

When he returned to his home in West University Place, Clay wandered out onto the deck in back. A few leaves had fallen into the swimming pool, so he picked up the long-handled net and removed them. The manual labor did nothing to stop his thoughts from repeating the entire conversation with his family.

Soul mates. Holy hell.

He'd always assumed he'd find his mate in the ranks of practitioners. Damn, he knew every single female witch in Texas and many other places. He'd even dated a few, but that had been more like going out with a sister. None had generated any sparks, but then, they wouldn't have. No soul mate, no sparks, by definition. He certainly hadn't taken any of them to bed. Female practitioners always went to their soul mates as virgins. No soul mate, no bed, either, for women. That's just the way the practitioner world was.

Few male practitioners, himself included, were

virgins. Usually quite the contrary. He chuckled as he
remembered his mother's comment when Daria asked
why it was the case. "All that testosterone," she'd said
with a matter-of-fact wave. He'd dated a number of
nonpractitioner women, and while he'd enjoyed their
company, both in bed and out, he'd never stayed with
one woman very long. He'd had no desire to—probably
part of the male side of the soul-mate situation.

What was Francie? Was she a virgin? Nah, she
couldn't be. Not at her age in these times. What about
his other conclusion? That some bozo must have misused
her to make her so skittish, to cause her to retreat into
those horrible clothes and behind those big glasses? He
still believed in that. Damn, he'd like to get his hands
on the bastard.

On the other hand, though . . . If the idiot hadn't
treated her badly, she might have believed she was in love
with him and might even have married him. Nonpractitioner women were known to marry the wrong men.
He'd never have looked at a married woman, and he'd
have lost her before he even found her. Now there was a
gut-wrenching thought.

So what was he going to do?

Run? Fight it? Deny it? Probably none of those
would do any good. At least not according to Daria and
Bent. A little jab in his center confirmed his conclusion.

Clay leaned on the net handle and stared at the
water rippling softly in the slight breeze. How did he

feel about the whole situation? He was thirty-four years old. Most men were married by then. He had to admit, the bachelor scene was beginning to pall. And coming home to an empty house, having no one he could share his life and accomplishments with, no one to share his bed—it had all become increasingly dissatisfying.

He grunted. Who was he trying to kid? Basically, it sucked.

No camouflage, no artificial barriers. Only the truth.

He had to be truthful with himself, as well as with Francie. He wanted her with a blazing, red-hot passion that lit up the sky and dimmed all other past attractions to the strength of one candle.

What was even better, he knew they were destined for each other. None of this "will she or won't she" non-practitioners had to go through. No hassle. *She was his.*

He felt an inner glow right in the middle of his chest. A warmth spread through him, and the itch turned into a happy little tingle. He rubbed the spot and felt himself grin. Evidently the imperative agreed with him.

Okay, what now? He had a job to do—catch the damn hacker. The question was, how to do it and handle the urge to claim his soul mate at the same time?

Did he himself have the strength to hold his attraction to Francie in abeyance, to stay away from her, not engage in any more kisses, certainly not take the physical side any further until this hacker mess was over?

Not without going crazy. He couldn't stay away from

her. He had to work with her to trap Brenner. Maybe he could treat her like he would if she were a practitioner. What was it his father had told him way back when? Oh, yeah. He could remember the exact words.

"Warlocks seem to be preconditioned—it's in our genes or something—to let our women come to us," his dad had told him. "My grandfather told me our patience comes from the way witches were mistreated in the past, when they were beaten or raped or worse. They have to be sure we're not out to hurt them. They have to trust us. You'll know when she's made up her mind."

Francie wasn't a practitioner, but the same rules had to apply. So he'd take it slow. Get to know her, let her get to know him, gain her trust. Definitely *not* heat up the physical side with more than a few kisses.

Did he have the internal strength to resist taking the physical to its logical conclusion? He groaned to himself. From all he'd heard about the imperative, it would be a close contest, a real trial of his self-control. But it would all be okay in the end.

Soul mates were destined to be together. She wouldn't be able to resist him.

He agreed with Daria and Bent: he had to tell her about practitioners and the whole bit. But they had to catch Brenner. Should the job be the first priority? Put off telling her until they had plenty of time and no distractions? God knew, it was going to be hard to concentrate on the hacker with all this soul-mate business churning him up.

Well, hell. He rubbed his chest as he realized he was already a goner, already accepting that Francie was, in fact, his soul mate. It had to happen sometimes, he guessed. Practitioners always found their soul mates. What had Bent said? The idea of it scared him half to death? Oh, yeah.

On the other hand, look at the benefits. No, benefit, singular, all in one package: Francie.

How would Francie react when she found out about him, his abilities, the practitioner world? About her being his soul mate? Bent had a point about women being different from men. He himself had seen it in his sisters often enough. Look at the fight Daria had put up, all her talk about wanting to be her own woman, not be subject to medieval matchmaking.

Francie was already skittish, although for reasons he didn't know—yet. He'd have to bring her around.

He wouldn't fail. He couldn't fail. After all, in the end, the soul-mate imperative would have its way. He felt a huge rush of confidence, and his magic center warmed up, as though it was smiling.

Maybe he could reconnoiter the situation, sound Francie out, bring up the subject of magic, see what she thought before he laid it on her. Prepare her, sort of. Pave the way. Yeah, good idea. Clay looked at his watch. Eight o'clock. He'd give her a call like he promised.

He walked inside to his desk, sat down, picked up

the phone, and punched the buttons.

Francie answered on the first ring. "Hello?"

"Hi," he said, wondering if she had been waiting for his call. "What are you up to?"

"Just checking my e-mail."

"I hope I'm not disturbing you."

"No, not at all. I was just sitting here by the computer."

He grinned to himself. She had been waiting— must be the SMI at work. She sounded a little flustered. "How's Tamara?" he asked to change the subject.

"She's fine. She dropped by this afternoon. On their date Kevin said something about 'big plans at work' but didn't elaborate. She thinks it's a sales promotion. I told her about my working late this week."

"Good. Let's hope he's anxious to hack into Brazos and takes the bait for Thursday." He paused, but she didn't fill in the gap.

"So, what did you do all day?" he asked to keep the conversation going. Why was he having such trouble talking to her? Why wasn't she responding to him like she did last night?

"Just the laundry, a little cleaning, grocery shopping, some other stuff, nothing special."

"I had dinner at Daria's. Gloriana, my other sister, was in town and wanted to get back home, so we ate early."

"That must have been nice."

Man, getting her to talk to him was worse than finding a bug in a computer program without a spell to help. "Yeah, it was. Daria's a good cook. Bent, he's her husband of two months, but I think I told you that already. Anyway, he has fit right into the family, and it's always fun to hear what Glori's up to." God, now he was running off at the mouth. He cleared his throat. Get to the point, Morgan. "We had an interesting discussion about magic."

"Magic?" Francie asked. "Like magicians? Magic tricks? Or more like TV with all those special effects? Or fantasy stories?"

"No, more like the existence of magic today, extraordinary abilities, inexplicable talents, both generally in the universe and specifically in people. To manipulate energy and matter. Not the goofy stuff in movies or the magical aspects of religion. Just ordinary magic." God, he was so lame.

"Uh-huh."

She sounded wary, or like she was humoring him. He rolled his eyes to the ceiling, happy at least she couldn't see his face. "So, do you believe in magic? If somebody might be able to work magic?" He almost crossed his fingers in hope.

"That magic exists? That a person might be able to do something by casting a spell? That sort of thing?"

"Yeah."

She was silent for a few seconds. "No, I can't say that I do."

Her words ricocheted through his system and left

him feeling like a spell had gone bad and erased all the data on his hard drive. He opened his mouth, but nothing came out.

Francie, however, kept talking. "I've always felt that the supernatural, outside of religion, was just a big fake. Anybody claiming 'magical powers' has to be a charlatan. I guess I'm just a skeptic. I mean, the idea of magic, outside of fantasy books and computer games, *Dungeons and Dragons*, that sort of thing, well, the idea is ludicrous. I like the computer games as much as the next person, probably more, and I enjoy reading fantasy. But what adult would think it real, or such a possibility exists? Wizards and witches and sorcerers? Puh-lease."

She paused, but he couldn't utter a word. His thoughts had spiraled off into the void. He managed to cough, but she had more to say and ignored his interruption.

"I'm afraid I'm too grounded in the real world to even entertain such an idea. What's the use in even daydreaming about how nice it would be to cast a spell and, oh, I don't know, make it rain, make Kevin disappear, or get my housework done? That will never happen. I've always believed you have to make your own way in the world and take it as it is. You can't hope for a magical something to help, a miracle to happen. It all comes down to your innate abilities and how hard you work." She paused, then asked, "What about you?"

He cleared his throat and managed to croak out, "Oh, I've kept an open mind."

She didn't reply, but seemed to be waiting for him to say something else.

Mercifully, his brain started working again, and he knew he didn't, absolutely did not, want to continue this topic of conversation. It wouldn't do his cause any good. He might be able to use her comment about "innate abilities," and God knew, casting was hard work, but he couldn't show her any magic over the phone. None she'd accept. From those words about being "grounded in the real world," he knew she'd have to see something with her own eyes to believe it. He obviously had to do some rethinking about his strategy and tactics for breaking the news to her. Time to change the subject. "Listen, do you feel all right?"

"Sure, why?"

"You sound a little down."

"No, I'm fine."

"You're sure?" He knew something was wrong. She had sounded more like herself when she was denigrating magic. Now she was back to those flat tones.

"Well . . . I guess I'm a little depressed from talking to Tamara. I just hate deceiving her. It was so hard hearing her talk about Kevin as though he's a great guy."

"You're doing fine, Francie. I know it's difficult, but we'll catch Brenner soon. We just need to set the trap." He injected as much heartiness as he could into his voice to counter the listlessness he heard in hers.

"I guess. I'd better let you go. I still have to do some

laundry."

"I'll see you tomorrow, right? We have the meeting with Herb at ten."

"Oh, right. Well, bye."

"Bye, and don't worry, everything will be fine."

"Bye." She hung up.

"Well, hell," Clay said as he put down the phone. "That went nowhere. Worse than nowhere, it went backward."

Something was definitely wrong. What was going on in her head? Besides no magic and no belief in magic. She didn't even want to entertain the idea it could exist.

Daria had had it easy. At least Bent had accepted the idea of magic and practitioners. But what had his brother-in-law said? He'd wanted Daria so badly nothing mattered except that?

What was going on with the imperative? Why wasn't it harder at work? Francie didn't seem to be in the same sort of state toward him. She seemed to be just the opposite. Retreating instead of advancing. Running away from instead of toward him. Was she afraid of him?

Maybe if he backed off and let the soul-mate imperative do its work, he wouldn't have any problem. When the time came, he'd explain everything logically, and the rest would be clear sailing. Wouldn't it?

Yeah, that would do it. Take it easy, reassure her, become part of her life. Not let her avoid him without getting some answers why. God knew, it wasn't going to be easy, a few kisses here, a hug or two there, while his body was screaming for hers, clamoring for release.

He could do it, he was absolutely certain. All the pain and anguish would be worth it in the end. The imperative seemed to agree with him; a warm feeling engulfed his magic center.

He went off to the kitchen to pour himself a Scotch and contemplate his universe. But the color of the Scotch just reminded him of her smoky eyes, and then made him think of her kiss, and that didn't do him any good at all. Thoroughly disgruntled, he tried playing a computer game and surfing the Web, but those didn't work as distractions either, so he finally went to bed where he could stare at the ceiling until he fell asleep. At least he'd see her tomorrow.

His last thought was, everything would be all right.

❉✦✳❉✦

Francie hung up the phone and sat back in her chair. She felt like she'd run some horrible uphill race. What was wrong with her? She was such a coward.

Just before he'd called, she had decided to reiterate that it could be nothing but business between them, no more of those kisses. She wouldn't see him alone outside of the office. She couldn't take it.

But there she'd sat, by the phone, waiting for his call like some hormone-addled teenage twit, and the mere sound of his voice had given her a thrill that blew all other thoughts out of her head. Maybe if she avoided being in his presence, she could control herself better. Keep it purely business.

She had told him one truth. The talk with Tamara had depressed her.

And what was all of that stuff about magic? In everyday life? Francie snorted to herself. Yeah, right. Just like in the role-playing computer games she liked. True, she did like to play a sorceress and throw fireballs, but pretending to do so was the extent of any magic in her life. Unfortunately. She'd sure like to cast a spell and make all this go away.

The painful itch returned suddenly with a vengeance, and she rubbed the spot vigorously for a minute. What she really needed was a spell to zap the bug who had bitten her. A good frying would teach it to fool around with Francie, Sorceress of the Gulf Coast.

Speaking of computer games, she had a little task to accomplish with a program for Conundrum, so she relentlessly quashed any other thoughts and turned to her programming. She was able to lose herself in the codes until it was time for bed. She took a couple of aspirins to thwart an incipient headache and managed to fall asleep by concentrating on relaxing her muscles slowly, from her feet up to her head, and not thinking about anything else.

It worked after a fashion. She did go to sleep about one in the morning, only to dream of being in Clay's arms while multicolored lights swirled around them. She woke to a curious state of both exhaustion and exhilaration, convinced of one certainty: real life might not contain magic, but her dreams most assuredly did.

CHAPTER SIX

Monday morning, Francie walked into Herb Greenwood's office at ten o'clock. Herb, Clay, and two men, one vaguely familiar and an unknown other, were standing by his desk. Consultants must not believe in casual office dressing, she surmised, because Clay looked gorgeous in a navy blue blazer, gray trousers, white shirt, and a red tie with an abstract design.

When her eyes met his silvery gaze, she shivered and pulled her baggy brown sweater tighter around her. She managed a weak smile. Three cups of coffee this morning hadn't been enough to prepare her for seeing him again. She turned to concentrate on the other men; it was safer.

"Oh, good," Herb said. "Now you're here, we can start. Francie, do you know Tom Robbins from the Legal Department?" He indicated the short, rotund, balding man with rimless glasses.

"Oh, yes, Mr. Robbins, I've seen you in the eleva-

DO YOU BELIEVE IN MAGIC?   101

tor." She and Robbins exchanged nods.

"And this is Lieutenant Bill Childress from the Houston Police Department," Herb continued. "Legal decided we should call in the police before we go any further."

Childress was a lean, nondescript man about six feet tall with short brown hair, wearing a rumpled brown suit. Francie thought he was probably just the sort of fellow people ignored or flat out didn't see, but she liked his penetrating dark hazel eyes and firm handshake.

Herb waved them to the round conference table and pulled up his desk chair for himself. "We've brought them up to date, Francie," he said before turning to Childress. "I understand you've worked with the Morgan family before, Lieutenant," he said as they all sat down.

"A few members of it," Childress replied. "I was on the case at the Glennell Company with Mr. Benthausen and Ms. Morgan. Clay's and her father, Alaric Morgan, helped us make the case, and I've known Clay for some time."

"I was on the periphery," Clay interjected.

"I do wish you had called us earlier on this one," Childress said in a somewhat exasperated tone. "I don't like to use civilians for undercover, but I guess we're stuck with your plan now."

"Well," Herb said, "let's take it from where we stand now. Clay, I think you said earlier you've let Brenner know he can get into Francie's on Thursday night."

"Francie, why don't you tell it?" Clay asked her. "It's your story."

Francie related her conversation with Tamara as succinctly as possible. She said nothing about her distaste for deception; after all, what good would it do?

"We can hope Tamara tells her boyfriend the coast is clear for Thursday, but we can't guarantee it," Clay added when she finished.

"Brenner hasn't been on Ms. Stevens's computer or tried to hack in from somewhere else since last Wednesday?" Childress asked.

"That's correct," Clay answered. "If he takes the bait on Thursday and dials in from Francie's, I'm going to play with him from here—let him in, throw him out, let him in, move him around, and generally frustrate the hell out of him. Francie thinks he's after sales and pricing information, and Herb and I agree with her."

"So afterward you're going to arrange to meet him and talk him into letting you into his scheme?" Childress asked.

"Let's just say I'm going to make myself attractive and available as a computer expert amenable to making a fast buck and not too fastidious about how I do it." Clay glanced at Francie and smiled before continuing. "I'll meet him through Tamara. Francie and I have established ourselves in Tamara's mind as a couple, don't you think, Francie?"

Francie thought about Tamara's claiming she and Clay were made for each other. "Yes," she answered, looking at Childress rather than Clay. "She thinks we are—a couple, I mean."

"I suggest we invite Tamara and Brenner for dinner Saturday night," Clay said. "We could go to a restaurant or eat in, your choice. It will give me the chance to put some ideas into his head. What do you think, Francie?"

His direct question drew her eyes to his. She tried to be matter-of-fact in her answer, but she could feel tension coiling in her stomach. "Why don't I cook something? Being in my apartment should give you more privacy for whatever you want to tell Kevin." And being in her own home would give her at least the illusion of being in control of the evening.

"Fine with me," Clay answered with a smile and a wink. "If we can also find out where he goes for a drink after work, all the better. I'd like to meet him on his turf later next week and see if he takes the bait. Could you ask Tamara about dinner Saturday?"

"I'll ask her tonight," she replied.

"If you do meet him alone, I want you to wear a wire," the police lieutenant interjected. "We need some hard evidence, and a recording could provide it."

"Certainly," Clay stated. "Wouldn't it be even more conclusive if I actually hack into Brazos with Brenner with me, telling me what to look for? Then, Bill, you could arrest him with his hand in the till."

"Let's see what we're dealing with first," Childress replied. "We don't want to put you in any danger."

Tom Robbins leaned forward. "We still don't know

if Brenner is invading our computers on his own or if he's in collusion with anyone at NatChem, do we?"

"No," Herb answered. "That's what we want Clay to find out. How we'll proceed depends on that information."

"Right," Childress agreed. "And it will determine who we prosecute."

"So," Herb said, "Francie, you'll set up the date for Saturday. Clay, you'll be here on Thursday night to handle Brenner."

"I'll be here," Childress said.

"Me, too," Francie said. "I'm working late then, remember?" she added when Clay raised his eyebrows at her. He didn't think she would miss the event, did he?

"Come about five on Thursday," Herb said. "I'll have some sandwiches sent in. I don't trust this guy. I'll bet he'll try to get in early. After all, he doesn't know what time Francie will be home. I want to nail this bastard to the wall."

The meeting broke up, and Francie slipped out of Herb's office while Clay and Childress were talking about recording devices. She breathed a sigh of relief as she went immediately to a meeting on another floor. If Clay came looking for her, he'd never find her there.

That evening Francie called Tamara after she returned home and invited her and Kevin for Saturday dinner. Tamara was ecstatic her friend was finally coming out of her "cocoon" and immediately accepted the invitation.

Francie waited until Tuesday morning, however, to call Clay, and she called him at home, not on his cell phone. It would be easier to keep her equilibrium if she didn't speak to him directly, or so she told herself. As she had hoped, she got his answering machine. The sound of his voice sent a shiver through her, despite her resolve.

"Hi, it's Francie," she told the recorder in as perky a tone as she could manage. "I asked Tamara and Kevin over for Saturday night. Come about six. I'll see you Thursday at the office." There, she thought as she hung up. That should hold him. She'd screen her calls at home tonight to continue her avoidance plans.

Tuesday evening Clay entered the gym at the Downtown Y and headed for the court where his team would be playing. He noticed a women's team on a far sideline waving at someone, and when he looked around to find their target, who should be walking toward him but Francie? She was waving at the women and not looking where she was going, so he deliberately stood in her way and had the satisfaction of having her run right into him.

"Clay!"

"Hi, Francie," Clay said as he held her upper arms to steady her for a moment. "I didn't know you played in the leagues here." He grinned as he looked her up and down. Mercy, he pleaded to any higher being who happened to be listening. She looked gorgeous in a thin T-shirt and shorts. Long, long legs, a stunning body, and a face to match, with no eyeglasses to obscure the view. Man, would he like to get her alone, but here they stood in front of God and everybody.

Then he remembered how she seemed to be avoiding him. "I heard the message you left on my home machine. Why didn't you call my cell?"

"Oh, uh, I couldn't find your cell number," she stammered. "Is six o'clock all right for Saturday?"

"Fine. I'll bring some wine and dessert, how about it? Red or white?" She was not meeting his eyes, and she was fidgeting with her towel, and he definitely did not like it. What was the matter with her?

"I don't know what I'm going to fix, probably something easy with pasta, so bring what you like to drink. Look . . ."

"Hey, Francie! Let's go!" Whatever she had been about to say was interrupted by a woman on the court.

"I have to go." She waved back at her teammate.

"I'll see you later," Clay said. "How about after the game?"

"Uh, no, I'm sorry. I'm going out with my team. It's a regular thing." She gave him what he thought was a nervous smile and started for the court.

"I'll call you," he said to her back and received a nod of her ponytail in return. Damn. His hands on his hips, he stood for a minute looking at her until he realized her entire team was staring at him. Not only that, but he was late for his own game. Afterward, he searched for her, first on the court, later in the lobby, but her game was long over and he couldn't find her.

Francie didn't answer her phone that night or the next; all he reached was her answering machine. Clay considered calling her at two in the morning, but decided it would only make her mad. He could bide his time. Thursday night would probably be filled with people, but Saturday . . . he'd be in her apartment, and they'd be by themselves at some point. He'd see to it. Then he'd get some answers about why she was avoiding him.

And maybe this damn itching imperative would leave him alone.

CHAPTER SEVEN

Thursday at five, Clay, Francie, Herb, and Bill Childress gathered in Herb's office. "The operators in the computer room will call when Brenner hacks in," Herb said. He pointed to the pile of deli sandwiches on his conference table. "Help yourselves. There are soft drinks on the credenza, but if you want coffee, I'll get a carafe from the lunchroom."

Nobody wanted coffee, and they all dug into the food. Conversation was nonexistent, which was just fine with Francie. She felt like she was still getting over seeing Clay at the Y. What a shock. No, several shocks. First, from literally running into him and feeling her own body zing to attention. Second, from all that barely clothed masculinity. Lord, have mercy, the man was as good-looking in shorts and a tank top as he was in a suit. Long legs, lean muscles, and a rangy build combined with black hair and silver eyes into a potent male presence. Last, from all the questions and teasing from her teammates she had to endure. Now, she just had to get through the evening.

They hadn't been eating more than twenty minutes when Herb's phone rang. He answered it, said, "We'll be right there," and turned to his visitors. "What did I tell you? Brenner's early."

They trooped down the hall and into the computer room. The operators were leaning over a terminal. Herb introduced Dick Fenimore, a tall, thin string bean of a man about twenty-five, with a shock of unruly red hair and wearing a T-shirt with a Nine Inch Nails logo, jeans, and running shoes; and Jim Kelly, a pudgy, already balding thirty-ish fellow in a Western shirt, jeans, and cowboy boots.

"Man," Dick exclaimed to Clay, "this tracking program you installed is so cool. I've gotta learn how to program like this."

"I can't believe this guy," Jim interjected with a West Texas twang. "He's such a bonehead. Neither of us can figure out what he's after. And what self-respecting hacker tries to dial in at five-thirty in the afternoon? Two in the morning I can understand, but five-thirty?"

"Move over, guys," Clay said. "Let's have some fun." He sat down at the terminal and started hitting the keys.

Over the course of the next hour and a half, Clay toyed with Brenner, moving him around the system, cutting him off, letting him back in after several tries, and generally making the hacker's life miserable.

With growing awe, Francie watched Clay manipulate Kevin. She knew she herself was no slouch with a program, but she had no idea how he had managed to do what he did. Remembering a phrase she had heard from a technical writer, she almost chuckled. "Flying fingers on the keyboard," the writer had said, admonishing Francie to slow down in her explanation about the workings of a complicated program. The description fit Clay's movements as he flipped between windows, typed in commands, ran the mouse pointer around the screen, and sent Kevin spinning off into the ether. If there were such an animal as a computer wizard, she thought, Clay Morgan was certainly one.

His abilities didn't change any of her own feelings about him, she told herself as the group rose from their chairs. She still had to remember this was all business. Nothing personal.

After Clay locked Kevin out completely, the foursome went back to Herb's office. "What do you think, Clay, Francie? What was Brenner after?" Herb asked as they took their seats.

"It looked to me like he was trying to find order entry and pricing again," Francie answered.

"I agree," Clay said. "He must have been doing some studying or research into your brand of software application, because he almost managed to open the order-entry system."

"Now as I understand it, you have a computer copy of every move Brenner made tonight?" Childress asked.

"That's correct, Bill," Clay said, nodding. "And it shows Brenner was using Francie's computer."

Childress's cell phone rang. The police lieutenant spoke into it for a few moments. "That was the officer we have watching Ms. Stevens's apartment. He took photos of Brenner at the computer. He said the man looked ready to punch in the monitor a couple of times. Brenner just left, obviously angry, from the way he peeled out of the parking lot. You can go back home any time, Ms. Stevens."

"Thanks," she told him. Turning to Herb, she asked, "Do you need me any more tonight?"

"Your dinner with Brenner is set for Saturday night?" he asked.

"Yes, that's correct," Francie replied.

"I'll let you know how it goes, Herb," Clay put in.

"Go on home, Francie," Herb said. "I'll see you tomorrow. Anything else, Clay?"

"Nope. I'll walk you out, Francie." He held the door and followed her out, leaving Herb and Childress talking about the surveillance.

"This isn't necessary, Clay," Francie told him as they walked to her cubicle. She busied her hands with her notebook and pencil so he couldn't hold one of them, but it didn't help. He put his hand on the small of her back, and she could feel the energy flowing between them, even through her sweater.

"Why don't we go out for a drink, or maybe some more to eat? I don't know about you, but a hastily eaten sandwich is not my idea of dinner."

She didn't, wouldn't, look at him and stepped away to enter her workspace. Why was she finding it so difficult to carry on a simple conversation? At least she'd prepared herself with an excuse just in case he had asked her out after dealing with Brenner. "Thanks, but I told Tamara I'd stop by her shop if I left work in time. She has a new shipment she wants to show me." She pulled her purse and a book out of her desk drawer.

"How was your game on Tuesday?" Clay asked as they walked toward the elevator.

"We won, but it wasn't easy." Basketball seemed like a safe topic. She grinned widely. "The team we played took the championship from us last year, and this was a grudge match. How about you? How did your team do?"

"We won, too."

"Good."

They reached the lobby. She tried again to discourage him from accompanying her. "I'm in the parking garage across the street. You don't have to . . ."

"Yes, I do," Clay interrupted. "I'm in the same place."

He didn't say anything—for which she was grateful—as they exited the building, crossed the street, and entered the parking garage. Francie took her keys out of her purse. She could feel her anxiety increasing. What if he wanted to kiss her again?

At her car, Francie unlocked her door with the remote control and reached for the door handle, but Clay put his hand on hers.

"Please don't do this," she said, as his touch made her nerve endings vibrate.

"Francie, we need to talk." His voice was low, and he raised her hand off the handle and cradled it between his larger ones. "About us. Our kiss last Saturday . . ."

"Clay, that can't happen again." She took her hand back and grasped her purse with it so tightly she probably made indentations in the leather.

He stared at her as if she'd grown horns. "What are you talking about?"

"I think we've had enough practice 'being together.' When we introduce you to Kevin, that should end our needing to 'date' or convince Tamara we're a couple. This is all only business, after all. When you make the arrangements with Kevin, I can step out of the picture, and we can go back to our separate lives."

"Our separate lives," he repeated in a hollow tone. "What about us, our relationship?"

"Clay, there is no *us*. Don't you see? This is all a charade, a play we've been putting on. Let's just get through this . . . this *mess* with Kevin. I can't think straight anymore, worrying about Tamara and trying to play a part. God, I hate deception."

"So do I. That's what we need to discuss."

She could see a little anger in his eyes, accompanied

by something else. Determination? Frustration? Confusion? No matter. "I disagree. I'm asking you not to compound the issue further by pretending feelings that don't exist."

"Feelings that don't exist? I know myself, Francie, and I don't have *feelings that don't exist.*" He said the last four words as if their presence in his mouth left a vile taste.

"Well, I'm not going to discuss anything with you standing in a parking garage. I have to meet Tamara. I'll see you on Saturday."

He clenched his jaw and stared at her for a long moment through narrowed eyes. Finally he nodded. "All right, Francie. Let's get through the dinner and then see where we stand."

She thought of telling him that they didn't "stand" anywhere, but kept her mouth shut and opened her door. She did not want to prolong the conversation.

He turned and left, taking long strides as if he couldn't get away from her fast enough.

She climbed into her car and sat for a moment, her forehead resting on her hands on the steering wheel. He wanted to talk about the kiss and where they stood? What did that mean? Why didn't the man understand that there was no *couple*, there never was and never would be? Had he convinced himself from two dates and a few kisses that they had a relationship? Not even real dates, but playacting, people impersonating a couple.

She sat up and shook her head. What did he mean

about discussing deception? God only knew, there was enough deception in this mess to fill Houston's baseball stadium. Why discuss it to death?

All she had to do was get through the dinner with Tamara and Kevin. Then she could go back to her own life, blessedly devoid of all this turmoil. She'd be in charge of herself again.

Maybe she'd even start dating for real. Find a nice man, an undemanding man, an honest one. A normal-looking one who didn't attract women like flies, one who couldn't charm the socks—and other pieces of apparel—off women. One she could trust. Maybe her computer buddies knew some guys who were interested in computers and liked the things she liked.

She raised her head and looked at her reflection in the visor mirror. In the dim light, her eyes looked huge and weird, slightly haunted. Her stomach hurt, too—little pulses of pain—probably from gulping down that sandwich.

"Idiot," she scolded herself. "You're a computer analyst, and you can't even think straight. You just have to hang in there a little longer."

She started the car, backed out of her space, and exited the garage. She almost drove onto the freeway before she remembered she had told Tamara she'd drop by. "Idiot," she said again, as she made the turn to take her to the shop.

She rubbed her stomach again. Maybe Tamara had

some antacid tablets she could take.

❧❀❦❀❧

On his way home, Clay played over the events of the evening. He thought he had worked Brenner well, giving the man nothing but grief. He'd be ready to find an expert when they met.

As for Francie . . . She had on those drab, baggy clothes again. She looked pale, like she wasn't getting enough sleep. And she was definitely staying away from him, tonight being only the latest example. As much as he wanted, needed to talk to her, he hadn't pushed in the parking garage. He definitely did not want to provoke a confrontation that would make her angry or drive her away. They needed to be calm and together on Saturday.

To be fair, he admitted she had to be feeling the strain of dealing with Tamara and her hacker boyfriend. That must be what was skewing her reactions to him, her soul mate.

But her statement about hating deception had given him pause. Was he deceiving her? Not about Brenner, of course. But about himself? About his motives? Did she still think what was between them was business, only business? Was "only business" really what she wanted?

How could she want him to go away if she were truly his soul mate? Especially after those kisses.

He certainly wasn't playacting. Was she? How could

she be, with the soul-mate imperative goading her on? She had to be itching and hurting, especially if she was denying her feelings. The ones that supposedly didn't exist. Did she think he was lying to her about those? His existed, all right. A small sunburst of pain spread out from his magic center as if to corroborate his thoughts.

What about his being a practitioner, he asked himself as he stopped for a red light. Was he deceiving her about that? He certainly wasn't telling her the whole truth, but as Daria had once said, the ability to cast spells and work magic didn't ordinarily come up spontaneously in conversation. And look where it had gotten him when he did broach the subject. Definitely not forward.

He had to overcome her nonbelief in magic, and he doubted that would be easy. Not after her out-and-out, bald statements about being "grounded in the real world," whatever that meant.

He had to show her what he was, convince her of his magical talents, but how? He could cast a ball of light and ignite a candle, but he didn't have the showy abilities his mother and Gloriana did. On the other hand, Francie had been watching him closely as he led Brenner around the system with the help of his spell-aided program. She had looked fascinated and delighted with his manipulations. He knew she would like to know how he did it.

Maybe that was what he needed to do. Get her over to his house and show her his fancier computer spells.

Those ought to convince her. Yeah, the more he thought about it, he really liked the idea. Computer wizardry would come to his rescue.

They had to talk about what was going on between them, and soon. But when she looked at him with those big brown eyes full of anxiety, he couldn't bring himself to force the issue. It was all he could do not to take her in his arms and kiss her senseless.

First came the dinner on Saturday and the chance to make her see that what was between them was definitely not business, but magic of the most ancient kind. He grinned in anticipation as he exited the Southwest Freeway and turned left on Buffalo Speedway.

His magic center seemed to like his plan. The good, ol' SMI was almost crooning along with him to the Brooks & Dunn song, "My Heart Belongs to You."

CHAPTER EIGHT

Clay arrived at Francie's just after six on Saturday night. He was pleased to see Tamara and Brenner were already present. He walked in with a bag holding the wine and a box of French bakery goodies, handed Francie the dessert, and kissed her lightly on the lips. When she frowned, he smiled and kissed her again. "Hi, Francie," he murmured, "I missed you." Damn, she had on those glasses and a dull, bulky sweater again.

Francie glared at him but wiped the look off her face as she turned to her other guests. "You know Tamara, of course. This is Kevin Brenner."

Clay shook hands with Brenner and exchanged greetings with Tamara. Brenner was a thirty-five-year-old, slightly beefy six-footer with thinning blond hair. He looked like he worked out in a gym, but had not gone for the total big-muscles, bodybuilder approach. Probably had played football in high school and college and kept himself up since, Clay surmised.

"I brought both red and white wines." Clay turned back to Francie.

"Fine," she replied. "The shrimp looked good at the grocery store, so I'm combining them with pasta and sun-dried tomatoes. I like red wine, and Tamara likes white, so everybody will be happy. Why don't you bring the wine into the kitchen, and then you can come out here and visit. Dinner will be ready in just a few minutes."

Clay followed her into the kitchen, put the white wine in the refrigerator, and asked, "Where's your cork-screw? I'll open the red so it can breathe."

"In the drawer on your left," she answered as she poured the penne pasta into the boiling water.

Clay opened the wine and put it on the counter. Turning, he lifted the lid over the sauce as Francie stirred the pasta. "Hmmmm. Smells good. Need any help?" He intentionally stood very close to her.

"No," she told him, with a well-placed elbow for emphasis. "Go visit. Do you want something to drink before dinner?"

"Nope, I'll wait for the wine."

Clay went back to the living room and sat in a chair across from the couch where Tamara and Kevin relaxed with drinks. A tray of veggies and dip was on the coffee table between them.

"Tamara said you were in computers, Clay," Kevin stated. "Some sort of consultant?"

"I fix problems for my clients. Hardware and software. What do you do?" He took a carrot, swirled it in the dip, and munched.

"I'm in sales, sales manager, in fact."

"So you're in the office more than calling on customers?"

"Yeah. Man, I'd rather be out, but the company decided to promote me, and I plan to go places with them, so I'm playing the corporate game."

Clay thought Kevin tried to look modest, but didn't pull it off. "Well, good luck. I'm out on my own because I couldn't stand the corporate game, not being my own boss."

"Francie said she met you at one of those computer seminars," Tamara interjected.

"Yes, the funny thing is, I almost didn't go to the class. I had just flown back from a pleasure trip to Vegas, spending some of my ill-gotten gains. If I hadn't gone to the seminar, we wouldn't have met. Guess my luck was running right for a change. Francie said she was helping you with your computer. How is it going?" Clay smiled encouragingly at the redhead.

"I feel much better about it now. I computerized my shop to make the accounting and inventory easier, but deciding what items to stock is still as much applying intuition and understanding trends as it ever was. All the computerization in the world won't help me with that. Sometimes I feel like a snail, creeping up on computers while the rest of the world passes me by. I was just never interested much, even with a computer whiz for a roommate in college. I don't know what I'd do without Francie and Kevin. They've shown me so much. Kevin's very good at finding information and my competitor's Web sites on the Internet." She patted Kevin's hand and smiled at him.

"I'm trying to learn how to program, too, but I'm not very proficient at it yet," Kevin admitted. "I know how to use our company programs and how to get around the Internet, but I'm nowhere near Francie's or your league. I've taken only a couple of programming courses, so I have a long way to go."

"Well, for what it's worth," Clay stated, taking some more dip on a carrot, "I couldn't do what you do, selling day in and day out, having to be nice to everybody, including the jerks."

"You must be a killer consultant, if you don't have to be nice to people," Tamara ventured.

"By the time some of my clients finally call me in, they've screwed up so badly, they're begging for help, and usually it's their own damn fault they're in the mess in the first place. They don't want me to be nice. Sometimes I think they need me to tell them off for their own internal reasons. It just means I charge them more, which I then lose at the crap tables." Clay shrugged to imply the loss of money meant nothing to him and began to relate some client-from-hell stories as Francie called for help putting things on the table.

Dinner degenerated hilariously into more stories, Tamara with rich ladies from hell who came into her shop demanding what looked worst on them, Kevin with customers from hell who changed their minds twenty times before delivery, and Francie with programmers and users from hell who didn't have a clue what the other was talking about.

Over dessert and coffee, Kevin asked, "You must run into all sorts of things that go wrong with computers. What's the worst?"

"People, always people," Clay answered. "If it's not somebody in the company, these days it's an outsider, usually a hacker, messing around in a company's files. You know, like the TV movie where the kid hacked into the Defense Department systems."

"Is it hard to hack?" Kevin asked with a disingenuous smile.

Good, just the question he'd been hoping Brenner would ask. "No. Getting in is the easy part. Finding what you want or gaining access to the applications can be the difficult part." Not really, of course, but Clay figured this inept hacker needed to hear it since he'd blundered all over the place inside the Brazos systems. "One of my sidelines is computer security, and I hack into my clients' computers to demonstrate their vulnerabilities. I don't mean to be immodest," he said with a smile meaning just the opposite, "but I can get into anybody's system, find what I'm looking for, and get out with the company none the wiser."

Let Kevin stew over this information for a while. It was time to change the subject, and he turned to the redhead across the table. "How's business, Tamara?"

"So far, so good," the little redhead replied. "The wealthier of my customers don't seem to be affected by economic downturns, although we haven't seen much of the south-of-the-border trade lately."

"Francie said she was going by to see your new shipment. I personally would like to see her in something new, like the blue outfit she wore to the theater. She said it was one of yours. Did you talk her into any other purchases?" He smiled at Tamara conspiratorially.

She smiled back the same way. "Almost. One cute outfit will look wonderful on her, but no sale. Work on her for me, will you?"

"Is there a commission in it for me?"

"Of course."

"Now look, you two," Francie broke in. "Don't gang up on me. My clothes are fine."

Everyone laughed at Francie's huffiness, and even Francie had to stifle a smile.

Then Kevin asked, "How's your computer game coming, Francie?"

Francie grimaced at the question.

"Computer game?" Clay asked.

She took a bite of the juicy apple tart he had brought for dessert, probably so she didn't have to answer right away. She hadn't mentioned the game before. The subject of games in general had not come up in their previous conversations.

She swallowed and said, "Some friends of mine from college days and I are creating a fantasy role-playing computer game. We want to see if we're the hotshots we think we are. To answer your question, Kevin, it's coming along just fine. In fact, they'll be over here tomorrow. We'll work on it all afternoon and into the evening."

"How long have you and these 'gamesters' been doing this?" Clay asked.

"For quite a while. We all have regular jobs and only work on it in our spare time." That was enough talk about the game. She glanced around the table. "Does anyone want more coffee or dessert?" When they all shook their heads, she rose. "Tamara, will you help me clear the table?"

"We can help, too," Clay offered. He watched Francie pick up plates. She was refusing to look at him again. What game? Why hadn't she told him about it? He'd be sure to find out later.

"Thanks, but no," she replied to his offer. "The kitchen's too small for more than Tamara and me. We'll just clear the table. I'll do the dishes later. You two relax."

Clay retreated with Kevin to the living room where they resumed their former seats.

"Make many trips to Vegas?" Leaning back on the sofa, Kevin was the picture of casual indifference, but the way his eyes darted all over belied his disinterest in Clay's answer.

Clay slouched in his chair and stretched his legs out in front of him. "As many as I can. I've had rotten luck lately. My next trip I'll recoup my losses for certain."

"What do you play?"

"Blackjack, poker, or craps."

"Man, I'm no good at gambling," Kevin complained.

"It's a lot like hacking," Clay said. "Either you've got the ability and the luck, or you don't. If you have the ability and the money, you can ride out the downturns in luck. It's not easy, enticing Lady Luck again, I can tell you. I may have to find some new clients before this bad run is over."

"A new source of revenue, you mean?"

"Yeah. I may have to go back to actually working for a living." He shrugged and Kevin laughed. The look in Brenner's eye told Clay the would-be hacker was beginning to get the message. Hell, he'd practically written it on the wall. Clay's estimation of Kevin's intelligence went down another notch.

The entrance of the women effectively stopped the conversation. Fine, Clay thought. Brenner needed to think about the situation before Clay gave him the next nudge.

"Kevin and I were thinking about going to a club. Would y'all like to come along?" Tamara asked.

"Thanks, but not this time," Clay answered after a quick glance at Francie, who gave him the tiniest of head shakes. "I've had a hard week, and I need my rest. I'm planning an early night." He made a face like he was tired as he said it, but shot a sly look at Francie.

Tamara gave him another conspiratorial smile and started making their good-byes.

After five minutes of pleasantries, Francie watched them go down the stairs. She took a deep breath as she closed the door. Maintaining a smooth facade during the dinner had exhausted her, and now she had to deal with Clay. Her arms crossed in front of her, she turned to him. "Do you realize what you said, what they think we're going to do next?"

"Of course." Clay immediately swooped, grabbing her around the waist, hoisting her up, and twirling her in a circle from the entryway back into the living room. "I thought they'd never leave," he said, grinning at her as he deposited her back on her feet.

"Clay, get hold of yourself!" Francie scolded, pushing back from him, but her heart was beating wildly. No man had ever picked her up as if she weighed nothing, much less whirled her around.

"I'd rather get hold of you," he laughed. He waggled his eyebrows at her. "And now, woman . . ."

"Yes?" She was trying not to think about what he would do next, what her body was telling her it would like him to do. Business, she had told herself repeatedly during the day, being with him was strictly business. Now as she looked up into his silver eyes, she realized how difficult it would be to hold on to her determination. She took another step backward.

"Let's clean up the kitchen, and then you can show me your game," he said with another grin. "I'll wash and put stuff in the dishwasher. You take care of drying and putting things away."

"Well," Francie said as she reached for a dishcloth, "you're certainly housebroken." She had never seen Kevin lift so much as a finger to help the women with or after dinner.

"With my mother, no one has a choice. Not if you want to eat again anytime soon." He winked at her as he opened the dishwasher before turning back to the sink.

Francie could only stare at his broad back for a moment as her system registered the effect of his wink. Why did she feel every move or gesture this man made? Finally she shook her head to clear it, reached for the pasta bowl, and resolutely repeated her mantra about it all being only business.

When the kitchen was spotless, Clay stopped Francie before she could leave the room. "Uh-uh, remember, no camouflage," he chided. He took her glasses off and laid them on the counter.

Francie blinked at him, feeling both intrigued and anxious. The first, because he was almost overpowering, standing this close to her, and she wondered again at the attraction between them that grew more powerful each time she was with him, no matter how strong her vow to guard herself. The second, because now she had to show him the game, and his opinion of it assumed great importance all of a sudden. What if he didn't like it? Before she could decide how his disapproval would make her feel, his next words took her mind in another direction.

"And speaking of camouflage, what do you have under this bulky thing?" he asked as he plucked at the hem of her sweater.

She felt her face grow warm as she realized what she did have on under the sweater—a set of champagne-colored, lacy lingerie. She certainly wasn't going to show him that. The game was a much safer subject. She frowned and batted at his hands. "None of your business. Come on and I'll show you the game. We're calling it 'Conundrum.'"

At her computer, Francie started the game as she explained the premise, the story line, and their progress. "We don't have music or voice or sound effects yet, and it took forever to decide on some of the graphics. We each had fun designing individual villains and monsters." She displayed the character creation screen. "What attributes would you like your hero to have?"

For the next hour, they played the game, discussing it and the programming behind it as much as actually playing. Clay had some interesting and helpful ideas about streamlining the code, and she wrote herself a few notes to tell the group the next day.

Finally she turned to him. While demonstrating

the game, seeing it in its entirety instead of the piece-meal way she usually approached it, she had concluded she and her friends had done a fine job. But she had to know his evaluation of their efforts, so she said, "I think you have a pretty good idea what we're about. What do you think?"

Clay leaned back in the chair and looked her in the eye. "I think you have a potential hit. The story line is intriguing, and not the run-of-the-mill 'save the king-dom' that has been overdone. Your monsters are really awful and awesome, your heroes and heroines look good, the puzzles players have to solve are ingenious, and the fights require the player to use strategy to win them. Your graphics are outstanding, and I can't wait until you pick the music and sound effects."

Francie couldn't help but grin. Praise from a com-puter wizard like Clay was praise, indeed. "Thank you, Clay. Your opinion means a lot to me."

"I tell it as I see it, Francie. Remember, no camou-flage, the truth." He leaned toward her, tilting his head with obvious intent.

Before he could kiss her, she ducked her head and swung back to the computer. "I'd better shut this down."

She didn't turn toward him, but could feel his eyes on her for a long moment. She stayed very still, only moving her hand on the mouse to click the commands.

He finally rose and placed his chair back against the wall. In a somewhat resigned tone, he said, "And I'd better get out of here and let you get some sleep."

"Did you accomplish what you wanted to with Kevin this evening?" she asked as they left the room.

"I think so. Brenner now knows I have a potential need for money to feed my gambling habit and I can probably program rings around him. I didn't try to do more than leave that impression tonight. The next step is to 'accidentally' run into him. Were you able to find out where he goes for a drink after work?"

"Yes, right before you arrived tonight. I said someone at work was asking where to meet a date on the other side of downtown. Where the NatChem offices are, but I didn't say that, of course. Kevin said he likes to go to a place on Old Market Square. He mentioned something about being a regular there on Thursday nights, when Tamara's shop is open." She grimaced, thinking of Tamara and the deception again.

At the door, before she could stop him, Clay put his arms around her and hugged her. His voice was low and comforting when he said, "I know how difficult this is for you. You're doing great, honey."

She almost relaxed against him—oh, how tired she was and how badly she wanted to accept his support—but her mind was in control tonight. She felt his embrace change to something harder, more urgent, and she stepped back. "Thanks, but it will be over soon, I hope, and my life can get back to normal."

He didn't take her hint—ignored it altogether, in

fact—and followed her as she retreated. She wondered, from the stark look on his face and the predator's glint in his eyes, if he'd even heard her. She put her hands on his chest to push him back, but when she touched him, heat spread like wildfire up her arms, and she could almost feel her bones melting. Pushing back was impossible.

Placing a finger under her chin, he tilted her head back and looked into her eyes. "Francie," was all he said before brushing her lips with his, then returning to claim her mouth.

A truly glorious joy swept through her at the touch of his lips. And she was lost.

"Yeeesssss!" went through Clay's brain like a sky-rocket as she kissed him back. On the back of his eyelids, he thought he saw the missile explode into the colors of the rainbow. Even expecting the upheaval to his senses, thanks to the last time he kissed her, he wasn't totally ready for the sense of power and sheer rapture that burst from his magic center to every molecule in his body.

He struggled for control and loosened the hold he had on her, although he had to fight his tight muscles and relax them one by one. Her scent, a combination of flowers and peach-smelling shampoo, didn't help.

"Lord, lady, what you do to me," he whispered, then cursed himself for saying anything at all as he felt her spine stiffen. He'd known she was resisting their attraction, but once she was in his arms and even though he only meant comfort at first, he'd simply had to kiss her again. He didn't care if it was the imperative or his own libido driving him. He'd needed that kiss. Whatever she did next, it was worth it.

She pushed at his chest, and he stepped back until they were no longer touching.

She closed her eyes for a moment, then opened and raised them to his. He could see tumult and desire warring with each other in the smoky depths and knew she was about to tell him again this was all just business. She was obviously in denial about both her feelings and his.

He didn't know exactly what to do about it or how to convince her otherwise. He didn't want her to run from him. All he could do was stick to his plan to take it easy. She'd come around eventually. He only had to persevere and let the soul-mate imperative work its magic.

But then she said in a firm voice, "I asked you not to do that again."

Despite his decision, anger and frustration at her small rejection spurred him to answer, "Consider it an experiment about those 'feelings that don't exist.' Whatever *you're* doing, *I'm* not playacting. I'll call you tomorrow." He walked out the door and closed it behind him.

Francie leaned against the door and listened to him walking down the steps. Damn that man! He'd done it to her again, kissed her and left her, refused to talk about her request, had not agreed to stop kissing and touching her. At least this time she was in better shape, her brain not so muddled, her body not so limp.

But she had let him kiss her again. She had cooperated—not merely acquiesced—but actively returned his kiss. Those feelings of utter bliss and excitement in his arms had robbed her of any thought, much less the ability to object.

This situation kept getting worse, not better. Where was her determination? Where was her strong will? They both disappeared in a poof when he turned those silver eyes in her direction, and especially when he touched her.

Maybe her earlier idea was the correct one: she was possessed by aliens—horny ones who wanted to experience humans having sex.

No, that was completely ridiculous. But what was going on?

Clay was smart. He knew the impact he had on her. From all the evidence, he was as affected as she was by their kisses.

But he wasn't really pushing—much. Okay, he'd kissed her tonight, but he'd left when she repeated her wimpy objection. He hadn't tried to force another kiss. Somehow she knew he wouldn't force her to do anything she didn't want to do. With any other man, she'd probably end up in a wrestling match. She should be thankful for that, she supposed.

All the evidence—his repeated kisses, his heated looks, his hard body—indicated he was attracted to her. He saw right through her camouflage. He was certainly a skilled lover; his ability to reduce her to jelly and heat her insides to lava proved that. His goal was obviously to get her into bed.

And then what? A few days of bliss, and he'd leave. Everything she knew about him told her so. Rumors had flown about him the last time he was at Brazos, about how he dated beautiful women but never settled down with one for any length of time. Several women had seen them together in the past few days and asked pointed questions about him, including, "Are you his next conquest?" Why should she believe any differently?

Well, she wasn't going to be another of his harem. She wasn't going to fall for him and let him break her heart. She'd learned that lesson well. She had to be strong. No, stronger. She had to push him out of her thoughts, out of her life, just as soon as possible.

"You can do it," she said aloud as she turned out the lights and headed for the bedroom. "You can control your own destiny. No man's going to give you grief, ever again."

The words were hardly out of her mouth before her heart gave a lurch and a burning pain flared right under her breastbone. Something she ate must be disagreeing with her—or more likely, this mess was giving her an ulcer. Wonderful. What next? Aliens popping out of her stomach?

CHAPTER NINE

On Sunday Francie and the "gamesters," as Clay had called them and she was beginning to think of them, were deep into the game program by late afternoon. Rick and Jim were discussing the best way to program a sequence, Tom and Linda were fussing as usual over a monster— one head or two, four legs or six—and Francie and Gary were designing a separate cave with a new puzzle.

Francie looked up from their design and studied her friends for a moment. They and their laptops were spread out over her living room, and you had to be careful where you walked because of the computer paraphernalia and extension cords everywhere. How fortunate she was to have them.

By some miracle, they had all moved to Houston after graduation. Everyone except Jim was gainfully employed. Jim's trust fund allowed him to dabble in a variety of endeavors, but he had spoken of being bored doing essentially nothing with a purpose, and Francie expected him to start his own computer-related company soon. With his abilities, Jim could organize Microsoft. Come to think of it, he looked a little like Bill Gates— the same narrow face and round glasses, only with curly blond hair. She smiled to herself at her thoughts.

She was especially grateful that her good friends were here right this instant. She needed them today to keep her mind off Clay. She had woken up later than usual this morning, and as she had lain there thinking about Clay and the way he made her feel, all her insecurities had returned with a vengeance.

She could tick them off on her fingers: Handsome men meant trouble and heartbreak. Men were only after one thing, and it wasn't her mind or her whole self. Sex was just a biological function, and she didn't need it, even if she was better at it than Walt had claimed. She was sufficient unto herself. Clay was just playacting, no matter what he said. He needed her cooperation and, like any man, would say anything to get it. He'd leave after they caught Kevin.

But he had not been lying about his physical desire, the answer came back in her head. It was obvious in the tautness in his embrace and the fire in his silver eyes— and the evidence pressing against her sex.

She had rubbed her stomach as she remembered, and for once, the alien in her chest seemed to be purring rather than aching.

Clay stirred her as Walt had never done. When he

touched her or took her in his arms, she hardly recognized herself.

And he treated her like an equal in all their discussions, especially the ones about computers. And he seemed sincere and honest. And trustworthy. He said no camouflage, only the truth. Could she believe him? Could she let herself go?

"What do you think, Francie?"

She almost jumped when she realized Gary was saying something about the cave. Resolutely pushing all her thoughts out of her head, she turned back to the computer to concentrate on the program.

At five o'clock, someone pounded on the door. "Who's there?" several people yelled at once.

"Pizza!" came the reply in a male voice.

"Yeah!" Gary said. "I'm hungry."

"You're always hungry," Linda stated. "I guess it takes a lot to fill your long, skinny body."

"Beer!" shouted the person on the other side of the door.

Everyone cheered loudly. "Let the man in!" Jim commanded.

Francie opened the door to Clay, who stood there with a double six-pack in one hand and a big bag with six pizzas in the other.

"I thought the group might need sustenance by now," he said, looking her up and down. Well, this was an improvement in her dress—jeans and a T-shirt. The T-shirt was oversized, but it clung in some interesting ways, and the jeans fit like a second skin. She still wore those useless glasses, though.

"You've got that right!" Tom agreed, standing and stretching.

Francie introduced him, as a "friend," to everyone, and they all gave him the once-over—very carefully. Like he could be Attila the Hun out to capture one of their own. He stifled a smile.

After the pizzas and beers were opened, and the group settled down to eat, he said, "Francie showed me your game and said you'd be over today. I'm impressed with your work."

"And you have a few ideas we ought to incorporate?" Jim asked with a slight sarcastic tone in his voice.

Clay had met Jim's type before and recognized territoriality when he saw it. Francie had spoken of him very highly during her demonstration last night. Sharp-faced, with cynical pale blue eyes watchful behind thin, round metal eyeglass frames, Jim was obviously the driving force behind the group and its endeavors.

If Clay could win Jim over, it would certainly help his cause with Francie—he hoped. "Hell, no," he replied. "But I do have some ideas for taking it to the market, and I know a couple of people who might want to invest in the effort. When you're ready, of course."

Silence descended on the group.

"If you don't want to do it yourselves, I also know a company who might be interested in buying it from you." Clay nonchalantly took a big bite of pizza.

"Wait a minute," Rick said. He ran a hand through his already thinning hair and peered intensely at Clay through his thick glasses. "Clay Morgan . . . Clay Morgan. Aren't you the guy with the rep for discovering what's wrong with hardware and software just by looking at the machine?"

"It's not that easy or simple, but I do fix systems," Clay admitted.

Gary swallowed his bite of pizza with a big gulp. "Hey, y'all, he's the one who fixed the mess at my company after that crazy manager tried to sabotage the system." He wiped his hand on his napkin and leaned over to shake Clay's hand. "Great work! Man, I thought we'd never get back up for months. You had us going again in days." He turned to the others. "Guys, this man can program rings around us. He really knows his stuff." With that accolade, everybody relaxed. "Welcome to 'Conundrum,'" Jim told Clay.

"Thanks. And if you need a beta tester, I'm volunteering." Mentally thanking Gary for his endorsement, Clay took a swig of beer and glanced at Francie to see how she was reacting to all this.

Francie avoided his gaze and concentrated on her pizza. She had been watching the byplay with some trepidation. The group had always looked out for each other from their first days as freshmen at UT. She hadn't been sure how her friends would receive Clay, but it seemed like they accepted him.

She could almost see the wheels turning in Jim's mind as he contemplated the future. They had never explicitly discussed what they would do with the finished game. The majority was in the project for the doing, not any monetary rewards. Maybe it would be Jim's task to market it. Such a job would certainly supply the focus and impetus he had been searching for.

After the pizza disappeared, Jim and Rick immediately captured Clay, demonstrating their latest progress, and everybody went back to work.

Francie glanced up from her design every so often, usually catching the eye of one of her friends. Everybody let her know by facial expression or gesture that Clay was all right with them. Linda went so far as to roll her eyes, pat her heart rapidly, and wink. Francie snapped her gaze back to the design, but she heard Linda's soft chuckle. Linda and Rick had been a couple even before they graduated, and she had always expressed worry about Francie, having witnessed her transformation after her fateful sophomore year. It was clear to Francie from Linda's expression her friend was not worried any longer.

Later, Jim followed Francie into the kitchen, ostensibly to help with the pizza boxes. "Francie, did Clay mean what he said about helping with financiers or buyers?"

"I'm certain he did, Jim. He wouldn't have said it otherwise. Are you going to talk to him?"

"Yeah, I think I will. It's past time we decided what

we're going to do with the game." He held the garbage bag while she stuffed in the boxes. "Clay's really something. Gary was right about his abilities. He gave us some outstanding ideas and came up with the solution to our biggest bug, and you know how it's been driving us nuts." He shot her a glance as he pulled the ties closed on the bag. "You two an item?"

"Well, I wouldn't go so far. We've only had a couple of dates."

"You know, Francie, if he does anything to hurt you, the guys and I will take care of him. I've always wished we'd had the chance to do something about what's-his-name back there at UT."

She couldn't help but smile at the idea of their taking on Clay. What good friends they all were. She put her hand on his. "Thanks, Jim. I appreciate your offer, but I don't think I'll need your help this time." Whatever she decided to do about Clay, she certainly didn't want her friends involved. "Come on. Gary and I have a cave to show everybody."

Around nine, after determining their tasks and goals for the immediate future, the group helped clean up the living room, packed their laptops, and prepared to leave. Jim secured Clay's promise to be at the next get-together in four weeks and talk about the game's future. The usual number of good-byes were called as people went down the stairs and toward their cars.

Francie shut the door and turned back into the

living room. She hadn't realized Clay was right behind her until she was caught, her back to his front.

"Did I pass?" he asked, nestling her close to his body.

She did not pretend to misunderstand, but she held very still and stiff. He wasn't going to repeat their last encounter. "Yes, you definitely passed."

"What do you think convinced them? My reputation? My superior knowledge? My take-charge but endearing personality?"

She pretended to consider his question. "Personally, I think it was the pizza. Oh, no, the beer. Definitely the beer."

"You're deflating my ego," he said as he nuzzled her neck.

"Then don't ask a leading question. It's too hard to resist. And, please, let go." She pushed back with both elbows and he released her. She walked to the far side of the room and moved the coffee table back to its usual location before looking at him.

He had a grim expression on his face, but his tone was mild as he sat on the couch. "We need to talk about Brenner."

"Kevin? Oh, ick." She made a face.

"I agree, but I spoke with Herb and Bill Childress this afternoon to let them know how the dinner went. We made some decisions."

"What are we going to do?"

"I'm going to meet him 'accidentally' Thursday night, talk about my money woes, and let him hire me to hack for him. If we make the deal, I'll bring him to my house next week and get into Brazos. Herb is setting up a dummy database of customer files, since we think that's where Brenner's been trying to go. I'm going to get as much information out of him as I can, especially whether he's on his own or doing this on orders from someone at NatChem. We'll record everything—audio when we meet in the bar and both video and audio at my place. And Bill will make the arrest, probably the next day, after he talks to his boss and the DA. This means you need to keep things from Tamara for just a little while longer."

Francie frowned as she calculated the timing. "That's almost two weeks before you can catch him. You can't do it any sooner than that?"

"Unless he calls me directly, we couldn't see how. If I'm going to meet him seemingly by chance, the bar is our best bet, but he only goes there for sure on Thursday, from what we know. We didn't see how a double date for the four of us would give him the opportunity or the privacy to make me an offer. And the time lag will make him even more desperate and more forthcoming about the scheme, we hope. Do you see any other alternative?"

Francie thought while she moved a chair, then leaned on the back of it and shook her head. "No, not really."

"Did you talk to Tamara today? Did she say anything about last night?"

"She stopped by this morning on her way to the

grocery store. You impressed her last night, and she mentioned going out together some other time. She said Kevin liked you, too. He talked about being envious of your ability with computers. She didn't mention if he said more about the 'big deal' he has coming up."

"Well, it's a start." Clay rose and crossed over to her as she straightened up. "When can we get together again? I have to meet with some clients Monday night. How about Friday night? I'll tell you how it all went with Brenner over dinner."

"I don't think that's really necessary. You've got your intro to Kevin now. Why continue to bring me into this?"

He frowned. "We need to maintain the fiction, Francie. It will look funny to Tamara if we stop seeing each other now, and she'll undoubtedly say something to Brenner."

"Okay," she sighed. She could probably take one more "date." "Dinner on Friday."

He chuckled. "Don't look so glum. This will all be over soon, and we can move on to other things."

He lowered his head with obvious intent, but this time she avoided him with a quick step to the other side of the chair. "No, Clay."

"No, what? No good-night kiss?"

"No. I told you how I felt about the situation. Last night you wouldn't let me get a word out before you left. I'm telling you as plainly as I can, no kisses, no touching.

Let's both keep clear heads and concentrate on catching Kevin. I dread every contact I have with Tamara, and I don't need or want more aggravation."

"If that's the way you want it." His eyes were silver ice and his voice lower than usual.

"Yes, it is." The words were no more out of her mouth a moment when a sharp pain hit her right in her middle under her breastbone. She gasped, looked down at her chest, and rubbed the spot.

"Are you all right?" he asked, with an odd quirk to his lips.

She raised her gaze to his face. The ice had melted, replaced by a mischievous glint in his eyes. She almost thought he looked victorious, but for what?

She nodded. "Fine," came out in almost a croak. She took a deep breath and cleared her throat. "Let me know what happens with Kevin."

"Will do." He walked toward the front door. "I'll talk to you tomorrow. Are you playing in your league on Tuesday?"

"Yes." She followed him and leaned on the door after he opened it.

"Good. So am I. Maybe we'll see each other. Play well."

"You, too."

He gave her a little two-finger salute and a wink, and he was gone.

She closed the door as a wave of relief washed over her. That was much better than last night. She'd resisted him and come out intact. She could get through this situation by being strong. She turned out the lights and headed for her bedroom, still rubbing the painful spot at the end of her breastbone—or was it right over her heart?

CHAPTER TEN

Monday night Clay went to dinner with some clients, and by the time he returned home, it was too late to call Francie. Reviewing the weekend, he thought he'd made some progress with her. Her friends liking him had to count for something.

She was, however, even more into this "don't touch me" and "don't kiss me" business. In fact, she seemed to be hardening her position. And not in the way a certain piece of his anatomy was "hardening."

At least, if her gasp and obvious pain Sunday night was any indication, the good ol' soul-mate imperative was at work. Now, if the SMI would just hurry things along.

Tuesday at the Y, his team demolished the opposition, a luckless bunch at the bottom of the league standings, and he was able to make the last ten minutes of Francie's game. He watched her feint and drive to the basket with a fluid motion. Damn, this woman was good. Her team was well coordinated also, running plays, feeding the ball to the open man—whoops, make that "open woman." A couple of the women, Francie included, made some sweet shots his own teammates might envy.

A fellow team member of Clay's sat down next to him on the bleachers. "You should have a layup as good," he teased Clay as Francie sank another two points.

"No, Hansen," Clay answered. "*You* should. She's playing your position, the center."

"Damn," Hansen said as Francie blocked a shot with a high jump and a long arm. "I need to meet this babe. We would have great things to talk about, like all sorts of *moves*."

Clay almost growled as he turned to glare at his teammate. "Lay off, buddy. She's taken."

"Oh, yeah? By who?" His eyebrows raised in question, he looked at Clay.

"Me."

"Oh." Hansen cleared his throat, watched the action on the court for another minute, and grinned at Clay. "Then you sure can pick 'em, Morgan. Good luck." He gave Clay a slap on the back and left.

When the game was over, Clay met Francie as she came off the court. "Good game," he told her.

"Thanks," she replied, wiping off her face and neck with her towel. "How did you do?"

"We won easily. Want to grab a bite?"

"I'm sorry. I'm going out with a few women from

the team."

"Oh, right, you always do that. What about tomorrow night?"

"Tamara finally decided last night she had to upgrade her accounting software and she wants a laptop for home. She and I are going out to look for it all on Wednesday evening."

Why hadn't she told him that earlier? "What about Brenner? Is he coming with you?" he asked.

"No, I don't think so. She didn't mention him." Her eyes opened wide as if she had finally caught up with his thoughts. "Oh! I'm sorry. I didn't even think about Kevin. Do you think he'll try to get back on my computer?"

"I don't know, but I think I'll hang out over at Brazos tomorrow, just in case. What's your schedule?"

"I'm going straight to her shop after work, and we'll leave for supper and the computer store after she closes up. I expect we'll get home around nine thirty."

"So, we can expect him early, if at all."

"Let me know, would you, if he's been there." She shuddered and twisted her towel around her hands. "I hate the thought of his being in my apartment, looking at my things, touching them."

"This will be over soon, Francie." He paused, then spoke. "But you have to do something for me until it is. Let me know where you and Tamara are every night." He could hear the exasperated tone in his voice, and from the look on her face, so could she because she paled, then flushed.

"I said I'm sorry, Clay. I'll warn you of our every move," she answered with her own edge. "Wednesday I'll be with Tamara, Thursday I'll be home, and Friday I'll be with you, keeping up pretenses. I don't know where Tamara will be on Friday. I don't know where either of us will be on Saturday, but she and I will set up the shop software on Sunday. Is that good enough for now?"

He knew that her answer came straight out of embarrassment since she'd missed the connection with Brenner and out of frustration with the entire situation, but he couldn't think of a way to mollify her without making it worse. He didn't want to give her any excuses for not seeing him. "That's fine," he said mildly. "I'll give you a call Wednesday night after ten to let you know if he's been in your place."

She folded her arms across her chest and hunched her shoulders. "Okay."

One of her teammates came up to them. "You ready to go?" the woman asked, looking Clay up and down.

"Yep," Francie answered. She introduced her friend to Clay, and they exchanged greetings. "I'd better go," Francie told him.

"I'll talk to you tomorrow," he said and watched the two women walk away. Damn. If he hadn't stopped by the game, would she have told him about her computer shopping and wide-open apartment in time for him to mount a defense? Or, even if she thought about Brenner, would she have continued her avoidance tactics, not even wanting to talk to him on the phone?

How could she be avoiding him so much? Why? Her date with Tamara should have given her the perfect "excuse" to call.

A painful question struck him: despite all the evidence, especially her rubbing an itchy breastbone, was this woman really his soul mate?

Soul mates were supposed to practically fall into each other's arms. Look what had happened to his own sister and her husband. What was going on with Francie? How could she be resisting him?

He walked toward the men's locker room, rubbing the spot on his chest that was alternating between an itch and an ache. Maybe what he was feeling was not the attraction of his soul mate, but heartburn. Either way, he was going to have an ulcer for sure before this was over.

※ ✦✲✦※

Wednesday night when the phone rang in Francie's apartment at ten fifteen, she jumped, then scrutinized the instrument with trepidation. She had acted like such an idiot yesterday with Clay, not realizing the opening she had given Kevin. She had been so embarrassed. But she had to talk to him now. Sitting at her computer, she had activated the program that displayed Kevin's shenanigans and had been studying his keystrokes. All the evidence proved he had been there again.

With a heavy sigh, she picked up the handset. "Hello?"

"Hi, it's me." Clay's voice came over the line, vibrated her eardrums, and resonated in every cell in her body.

"He was here again."

"Yes. Have you called up the little application I left on your machine?"

"I'm looking at it now. You threw him all over the place, didn't you?" She had to admit Clay could play Kevin like a fish on the end of his line. In fact, as she'd noticed before, Clay's skill with the computer seemed almost magical. But she didn't tell him that because his ego certainly didn't need stroking. She did ask, "How do you do it?"

"Magic."

"Oh, really." She couldn't help the sarcastic tone. What was it with Clay and this magic business? But wasn't it just what she had been thinking?

"I'll show you some time," he said with a funny note in his voice she couldn't identify. It wasn't sarcasm. Teasing? No, it was more like he had a secret. But she didn't have time to follow up because he was speaking again.

"Bill had one of his people take some photos of Brenner at your place again. From what the cop could see, Brenner was fuming when he left. He ran over a curb and almost had an accident. Did he do anything to your apartment in his frustration?"

"No, and I checked pretty thoroughly." She had

even left some spy-movie-type traps—tape or hairs on drawers, especially her lingerie drawers—to make sure Kevin hadn't been searching her belongings. But that was too embarrassing to tell Clay. The last thing she wanted to discuss with him was her underwear.

"Good. If we do this right, it should be the last time he's in your apartment uninvited. By the way, does Brenner know what Herb or anyone else at Brazos looks like?"

"I don't think so, except he might know some of our salespeople, the ones he competes with directly. Tamara doesn't know Herb or any of my coworkers, except by name when I've talked about them. Why?"

"Because I'm going to have someone with me at the bar tomorrow night so it will look like I met him there for a drink. The person will leave just after Brenner arrives so our hacker can approach me with no one else around. Herb wants to be the person."

"Oh, puh-lease. Herb's doing undercover work now?" She rolled her eyes at the very idea of her boss playing spy.

"I think he just wants a look at the guy. You know how he's called the hacker every name in the book. I'm going to let Bill handle this. He can use the power of the police department to keep Herb out."

"I hope Bill succeeds. What about you? Are you going to, what do they call it on the cop shows, 'wear a wire'?"

"Yeah. Fortunately it's a fairly quiet bar, according to Bill, so recording should not be a problem. Do you have any advice for me about Brenner?"

"No, not really." She thought for a moment. "Oh, there is one thing you might like to know. I think Tamara may finally be getting tired of Kevin. You know I told you how she's never with one man for very long?"

"Yeah. What happened?"

"Kevin evidently became the 'big expert' when he found out she had decided to get a laptop. Acted like she didn't have a brain in her head. She and I had discussed the topic enough so she could tell he didn't know what he was talking about. She said she finally convinced him she wanted *me* to go with her to buy it, not *him*. Then she complained how the zing had gone out of the relationship."

"The zing?" Clay put in. He sounded delighted with the word.

"Tamara's big on zing. If she's not excited to see a man, doesn't feel a zap to her system anymore, she drops him. I don't know how she does it, but she usually leaves him thinking it was *his* idea to stop seeing *her*."

"How about you, Francie?" His voice dropped to a low rasp that skittered along her nerve endings. "Are you 'big on zing'? Do you like to feel a 'zap to your system'?"

She was speechless for a moment as every synapse in her body seemed to fire at once. Zing, phooey. More like a lightning storm. Then a sudden feeling of euphoria and happiness made her giddy. "Uh . . ."

She had to answer him somehow. What could she say that wouldn't push her into deeper trouble? She decided to fall back on a tried-and-true tactic: ignore the question and divert the questioner. "You know how red-heads are, much more volatile than the rest of us. Look, what time will you call me tomorrow?"

She heard what sounded like a sigh or a chuckle on his end, but his voice was normal when he answered, "I don't know how long it will take Brenner to get down to the question, but I expect I'll be home by nine. I can't see us becoming drinking buddies."

"Good. I want to know what happened." She didn't give him time to respond, just kept talking. "I'd better get to bed now. I have a lot of work to do tomorrow." She was almost weak with relief he had not pursued the "zing" question.

"I'll call. Sleep well. Good night."

"Bye." She hung up the phone and slumped back in her chair, one hand held to her solar plexus where a distinct pain made itself felt—again. What was going on? First an itch, now a pain. Was she really coming down with an ulcer from all this anxiety? She drank some hot chocolate before she went to bed. It seemed to help.

CHAPTER ELEVEN

Thursday evening about six, Clay and Bill Childress sat at a table in a Market Square bar, located in one of the few original buildings left in the northern end of downtown. A mix of business people and blue-collar construction workers occupied many of the tables and all the stools at the bar. The lighting was only slightly subdued, and everyone could be seen clearly. The hum of conversation was low.

"I hope Brenner gets here soon," Clay told the detective. He shifted the props, a notebook and file folders open on the table, and then took a handful of the popcorn for which the bar was known and ate some of the fluffy kernels. "I'm filling up on this stuff."

"Relax. The man just walked in the door. Remember, the microphone is picking up everything just fine. Don't lead him too much. Let him initiate the offer." Bill pretended to look at the papers in front of him.

Clay and Bill waited until Kevin had said hello to

a couple of people and ordered a beer at the bar. When Kevin turned around to survey the crowd, Bill rose, closed the folders, picked them up, and held out his hand. "I'll be calling you, Clay," the lieutenant said, loud enough to be heard at the bar.

"I'll look forward to it." Clay rose to shake hands, then sat down as Bill exited. He closed the notebook and, settling back in his chair, picked up his Scotch. He hoped to God he looked like he was in no hurry.

"Clay?" a voice asked beside him. "Clay Morgan?"

Clay looked up to see Kevin standing there. "Hi, Brenner. How's it going?"

"Fine, fine. How's business?"

"Okay. I just met a prospective client for a drink. Now, if he will only make up his mind about using me. . ." He let the sentence fade off.

"Yeah, I know what you mean. Waiting to know if you made the sale is the hardest part."

Another man went by Kevin and lightly punched him on the arm. "Hey, Brenner, how's it hangin'?"

"Fine," Kevin threw over his shoulder and turned back to Clay.

"You come here often?" Clay asked.

"Yeah, usually on Thursdays when Tamara works late at her shop."

"It's a nice place," Clay said, glancing around. "Why don't you join me if you have no other plans? I hate to drink alone."

"Don't mind if I do." Brenner took the chair Bill had been using. He took a couple of swallows of beer. "How's Francie?"

"Good. How's Tamara?"

"Fine. That was a nice dinner Francie fixed."

"Yeah. We had a good time."

"We did, too."

Clay ate some more popcorn. "How's business?" he asked.

"Pretty good." Brenner shrugged and shook his head. "But this being a manager sucks. I wish I was still out in the field. Some of the guys on my sales team can't make a sale if it's handed to them on a silver platter, know what I mean?"

"Man, how you can sell all the time, wait for somebody to decide to buy, face rejection over and over, is beyond me," Clay said, shaking his head. He pointed at the notebook on the table. "Take this meeting I just had. Bill's company needs me. They need me bad. But all they care about is how much I'm going to cost, and he's trying to nickel-and-dime me to death. If that's not bad enough, I think he's talking to one of my competitors, trying to play us off against each other. That ever happen to you?"

"All the time. All the friggin' time." Kevin frowned at his beer.

"If I knew what the other consultant was charging, I'd be able to undercut him, I'm sure. But . . ." Clay shrugged his shoulders.

"Can't you find out?"

"Not easily. Not unless I have a friend in the company with access to the information. If any of this made it into the company's computer system, I'd have a chance, but all this is done verbally, maybe a few e-mails, but mostly with proposals on paper, and by the time the contract's entered, it's too late."

"How would you find out? If you had the chance, I mean."

"There are ways, my friend. There are ways," Clay said with what he hoped was a sly smirk. He finished his drink and signaled the waitress for another round for them both. "But these bozos will just fart around and not make up their minds for another two or three weeks. I don't have the time. There's a big game coming up in Vegas in three weeks. I'm going to have to hustle up another client pretty quick if I want to make it."

"How's your luck been holding?" Kevin asked. "You said something last Saturday about having a bad run."

"Man, it's worse than bad. My ready cash is tapped out. I was hoping this guy I met tonight would be able to bring me in tomorrow, Monday at the latest. The job's not a difficult one. I figured I could be well into it, probably halfway done, by the end of next week. Then I could bill them for work done to date. Knowing the money's coming in would allow me to dip into my reserves and head for Vegas. But, no billing, no Vegas, no game. A chance to make a heavy score and I'll miss it, damn it."

He leaned back while the waitress served their drinks and continued when she was out of earshot. "One very important tip about gambling, Brenner. Always keep your reserves separate from what you gamble with. Never, ever bet your going-home money or the mortgage payment. Discipline, it's all about discipline." He stared into his Scotch and nodded sagely.

Kevin took a gulp of beer and frowned as he moved the mug around in a circle on the table. Clay could almost see the wheels turning in the man's head.

"Can I ask you a question, Morgan?" he said finally. "About computers? Sort of off the record?"

"Sure. What do you want to know? I won't even charge you for it," Clay answered with a negligent wave of his hand.

"How would you find out about your competitor's bid—if the info was in their system, I mean?"

"How do you think?" Clay repeated his smirk. "Remember what we talked about at Francie's?"

"Yeah," Kevin nodded. "That's what I was thinking about. Is it difficult? Getting into a company's files without them knowing it?"

"Like I told you on Saturday, it's more tricky than difficult—when you know what you're doing, of course. It's a matter of routing yourself through several different servers on the other side of the globe. See, what you do is . . ." Clay continued his explanation, degenerating rapidly into technobabble until Kevin's eyes were glazing over. "That's basically how you do it," he concluded.

Brenner hunched over his beer, moved a little closer to Clay. "What if I knew of a job right up your alley?" he asked in a low voice.

"Yeah? Who with?"

"Me. I need to get some information about one of our competitors. They've been eating our lunch lately, and we think it's by their pricing, but we're not sure. It could be some special delivery considerations. None of my salespeople is able to find out. I'm saddled with incompetent idiots who couldn't sell refrigerators in the tropics."

To cover his grin at Brenner's statement about "incompetent idiots," Clay sipped his drink, put the glass down, and leaned toward Kevin to place the microphone under his jacket closer to his target. "So, you're looking for what, exactly?"

"I need someone to hack into our competitor's customer files to see what they're buying, at what price, and at what shipping costs."

"You just want the information, right? You don't want to change any data, mess anything up?"

"Right. I don't want them to know I've seen the information." Kevin took a swallow of beer as if his mouth had suddenly gone dry. "So, what do you think? Can it be done?"

Clay leaned back in his chair, stared at Brenner until the man began to fidget, then sat forward again. "How much?"

"How much?"

"How much are you willing to pay for this information?"

Kevin gulped, then assumed an indifferent expression contradicted by his tight grip on the beer mug. "Name your price."

"Who do you work for, and whose pockets do I have my hand in, yours or your company's?"

"Why?"

"Because theirs are deeper than yours." Come on, Brenner, make the connection.

"Oh. You'd charge them more."

Clay just nodded.

"Mine," Brenner said, leaning a little closer. "I work for NatChem, and they don't have anything to do with this. I have a real bastard for a boss. Man, he's on my ass like there's no tomorrow. I need the information to turn my sorry sales team into winners instead of losers. It's my only ticket to a promotion."

Clay gave Brenner a hard look. "*If* I agree to do it, I need to know something first."

"Name it."

"Did you try hacking on your own?"

"Yeah, but I got nowhere. Why?"

Clay shook his head disgustedly. "Because I have to know how much crap you left behind. How did you get in? Whose computer did you use?"

"It's okay," Brenner said earnestly. "I used . . ." He paused. Clay could tell the exact moment when Brenner decided not to inform him it had been Francie's. "I used someone else's computer. There's no way to trace anything back to me." He held up his hand. "I swear."

Clay ran his hands through his hair. "All right," he said. "I'll only do this one time. I'll need you with me, showing me what information you want. And, in the meantime, you stay off the other computer. The last thing I need is for you to make a dumb-ass mistake and alert them about an intruder."

"Fine with me," Brenner said, his eyes beginning to light with excitement as he realized Clay was going to do his bidding.

"Five thousand," Clay stated.

"Excuse me?" Brenner looked astounded.

"Five thousand, cash, hundreds is fine. Payable up front."

"Oh. That much?" He took a big gulp of his beer.

"And," Clay held up his hand and pointed his finger at Kevin, "*nobody* ever mentions this again."

Brenner's gaze fell to his beer, roamed the room, and finally met Clay's. He shook his head as he said, "Uh-uh. Never."

"Shit, do you want to do this or not?" Clay let his irritation show. Brenner looked like he finally realized the implications of what he had just asked Clay to do. Or maybe it was the cost. Either way, they had their hacker.

"Yeah. Yeah, I do." Kevin nodded and hunched over his beer again. "But it will take a couple of days for me to come up with the money."

"We'll do it next Wednesday, my place. I need to use equipment I trust." Clay pulled out a card and wrote his address on it, under the phone numbers. He handed it to Brenner. "Be there at seven. With the cash. Know exactly what you're going after. The less time we spend in their system, the better."

"Right, right," Brenner agreed, nodding his head like a bobblehead doll's.

"By the way, whose system will we be getting into?"

"Brazos Chemical."

"Francie's company?"

"Yeah. Is that a problem?" He fidgeted as he asked the question.

Clay paused a beat, until Brenner turned pale. "No."

"Thanks, man. I appreciate it." Brenner let out a huge breath and looked at Clay like he was the answer to the salesman's prayers.

Clay stood up and picked up the notebook. As he put some money on the table, he leaned down close to Kevin and stated, "Don't mention this to anybody, especially not your girlfriend or mine."

"No, no. Not a word." Brenner held up his oath-taking hand again.

Clay nodded, said, "See you next week," and walked to the exit. As he opened the door, he glanced back at

Brenner. The hacker was grinning like a fool as he swaggered to the bar calling for another round.

Outside, Clay took a deep breath as he walked to the truck where the police were recording the conversation. Even though he himself had done nothing wrong, he had not enjoyed the experience of pretending to be unethical. "How'd I do?" he asked as Childress opened the door for him.

"Just fine. It came through loud and clear. Once we tape the hacking, we should have a strong case."

Clay took the microphone and transmitter from beneath his shirt and handed them over to the technician running the equipment. "You'll be at the house to set up on Wednesday?"

"That's right. Bright and early in case we have any problems."

CHAPTER TWELVE

A message was waiting for Clay when he returned home. It was Francie. She had called about four in the afternoon.

"Hi," she had said in a perky sort of voice. He could hear the edge in it again. "I'm reporting in, as requested. I've had a change of plans. I'm over at Tamara's shop tonight. We're looking at her records and deciding what we need to enter into her accounting software on Sunday. Since Kevin is with you, I thought it would be okay."

"Fine," he told the machine. Why wouldn't the woman call his cell so he could talk with her in person? Her avoiding him was really getting on his nerves—not to mention frustrating his libido. His good humor at trapping Brenner dissipated and degenerated into discouragement.

"I'll see you tomorrow about seven? How about something casual, like Mexican food?" There was a pause. "I hope everything goes all right tonight." Another pause, like she was trying to think of more to say. "Well, I'll see you then. Bye." The machine clicked and told him, "No more messages," in a firm masculine tone.

Clay replayed the recording a couple of times. Hearing her voice did not lighten his dark mood, but it did cause repercussions elsewhere in his body. He knew a cold shower wouldn't help, so he simply went to bed and read a sci-fi book until he fell asleep.

Over his coffee the next morning, he thought about their upcoming date. He had to play it light, not spook her or give her any excuse to avoid him. He had reached a decision while shaving. He was going to get everything out in the open. If he accomplished nothing else tonight, he had to talk her into coming over to his house on Saturday, and he knew just the way to do it—by appealing to her programmer curiosity. The lure of learning how he manipulated Brenner would be irresistible to her.

Once she was in his home, they had to talk about practitioners, what it meant to be one, what he could do with his particular talents. Surely he could convince her that magic existed. After she saw what he could do with a computer, she wouldn't be able to doubt magic or him.

What about telling her about soul mates? How much should he spring on her at once?

No, he'd better concentrate on getting over the first hurdle: changing her mind about the actuality of magic and practitioners.

He could call Daria and Bent and ask for their help, but it seemed a cop-out. Daria had enlisted almost the whole family to explain practitioners to Bent, but she'd had no choice. Daria couldn't cast a spell on any person or any object, and Bent, as her soul mate, was oblivious to the spells she threw on herself. She'd had to bring in people like their mother, who could demonstrate magic by causing plants to grow or a ball of light to appear.

It was not the case for Clay. While he himself wasn't so hot on the showy stuff, light balls and candles being his best—well, really his only—"tricks," he could show Francie solid proof he could cast spells. As a programmer, Francie would be able to see and understand his magic. If he couldn't make his own case with all of his abilities and especially with the help of the soul-mate imperative pushing them together, he might as well give up.

A sharp pain stabbed through his center with his last notion and left him gasping for breath. "All right, all right," he said out loud. "I won't give up." The pain subsided.

"Why can't practitioners be like everybody else?" he grumbled as he poured a second cup of coffee. "Nobody else but us has to go through this soul-mate business."

No one answered his complaints, so he rubbed the spot and left the house for a client's office. At least the problem there would keep his mind off Francie. But as he drove, he ran through his mind scenarios of how he would tell her and what she would say.

And he reassured himself confidently that everything would come out all right.

It had to.

❧✷✷✷✺

He was his usual prompt self, knocking on her door at seven, eagerly anticipating the look in her eyes when she saw him—the one she couldn't hide that told him she was just as excited to see him as he was to see her.

When Tamara opened the door, disappointment hit so hard that he had to work to keep the smile on his face.

"Hi, Clay," the small redhead said with a big grin. "Come on in."

He entered the apartment and glanced around. "Hi, yourself. Where's Francie?"

"She's on the phone."

"No, I'm not," Francie answered from the kitchen. "It was another telemarketer." She walked into the living room shaking her head. "I'm on the no-call list, but get them just the same," she said with a frown, but she smiled when she saw him. "Hi, Clay."

"Hello to you, too." Her eyes definitely lit up, he was certain. A small flame kindled in the smoky brown. Knowing she couldn't protest with Tamara there, he took a step toward her and gave her a hello kiss. When she made a little gasp, he kissed her again. Tamara didn't have a monopoly on "zing." He felt the effect of the touch of their lips all the way to his toes.

He looked Francie up and down. She had on a denim skirt, a Western-style blue shirt with pearl buttons, and a light tan jacket. Her hair was down around her shoulders. Gold hoop earrings peeked out from under the blond curls. And, wonder of wonder, no glasses.

"You look great," he said.

"See, Francie, I told you so," Tamara said. "What we dug out of the back of your closet works fine."

"All right, you two," Francie scolded. "Enough talk about my clothes. Let's go, Clay. I'm hungry."

"Y'all have fun," Tamara said as she walked out the door ahead of them.

"You, too," Francie said. "Let me know what you think of the new club."

"Yeah," the redhead answered with a shrug. "It'll be just like all the rest, I'm sure. Bye, Clay. It was good to see you again."

"Bye, Tamara," he answered as he and Francie walked toward the parking lot. "What's going on with her?" he asked once they were out of earshot.

"She's not particularly looking forward to going out with Kevin tonight. He groused at her on the phone last night about her choosing me to help her with the computer. She also said she's getting tired of the club scene. It's all they ever seem to do. Or go to baseball or football games if he can get tickets as part of his sales pitch. Then they have to sit with his clients, who are always men, no women, and a couple of them have treated her like his bimbo."

Clay opened the Jeep door for her, closed it after her,

and came around to get behind the wheel. As he closed his own door, he asked, "Do you know if he mentioned seeing me at the bar?"

"No, or rather, she didn't say anything about it. Mostly she complained. I really think she's going to dump him. All the usual signs are there in her attitude and conversation about him. She's really bummed because he's not even taking her out to dinner tonight."

Clay stopped in the act of turning the key in the ignition. "Do you want to ask her to come with us?" He would rather have Francie all to himself, but he knew how much she cared for her friend.

"Clay, that's sweet of you, but I already did and she turned me down."

"Okay." He started the car and turned to her. "Where would you like to go?"

"My favorite Mexican place is on Westheimer, close to Hillcroft."

"I know the one. They have excellent carne asada and tacos al carbon." He pulled out of the lot and into the street.

At the restaurant, Clay felt like they were both working on avoiding the topic of the hacker and all it entailed. Instead they talked about everything else—his clients, the gamesters and Conundrum, their basketball leagues, the latest cell phone enhancements, current events and the economic outlook. As a result, he had relaxed and so, he thought, had she. She hadn't shown any of the hesitance or reluctance evident when they spoke on the phone. It felt like a real date, two people enjoying themselves and being together.

After chips and hot salsa, succulent carne asada for him and spicy chile rellenos for her, accompanying side dishes of rice, refried beans, and guacamole, and two margaritas each, Francie leaned back from the table and looked around the gaily decorated restaurant. "I couldn't hold another bite," she told him.

"What? No flan for dessert?" he teased. He himself was stuffed. He signaled for the waiter.

"No, thank you. That was delicious. I had a craving for Mexican food."

"I know what you mean. Once you said the words, I could almost taste the salsa." The waiter brought the check, Clay paid, and they left.

In the car, he asked, "Would you like to go to a movie or a club? We're dressed for something country-and-western." He really wanted to take her home and kiss her silly. He still had to ask her over for tomorrow, he reminded himself.

Francie looked over at his jeans, black shirt, leather jacket, and boots. He did have something of the look of a gunfighter. She hadn't paid much attention to his clothes up to now, caught up instead in the look in his silver eyes smiling into hers, the touch of his large hand helping her in and out of the car or guiding her to and from the restaurant. And in the struggle to maintain a level head when he was around.

The thought of dancing with him, being in his arms again, brought her back to reality. She had to resist this man's charms or risk losing herself again. But she didn't want to get into an argument, so she answered nonchalantly, "No, not really, I'm not much for clubs. And you never told me in detail how it went with Kevin. I do want a complete account of the meeting."

"Okay. Let's go back to your place."

As they were walking up the stairs toward Francie's apartment, Tamara and Kevin came out of the door across the courtyard. The two pairs exchanged hellos and a wave, but did not stop to speak.

Francie watched them leave the courtyard and shuddered. "That man just gives me the creeps. I didn't like him before this mess, and now, I don't want to be in his presence." She unlocked her door and let them into the apartment. "Would you like something to drink?" she asked as they both took off their jackets. She hung hers in the closet by the door, and he laid his over the back of a chair.

"No, nothing for me, thanks." He looked at her as she wandered around the room, straightening the items on a table, fluffing a pillow. It was time to take control, or she'd sit down in that overstuffed chair and be out of reach. Even though she'd said "no kisses, no touching," that didn't mean they had to act like adversaries and speak across the coffee table. He sat on the left end of the couch and patted the cushion to his right. "Come sit down here, and I'll tell you all about the meeting."

She actually did as requested, and he waited until she made herself comfortable. Good, just where he wanted her. Hiking his knee up on the seat, he turned so that he faced her. Her position mirrored his, except she kept her legs together.

Stretching his arm along the back of the couch but controlling the urge to touch her, he began talking. He told her everything from the beginning, about being wired for sound, impatiently waiting with Bill Childress for Kevin to show, dropping sledgehammer hints to the hacker, making the deal, setting the appointment for Wednesday.

"So?" he asked when he had finished. She hadn't interrupted him at all. "What do you think?"

She made a face. "I think he's a disgusting slimeball. And you're certain he's not in collusion with anybody else?"

"It doesn't look like it. I think he was telling the truth about that. Unless the managers over at NatChem are crazy, and they'd have to be to assume Brenner could pull off a hacking job, I can't see them authorizing criminal activity."

Francie looked at her hands clasped in her lap, then up at him. The worry in her eyes was almost palpable. "What about Tamara? Could he have been using her all along as a ploy to get to me?"

"No. Don't start thinking any of this is your fault.

How could he have known beforehand you two were friends? From what you said, they went out for a couple of months before he started using your computer to hack. If Brenner's goal all along had been you or your machine, he'd have been pushing it long before. This was probably a crime of opportunity precipitated by his troubles at work. He saw the chance and took it. Did you ever dial into Brazos while he was present?"

She frowned in remembrance. "Yes, there was once when they came over to use my computer to surf the Web, and I was online with Brazos."

"See." He nodded; her comment clinched his hypothesis. "Brenner lucked out. His girlfriend had a friend who worked for the competition. He had a lagging sales team and wanted inside information about her company. He could use a machine that already had access, he knew when you wouldn't be home, and he thought it would be easy. I'll bet he tried at least once to get in using your password, and when he couldn't figure it out, he took the hacker's route. You and Tamara are innocent bystanders."

Francie sighed and slumped against the sofa back. "Tamara. She's going to be so angry at Kevin when she finds out what he's done. I only hope she won't be too upset with me for not telling her. I still feel like I'm deceiving her. At least it looks like they're breaking up."

"If she gives you too hard a time, let me talk to her." Clay reached out his arm on the couch and put his hand on her shoulder, partly to show support and partly because he couldn't resist the need to touch her any longer.

She shook her head and smiled sadly. "Thanks, but I couldn't ask you to do that. We'll work it out. We've been friends too long not to."

"Atta girl." He gave her shoulder a little shake of encouragement before moving his hand back to the sofa. It was time to change the subject. He knew *he* didn't want to talk about Tamara or deception, and Francie was looking pretty dejected. He smiled and tapped her clasped fists with his free hand. "In the meantime, I've got an idea."

"What?" she asked in a listless voice, but she raised her eyes to his.

"Tomorrow afternoon, why don't you come over to my house and I'll show you how I foiled Brenner's hacking attempts."

The idea seemed to perk her up. She gave herself a little shake, as if she were casting off her worrisome thoughts, and she smiled again, this time in delight. "How you detoured him when he was heading straight for the customer files?"

"Yep."

"How the application on my machine works to track him?"

"Sure. We wouldn't exactly be getting away from our problem, but it would give us something to do. I have a couple of other programs you might like to see, as well."

A skeptical look crossed her face, but she was still smiling. "Is this the computer version of luring me over to 'see your etchings', as the lotharios say in the old stories?"

"Of course not," he replied in fake indignation and went on with a lecherous leer. "Or would you like to see my etchings?" He waggled his eyebrows at her.

"Just the programs will be fine," she answered primly, and they laughed together.

"No, seriously," he continued, pleased that she seemed relaxed enough to joke. Maybe he was making progress. "You're one of the few people I know to whom I can show off and who will understand what I'm doing. Afterward we can broil some steaks on the grill. Suppose I pick you up about two o'clock."

She shook her head. "No, I have a hair appointment at one. I'll come to you."

"Please don't tell me you're going to get a haircut." He couldn't resist; he had to touch her. Raising his hand and fingering the blond curls, he wrapped a silky strand around his fingers. He could feel the connection between them, energy flowing as if his touching her hair had completed a circuit. He bent toward her. She was so close. Maybe just one little kiss wouldn't hurt or cause her to reject him again.

The energy flow became stronger. He looked into those smoky brown eyes and leaned closer, close enough to see himself reflected in them.

She went still for a second, and when she shivered, he knew she also felt the current.

"N-no. Not much of one. J-just a little trim," she stuttered, her gaze moving from his down to his lips. Her own lips parted.

"Good," he whispered as he completed that circuit, too.

Somebody groaned as their lips met. Somebody took in a deep breath. He could have sworn a hum floated in the air. Multicolored lights seemed to sparkle on the back of his eyelids.

Clay moved his hand from her hair to her head, threading through the thick blond waves, cradling her skull. He slid his other hand from her hands up her arm and around to her back, coming to rest at her waist. He sipped at her lips, his tongue asked entrance, and when she gave it, he swept inside.

Francie stiffened for the barest part of a second, then softened and reached for him, both arms going around him, one at his neck, the other his chest. Her tongue played with his and caressed his lower lip.

He could feel her full breasts against his chest, her nipples already tight. He could have howled at the pleasure the sensation created.

It wasn't enough. He had to feel her along his whole body. Not breaking contact anywhere, he lifted her closer and leaned back toward the sofa's arm. She held tight and followed until he was almost flat on his back and she was on top of him, her legs between his.

His hands roamed over her, from her head to her thighs, kneading, massaging, holding her tight against the granite hard erection straining against his jeans. He deepened the kiss, thrusting his tongue as he rocked their hips together. She responded by fisting one hand in his hair and purring, a vibration he felt resonating down his body to lodge in his now throbbing cock.

When he brought a hand up to her breast, she tensed again, then pressed herself into his palm and took over his mouth with her own tongue. He felt her heartbeat accelerate, beat to the same rhythm as his. He kissed her forever, until both of them were laboring for breath as though they'd run a marathon.

He finally ended it with a series of small kisses, then tucked her head under his chin and held her tight. She lay over him like a blanket, utterly relaxed, while she regained her breath.

Holy hell, the words somehow ran through his bloodless brain. No woman had ever affected him like this. He had practically climaxed in his jeans—how he'd avoided it, he'd never know. And Francie had been right there with him.

If this was what happened with a single kiss between soul mates, what would actual lovemaking be like? It would kill him, for sure.

Eventually—he had no idea how long it took—their breathing returned to normal, and Francie began to stir.

He sat up—carefully—and pulled her legs around so she was sitting again, but still between his legs, one of which was braced by the couch back, the other with his foot on the floor.

Her hands on his chest, she raised dazed eyes to his and licked her lips absently. She had been affected as strongly as he. Good. He wasn't in this by himself. They were, had to be, soul mates. His doubts had been foolish.

Right now, he had to get out of here before he gave in to the compulsion to carry this activity to its natural conclusion. He didn't want to give her the opportunity to tell him that this was all "business," or that she was too worried about Tamara to think about any remotely possible relationship with him. He absolutely did not want her to regret their actions or to refuse to come over tomorrow.

One thing this episode had taught him: he had to tell her everything, *yes, even about soul mates*, and he had to do it tomorrow. He didn't think he could take another of these sessions without rupturing something.

Her eyebrows drew together in a slight frown, and the smoke began to clear from her eyes. He had to be extra careful as her wits returned to her.

"Clay?" she whispered, "what happened?"

"Shhhh." He leaned in to kiss her forehead. "It's all right. We just got a little carried away, that's all."

"Oh." She must have realized her hands were stroking his chest because she snatched them away, back to her lap. "I didn't mean for that to happen. I'm sorry."

He chuckled at her apology. "Don't be. I'm not." He scooted back on the couch and levered himself to a standing position.

Francie rose, pushed her thoroughly mussed hair back from her forehead, and took a deep breath—oh, what that did to her glorious breasts and his now painful cock. She straightened her clothing and looked up at him again. She frowned, but was obviously still disoriented. "Clay, I don't . . . we can't . . . this won't . . ." she began.

He placed a finger on her lips to shush her, then tucked another unruly lock of her hair behind her ear, his fingers lingering on her cheek. "We have a great deal to talk about tomorrow, Francie." He couldn't stop himself from kissing her again lightly. "I'll see you between two and three, okay?"

"Okay." She sighed, then frowned again.

Taking advantage of her still-confused state of mind, he kissed her again for luck, grabbed his jacket, and walked out the door.

He grinned all the way home. The soul-mate imperative was definitely working. He could feel his magic center grinning.

He was totally certain.

Tomorrow she'd be his.

CHAPTER THIRTEEN

The next morning, Francie opened her eyes before her alarm clock buzzed. Instead of her usual grogginess, she was completely awake, she realized as she stretched. She couldn't remember the last time that had happened. It didn't mean that she had to get up, though. Today was Saturday, after all. She turned the pillow over, rearranged the covers, and wallowed in the luxury of being able to remain in bed.

She closed her eyes and tried going back to sleep, but the evening before persisted in replaying itself in her memory. She had thoroughly enjoyed dinner and conversation with Clay. It had been almost like a real date, not something to keep the fiction of their relationship alive for Tamara and Kevin. She was glad this deception was almost over. She hated Kevin for what he was doing to Tamara and, by extension, to herself. If it hadn't been for Clay and his computer wizardry, she might have been blamed for Kevin's chicanery. As for Clay . . .

She pulled her mind away from him and toward the problem of the hacker. Setting up the trap the way he did, Clay was certainly handling Kevin well. Now if everything went as planned, the police would catch Kevin on tape and arrest him and this farce would be finished. He'd be out of Tamara's life for good.

She made a mental note: after Kevin was gone, both she and Tamara should have their locks changed.

And what about Tamara? *Please*, she pleaded, *let Tamara understand why no one told her what Kevin was up to. Let her remain my friend.*

As for Clay . . . Here she was, back to him again. The man walked in and out of her thoughts like he owned them, like he had set up housekeeping in her head, she grumbled to herself. But . . .

What in the world had happened to her last night? They had been sitting there, carrying on a conversation about Kevin, then he invited her over to show her how he programmed his hacker-catching applications. She was feeling really good, with a warm glow in her middle from good Mexican food and the anticipation of learning his methods. Nothing itched or ached.

Then he was touching her, and she could have sworn energy was flowing between them. What a crazy idea!

If that were not enough, and despite her intentions to keep her distance, he'd kissed her, and she'd simply . . . simply disintegrated.

Wow, had he kissed her. This one had been devastating. Overwhelming. Enchanting. Wonderful. Magical. Just as his other kisses had been.

No, more so.

When his lips touched hers, her brain turned into mush, and her body into a willing participant in whatever he wanted to do with it. More than willing. Eager, enthusiastic, enraptured. The man cast a spell, and she was bewitched.

Her body had felt wonderful, warm, happy, right where it wanted to be. Her insides seemed to be singing, her heart was blissful. Colored lights surrounded them, rippling through rainbow hues, intensifying as his kiss had.

Where had her mind been? Off in outer space with the aliens again. She couldn't have stopped that kiss. She'd have to be paying attention with a conscious mind to do that. Conscious? Phooey! She couldn't even remember going to bed, but she must have because here she was, and it was morning.

She moved restlessly on the smooth sheets and rubbed her rib cage, then crossed her arms over her chest, her hands holding her breasts. They tingled. She rubbed herself through her nightgown, but it made the tingling worse, and she quickly let go when she realized what she was doing.

"Oh, God," she groaned aloud. She was turning into a sex-crazed, blithering idiot. She drew her legs up and hugged her knees.

Why was she so attracted to this one man? She'd never, ever had such a reaction before. Sure, he was tall and good-looking, but so were many others. She especially liked his silver eyes and the way they lit up, then darkened when he looked at her.

He was honest and had loads of integrity, she was certain in her bones about that. What was the rule for when they were alone? "No camouflage, only the truth?"

They got along well together. She was surprised to have so much in common with him—computers, basketball, political opinions, so many of the same likes and dislikes. He came from a stable family, and she liked that because she did also. He was kind; look how he had immediately asked if she wanted to bring Tamara along for dinner last night. Would any other man have made the offer? And meant it?

He was certainly intelligent. And he respected her own smarts. What had he said about her being one of the few people who could understand his programming? A high compliment, indeed.

Her friends liked him. Their acceptance said a lot to her. None of them had ever liked Walt.

Clay was also sympathetic. He understood her anguish over Tamara and the possibility of hurting her best friend. And he soothed her fears and wouldn't let her take on the blame for Kevin's actions. He seemed interested in her, for herself, not just because of the excitement of catching Kevin.

Could she be reading the situation wrong, by thinking he would leave after this mess was over? Might he still want to be together?

He wasn't like Walt, not by a long shot. Was she assuming he would be? Just because he was good-looking? Just because she had been hurt once before? The answers in her head were leaning heavily toward "yes."

He wasn't pushing her into bed like Walt had. In fact, he was always the one to halt their kisses, despite his obvious desire. He hadn't been faking his reaction. Why then was he taking it so slowly, especially when she wouldn't have done anything to stop him? Last night she had practically crawled all over him.

Practically? Be honest. She had been on top of the man and had almost had an orgasm right there on her couch.

Maybe it was better for both of them he had left when he did. Despite the attraction, despite the . . . oh, she might as well admit it, despite *her* raging desire, *her* almost frantic need, she really didn't know if she was ready to make the leap to bed. Something she couldn't identify, couldn't quite get at, was holding her back. What was it?

No voice spoke from above, or even in her head, to give her an answer. No surprise there. She had to laugh at herself for even asking the question. Her stomach gave a little flutter, and she rubbed it slowly. Even her incipient ulcer seemed calm today.

Okay, what did all this mean? What conclusion did she come to after all this thinking? Oh, how she wished she could talk all this over with Tamara. Her friend certainly had more experience with men and might understand more about what was going on.

Everything seemed to come down to the question: What was *real* here?

She had always prided herself on her ability to see things as they actually were. To base her thinking and her actions on reality, on facts, where the only fantasy was in the games she played and the books she read. Granted, the episode with Walt had taught her how to do that. Painfully. So painfully, in fact, she had cut herself off from men and the possibility of being hurt again.

Maybe she had been wrong to do it. Tamara had certainly fussed at her often enough about her self-imposed "seclusion." Now, with Clay, she was beginning to feel like she was waking up after a long sleep. Returning to the world of men and women and possibilities. Not of being hurt, but of finding someone just for her. A mate.

A *mate*? What an old-fashioned word. Where did the thought come from?

What about the other old-fashioned word, *love*?

Love. Was she falling in love with Clay?

No, certainly not. Not on the basis of a few dates and four kisses. Not a conclusion she even wanted to ponder.

Coward! jeered something inside her. She ignored it.

Rubbing the pesky itch again plaguing her, Francie rose from bed and headed toward the shower. She had to get moving if she was due at the haircutter's at one and then Clay's. As she dried off, she let herself wonder about his house. Would it be a typical bachelor place, with little furniture and no decorations, a refrigerator full of beer and leftover pizza? He'd have a killer computer setup, of course. She couldn't wait to see how he programmed that trap for Kevin.

As she turned on the water, she wondered briefly what he wanted to talk about so much today.

CHAPTER FOURTEEN

Francie pulled up in front of Clay's at two thirty. The address had been easy to find in West University Place, south of Bissonnet between Weslayan and Buffalo Speedway. She had always thought the little city surrounded by Houston and Bellaire would be a nice place to live, but she didn't know anyone who actually resided there. During the morning her curiosity about Clay's home had grown from a small spark to a good-sized blaze, so after stopping the car, she turned off the ignition and sat a moment studying the house.

Like so many of the older houses in West U, this one was essentially an ordinary two-story box with a lawn and shrubbery beds in front. Two large oak trees with shiny dark green leaves rose from the grass strips between the sidewalk and the street. The siding on the house was a smooth cream color, and the front door and open window shutters echoed the leaves' dark green. A driveway on the left side led to a solid wooden gate, which appeared from its hardware to be mechanized to swing open.

Though the house presented a conventional, even bland face to the world, Francie liked it immediately. In a funny way she didn't stop to analyze, the structure seemed to welcome her, call to her, tell her she would be happy living there. "Talk about curb appeal," she said to herself as she climbed out of her car.

She noticed a curtain twitch as she came up the walk, and Clay opened the door before she could push the bell. She couldn't help but smile. He just looked so good in a button-down blue plaid shirt, jeans, and running shoes. His silver eyes seemed to light from within as he returned her smile.

"Hi. Come on in." He stepped back from the door. "Welcome to my home."

"Thank you." Francie stepped into the entryway and looked around. "My goodness," she said as she felt her eyes opening wide. Whatever she had expected his house to be like, it wasn't what opened up in front of her.

West U box, indeed! Instead of walls defining living, dining, and whatever else, the downstairs seemed to have almost no interior barriers. The staircase rose— or floated—straight from the small entryway with no visible means of support except the posts at either end and the frame holding the individual treads. Under the stairs, an abstract metal sculpture gleamed in the beam of a small spotlight.

A dining area on the left held a glass-and-chrome

table surrounded by antique-looking chairs. The chandelier over the table mixed metal and lights to leave the impression of a star-filled galaxy. Against the back wall—yes, there was an interior wall with a door leading into the kitchen—stood a tall, deep-red cabinet in chinoiserie style. The light-colored hardwood floor reflected the light pouring in the front window.

To the right of the entry stretched a room that ran from the front to the back of the house and ended in sliding-glass doors. Topped by a severely plain mantle and flanked by oak bookshelves and cabinets, a fireplace sat in the middle of the long outside wall. A leather couch, again in the smooth cream color, faced the fireplace, flanked by a couple of dark blue wing chairs. A glass slab perched on what looked like a tree stump served as a coffee table and sat in the middle of the grouping. Lamps and side tables were where you would need them. Except for the large Oriental carpet in shades of vivid red and blue covering most of the floor, the colors were neutral, and the walls repeated the cream background.

What really drew her eye, however, was the vibrant artwork—a thorough mix, from impressionistic to surrealistic, from representational to abstract, from oil paintings to three-dimensional collages. No old masters for Clay. The colors leaped off the canvases, but somehow didn't clash with each other or the furniture. Despite the disparity of styles, the furnishings coalesced into a space infinitely interesting, but pleasing and comfortable at the same time. She could live here easily.

Francie brought her startled eyes back to her host. "My goodness," she said again.

"That's what everybody says when they walk in the first time," he answered with a smile as he closed the front door. "Put your purse on the couch, and let me show you the rest."

He took her to the sliding-glass doors and out onto a patio stretching across the back of the house. Comfortable-looking furniture and several large pots filled with red geraniums or purple pansies sat on the reddish-brick patio. Steps led down to a small patch of Saint Augustine grass. "I added about five feet onto the back of the house, which reduced the space for the yard by a considerable amount. I spend a lot of time out here in the summer," he said with an encompassing wave of his hand.

A tall wooden fence surrounded the enclosure and guaranteed privacy. Along the fence was a lush jungle, even in late September, full of azalea, oleander, and forsythia bushes, banana trees, and one large clump of pampas grass. A gigantic oak rose from the right-hand corner, opposite the two-car garage set against the back property line on the left. Under the tree lay a swimming pool of irregular shape. The turquoise waters looked perfect for paddling around in, or just lounging on a float, under the tree's shade, a tall glass of something cool in one hand and a hot novel in the other, during one of those blistering Houston summer days.

"This is wonderful, Clay!" Francie exclaimed as she tried to take in everything at once. "It's like being somewhere else, not in the middle of a city at all."

"My mother and sister Glori are the ones to thank for the plantings. I told them I wanted a carefree yard, perennials, absolutely no annuals. And hardly any grass to cut back here, either. I had enough of tending plants growing up on the farm. So, of course, what do they do but rope me into helping Daria take care of her garden, which is full of annuals," he complained with a flap of his arm.

"Poor baby," she commiserated. Personally, she'd love to have a garden to tend. This one could use some more flowers. "How did you manage such a complex shape to the pool? It looks like it could be a pond in the woods."

"The space is too small for a conventional pool, so I spread a garden hose around until I liked the shape, then called in a contractor. It's more a sit-and-soak pool than a swimming one, but it also has one of those pumping machines to allow you to swim against a current without going anywhere. I like to swim laps, but the Y is always so crowded."

She asked some questions about the plantings, and after he answered them, he said with a gesture toward the kitchen door, "Let me show you the rest of the house."

He led her inside through the kitchen, a room gleaming with stainless-steel appliances, shiny dark gray granite counters, white cabinets, and colorful Mexican tilework on the backsplashes. He didn't give her any time to admire the functionality of the kitchen or to inspect the herbs in the pots on the windowsills, but took her through the dining room and up the stairs.

Francie didn't complain, but followed willingly. She didn't know which she was enjoying more, seeing the house or watching Clay show her around. He was so obviously—and justifiably—proud of it.

"The second floor was a hodgepodge of small rooms, so I moved some walls up here, and now there are three rooms and two baths." Standing in the upstairs hall, he pointed toward an open door at the front of the house on the dining-room side. "That's a guest room of sorts, with a bed but little else. Any family who come into town usually stay with Daria, not me. She has more room, and the food's better over at her place. There's a bath between the guest room and this one." He gestured toward the room at the back of the house. "This one's my office."

He walked into the room, stood in the middle, and turned to face her, his arms outstretched. "What do you think?"

Francie looked around at the three computers, one with at least a twenty-inch-wide-plasma-screen monitor, a laptop docking station, a scanner, a copier-fax, a color printer, a webcam and microphone, a server box, ergonomic chairs, shelves neatly arrayed with CD disks and manuals, and futuristic halogen-light lamps. The artwork here consisted of sci-fi movie posters and photographs of the earth and of star systems that could only have been taken from outer space. "It looks like Mission Control," she answered. "I love it. You even have your own network, I see."

"Yep. The network's wi-fi, of course." Clay recited the server's hardware specifications, operating system features, and memory capacity, and answered her technical questions while a feeling of joy grew within him. By the end of his answers, he knew he was grinning like a fool, but he couldn't help it. She liked his house. She liked his computer setup. Why he had been so apprehensive this morning as he was cleaning up, he didn't know now. Of course she would like it. She was his soul mate. But there was one more room to go. "This way to the master suite."

He preceded her out into the hall again and across to the other side. They walked into a room that, like the living room below, stretched from front to back, or almost. "The bathroom and closet are on the front of the house," he said, pointing at the doors, then he shut up and watched her reaction.

Francie first walked to the sliding-glass doors and looked out at a small balcony holding a lawn chair and a small round table. "I didn't notice the balcony when we were downstairs. What a good idea, and the doors let in so much light," she said before turning to the interior.

He watched her eyes roam over the large bed with

its navy spread and the picture—a charcoal-and-pastel drawing of nudes, a man and a woman in an embrace—above the severely plain oak headboard. Did her eyes linger on the bed, or was he mistaken?

She moved past the bed into the sitting area by the fireplace, a duplicate of the one below. The overstuffed chair and its ottoman, both in burgundy, received her scrutiny, as did the oak dresser against the wall and his other artwork. Her eyes went to the bed again, and her face took on an introspective expression.

"Francie?" She jumped slightly when he said her name, and her eyes came back to his.

"Oh. It's a lovely room, Clay," she said hurriedly, almost nervously.

He watched a blush color her cheeks and wished he had the talent to read minds. On the other hand, he was happy she could not read his, which had been busy conjuring the image of her lying on that bed, his bed, her blond hair spread out on that pillow, his pillow. First things first, he admonished himself. "Come on, let's get something to drink. Then we can talk."

They went down to the kitchen, and Clay busied himself taking glasses from the cabinet. "What would you like? I have soft drinks, wine, beer . . ."

"Just some water will be fine." She ran her hand over the smoothness of the granite countertop. "You have a beautiful home, Clay. So much light, such comfortable furniture, and your art is extremely interesting."

"Interesting as in the 'interesting' you say when something is truly awful and you don't know what else to say?" he teased as he handed her a glass filled with ice cubes and water.

"Oh, no." She shook her head. "Not at all. Interesting as in you could look for a long time and not tire of it."

"I'm glad you like it." He watched her golden hair swing from side to side and repressed the urge to take it between his fingers. He was happy to see she hadn't cut off more than an inch. Her color had returned to normal, and she didn't seem as nervous as she had in his bedroom. He was the jittery one now, his hand jerking a little as he picked up his own glass. "Let's go into the living room. I have some things to tell you before I show you the computer apps."

He led her into the living room. "Please, sit down," he said, but after she sat in one of the wing chairs, he found he was too uneasy to sit. Take it easy, he counseled himself as he put his glass on the coffee table. Before she'd arrived, he'd rehearsed his explanation in his head about fifty times. He knew what he had to say. She was sure to believe him about magic and soul mates once she'd seen what he could do with a computer. She'd be his before the night was over. Why, then, was he so nervous? He stood by the fireplace and rearranged several of the small crystal-filled geodes standing on the mantel.

"Clay?" Francie asked. "Is anything wrong?" She took a sip of water, placed her glass on the nearby side table, and peered up at him.

"No, of course not. I'm just trying to organize my thoughts." God, he was such a jackass. Just gut up and tell her, idiot. He ran a hand through his hair, took a deep breath, and said, "I have something very important to tell you, Francie. It's complicated, and I'd appreciate it if you'd wait till I've finished before asking any questions. Okay?"

Her eyes grew round, and she looked like she really wanted to ask a question, but all she said was, "Okay."

"First, I have to ask you to keep what I'm going to say absolutely confidential. You can discuss it with my family, but nobody else, not even Tamara. Don't worry. It's nothing illegal. It's just private information. Okay?"

Francie frowned, but she agreed with a softly spoken, "Okay."

"Okay." He flashed her what he hoped was an encouraging smile, but probably came across more like a grimace. "You know how I answer people when they ask how I do my programming, how I figure out what's wrong with a computer?"

She smiled and seemed to relax. "You tell them it's 'magic.'"

"Right. The thing is, Francie, I'm not lying. *It is magic.*" Her eyes widened again, then narrowed, and she shook her head in a "not again" manner. He made placating gestures with his hands before she could scoff. "Now, just hear me out before you jump to any conclusions. I'm not crazy. You see, it's like this." He sat down in the chair across the coffee table and leaned forward, his elbows on his knees and his hands open to her.

"My family and I belong to a group of people who call ourselves 'magic practitioners.' We have the ability to manipulate little pieces of the world by casting spells, and we use our talents to make our livings. We're 'practitioners' because we practice magic the way doctors and lawyers practice their vocations. Basically, the ability to do magic is genetic, passed down from adults to their children. But to develop your talents, to use them, well, takes training, study, practice, and a lot of it."

He stopped to take a breath. She was just sitting there, her eyes wide, without much expression, and he couldn't really tell how she was taking his statements. Confident in his cause, he could only go on with his explanation.

"All this doesn't make us any different from anyone else, fundamentally. We're normal human beings, with normal life spans, subject to all the cares and woes of other people. We have these abilities, but they don't make us all that different, either. Take prodigies and geniuses, or even extremely smart people, for example. There are a whole bunch of them out there who have no magic ability at all, but what they do, how they play an instrument or manipulate mathematical formulas or know exactly how to put something together, appears 'magical' to others. We practitioners just carry the idea a little further."

Still no reaction from Francie. "Are you with me so far?" he asked. She only nodded once, slowly, and her eyes never left his. She swallowed. She seemed to be intently interested. That had to be good. He simply had to follow his script.

"There are all sorts of talents, some for just about any work a person can do. Some practitioners have a talent for one of the sciences, or business, or medicine, or a sport, or cooking, or even plumbing, would you believe. Some have strong abilities, and others are less powerful, but they all can cast spells to help them with their work.

"Take us Morgans for example," he continued, thinking he sounded like he was lecturing in a very weird college course. "My specialty, as you have probably figured out by now, is computers, both hardware and software. I use spells to cause programs and machines to do what I want them to do. You saw my work in action with the program that put Brenner's keystrokes into a file on your computer. I'll show it to you in a little while." He risked what he hoped was a reassuring smile.

Still no reaction, although she clasped her hands tightly together.

"Daria, whom you met in Herb's office, has a different, possibly unique, talent. For some reason, she can't cast a spell on any person or any object, but she can spell *herself*. That's how she's able to operate as a management consultant. Her spells make people see her as she wants them to—as someone they can trust and must tell the truth—and she finds out how her clients' employees are working, or not working, together.

"Do you remember the day we met? She was talking to you and you jumped, like something had startled you or a little flash had gone off?"

Francie looked to the side and her eyes went unfocused, like she was thinking back. Finally she nodded again. "Uh-huh."

"It was a spell going active. You blinked. Sometimes people can react to a spell. That's what you did."

That last statement brought her eyes back to him, and she seemed astonished, almost alarmed.

"Don't worry," he said. "It just means you're sensitive to magic. A number of people are." Francie might not have any witch blood in her, but she might have a latent talent. It showed up outside the bloodlines from time to time. Or it could be because of the soul-mate connection. Either way, the thoughts pleased him inordinately. Now, where was he? Oh, yes, back to the family.

"I'm a little like Daria, in that I can't put spells on people, although I can cast them on anything with a computer chip in it and also on some other machines. I can do a couple of simple general spells, too. I used to drive my parents crazy manipulating clocks when I was little." He chuckled, but she only smiled weakly at his statement. He could do nothing except plunge ahead.

"My father is an auditor. He casts spells on a company's financials to point out discrepancies, imbalances, and improper accounting methods. He's also able to find embezzlers with his spells. He has to have hard copy, all the accounts on paper, however. He can't do a thing with computers, although I've certainly tried to work with him on it." Clay smiled to show he was teasing about his father.

Francie didn't move, just blinked at him.

"My mother and other sister use their abilities to grow plants. They can boost plant growth, make potions, and do all sorts of things. They're more in the traditional domain, the usual picture of what magic users should be like—witch women, healers, that sort of thing. Which brings up another point. This is in no way 'black' magic, let me assure you. Don't think in terms of the fantasy you've read, or you'll have the wrong idea entirely." He waved his hands in a negative manner.

"I should mention, I guess, we call ourselves 'witches' and 'warlocks,' but those aren't really the proper terms. Those words carry all sorts of historical and fictional baggage that doesn't apply to what we are. We also don't do the kind of magic like you see in stories or movies. We can't change the weather, or teleport all over the place, or conjure up food or objects out of nothing. We certainly don't transform people into toads or anything else. Our magic is just 'workaday' stuff. I'll show you later how we actually 'do magic,' and you'll see what I mean."

Clay took a moment to sip some water. After putting the glass back on the table, he studied his hands for a moment, then focused on her. From the attentive expression on her face, she seemed to be taking it all well. But the hardest part was coming up.

"Right now, I'm sure you're wondering what this has to do with you. Why I'm telling you all this." He paused, but she didn't move.

Those big brown eyes huge in her face, she simply stared at him.

"Because it affects you and me. Remember our promise, 'No camouflage, only the truth'?" He nodded at her, hoping she would nod back. She looked down at her hands, but she finally gave a little jerk of her head that he took for an affirmative answer. He leaned closer to her, wishing he had suggested they sit on the couch. Surely touching her would make it easier to explain, would give him more clues to her reaction.

"Among practitioners, we have an aspect to our lives, an essential condition, a necessity, a need, a compulsion—hell, I don't know what all it is—but it's called the 'soul-mate imperative.' According to this idea, every practitioner has a soul mate and will find that person. Our definition of a soul mate is not much different from the nonpractitioner world. Soul mates get along with each other very well, have similar opinions, likes, dislikes, interests. They're attracted to each other—sexually. Like you and I are, Francie."

She looked more alarmed at his last statements, but he had no choice now but to keep going. "The imperative is both an event—soul mates finding each other—and an ancient force that brings the two together. It lets you know who your soul mate is and makes sure you come to each other.

"In the practitioner concept, when you find your soul mate, what you feel is more powerful than the attraction nonpractitioners have. The desire, the need for the mate, is irresistible. I think you already know what I mean. When we've kissed, it's been all I could do to stop, Francie. I can't get enough of you. I think you haven't wanted to stop, either. But I knew I had to, because you need to understand about the imperative and what it means *before* we make love."

Unable to tolerate the distance between them any longer, he moved around the coffee table to kneel in front of her. He put his hands on hers that were fisted together in her lap. Her fingers were cold, and he rubbed them to warm them up. She glanced at their joined hands and then brought her eyes up to meet his, but he couldn't read her thoughts.

It didn't matter. He was almost finished. They'd be in each other's arms in just a minute.

"What it means," he continued, his voice raspy with the effort it was taking to say the words, "is that the two soul mates are bound together, and the bond grows stronger and stronger over time. The binding is both activated and consummated the first time they make love. Then they're with each other forever."

She frowned, even harder than before, and he hastened to reassure her. "I know you're going to say you're not a practitioner, but neither is Daria's husband. Practitioner or not doesn't matter. If one of the pair is, then all the soul-mate rules apply. It's a lifetime commitment, Francie.

"Once the imperative has identified two soul mates, it brings them together, somehow. I have no idea how. The SMI is alive. You can feel it working, right at the end of your breastbone, right where a practitioner's magic center is. It itches, right?"

Her brown eyes went wide at his question, and she looked down at herself, then back at him. "It's not a bug bite?"

"No, and it's not an ulcer, although it can feel like both. If it doesn't get its way, it can make your life miserable until you give in. Daria and Bent tried to fight, but the imperative had its way. Now they're happier than they ever imagined they'd be. We can be the same way." He gave her hands an encouraging squeeze. She just stared at him. Time for his big finish.

"I'll admit the idea knocked me on my ass at first, just like it's probably doing to you right now. I've been thinking about you and me for days. I finally realized I don't want to fight the imperative. All I could do was tell you what was happening to us. I want you so badly, Francie." He brought her fists up to his lips and kissed her knuckles. "What do you think of all this, darlin'? Will you be my soul mate?"

CHAPTER FIFTEEN

Silence. They stared at each other.

As she looked at Clay, right into his eyes where his pupils had darkened to leave only a rim of silver, Francie felt like the earth had just tilted on its axis. She had sat there, listening to him talk about magic, about people called practitioners, about using spells to do your job, and finally about soul mates, but not just ordinary soul mates. Oh, no, these soul mates were destined for each other, preordained by some mystical, magical "imperative" that left them no choice—no choice but what? To have sex?

He actually thought she would swallow this tale—hook, line, and sinker?

Magic? Practitioners? Soul mates? Some mysterious force called the "imperative"?

Did he take her for a fool? This was the biggest bunch of hooey she'd ever heard. All this buildup to what? Fantasy land? What was he trying to pull? She didn't get angry very often, but when she did . . . She felt her temper blow sky high.

She stood up abruptly, forcing him back on his heels, and snatched her hands out of his before he could tighten his grip. She whirled around behind the chair to create a barrier between them. The increased space did nothing to calm her down.

"Magic? Spells? Soul mates? You honestly expect me to believe all this?" She had to struggle to keep the shrillness out of her voice. "I have never heard of such a thing. Magic? Get real! Witches and warlocks? Puhlease! Where's your magic wand and your wizard robe? Who do you think you are? Harry Potter? Gandalf?"

She glared and tried for a more reasonable tone, but her next words came out sounding like disdainful ridicule to her. "Clay, you've been playing too many *Dungeons and Dragons* or computer games."

After this response, he sat back on his heels and looked at her like *she* was crazy. Well, what did he expect of her?

She waved a hand at the whole idea. "Magic, spells, and all that, does not exist in the real world. Oh, it's fun to pretend, but what you're telling me isn't true!"

She gripped the tall back of the chair to ground herself and took a deep breath. She had to apply reason to this fantastic tale. "I've always prided myself on having a clear view of reality, of how the world works. Now you tell me there are people who cast spells to do their work?

You honestly expect me to believe that? Spells to cook? To do accounting? To make toilets flush? You truly believe you cast spells on your computer? This is the most bizarre thing I've ever heard."

Clay rose to his feet and spoke slowly and distinctly. "Magic does exist. It's not make-believe. It's true." He stretched a hand toward the stairs. "Come upstairs to the computer, and let me show you."

He was talking to her like she was a child or mentally deficient, and she didn't like it. What had happened to his treating her like an equal?

"No," she answered. "I don't want any demonstrations. I know your programming capabilities. You could have rigged that computer to do anything you wanted it to do."

"All right," he answered, still in his infuriatingly reasonable tone, "we'll go to your place."

"No, not at my place, either. You've been on my machine. Who knows what you might have done there or uploaded from Brazos when you were tracking Kevin?" She leaned over the back of the chair toward him. "Why are you doing this, Clay? How can you claim with a straight face you can do magic?"

He put his hands on his hips and gave her a determined look. "Because you're my soul mate."

She opened her mouth to answer, but he held up a hand. "As to the magic . . ." He snapped his fingers.

A glowing ball of light appeared right in front of her

nose. It was blue, and it crackled faintly.

Francie jumped and felt her eyes cross as she looked at the object. Rearing back, she swatted at the globe. It moved out of her reach before she could touch it, and when Clay snapped his fingers again, it vanished.

She glared at him. "You can't fool me with some old illusion. You're just an ordinary magician, that's all, no different from Blackstone or David Copperfield or one of those guys who plays Vegas. For all I know, you've got some lasers rigged for a hologram." She swiftly searched the corners of the room, but saw nothing to back up her accusation. Well, no matter.

She crossed her arms in front of her. "Magic. Puh-lease." Then her brain latched onto something else he had said. "Wait a minute. Are you telling me that in our first meeting your sister put a spell on me to see if I was telling the truth?"

Clay waved both hands in the negating gesture he had. "No, that isn't what I said. Daria can't put one *on you*, just on herself, and then you see her as she wants you to." He put his hands back on his hips. "Because of her, we *knew* you were telling the truth, you weren't part of Brenner's scheme. Sure, we would have found it out eventually, but this way we cut right to the crux of the situation."

"Didn't Herb at least trust me?" A sharp iciness ran down her spine as she realized that if her boss hadn't be-lieved she was innocent, then Kevin might have truly succeeded in framing her.

"Yeah, he did. *I* was the skeptical one. Lay it on *me* if you're looking for someone to blame. But I didn't know you then. I do now."

Francie almost slumped in relief, but his next words stiffened her backbone.

"Look, you can't have it both ways, first magic doesn't exist, then Daria cast a spell on you. Now which is it?" His expression was changing from earnestness to triumph.

She wasn't ready to concede anything at this point. She knew she wasn't being exactly rational, and she couldn't seem to get her mind to stop whirling and start concentrating in a straight line. Her stomach aching again didn't help, either. Her thoughts veered off on another tangent, and rather than answer his question, she went with them.

"What about this soul-mate rigmarole? Ancient force, imperative?" she asked. "Are you making up all this fantasy just to get me in bed? That's laughable! What is it with good-looking men? You seem to think women will believe everything you tell them. I thought I'd learned my lesson with Walt."

Clay looked thoroughly perplexed by her change of subject. "Walt?" he exclaimed, throwing his hands up in the air. "Hell, who's *he*? What's he got to do with *us*? The soul-mate imperative is not 'rigmarole.' It's very real. I know you've been itching and hurting. Can't you feel it, Francie? Can't you feel the attraction between us?" He held out his hands and took a step toward her.

She countered with a step to keep the chair between them. "Such a thing doesn't exist, either," she answered. "This is all just a ploy to have sex. Sure, I'm attracted to you. That's just hormones. I haven't been with anyone in years—"

"Years!"

"—and it's just my body complaining or my biological clock or something." She shook her head. "And for me to be thinking just this morning I was coming to like you, we were getting along so well, you were all right, we might have a future. Then you pull this, this 'tale' out of thin air. God, I can't believe what a fool I've been."

She pointed her finger at him. "You've got sex on the brain, Clay. And when I told you this phony, fictitious 'relationship' was just business, all I did was arouse your predatory instincts, didn't I? Activated the hunt. You want something you couldn't have, *me*, so you make up this convenient, cockamamie story about how we're 'fated' to be together because of some magic-practitioner nonsense, just to get me in bed. Expect me to fall into your arms. Have you used this line much in the past? Does this story really work for you?"

He opened his mouth to reply, but she kept talking. She was on a roll and couldn't seem to stop her thoughts and fears from tumbling out. At least she was too angry to cry. Cry, hah! She wouldn't give him the satisfaction.

"And what will happen after that? You'll betray me or leave me. I'll be stuck again picking up the pieces. It's all just a game with you, isn't it? Well, I for one am not going to play it, not this time.

"*I'm* leaving. Don't call me, don't come around. You got what you want. You have Kevin in your sights. You don't need me anymore. Don't worry, I'll keep your secret. I wouldn't want it to get around that Brazos had hired a crazy consultant."

She whipped around the couch, grabbed her purse, and ran out the door.

Clay stood there stunned for a couple of seconds. What had just happened? What was wrong with the woman? Where had she gone? Oh, shit! She had walked out on him! He practically vaulted over the furniture and shot out the door she had left open in her haste. "Francie!"

She had climbed into her car and was starting the engine. He ran to the passenger door and pulled the handle, but it was locked. "Francie!" he yelled again as he beat on the window.

She paid no attention to him, just put the car into gear and hit the gas before he could get a grip on the handle or the outside mirror. He watched her drive off and turn at the corner.

"Damn!" Clay ran back into the house, closed and locked the front door, and headed out the back for his own car. She had to be going home. When he reached her apartment complex, the first thing he did was check her parking slot. Her car was there. He ran up to her door and rang the bell.

Nothing happened. Not a peep issued from the interior.

"Francie!" He rang the bell again and pounded on the door. "I know you're in there. We're not finished. We need to talk this through." He pounded some more. "Francie, answer me!"

The door swung open. Francie stood in the entrance with her hands braced, one on the door, the other on the jamb. Clearly, if he wanted in, he'd have to move her out of the way physically.

"Francie, we have to talk," he said in as reasonable a tone as he could muster, while he fought to keep himself from throwing her over his shoulder and carrying her off to bed.

"No, we don't," she said, shaking her head. "Go away!"

"But you're my soul mate," he said. "How can you say that? You can't reject me!"

"Just watch me. And furthermore, you're crazy. Nobody can cast magic spells. Magic doesn't exist!" She slammed the door in his face.

"Francie!" he roared and pounded on the door again.

"Hey, buddy!" An older man stuck his head out of the apartment to the left. "What's the matter? What's all the racket?"

Clay stopped pounding. "Nothing. I just need to talk to the woman inside, that's all."

"Well, it sure doesn't look like she wants to talk to you, does it, if she won't answer the door. Now cut out all this noise. I have to work the late shift tonight, and I need to get some sleep."

Clay stared at the man for a moment, then looked back at Francie's closed door. The guy had a point. It wouldn't do any good to break the thing down. It would only make her madder. All he could do was leave before her neighbor—or she—called the cops.

"Francie, I'll be home if you want to talk," he said loudly. "And we do have to talk. You know it as well as I do." He looked at the neighbor. "Sorry for the disturbance."

"No problem," the man answered and shut his door.

Clay thought about leaving a note, but he didn't have a card or pen on him, and he wasn't sure it would do any good anyway. So he stalked down the stairs and back to his car.

What was wrong with the woman? Why didn't she believe him? He climbed into the vehicle and headed home. He couldn't believe her reaction. It was the last thing he would ever have expected.

His gut was hurting, probably from all the stomach acid the argument had churned up, but his magic center was quiet, as though it was waiting for something.

They were soul mates, weren't they?

Weren't they?

Damn right, they were.

CHAPTER SIXTEEN

Back in her apartment, Francie sat slumped on her bed, staring into space. Clay must have left, she figured, when the pounding on the door stopped and he yelled that stuff about how they had to talk. She gave a big sigh, but it didn't feel like one of relief. It felt more like one of emptiness.

He wanted to talk. Oh, God, he'd be calling her. She roused herself and pulled the plugs on the phones in the kitchen and her office, leaving only the answering machine hooked up. Returning to the bedroom, she disconnected the phone by her bed, then took off her shoes and resumed her place on the spread.

What good would talk do now? The man was definitely deranged, mentally unsound. Nutty. Off his rocker. He had bugs in his hardware and was many code lines short of a working program. She was better off having nothing to do with him.

Wasn't she?

Yes, she nodded and, threading her fingers through her hair, rubbed her scalp vigorously. Yes, of course, she was.

What a fantastic tale he had told! Magic—what did he call them—practitioners? Magic practitioners who applied spells to their jobs to do them better. How could he have thought she'd believe him? Sure, there were very smart people or those with an intuitive feel for their work who produced wonderful ideas and products. She knew several of them. Her fellow gamesters, for example.

And Clay? She had to admit he seemed to take computer programming and manipulation to new heights. She frowned at her last thought. What he did couldn't be magic.

Magic didn't exist.

And his explanation! He hadn't given her the chance to process the information about this so-called magic. He hadn't let her ask a question—he obviously didn't want her to since he'd asked her to hear him out first. Instead he had gone from magic to talking about "soul mates," for crying out loud. If that didn't sound like a line straight out of a bad sitcom, or an even worse singles bar, she had never heard one. Sort of a someday-my-princess-will-come story. Was the idea, the claim they were "fated" to be together, supposed to make a woman fall into a man's arms? Or rather, his bed?

His bed . . . How enticing it had looked, up there in his bedroom. She sighed again and rubbed the painful itch—

the ache had never let up from the time it flared back at Clay's house. Now a dull throb accompanied the irritation.

"No, no, no!" she said aloud and shook her head until she felt her hair flying about her face. Thinking about his bed was not a good idea.

Back to his soul-mate . . . imperative. Hah! She was supposed to believe that some outside force, an arcane, magical, mystical coercion, was pushing them together? Or was it an internal chemical compulsion? Or just good old-fashioned lust? Didn't matter which. It came down to the same thing: All he really wanted was to jump her bones.

She rubbed the aching spot between her breasts. This torment was no ancient force, and it certainly wasn't an alien. She was developing a real-life, non-pretend ulcer, and no wonder with all she'd been through lately.

Mr. Clay Morgan was quite a seducer. First he kissed a woman until she turned to jelly, then he walked out the door as calmly as could be, and he repeated the pattern until she was a quivering mass of frustration.

Then the coup de grâce: *Guess what? We're soul mates. Magical soul mates. Don't fight it. I want you.*

Why on earth he'd thought he needed such an unbelievable story about practitioners and then the soul-mate idea to get her into bed was beyond her. At least he hadn't uttered the horrible ancient cliché, "It's bigger than both of us."

In all of his preposterous explanation, he had not

said one word about caring about her beyond the physical. Not one word about love. *No, be fair*, she chided herself. He had used the word once, but in "making love," not as in "I love you."

I love you.

Oh, God. Did she want him to say that? Did she want to say those words back to him?

No, she couldn't be in love with him. Not when all he talked about was sexual attraction and this weird "imperative" to be soul mates.

But, oh, she did like the man. Liked looking at him, talking to him, being with him, touching him, kissing . . . No, don't go there! She shook her head again and concentrated on the opposing argument to her reflections.

What she felt was just an infatuation, that's all. She hadn't been involved with a man in so long her hormones had finally rebelled and taken over her mind for a while.

She could get over Clay. She *would* get over him. She simply had to stay away from him. They had nothing left to talk about. There was nothing to "get over."

The pain in her chest intensified to a true heartache, and she collapsed back on the bed and curled up in a ball. With an immense feeling of loneliness settling in her bones, she fought tears until she fell asleep in the late afternoon.

She opened her eyes Sunday morning feeling like her system had totally crashed, her usual morning grogginess infinitesimal compared to this mega-headache and feeling of immense exhaustion. She looked at the clock: ten in the morning. She had slept, if she could call it that, over fifteen hours. Carefully, she extricated herself from the tangled bedspread, groaning as her stiff body protested.

She stumbled into the bathroom and almost gasped when she saw her reflection in the mirror over the sink. Her hair was a tangled mess, her makeup was smudged, and large black circles hung under her swollen eyelids like the curtains on the stage at Jones Hall. She vaguely remembered waking up from time to time to a wet pillow, so she must have been crying in her sleep.

As she removed the clothing she had slept in, memories returned of the dreams that had caused her tears. She and Clay making love, an act so beautiful she had to cry. Clay standing naked before her, looking like Desire Incarnate, holding out his hands to her, but try as she might, she couldn't move to meet him. Clay saying, "If you won't believe me, then you can't have me," and her wailing, "I want to, but I can't!" Clay, his face a mask of pain, stating, "You're my soul mate. Of course, I love you."

Francie doubled over in anguish as the last recollection flashed through her mind and pain radiated from her middle. Laboring for breath, she somehow collected herself and stepped into the shower. The hot water rushing over her body didn't restore her equilibrium completely, but the heat helped to soothe her too-tightly-wound muscles. Finally somewhat refreshed, she shut off the spray and toweled herself dry. After swallowing some aspirin, she ran a comb through her hair. She put on her robe and slippers and shuffled toward the kitchen, determined to go about her usual chores and put all the rest out of her mind.

The doorbell rang.

The sound practically threw her against the wall. Oh, God, what if it was Clay? Heart racing, she clasped the robe tighter around her body, tiptoed to the door, and peeked out the peephole.

"Thank you, Lord," she whispered. It was Tamara. Only Tamara.

Francie opened the door. "Hi." The single word came out in a croak.

"You look awful," Tamara stated after giving Francie a fast once-over.

"I know," Francie replied.

Tamara looked like she always did, well put together in a crisp bright blue shirt and pressed jeans. "I broke up with Kevin," she announced with a cheery smile.

"I broke up with Clay," Francie responded with no smile at all.

"I brought Oreos and ice cream." Tamara held up a large grocery bag.

"Come on in."

Francie stepped back, and Tamara headed straight for the kitchen.

Francie put on the coffee while Tamara gathered plates, silverware, napkins, and two large dishtowels—their usual ritual for commiseration when Tamara broke up with a boyfriend. This was the first time Francie found herself in total sympathy with her friend.

"I bought pints of Chocolate Fudge Brownie and Cherry Garcia for you, and Phish Food and Uncanny Cashew for me, as usual," Tamara said. "Which do you want first?"

"Cherry Garcia."

"Fine. I think I'll start with Phish Food." She put the remainder of the ice cream in the freezer and placed the bag of cookies on the table.

They both sat down at the table, wrapped the pints in the dishtowels, took off the lids, dug out one spoonful, and held the spoons up to each other.

Together they repeated their standard litany: "Here's to the only men who truly understand us. Ben and Jerry." They ate the ice cream.

After several moments of savoring the creamy goodness, Francie asked, "So, what happened with Kevin? You don't seem to be very upset about it." With any luck, she could keep Tamara talking about him and not asking any questions about Clay.

"Remember how I said the zing was gone from our relationship? Well, the zing turned into a thud. I finally had it up to here with him." She waved her spoon in front of her throat. "First, he once again didn't take me to dinner, but I told you about that on Friday. He was acting strangely at the club, too, first excited and talking big about his prospects at work, then anxious and worrying about money over some deal he has going. He never asked me how I was, or how the shop did last week, or even about my new computer. We hardly danced at all."

Tamara stopped to eat more ice cream.

"Did he explain why he was excited or anxious? About either the prospects or the deal?" Francie put in, hoping they wouldn't go into *those* subjects.

"No. He acted really mysterious about both. As I sat there and listened to him, I realized this was one of the few times we'd been at one of the clubs without seeing someone we knew to sit with and talk to. Without somebody to run interference for him, you know, carry on the conversation, Kevin is boring. Booorrrring."

She shot a glance at Francie over the top of the ice-cream container. "I know, you've thought it from the beginning. At the start, he was so attentive to me, and I was looking for nonserious companionship, so I didn't pay any attention to the negatives. The more I think about it, however, the more it looks like he was using salesman tactics on me. You know, let the prospect talk, find out what she likes, what she needs, say what you need to close the sale. All men do it to some extent, I know. Kevin carried it to an extreme. He seemed really interested in the shop until recently and even gave me some good suggestions about making sales. I was perfectly willing to fill in any conversational gaps that developed. And then, he is a good dancer, I'll give him that, and I do like to dance.

"But lately, we've had less and less conversation about anything but him. He's been drinking more and dancing less. Friday night the reality of the situation finally hit me. So, I decided to think about it and him and us. When he took me home and wanted to stay the night, I pleaded exhaustion, a busy day coming up at the shop on Saturday, and I don't know what all to get rid of him. He wasn't happy about it, but he left with good enough grace."

Francie reached for the coffee pot and poured them each a cup. "What happened on Saturday?"

"I thought about him all day, every moment in between serving customers, and came to the conclusion you have been right all along. Kevin is not the man for me. Going back over all our 'conversations,' it became clear we never talked about anything but our jobs—especially *his* problems—or his pontificating about something, be it the economy, sports, or the latest scandal. When we watched TV, it always had to be what he wanted. We never went anywhere except to bars or clubs or ball games with his clients. He may be a good dancer, but that's not enough to sustain a relationship."

She grimaced and shook her head. "And I gave in to him all the time, never stood up for what I wanted to do. I have turned into a wimp. I can't believe it. This is so unlike me. For example, do you know he works for NatChem?"

"Really?" Francie managed to put a look of surprise on her face. "Why didn't you tell me?"

"Because Kevin asked me not to, said it would make things awkward between you and him. I thought the idea was ridiculous, but went along with it. I'm sorry."

"Oh, don't be," Francie admonished with a shake of her head and a waggle of her spoon. "Knowing his employer wouldn't have made any difference at all in my opinion of him. Whatever he did or whomever he worked for, he still wasn't good enough for you. And certainly not smart enough. What did you decide after all this thinking?"

"He came over again Saturday night. This time he was supposed to take me to dinner—a casual dinner, he said. It probably would have been to a cheap Mexican or Chinese place, after all his grumbling about money. I didn't give him a chance. Just told him flat out I didn't think our relationship was going anywhere and we'd both be better off if we didn't see each other anymore."

"How did he take it?"

"He was angry, of course. Ranted and raved a bit. Claimed he was just about to 'make it big' and I'd be sorry."

"He didn't get violent, did he?"

"No, but he turned awfully red in the face at one point. I wasn't afraid, though. Then he said something nasty—accused me of being frigid, would you believe?—

and left." Tamara started laughing. "Can you imagine? Me, frigid? How unimaginative and banal can you get? Not to mention wrrrroooonnnng." She smirked and took another bite of her ice cream.

"You certainly don't seem to be upset about him, like you have been with guys at times in the past," Francie observed, not wanting to hear about how good or bad anybody was at lovemaking.

Tamara looked startled for a moment, then shrugged. "You're right. Which just goes to show you I was right to kick him loose. It hurt more to break up with Rich and then Dave, but they are truly nice people. We just didn't suit each other somehow, once the excitement was gone. And we both knew it, each time. Kevin? No way could we even remain friends. I really picked a loser with him. But, that's all behind me now. I feel like I shook a big load off my back."

"I don't know how you do it, dating all the men you do. I've thought you were actually in love with at least two of them—the kind of love that leads to marriage, I mean. Then you broke up with them and didn't seem any the worse for wear."

"Because I haven't been in love, not the gut-wrenching, can't-live-without-him, totally bewitched, completely committed type. I know that kind of love exists, and I'm looking for it. I'm going to find my soul mate one of these days, I just know it."

Soul mate. Even Tamara was looking for a soul

mate. Francie winced inwardly. Soul mates were the last things she needed to think about. Or talk about. So she said simply, "Good for you, Tamara," as she opened the cookies. She took one out, used it to dip out a scoop of Cherry Garcia, and took a bite. The crunch of the cookie combined with the smoothness of the ice cream to enhance all the flavors. "Oh, this is so good."

Tamara unscrewed her Oreo, licked off the creamy filling, and took a bite of the chocolate wafer. They sat for a moment, cookie-crunching the only sound.

After finishing her ice cream, Tamara set the container aside. She rested her elbows on the table and leaned forward, worry on her face. "All right," she said, "now what's all this about your breaking up with Clay? I thought everything was going smoothly with you two."

Francie finished the Oreo she was eating and took a sip of coffee. When Tamara had that look in her eye, she wasn't going to let anyone off the hook until she knew the whole story. Well, she wasn't going to get it this time. "Let's just say we had a difference of opinion and leave it, can we? I really don't want to talk about it."

"Oh, Francie, I'm so sorry. I hoped you were finally coming out of the fort you built around yourself and beginning to live a little. Clay seemed so perfect. Good-looking, intelligent. You had the same interests, computers, even basketball. You were enjoying your dates, weren't you?"

"Yes," Francie said with a sigh.

"What'd he do, come on too fast?"

"No, yes, oh, I don't know. I kept thinking about Walt and . . ."

"Walt!" Tamara rolled her eyes. "Clay is not anything like Walt, I can tell you that for sure. There was something phony about Walt's oversized ego from the beginning. And the way he was so condescending. I couldn't understand the attraction. Just like you told me about Kevin, I told you about Walt, remember?"

"Uh-huh." Francie put her elbow on the table and her chin in her hand. "I guess we ought to start listening to each other, shouldn't we?"

"Right. From now on, we won't go out with any man till the other checks him out." Tamara cocked her head and gave Francie a penetrating stare. "You got scared, didn't you? Scared of Clay's appeal, his attractiveness, that you wouldn't measure up, didn't you?"

"What are you talking about?"

"You haven't been around a man coming on to you in a long time. And Walt did a number on your self-esteem. And here comes Clay. If he is half as sexy as he looks, I'll bet he's not shy, either. But, because your last encounter with sex was such a disaster, you assumed this one would be, too. What did he do that scared you so? Was it really that bad? Could you have overreacted and made a mistake about him?"

Tamara was coming too close for comfort, Francie realized. The two of them knew each other so well, they could have been twin sisters. But she didn't want to think about the possibility of having overreacted. A straightforward "let's go to bed" she could have handled—and probably would have raced him up the stairs after a couple of those mesmerizing kisses. But all this "practitioner" and then "soul-mate" business . . . No, she couldn't tell Tamara about that. Even if she hadn't promised Clay to keep it secret, the story was too outlandish to repeat. So she lied.

"No, no, it wasn't about that at all." She'd let Tamara define "that" any way she wanted to. "We just got into a crazy argument, and it escalated, and he said some things, and I said some things, and . . . and . . . Oh, damn." As tears filled her eyes, Francie grabbed a handful of paper napkins and hid her face behind them.

"Oh, Francie." Tamara came around the table and gave her a big hug. After Francie calmed down, the redhead returned to her chair and asked in a soft voice, "Are you going to see him again? Try to patch it up? Making up can be fun, you know." A wink accompanied her last sentence.

"I honestly don't know. But, Tamara," Francie leaned over the table and pointed a finger at her, "don't you try to mediate. Don't call him or tell him anything if he comes by your shop. Just tell him you're neutral. Don't let him talk you into bringing me a message. Promise me."

Tamara frowned, and her lips thinned, but she said,

"Okay, okay. I won't meddle. But I have to tell you—and I feel it in every one of my red hairs—if you don't try, you're making a mistake, a big one, and I hope you don't live to regret it." She slumped back in the chair, then straightened up and snagged another Oreo out of the bag. "So, do we start on the next pint, or what?"

"Thank you, Tamara, you're a good friend."

"So are you."

They grinned at each other, although Francie could feel her lips wobble.

"However, I don't think I can eat more ice cream or anything. How about you?" she asked.

"No, me, either," Tamara replied with a grimace. "We just can't hold it like we used to."

"Not if we want to fit in our clothes, we don't." Francie rose and started clearing the table.

Tamara helped put cups and spoons in the dishwasher, then turned to her and put a hand on her shoulder. "Francie, are you all right? Seriously?"

"Yes, seriously, I'm all right. Now. Thanks to you and Ben and Jerry, not to mention Mr. Oreo." She put on a cheerful smile. "I feel fine. I'm energized."

"Do you feel up to entering my accounting information in my computer as we planned, or shall we just blow it off?"

Oh, damn. She had forgotten her promise to Tamara. "No," she said as brightly as she could, "let's do it. Give me a minute to dress."

"I'll get my things and meet you out front." Tamara started for the door.

"Great."

As Tamara stepped out of the apartment, Francie said, "I'm really glad you got rid of Kevin." She just wished she could tell her friend why.

"Me, too. See you in a few minutes," Tamara replied as she went down the stairs.

Francie shut the door. Leaning against the wall, she contemplated her options. Helping her friend would keep her mind off . . . other things, and she wouldn't be at home to answer the phone—or, God forbid, the doorbell. Also, the whole crazy situation looked better somehow after talking to Tamara. She could get through this; it would just take time. She pushed herself off the wall and headed to her bedroom, determined not to think about anything.

By early evening, she was exhausted. She and Tamara had entered most of the accounting data by mid-afternoon, and she had left Tamara at the shop checking inventory. At home she'd thrown herself into a frenzy of cleaning, going even so far as to wipe off the shelves in her refrigerator. She stopped short of scrubbing the oven; she wasn't that miserable, she lied to herself.

She'd managed somehow to ignore the constant pain in her stomach, and the milk, ice cream, and aspirins she'd poured down it seemed to help.

In her office, she'd plugged the phone back in and

called her parents in Dallas—this being the night for their usual biweekly rendezvous. Somehow she had managed to sound normal and chat as if nothing at all was wrong, although she was afraid her mother was getting suspicious by the end of the conversation. After the call, she'd stared at the answering machine where a red "7" blinked. Telling herself she wasn't a coward, she hit the play button.

"Francie." His voice came through loud and clear, and an agonizing pain stabbed her middle, next to her heart. She hit the delete button. Then she hit it six more times. She unplugged the phone and marched out of the room, intent on finding something else to clean, anything other than him to occupy her mind.

By the time she went to bed, she had arrived at an equilibrium of sorts. First, she refused to think she had overreacted. Second, his claims were too fantastic to believe. Third, Clay was an alluring man. The attraction was merely chemistry. Fourth, all she had to do to get through this—whatever "this" was—was stay away from him.

Soul mates, what a ridiculous idea.

She wasn't in love with him.

She wasn't.

Was she?

CHAPTER SEVENTEEN

"Damn it! This is not the way things were supposed to turn out." Clay glared at the phone in his home office. It was ten o'clock on Sunday morning, and after his last call, the seventh since yesterday, the third today, he was giving up. She obviously wasn't going to answer, much less call him back. Even his magical skills couldn't overcome her decision.

He zapped the phone with a spell and it rang. At least the thing still worked, he thought glumly, reversing the enchantment to turn off the noise.

What was he going to do? His soul mate had rejected him. Told him he was crazy. Then she'd run. Actually, literally, run from him.

And what was all that crap about a guy named Walt? He must be the asshole who hurt her in the first place, who made her hide behind those clothes and glasses. Clay flexed his fingers, formed fists. Man, if he could only get his hands on good ol' Walt.

Face reality, he told himself. That was what she had said.

But reality *was* magic. He conjured a light ball and bounced it around the room, off the top of the bookshelves, in and out of the trash can. Francie had denied the evidence right in front of her face. He dissolved the blue globe with a snap of his fingers.

What *was* he going to do? He knew what he *wasn't*. He wasn't going to beg. He wasn't going to go over there and beat on her door. He wasn't going to send her e-mails or show up at her office, either. Those things smacked of stalking, and he didn't think they'd do any good, anyway.

He'd wait her out. Wait for the soul-mate imperative to kick in.

Could he stand waiting? He already had a hurt in his center that nothing alleviated. "It's not *my* fault," he said to his chest, but nothing happened.

"Hell." He ran his fingers through his hair. He had to do something or he would go crazier than Francie thought he was.

He picked up the phone and dialed.

"Hello?"

"Daria, it's me. Can I come over? I need to talk to you and Bent. It's about Francie."

His sister sounded puzzled, but mercifully she didn't question him. "Sure, come on."

"Thanks. I'll be there in a few minutes." He hung

up and headed out the door.

Bent answered the doorbell. "Hi," his tall, auburn-haired brother-in-law said as he looked Clay up and down. "What's up? You look like what Zorro drags in."

"Thanks a lot," Clay replied as he stepped into the house.

"Problems on the soul-mate front?" Bent asked as he closed the door. "I can relate to that."

Clay followed Bent into the kitchen, where the cats were lounging on a windowsill and Daria was taking a coffee cake out of the oven. "Oh, my," she said after she inspected her older brother.

"Don't say it," Clay interrupted. "I look awful, or so Bent already informed me."

"Sit down. Did you have any breakfast?" When he shook his head, she said, "You'll feel better with some food in you. Bent, why don't you pour us some coffee?" She cut the cake and served it.

The cake with its cinnamon and pecans tasted good, and Clay's appetite revived as he ate. He hadn't had anything since last night, but he couldn't remember what he had eaten then. A sandwich, maybe. Yeah, he'd fixed himself a sandwich around eight, after the second or third call to Francie. It had tasted like cardboard. He finished off his piece of cake and took a big gulp of coffee.

Daria and Bent put down their cups and gave him inquiring looks.

"I told Francie yesterday about magic, practitioners,

soul mates, everything," he announced, the words like bitter gall in his mouth. "She didn't believe me."

"Oh, damn," Bent said. "What'd she do?"

"Ran out of the house like the banshees of hell were after her. I followed her home, but she wouldn't let me in the door, and she won't pick up the phone, either yesterday or today. What's the matter with the woman? She's my soul mate. She's not supposed to act this way." He couldn't bring himself to look either Daria or Bent in the eye. He'd failed, and he hated failing at anything, much less admitting it to anyone.

"Take it easy, Clay," Daria said, putting a hand on his arm. "Let's go back over what you said. Maybe she just didn't understand."

"Oh, she understood all right. Said magic doesn't exist. Accused me of stringing her a line."

"Tell us what you said. What an explanation sounds like to a man is not always the same as it is to a woman," Daria replied.

"She's got a point," Bent put in. "Remember, I said something along those lines to you earlier."

"Yeah, right, okay." He repeated his "script": practitioners do magic; they're not different from other people; they have different talents. Soul mates always found each other, and the imperative bound them together the first time they made love. The sexual attraction was extremely powerful.

"Then I asked her to be my soul mate," he concluded.

He couldn't bring himself to mention he'd been on his knees when he asked her; that was too embarrassing, especially given her reaction.

"What did she say?" Daria asked.

"She told me there was no such thing as magic, and I'd been playing too many fantasy computer games. I cast a light ball right in front of her nose, and she accused me of being a Vegas magician. She wouldn't give me a chance to demonstrate on the computer. Then she decided the soul-mate imperative was just a big line to get her into bed. She compared me to some guy named Walt. And, to put the star on top of the wizard's hat, she told me I'd leave her or betray her as soon as I got what I wanted." He heard himself almost yelling as he said the last sentence, and he made himself stop. He collapsed back in his chair. "And then she ran out."

"You told her this all at once," Daria said. "Did she ask any questions?"

His sister had that intent look on her face she used when she was analyzing personnel interactions for a client. Good, he had been right to come over. She could get to the bottom of this if anybody could. "Yes, I laid it all out," he answered. "Just about the way Mother and Dad did for Bent, only shorter."

He took a gulp of coffee. He wasn't going to admit how nervous he had been. "I thought it better to tell her everything, including the part about soul mates, before she asked any questions." He shrugged. "Give her the big picture. Like I do when I'm making a presentation to a client. Let her understand how it all fits together so she could see all the ramifications. She hates what she calls 'deception,' and I didn't want her to get the idea I wasn't telling her all of the truth."

Daria and Bent looked at each other, one of those husband-and-wife glances that practically read each other's minds. Clay began to have feelings of trepidation. Had he done something wrong? He couldn't see how he could have. But what was he supposed to have done?

"Let's look at this from another angle—that of our first nonpractitioner," Daria said, turning to her husband. "Bent, how would you have felt if we had told you *everything* that day, instead of concentrating on the existence of practitioners and leaving soul mates for later?"

Bent rose from the table and walked over to look out a window, put his hands in his pockets, and rocked back and forth on his heels, his usual stance when thinking hard. After a minute, he turned around. "I think I would have been totally overwhelmed. Learning you all could do magic and then seeing spells happen in front of me were mind-boggling enough. It took me several days to get used to the idea. If you had sprung soul mates on me on top of that, well, I don't know. Remember, when you did tell me about them, it threw me for an even bigger loop."

He grinned as he sat back down and looked at Clay. "You know, I fought the imperative, and it was the damn thing's own fault because, from what we can figure, it kept me from making a commitment to any woman before I met Daria. I, of course, had decided that getting seriously involved just led to my pain and suffering and was determined to never attempt it again. It took me a couple of days to come to terms with the idea, realize Daria was the best thing that ever happened to me, imperative or not, and I didn't want to lose her. My waffling did confuse the hell out of Daria, and it pissed off Lolita so much she bit me. But that was *my* reaction. In Francie's case, you may have another type of problem."

"I think you're right, Bent," Daria said. "Francie doesn't fear commitment if she's worried about your leaving, Clay. She wants it. The main problem from my point of view is that she isn't receptive to the *idea* of magic. I assume she likes to play those fantasy computer games the way you do, or she reads sci-fi and fantasy, so it's not like she's unfamiliar with the fictional version. Clay, did she give you any indication before your talk as to how she viewed the subject of the real stuff?"

Clay winced in remembrance. "Yeah, she did. I brought up the subject, casually, as an abstract, and she said she didn't believe in it at all. Something about how she was 'grounded in the real world,' whatever that means."

"Uh-oh." Bent shook his head.

"Yeah, well, that's what she threw back at me at first. Then she did a one-eighty and was worried that *you*, Daria, might have cast a spell on her in our first meeting. I told her she couldn't have it both ways, no magic one minute and a spell cast on her the next."

All the disappointment of the previous day came back to him, and he flapped his arms in frustration. "She didn't answer, but went off on another tangent about soul mates. Said it was all 'rigmarole.' Said the only purpose of my story was to get her into bed. I had 'sex on the brain.' Acted like she hadn't heard the part about commitment."

The more he thought about her rejection, the angrier he was getting. He folded his arms across his chest to regain his control. He'd like to hit something, and he knew exactly what, and it wasn't Francie. "And to compare me to this 'Walt' character! And to claim I'd leave her! Or cheat on her! What a load of shit!"

"Clay," Daria said, "let's take this apart, one piece at a time. First, are you *sure* she's your soul mate?"

"Yeah, I'm sure. I have all the symptoms Mother and Dad told us about, and the ones you and Bent mentioned. Outside of this fiasco, we think the same way, have the same likes and dislikes, all that stuff. Hell, she even plays basketball." He took a deep breath, willing himself to calm down. "Daria, this isn't some infatuation. It's not just lust. I've never felt this way about a woman before. We just . . . Well, never mind. Leave it at that." He wasn't going to tell his sister about their practically setting fire to the place, they were so hot together.

"Okay. You're soul mates, it's a given." She leaned back in her chair and thought for a few seconds. "That takes us to Walt. It sounds like you stirred up an old hurtful episode involving this man. He must have treated her very badly, and she's still carrying the baggage from the old relationship, so she's distrustful of any man, not just you."

"Wonderful." Clay couldn't help snarling the word.

"Did she give you any indication what he'd done?" Bent asked.

"I got the impression he left her, but I may not be correct. She used the word *betray* in there somewhere," Clay said. "Whatever it was, I think it drove her into those baggy clothes and those glasses she doesn't need, and she's been there ever since."

"What he actually did may not matter if she's generalized the event to encompass all men," Daria said. "What about love? Did you say anything about love, about how soul mates love each other?"

"No." He'd planned on saying the words just after she said yes to being his soul mate.

"No?" Daria's eyebrows almost hit her hairline. Bent looked skyward and shook his head slowly.

"You didn't tell her you love her." Daria made it a statement, not a question.

"She didn't give me the chance!"

"Clay, a woman likes—phooey, she *needs* to hear the words." Her tone implied he was feebleminded.

"I know. But she kept yelling about all this other stuff and . . . Hell!" He ran his hand through his hair, then pointed his finger at his sister. "Look, it wouldn't have mattered *what* I said after she threw all her weird ideas at me. I'm telling you that *she* wasn't listening *to anything* I said. Are *you*?"

What was it with women? Didn't any of them listen? Why had he thought Daria would be any different or that she could explain Francie? He wasn't going to let Daria turn it around so everything became his fault. He was doing the best he could, damn it. Francie was his soul mate, for crying out loud. He bent over the table, glowering at Daria, who leaned toward him and glared right back.

She opened her mouth to answer, but Bent intervened, gesturing for a time-out. "Wait. Hold on, you two. Let's get back to the origin of the problem, shall we?"

Clay's respect for his brother-in-law went up a notch. Nobody but their parents would have stepped between him and Daria when they were arguing, not even Glori. "Yeah, you're right." He made a conscious effort to relax his tense body and sat back in his chair.

"Okay," Daria agreed after she took a deep breath. "Some incident—probably involving this Walt—caused her to distrust men, but I don't think distrust will be a problem, once we solve the main issues. She has to accept the existence of magic and practitioners first. If she does, then being soul mates is easy to believe, especially with the imperative driving her toward you. Once she agrees about being your soul mate, the distrust, at least of you, should vanish, I would say. One step follows the other, logically, that is."

"Assuming she will think logically," Clay grumbled. "I haven't seen much evidence of that."

"Why did you try to explain practitioners by yourself, Clay?" Bent asked. "If Francie had already said she didn't believe in the possibility of magic's existence, and if your talents are like Daria's, not immediately obvious, I would have thought you'd bring the whole family in, the way Daria did with me."

Clay stood up and paced around the room. Trust his CEO brother-in-law to ask the question he didn't particularly want to answer. His decision to go it alone now looked like the absolutely wrong one. Unfortunately, he had no response except honesty, and he had to unlock his clenched jaw before he could speak.

"Okay. All right. Because I thought I could do it all myself. Because I'm a total idiot! I thought once I showed her my computer skills, she'd have no choice but to believe me." And come to his bed last night, although he didn't say *that*. Instead he finished with, "But she didn't give me the chance."

He slumped back down in his chair and rubbed his suffering breastbone. "She just ran." Damn, he sounded pathetic, even to himself.

"There is a bright side to this," Bent said. "I can testify to the fact that her running won't do her any good. The imperative will make her life miserable until she comes to terms with it and with you."

"Yeah, but how long will it take?" A flicker of hope fluttered in his chest, but died at Daria's next words.

"My intuition says it won't be quick," she said. "If, as we surmise, this Walt business triggered her apprehensions about you, I think she will need to settle that old ghost herself. As far as magic is concerned, would you like Glori and me to pay her a visit? We could throw on our illusions, and Glori knows more showy spells than Mother does. If she can't convince Francie, there's always Mother and Aunt Cassie."

"No." The idea of his two sisters, much less his mother and aunt, demonstrating spells for Francie scared Clay silly. She'd run so far he'd never find her. A visit from the family would have to be his last resort. He returned to his original idea: surely if he could talk to her, show her some programming on a "neutral" computer, it would do the trick. "Thanks, but not yet. I'd rather keep you two in reserve. The imperative convinced Bent. Maybe it'll have the same effect on Francie."

"Man, I hope so, for your sake," Bent said.

Daria looked dubious, but smiled and patted him on the hand. "We're here if you need us."

"I thought this soul-mate process was supposed to be easy," Clay complained. "Look at Mother and Dad. They didn't have this kind of trouble."

"Speaking of our parents . . ." Daria raised her eyebrows.

"No. Definitely not. Do *not* tell them anything

about this." Holy hell, his parents descending on Francie would send her right off the deep end. He thought of something else. "And do not tell Glori, either. I can't take any of her teasing right now."

"All right. I'll cover for you. How's your sting going? Any possibility it can help you with Francie?"

"No, she's out of that, thank goodness." Clay told them how the plans for trapping the hacker were progressing. When he was finished, he rose. "Thanks, both of you, for listening to me."

"We didn't do much," Bent said as they walked to the door.

"You helped me clarify the situation," Clay replied, realizing he told the truth. He did feel a little clearer in the head now.

"Give it time, big brother." Daria gave him a hug. "If you want us to talk to Francie . . ."

"I'll let you know." He walked to his car and gave them a wave as he drove off. On the way home he remembered he might see Francie at basketball on Tuesday. He'd leave her alone until then, let the imperative chew on her for a while. She'd be softened up, and he should be able to talk to her at the Y. Maybe if they were in public, she'd hear him out.

He was her soul mate. She was his. He loved her. She loved him. He was certain about that.

Wasn't he?

Damn right, he was.

CHAPTER EIGHTEEN

The week had certainly not started well. On the way to her basketball league, Francie reviewed the past two days.

Monday had been bad enough.

"Are you all right?" Janet, the office mother hen, had asked with a worried look.

"Where are those great new outfits you've been wearing? This is so dull, it makes you look like a frump," Sue, the office fashion plate, had opined, rubbing Francie's sleeve between two fingers as though the material was shoddy.

Even Herb. "Look, I understand how difficult this has been for you, with your friend in it and all. If you need to take some time off, I think we have the hacker problem in hand," he had suggested, taking her aside.

"You look like you're coming down with a cold," pregnant Peggy said as she offered her a cup of her "special" tea. "This has all sorts of vitamins and minerals in it."

Francie accepted the tea, agreed about the cold, and gave everybody else vague answers as she wrapped her bulky brown sweater closer around her drab green dress and pushed her smudged glasses back up her nose.

At least the "cold" fib explained her red eyes and runny nose. Maybe she *was* catching something, the way her eyes kept tearing up. It didn't, however, explain the pain in her middle. She'd have to make a doctor's appointment soon.

Tuesday had been worse.

Those disturbing—and arousing—dreams of Clay had returned overnight, and she woke to tangled sheets, her usual morning sluggishness intensified to hurricane strength. The pain under her sternum had become a constant nothing could alleviate, neither antacids nor aspirin nor milk. Only her sense of duty and responsibility to her job drove her out of bed.

To wake herself up, she had chugged coffee until she was floating. Anything was better than sliding into a drowsy state where those damn dreams resurfaced and set her body to tingling, then aching. Luckily, someone had brought doughnuts to the regular Tuesday morning meeting, and the glazed pastry added another layer of protection.

She rode the resulting sugar and caffeine high to lunch—a deli sub and two candy bars—and into the afternoon when homemade brownies and more coffee carried her through another interminable meeting. Ruthless concentration forced all extraneous subjects

out of her head, or so she thought until she caught herself doodling little wizard and witch hats, complete with
moons, stars, and lightning bolts, in the margin of her
notes. By five o'clock, feeling at the same time exhausted
and raring to go, she was surprised to discover how many
tasks she had actually accomplished. Just the game to go
now, and then she could crash.

The contest against their main rival was a fierce one,
with both teams playing at the top of their form. Her
team won by a single basket—hers.

Nothing could have stopped her tonight, Francie thought, as she accepted the congratulations of her
friends. Not the opposing center, a woman even taller
than she and rumored to have been scouted by several WNBA teams. Not their smaller guards with their
quick hands and fast breaks. Tonight she could have
taken on Michael Jordan and won.

"Way to go, Francie!" one of her friends said as they
gathered their towels at courtside.

"You were pumped, girl!" exclaimed another. "Where
are we going to celebrate? I could use a nice cold beer."

Several women called out the names of nearby res-
taurants.

"Where do you want to go?" a third asked Francie
directly.

"Count me out on dinner tonight, y'all," she said.
When everyone tried to convince her to go with them,
she responded, "I've been eating all day, mostly junk

food and chocolate, and I'm still jazzed. I have to work off some of this energy or I'll never get to sleep tonight."

She remained adamant in the face of their attempts at persuasion, and before long, her friends left to shower. She picked up her towel and one of the balls and headed toward a court in the back of the sports complex usually free at this time of night. She hadn't been lying to her friends about her energy levels, but she also couldn't put on a falsely happy face over dinner. She simply wasn't that good of an actress. Besides, she did need some free throw practice and her longer shots could use fine-tuning.

She threw her towel on the bench and dribbled the ball to the free throw line. She had the court to herself, thank goodness, and the configuration of the walls muted the noise from the other matches still underway. She couldn't have wished for more privacy. The thunk, thunk, thunk of the bouncing ball soothed her frazzled nerves, and she sighed in contentment as she took hold of it. She centered herself, lofted the ball, and grinned at the result. Nothing but net.

How could she look so good, Clay asked himself. He watched her from the edge of a neighboring court as she retrieved the ball and bounced it back to the line. Those long legs, that blond ponytail, those gorgeous breasts, that delectable butt. Then he focused on her face and smiled in bitter satisfaction. The circles under her eyes told him she hadn't survived the past couple of days in any better shape than he had.

He had caught the last minutes of her game. She had been all over the court, acting more like a guard than a center. She hadn't hogged the ball, however, but always found the open woman who had the sure shot. The game had come right down to the buzzer, and he had cheered when she sank the winning basket. How she still had the strength to practice was beyond him.

He saw her rub her breastbone, and an idea began to form in his head. If she were as exhausted as she looked, it might work to his advantage. His game had been easy, and he was relatively fresh. There might be a way to force her to talk to him.

He sauntered over to her, coming up from her rear. "Good game, Francie," he said when he was about five feet from her. She must not have heard him coming because she jumped and whirled around in a defensive stance, elbows out, ball protected.

"Oh. Clay." She didn't sound happy to see him. She relaxed slightly, but she didn't meet his eyes. "Thanks." She turned back around and bounced the ball as if she were going to shoot again.

"Francie, we do need to talk. I really need to explain, and you need to understand what's happening here to both of us."

She shook her ponytail at him and dribbled the ball some more.

"I'm not crazy, I promise. I'll go to any computer you can think of to prove my point. I really am a magic practitioner and a computer wizard, and we really are soul mates." Hell, he sounded pitiful, almost like he was begging. He could hear the exasperation in his voice when he said, "Will you please look at me?"

She turned back around, her chin raised and her face composed. "Go away," she said with a level tone. "There is no such thing as magic. I do not believe in it. We have nothing to discuss." She faced the basket again.

He walked around in front of her and put his hands on the ball she held at waist level. Good. That forced her to raise her eyes, and he locked his gaze to hers. Damn. He didn't know her smoky brown eyes could be so icy, so frozen. Double damn. He was close enough to smell her, an overheated scent of pure woman, pure Francie, that would be the same, he knew, when they came together as soul mates. But later. *Concentrate on your objective, Morgan.*

He kept his voice low and even. Reasonable. As persuasive as he could make it. "Francie, you know we have plenty to talk about. And we need to settle some things. The soul-mate imperative is working on both of us. The pain in your chest?" He pointed to hers, then rubbed his own. "I've got one, too. That's the imperative telling us we belong together."

She snatched the ball from his hands and took a step back. "I don't want to talk to you, and I don't want to see you. There's nothing between us, not this so-called imperative, not make-believe magic, not anything. Now, go away. I have to practice."

What was the flicker in her eyes? The brown had almost melted for a second. Fear? Anger? Embarrassment? No matter. Ignoring her comments, he pressed ahead with his plan. "I have a proposition for you."

She shot him a squinty, suspicious glance. "What kind of proposition?"

"Play a game of one-on-one."

"Whoever gets to eleven points first wins? Each basket worth one point?" Her gaze grew more squinty, more suspicious, but she looked intrigued.

"Yep. Whoever wins the point, the other gets the ball. The ball handler starts from center court after each basket, the opponent from the foul line."

"What's the bet?" Her eyebrows went up and he thought he had her.

"*I* win, you talk to me and let me show you what I can do with a computer. *You* win, and I leave you alone. *You* win, and you'll have to come to me if you want to see me."

She scrutinized him carefully, clearly trying to find any loopholes in his offer. "You have height and reach on me. How many points will you spot me?"

"Not a one. I've seen how fast and accurate you are. What's the matter? Don't you believe in women's equality?" He couldn't help the jeer. Even though he knew he could beat her, probably easily, he couldn't help wanting to rub her nose in it just a little. He knew exactly where he wanted that nose, and those hands, and . . . Don't get distracted, he told himself. "I will, however, give you the ball first."

"How magnanimous." She dribbled the ball for a moment, then held it and met his eyes. "You won't bother me anymore?"

"Well, I can't promise completely," he said with a smile. "But if I do, it won't be from something *I've* done. It will all be in *your* head. I won't call or come by or e-mail."

She studied him for a few seconds. "All right, you're on." She shot the ball over his head. It swished through the basket. "One point for me. Your ball."

Grinning at her audacity, he threw his towel over to the sideline and retrieved the ball.

This was not going to be the cakewalk he had envisioned, Clay acknowledged several minutes later. The score was five to five. She was even quicker than he anticipated, and she had a sweet, surprising shot from three-point range. By not pressing her closely, not getting in her face, he was letting her play *her* game, not his. Time to change tactics. He had to force her to come in under the basket where his greater height would be more to his advantage. Make her work to win the point instead of sit back and lob those bombs of hers. Maybe a little intimidation was in order.

She brought the ball in from center court, dribbling easily. He met her at the top of the foul line circle with arms spread high and wide. He came close, looming over her, blocking her way, windmilling his arms to deflect any shot. He set himself to take her charge, not that it would matter if she did run into him. Nobody was calling fouls.

Instead of continuing straight at him, she went to her left and he followed, but her move turned out to be a fake, and she reversed, darting right, ducking under his arm. Three steps and two dribbles took her to the net, where she jumped up and laid the ball in, just caressing the backboard.

Her six, his five.

He walked across the half-court line, bouncing the ball slowly as he worked out his next approach. Francie looked ready for anything. She also looked gorgeous, with her blond hair beginning to come down and her smoky brown eyes flashing with determination. She was veering sideways to his left. He should have an easy path to the right. Just as he decided to move, she suddenly launched herself at him, grabbed the ball on its upward bounce right out from under his hand, pivoted into a jump, and nailed the shot. He stood there flat-footed, feeling like a fool.

Her seven, his five.

He growled to himself. He had to admire—grudgingly—her speed and daring, and he swore at himself for his lapse. Two could play at the fast game, but he preferred power. This time he drove straight for the basket, shouldered her aside, leaped up, stuffed it. As he threw the ball back to her, he thought he heard some cheers in the background, but paid them no attention. He blocked everything extraneous from his mind: the noise from other games, the sound of the bouncing ball, the squeak of his shoes on the court. Hunching over slightly, he concentrated totally on his blond nemesis.

Her seven, his six.

She evidently decided to try his tactic, because she took off from the center circle straight for the key. He took two steps right into her body. They crashed into each other, momentarily plastered together from chest to knee.

"Holy hell!" He staggered back two steps. He felt like he had just run into a lightning storm. A huge bolt had smacked him right on the top of his head, blazed down his body, bounced off the rubber in his shoes, and departed the same way it came in. A double whammy. His nerve endings sizzled. He was certain that his hair stood on end. He inhaled deeply to see if he could still breathe.

He blinked to focus his muddled eyesight. Francie was just standing there, evidently as stunned as he was. The ball was bouncing toward the sideline. He shook himself, ran down the ball, loped to the basket, and scored.

Seven to seven.

He watched Francie recover enough to retrieve the ball and walk back to the center line. She looked like she was back in control, although her game face gave him no clue as to what she was thinking. Well, he'd see about *her* control. That zap had to be from the soul-mate imperative, a reminder they hadn't been together for a while. Maybe he could put it to good use.

She dribbled forward, turned, and backed toward him, keeping the ball in front of her, working her way to his left. He crowded her closely, very closely, extremely closely, until he was leaning over her, practically draped across her. Touching her from butt to shoulder. The contact made his blood bubble hotly, but he forced himself to maintain control.

He felt her shiver, falter, miss a bounce. He took over the dribble, grabbed the ball, whirled, shot.

Her seven. His eight.

Only three more points to go, he congratulated himself as he moved to the foul line. This was the answer. The soul-mate imperative reduced her to putty. All he had to do was let the old SMI work for him. He smiled in anticipation.

What had just happened? Francie asked herself. She stood in the center circle bouncing the ball, using the ball-change time to calm down. Think, woman, she ordered. Forget about the noise, the movement on the sidelines. Concentrate.

She'd been proud of the way she had reacted when he walked up behind her, and feeling as unconquerable as she had, she couldn't resist his challenge. She'd been doing fine, leading in points—until they'd run into each other. Then, wham! A thunderbolt struck, and a wave of longing crashed through her, stole her breath, blackened her sight, and left her too weak to move. She'd stood there like a post while he scored.

And double *wham* with that sneaky, underhanded tactic, laying his body, his scorching, outrageously sexy body, right on top of hers, forcing her to feel him against every inch of her back, forcing her to breathe in his over-heated, thoroughly alluring scent. No wonder she had lost the ball.

Two things were clear. First, touching him had the same effect it always did, shutting down her mind and turning her body to goo. And second, he knew it. Just look at him standing on the foul line with a smirk on his handsome face, a twinkle in those silver eyes, a light sheen of sweat glistening on his muscular body. He thought he had her beat.

Well, not this time, buster.

She started forward, sidling around to the right, her left side toward him. Sure enough, he moved to block, just like last time, intentionally bringing his body into contact with hers. She felt the zing spread to her fingertips.

He must have, too, because he breathed into her ear, his voice an insidious purr that vibrated her diaphragm, "What's the matter, sweetheart? Can't you take it?"

She turned her back completely to him and bent over, keeping the ball bouncing as far away from him as she could. He repeated his previous maneuver, envelop-ing her body with his. When his crotch hit her butt, she wiggled. Once. Twice, for good measure.

He froze and she heard his sharp intake of air.

She slid out from under him, drove to the basket, and laid in a goal.

Eight even.

His ball, his turn at center court. He was scowling as he rolled his shoulders. She could see him gathering his control about him like protective armor. She had to act fast, not let him regroup.

He stood holding the ball between his right hip and his right elbow, clearly contemplating his next move. She stormed him, flattened her body against him, pressed herself right into him, rubbed her front across his. Pumped her hips once, straight into his groin.

He stiffened, turned to stone.

She seized the ball, ran right up the key, and tipped in the point.

Her nine, his eight.

She threw the ball back to him, standing on the free throw line, and she couldn't resist the smug grin, the taunt. "I can take it, *sweetheart*. Can you?"

He caught the ball, lowered his head like a bull, and used his weight to blast by her and slam-dunk the ball. The hoop and backboard rattled.

Nine all.

Looking, in her view, entirely too confident, he tossed the ball to her. The wolfish smile on his face made her insides flutter and she frowned. She had to concentrate harder. This was no time to be distracted, not by his effect on her or by all the noise reverberating around the gym. Another team's game didn't matter. Her contest did.

She tried her reverse assault again, but this time, he ran his hands from her shoulders, down her back, and around to and over her breasts. At his touch on her nipples, she jerked back into him and lost the ball. He recovered it before it bounced out of bounds, and drove the basket, pushing her out of the way when she tried to block.

Her nine, his ten.

Her ball. He rushed her at the center circle, wrenched the ball away from her, and held it in one hand high above her. Arrogantly, insolently, he grinned down at her. Until she ran her hands down his chest and then lower. And lower still. His face lost its grin, and his arms fell to his sides.

Hah! She snatched the ball and took off for the basket.

Ten all.

They stared at each other for a long moment, he at center court, she on the foul line. Last point. Winner take all. She knew what she had to do.

She charged. He crouched slightly, held the ball in his right hand high and to the rear. His left arm was stretched out toward her to fend her off. She grabbed that arm, pushed it to the side, slid under it, and plastered herself against him. Her free hand in his hair, she hauled his head down and planted her mouth on his.

Think, Francie, she ordered herself. Don't let him take over.

It was hard going.

She heard him groan, an agonized, tortured sound that her own throat repeated. He dropped the ball, clamped her in his arms, and plundered her mouth. He tasted better than Cherry Garcia, and his arms felt like heaven. Her heart almost burst with longing. Her body rejoiced, threatened to melt around his.

No! She couldn't let him come to his senses first; she had to keep her brain working. Overruling her traitorous heart, her spineless body, she broke the kiss and pushed back away from him.

With a dazed, unfocused look in his eyes, he let her go.

The ball was at her feet. She scooped it up, sprinted to the basket, leaped high, higher, higher still, and—hot damn!—stuffed it in the net. Her first ever slam dunk. Eleven points. She'd won!

When she landed, she spun around to face him. A desolate look on his face, a dejected slump to his body, he stood where she had left him. They stared at each other for what felt like eons.

Finally he moved, walked slowly to her, stopped three feet away, and spoke with a raspy voice, "You win, Francie. I won't bother you anymore."

She'd won, but *what* had she won? The question reverberated in her head.

The answer almost buckled her knees. She abruptly

felt terribly, completely alone, and her mood plummeted from exhilaration to despair as the idea, the reality, of losing him washed over her.

Before she could say anything, before she could begin to comprehend the horrible hollow emptiness that suddenly opened in the middle of her chest, they were engulfed by a laughing, yelling crowd.

CHAPTER NINETEEN

When she finally made it home, Francie dropped her gym bag and collapsed on the sofa. She should be extremely embarrassed, she thought, as all the shouts from the spectators rattled around in her brain. "Wooooeeeee! Sexxxxy!" had been one. "I'll play the winner," came from a number of male throats, while the women yelled, "Dibs on the loser." "Grrrrrreat moves!" "Let's hear it for co-ed basketball!" "You can guard me anytime." And those were the mild ones.

Somehow, she'd broken through the crowd and run for the locker room. Her teammates followed. From what they'd said, she'd gathered they had returned to the court to try again to persuade her to come with them. They had been caught up in the match and stayed to support her. Their presence had attracted the attention of several men, and before long, a sizable number of people were laughing, cheering, and generally whooping it up.

They had all watched her rub herself all over Clay,

kiss him like a slut, and behave like a complete idiot. The Y would probably expel her, rescind her membership, toss her out on her ear. Which might be for the best. She didn't know how she could ever show her face there again.

But, damn it, she'd won. He had been cheating as much as she was. *Sweetheart, who couldn't take it in the end?*

She'd won. She'd made her first ever slam dunk, to boot. She should be swinging from the chandelier in triumph. She should have asked the Y to give her the net. She should be happy, gleeful, rejoicing.

But instead, she felt like she'd been trampled right into the court's hardwood floor.

What about Clay? She hadn't seen him after the swarm of onlookers parted them. He'd looked so shocked, so dejected, so disheartened. What would she have said to him? Crowed in victory? Told him her winning didn't matter, she'd talk to him anyway?

No! It did matter. How could she talk to him about magic that didn't exist? Even theoretically.

But, what if it did? What if, contrary to everything she had ever learned in science classes, contrary to her own view of the world, Clay really could put spells on computers and cause them to do his bidding?

She hadn't given him the chance to prove his claims. Instead she'd gotten scared, but frightened of what? Going to bed with him? Having sex? Somehow, given the effect they had on each other, "having sex" seemed like an extremely puny description of what might happen.

So, what had caused this reaction? Memories of Walt? Fear Clay would do to her what Walt had? Looking at the situation as dispassionately—what a word—as she could, she had to admit fear was probably at the center of her reaction.

And what about the electric, searing attraction with Clay? He claimed that soul-mate-imperative "force" was causing it, or bringing them together, or causing her pain. She still couldn't accept its existence or influence. Hormones, it was all hormones, and pheromones, and chemical changes in the brain caused by infatuation. Not some ancient magical compulsion—simply a legend whose power was imaginary.

And now? She had "won." He said he would leave her alone. She hadn't understood when he said his bothering her would be *only in her head*, but she did now. That's exactly where he was, embedded in her brain cells.

What about in the chambers of her heart? She bent over as agony lanced out from that much abused organ. A tremendous sob wracked her body. She gave in to it and let herself cry until she had no tears left, just a chasm of desolation in her chest.

Eventually she roused herself. The crying jag had had one effect: her mind was numb now, and she was too exhausted to think about Clay. She'd decide what to do after she had had some sleep.

She looked at the clock: midnight. She was still

wearing her basketball outfit, having thrown her street clothes into her bag in her rush to leave the Y. Feeling like a twenty-pound weight was attached to each limb, she made her way to the bathroom, stripped, and stood in the shower for a while.

That helped, but only marginally. The pain in her chest persisted, but had subsided to a low constant throbbing in place of the sharp stabs.

Maybe she'd call in sick in the morning. What did she have to do tomorrow? No meetings, only . . . Only the setup for Clay to trap Kevin tomorrow night. But she wasn't part of the technical tasks. And she didn't want to hear about how good Clay was, how great a computer *wizard*. And she definitely did not want to see him. She'd better call in right now.

She turned off the water, hurriedly toweled herself dry, and headed for the phone. After leaving voice-mail messages for Herb and several others, she finished her nighttime routine, took a couple of aspirin, and fell into bed. And finally into a fitful, but thankfully dreamless, sleep.

※※※※※※

"Fuck, fuck, *fuck*!" Clay slammed his kitchen door and threw his gym bag on the floor. He badly wanted something to hit, but now that he could let his fury out, he had no target. He'd had to hold it in at the Y, where he'd managed to joke and laugh with his buddies, all of whom claimed to be extremely jealous of his match, and all of whom heckled him unmercifully about losing. He didn't know why his jaw hadn't cracked under the strain of his gritted smile.

What the hell was he going to do now? It was unheard of for one soul mate to reject the other. If a practitioner married someone who wasn't his soul mate—which happened in the past as families made dynastic decisions instead of letting hearts and the SMI rule—he spent the rest of his days in loneliness, unhappiness, and despair.

Why couldn't his own soul mate have been a practitioner? She would have understood. They wouldn't be going through this torment.

He'd been so certain he would win that idiotic game and then demonstrate to that skeptical woman he could do magic. Instead, what had happened? Damn the imperative! How could it fail him when it counted the most?

He filled a glass with water and drank deeply. He had to hand it to Francie, she had turned the SMI around on him with a vengeance. He'd been able to handle its effects before, but this time, he'd just petrified, frozen, solidified while she literally ran rings around him.

Damn! She had felt so good in his arms during that kiss. His body began to stir at the memory, and the now-familiar ache began to build in his chest. He sat heavily on one of the kitchen chairs.

Get hold of yourself, Morgan, he admonished himself. *Think. What are you doing to do now?*

He rubbed a hand over his face and concentrated. First, he refused to give up the hope, no, the *certainty* Francie would be, no, *was* his. Despair and desperation did not appeal to him, and after all, he did have the SMI on his side. The imperative was alive and well. If nothing else, their reactions to each other during the game proved it.

He'd honor his word and stay away from Francie. Let the imperative work on her and hope it didn't kill him in the meantime. He didn't like his next idea, but he'd have to ask Daria and Glori for real help. What choice did he have? Maybe a woman could get through Francie's defenses. Besides, he'd promised to stay away, but he hadn't said a word about his sisters. For now, should he call Daria tomorrow?

Tomorrow. Oh, damn.

Tomorrow the cops were coming early to set up for Brenner and the hacking session that evening. Brenner. What a jackass. Clay clenched and unclenched his fists and wished he could take out his frustration on the hacker's face.

But beating up Brenner would serve no other purpose. Difficult though it may be, he'd have to be civil tomorrow. He'd better wait until Thursday night to call Daria. He'd never be calm in the evening if he had to discuss the Francie situation with Daria in the afternoon.

Clay rose, grabbed the gym bag, and walked upstairs to his bedroom. Once there, he realized there was no way in hell he could go to sleep. His body was in no mood to relax.

He changed into swim trunks, grabbed a towel, and went downstairs and out into the backyard. The night was cool, but the pool was heated. He turned on the pool lights and the motor to create a current to swim against. The well-insulated motor emitted only a quiet hum as the jets kicked the placid surface into a froth of white water.

Clay swam until he was so waterlogged he thought he'd sink. At first he'd concentrated on swimming technique, then occupied his mind with inventing curses he'd like to throw on Brenner and "Walt."

Finally, he came to a sort of equilibrium based on the mantra, "Francie is my soul mate. Everything will be all right." He flopped onto his bed about three in the morning and immediately slept. Mercifully dreamlessly.

CHAPTER TWENTY

Clay's doorbell rang at eight, only fifteen minutes after he had levered himself from his bed. He ushered in Bill Childress and the police team who would install the cameras and recording equipment. Bill introduced Stan Hardy, the West University Place officer who accompanied them.

"We thought it best to involve the West U police to keep the lines of communication clear and in case we need their help," Bill explained.

After showing the technical team his office setup, Clay left them to it and took Bill and Hardy to the kitchen for coffee.

Over cups of the life-giving brew, Bill eyed Clay and asked, "You okay?"

Just what he needed, an observant cop, Clay grimaced to himself, but hid the feeling behind his cup as he took a swallow. "Yeah, I'm okay. Hard night."

"Anticipating Brenner? I don't think you'll have any

problem with him."

"Neither do I." He definitely didn't want to get into his problems with Francie, so he answered simply, "It's a personal problem, but it won't mess with what we're doing here."

"Fine."

"How are things at the cop shop?"

"Pretty good. Did you see where we caught that ring of carjackers?"

"Yeah." Clay asked some questions about the capture, and they went on to discuss local politics and sports.

Before long, the leader of the tech team, Joe Ramirez, walked in. "We're just about set up," he said.

"You're welcome to coffee," Clay said, pointing at the pot and cups he'd put out.

"Thanks." Ramirez poured himself some and sat down. "Tonight we're going to park the van around the corner," he said. "In a few minutes, we'll run a test. First, Benny and Phil will impersonate you and Brenner, and you'll watch from the van. Then you and Bill play the parts. We'll tape you and look at it to make sure all the angles are covered. That's a nice setup you have up there, by the way."

"Thanks," Clay said.

They discussed computers until Benny stuck his head through the door. "We're ready."

Clay, Bill, Stan, and Joe watched and listened from the van while Phil and Benny played their parts. Clay and Bill noted camera angles and mike sensitivity. Then Clay and Bill rehearsed the scenario. Everything went smoothly, and they reviewed the tape on Clay's TV set.

"It looks to me like the only thing you have to remember is to keep Brenner on your left side," Bill remarked as Clay shut off the set and handed the tape to Joe.

"That won't be hard," Clay said. "Brenner's due at seven. What time will you get here?"

"Around five," Bill answered. "Just in case he's early."

Brenner did show up early, about fifteen minutes. Fine with him, Clay thought as he opened the door. He wanted to get it over with. "Come on in," he told the hacker. "Up here." He led the way up the stairs.

Brenner looked nervous, but he followed Clay with no hesitation. When they reached the office, Brenner's eyes grew wide as he looked around. "Wow! You have some great equipment here."

"Yeah," Clay said. "Sit down there and don't touch anything." He pointed at the chair they had carefully positioned for maximum camera exposure. Brenner sat and Clay took his seat at the keyboard and large monitor.

"Do you still want me to hack into Brazos Chemical?" he asked. He knew he sounded surly, but Brenner didn't seem to mind.

"Absolutely," Brenner answered, but he had to swallow before he spoke.

"You're sure Francie Stevens doesn't know about any of this?"

Kevin smirked. "Still after her, are you? No," he said quickly when Clay glared at him, "Francie doesn't know a thing. Do you think I'm crazy? She's not part of this at all."

"What about Tamara?"

"Her neither. Especially Tamara. She turned into a real bitch, let me tell you."

Good, Clay thought. Those statements should negate any future attempt by Brenner to implicate Francie or Tamara in this mess. "Did you bring the money?"

"Oh, yeah," Kevin said and pulled an envelope out of his jacket pocket. He handed it over. "It's all there, all five thousand."

Clay took the bills out of the envelope and riffled through them, making certain the camera got a good shot. "Fine." He returned the money to the envelope and placed it on the desk to the side.

He turned to the wide screen, which displayed a number of both large and small overlapping windows, some with graphics, some with text only. Two contained scrolling code in a bilious green type on black backgrounds. Clay was rather proud of his display, a combination of spreadsheet, word-processing, and graphics programs that looked complicated and would certainly be confusing to someone like Brenner.

"I've routed us around through several Web servers already." He pointed to a couple of screens as if they belonged to the servers. "If, by some fluke, they detect us, they won't be able to tell where we are."

"Sounds good," Brenner offered, nodding in agreement.

Clay hit some keys, clicked the mouse, and set off a little spell at the same time. A new window appeared with the Brazos Chemical Company logo and password fields for logging in. He filled in the fields with gibberish and a menu came up. "You want sales information, right?" He clicked around the menu, typed in some "code" into another three entry fields, and called up the fake database Herb had created. A table displayed with client names and addresses.

He snuck a glance at Brenner. The asshole's attention was riveted on the screen.

"Holy shit. You're good," Brenner said, an awed expression on his face.

"Yeah, I am." Clay flipped through another couple of windows until a panel asked for the range of customer names and other query information.

"What time period?" Clay asked.

Brenner looked confused. "What do you mean?"

"How far back in time do you want to go in the records?"

"Oh. How about six months?"

A spreadsheet-like window displayed a table entitled "Outstanding Orders" with each customer's information. "Is this what you meant?"

"Oh, man, yeah," Brenner whispered as if he were afraid the display would disappear with a poof. He reached a hand toward the screen and pointed down. "Can you come down the list a little lower to Middlefield Manufacturing?"

Clay scrolled the table and found the company. He glanced at Brenner.

The salesman leaned forward, eyes gleaming with greed. "Come over to the right."

Clay followed the instructions. The products Middlefield had ordered and the prices they had paid appeared.

"Where's the delivery charges and conditions? I need those, too. And the payment terms. Can you print any of this? This is great." Brenner practically jumped up and down in the chair as Clay manipulated the code, and windows with the requested information came on the screen.

"Do you want the whole damn customer list? We could be here all night," Clay grumbled.

"No," Brenner answered and scrabbled in his jacket pocket. "Here's who I need." He handed a piece of paper to Clay. Twenty company names were written on it.

"Okay. Pull the sheets as they come off the printer and tell me if you're getting what you want." He incorporated the names into his search spell, and the screen displayed only those companies Brenner wanted. He hit two keys, and the laser printer started spitting out paper.

"Don't forget the delivery instructions," Brenner said as he scanned the first pages. "Damn. This is just what I wanted." He read another page. "Shit, we can beat these prices. They must be making the sales on the delivery terms."

Clay finished printing the delivery and payment data. "Anything else? Say so now."

Brenner gathered up the pages and flipped through them. "No, no, this is great. Just right. With this info, we'll be able to steal Brazos's customers right out from under them. Man, I can't thank you enough."

"You already did," Clay said, waving the envelope with the money and putting it in his pocket. "Remember, this was a one-shot deal. I never want to see you again. And keep your mouth shut about the origin of this shit." He shut down the windows, then the computer, and rose.

"Right." Brenner stood, then followed Clay down the stairs. "Thanks, Morgan," he held out his hand as he stood in the open doorway.

With disgust, Clay looked at the offered hand, but shook it anyway to play out his role. He watched the salesman climb into his car and drive away.

Within seconds the police van stopped in the spot Brenner's car had occupied. Bill and the team came into the house. Phil and Benny went upstairs to retrieve their equipment.

"How'd we do?" Clay asked.

"Just fine," Bill answered. "What do you think, Joe?"

"The volume and pictures came through loud and clear," Ramirez answered. "The man incriminated himself, no question about it. I'll have extra copies for you tomorrow."

"Good. We're planning on arresting him tomorrow," Bill said.

Clay handed him the envelope. "Here's your additional proof."

"Thanks for your help, Clay," the detective said. "I'll keep you and Brazos apprised of what happens."

After Phil and Benny came down with the cameras and microphones, Clay shook hands with the cops and watched them drive off. Thank God that was over, he thought as he closed the door. Now he could get back to his more pressing problem. He went into the house, picked up the kitchen phone, and dialed.

"Hello?" Daria sounded disgruntled.

"Hey, it's me. What's the matter?"

"Oh, I'm just paying bills. You know how I hate to do that. What's up?"

"Will you be home tomorrow? I need to ask a favor." He tried to keep his voice utterly flat.

"Sure. I don't start my next job for two weeks. What can I do?"

"I'll tell you tomorrow." He wasn't going to get into it over the phone.

"Okay, Mr. Mysterious. Say, how are things with Francie?"

"I'll tell you tomorrow."

"That bad, huh?"

Sometimes he swore Daria could read his mind,

but he still wasn't going to tell her anything now. "Ten o'clock all right?"

"Fine. Come tell me everything."

They exchanged good-byes. Clay hung up the phone and stared at it for a long moment. Should he call Francie to let her know Brenner had taken the bait and would be arrested tomorrow? No, better not. He'd given his word.

Instead he called Herb and told him what had happened. "Great work," Greenwood said. "I wish I could be there when they arrest the bastard. I'll alert Legal."

"Thank your computer operators for me. The fake database they created worked fine."

"Will do. I hope Francie comes in tomorrow so we can celebrate."

"You hope she comes in?"

"Yeah. She called in sick today. Left me a message in the middle of the night. She sounded awful, but she looked like she was coming down with a cold on Monday."

An interesting bit of news, Clay thought. Either the game or the SMI had done her in, and he knew which one he'd put his money on.

"Anyway," Herb continued, "why don't you come by next week and we'll talk about increasing protection on the system. If a jerk like Brenner can get through, our defenses aren't worth squat."

Clay discussed the Brazos system with Herb for a while, then said good-bye.

After hanging up the phone, Clay looked around his

kitchen. It was only nine o'clock, too early for bed, even if he had had only four or five hours of sleep the night before. Not to mention he was still keyed up from playing crook with Brenner. So he went back to the computer, started up a complicated sword and sorcery game, and took some pleasure in chopping off the heads of goblins, ogres, vampires, and other assorted monsters.

He pretended they were all Walt.

CHAPTER TWENTY-ONE

Clay arrived at Daria's the next morning at ten.

"Don't tell me," he said when she opened her mouth as soon as she saw him. "I look like shit. Neither you nor Bent told me the imperative was so vicious."

"It was pretty hard on Bent, but he gave in pretty fast," she said as she led the way to the kitchen. She waved Clay to a seat at the table and, after pouring them both some coffee, sat down beside him. "All right, what's going on?"

As he tried to decide where to start, Clay took a swallow of his coffee and looked around the large kitchen, so reminiscent of his mother's at the farm. White cabinets, maple butcher-block counters, and herbs growing in pots in the windowsills combined to create a feeling of warmth and home. Then Lolita walked in, jumped into his lap, curled up, and started purring. He sighed. Even the cat thought he needed commiseration. Might as well lay it all out for Daria.

"I blew it, big time," he said. He told her everything, how he'd been certain once he had Francie at a computer, she'd have no choice but to believe him about magic and soul mates. Then how he'd tried to force Francie to talk to him by means of the game, and exactly how Francie had won. "And the worst part was she used the damned imperative to beat me. I thought the lousy thing was supposed to be on *my* side!"

Daria chuckled, then put her hand on his. "Oh, Clay, I'm sorry for laughing, but I wish I could have seen that game. What's your plan now?"

"I gave her my word I wouldn't call or come by or e-mail. I'd leave her totally alone. I said if she wanted to see me, she had to make the first move." He rubbed a hand across his chest, right over the pain. "But that woman is so stubborn, I don't know if she'll give in to the imperative and come to me. She was so adamant about magic not existing, she might not be able to take her words back, to admit she was wrong. I don't know if her pride or her embarrassment is stronger."

"It sounds to me like your light ball wasn't nearly enough. She needs some real demonstrations, something more 'tangible,' as it were, something more mundane, less esoteric than computer programs. Some proof she can't refute or deny." Daria tapped her fingers on the table while she thought for a moment. "This may be splitting hairs, but while *you* can't see her, you didn't promise anything about any of your family staying away.

What if Glori and I pay her a visit? Glori could do her bit with plants and maybe some healing—Francie's bound to have a raging headache by this time. Both of us can also cast illusion spells. Glori does a nice black panther, and my dragon is quite spectacular, or so I'm told."

"That's what I hoped you'd suggest," Clay said, slumping in his chair in relief. He knew he'd pay for this where Gloriana was concerned. She positively reveled in teasing him for every perceived fault he possessed. But he knew he'd get revenge. Just wait until Glori found *her* soul mate.

Then he had another thought. "I hope she'll see you."

"Oh, she'll see us all right, one way or the other." Daria smiled the way she did when she was plotting something against him. "As I think of it, I'm getting a little angry. Who is this woman to refuse my brother? Don't worry, Glori and I will make her listen. By the time we're finished with her, she'll be a believer."

Clay winced. "Uh, just don't get carried away. I do want her talking to me, you know."

"I have a spell, sort of an I-am-someone-you-must-absolutely-talk-to bewitchment that should do the 'trick'—so to speak. That will get us in the door, and if it doesn't, I'm sure we'll think of another ploy."

Clay stared at her for a moment, playing scenarios in his mind. "I don't know. She hates deception of any kind, I do know that. I've told her you can't cast a spell on anybody except yourself, but I don't know if she even heard me or if she believes it."

He shook his head in frustration. "Here we are at that paradox again. If she doesn't believe in magic, then she doesn't believe you can throw a spell of any kind, but if she agrees magic *does or might exist*, then she could be afraid you *have* spelled her. Either way, she could think you were trying to deceive her, and she could refuse to see you."

"All right, we'll play it by ear. You know . . ." she paused, then continued with a grin, "we can't forget our biggest ally here, the soul-mate imperative itself."

Clay returned her grin, feeling better for the first time in days. "You're right, and that's the conclusion I came to. The old SMI must be giving her grief. It's certainly taking a toll on me. She has to want the pain to end, and it's a good reason to talk to you."

"I'll call Glori tonight and ask her to come for the weekend. We'll try to see Francie on Saturday." Daria rose and went to the counter. She picked up the pad and pen by the phone and brought them to Clay. "Write down Francie's address and phone number for me. I'll do a little reconnaissance today or tomorrow."

He wrote down the requested information and described Francie's apartment. "Her parking spot is to the right. She drives a silver Honda," he said. "Her boss told me she stayed home yesterday, but I don't know if she's still there."

"Probably not. If she's anything like you, and we

know she is, she'll be at work today, just as you would. I'm sure she's as much a workaholic as you are."

"Hey, when I have a job to do, I do it," he protested.

"Exactly." She studied him for a moment, then asked, "How are you in all this, Clay? You're my brother, and I worry about you. How do you feel about the imperative? About Francie?"

"I'm okay," he shrugged, then knew from Daria's skeptical expression he'd better elaborate. "I had some doubts at first, fought against it, but nothing like what you did. Like Bent said, men and women are different. The more I was around her, the more I wanted her. The more it felt 'right' when we were together. Before I knew it, I was thinking in terms of forever. Having seen you and Bent go through the experience gave me some warning about what to expect, but the reality was a hell of a lot stronger than I thought it would be."

He rubbed his aching middle and grimaced. "If Francie doesn't give in soon, the SMI is going to be the death of me."

"Don't worry," Daria consoled him. "According to Mother, the imperative's never killed anyone."

"Yet."

CHAPTER TWENTY-TWO

Thursday evening Francie arrived home in what was becoming an incurable state of exhaustion. She was really going to have to see her doctor soon. Now she seemed to have not only an ulcer, but probably mononucleosis or chronic fatigue syndrome. Or was she just turning into a hypochondriac? She had no sooner changed into comfortable, soft, baggy sweats and tied her hair back with a big clip than the doorbell rang.

Was it Clay? Her heart leaped and landed running. Oh, great. Now a heart attack, too.

But when she looked out the peephole and saw only Tamara, she relaxed—until she realized her friend should still be at the shop. Tamara looked angry. Had she heard about Kevin?

"Oh, damn," Francie muttered under her breath. She didn't know if she had the strength to deal with the Kevin problem, but it was on her now. She opened the door.

"Hi, Tamara. Come on in." She stood back while

Tamara, hands clenched at her sides, stalked over the threshold and into the living room.

The redhead turned to face her as Francie closed the door. "The police came by to see me today. They arrested Kevin this morning." Tamara's tone was distinctly flat, a signal she was definitely angry.

"I know. I heard at work," Francie said softly. She came around the sofa, but remained standing.

"Lieutenant Childress told me Kevin had been caught hacking into your company's computer system and wanted to know if he had ever mentioned to me his doing anything like that." Tamara plopped down on a chair. "Of course, I told Childress Kevin had never said a word about it to me."

"Of course. I know you would never be a party to dishonesty of any kind." Francie sat gingerly on the edge of the sofa cushion. Was Tamara angry with her, or just Kevin?

"I couldn't believe it at first," Tamara continued, shaking her fists in the air. "How could Kevin do such a thing? I had no idea he was proficient enough to hack, no idea at all he would try such an idiotic idea on Brazos. Childress said Kevin even hacked from your computer here!" She slumped farther back in the chair, crossed her arms over her chest, then sat up straight. "You said you knew Kevin was arrested. Did the police come to see you, too?"

"Well, actually . . ." Here it comes, Francie thought,

she had to tell her all about it.

Tamara evidently jumped to the proper conclusion because her eyes locked on Francie's. "Wait just a minute. Of course, the police came to see you. They knew all along what Kevin was up to, didn't they? Childress said something about their laying a trap for him. You were helping them, weren't you? You and Clay. It was all a setup—you and Clay, having Kevin and me over for dinner, all the rest of it. You knew all along what a loser and a crook and a thoroughly dishonest bastard Kevin is!"

She stared at Francie for a long moment, then said in a sad, harsh voice, "Oh, my God. *You knew* what was going on. Why didn't you tell me?"

"Yes," Francie said, speaking in as calm a tone as she could muster. "I knew. I knew from the beginning." She leaned forward, stretched out a hand, palm up. "But, Tamara, I couldn't tell you. I wanted to, from the start, but Clay had to get close to Kevin, and I knew you would have thrown Kevin out the minute you found out what he was doing, and that would have ruined our plan." She let her hand fall into her lap. "Kevin tried hacking into Brazos first from my computer."

"But how did he get in?" Tamara's expression showed her shock.

"He must have copied your key to my apartment because he came while neither of us was at home. First he tried to use my dial-up capabilities to get into our sales records, but he didn't know my password. Then he tried a hacking program he found on the Internet. He actually entered into our files, but he couldn't find what he wanted.

"Clay consults for Brazos, and when Kevin was making one of his forays, Clay traced Kevin back to my machine. Clay and my boss had me followed and spotted Kevin here on my machine while we were at the book club. If it hadn't been for Clay, Kevin might have framed *me* for his hacking, claimed *I* gave him permission to use my computer, and he might have included *you* in the scheme because you had my key."

"But why didn't you tell me?" Tamara repeated. "At least give me a clue? Instead of letting me go ahead seeing him, having a relationship . . ." her voice turned distinctly cynical, ". . . with all that word implies. Didn't *you* of all people trust me?"

"Of course, *I trust you*, Tamara, but you know yourself you don't lie well. Remember those times in college when you tried to lie about your age? You can't even tell one of your customers a dress looks good on them when it doesn't.

"We *had* to give Kevin the idea Clay would be open to something illegal like hacking and then give him the opportunity to bribe Clay to actually do it. If you broke up with Kevin suddenly and inexplicably before they met over here, Clay had no introduction to him that didn't look phony. The cops wouldn't have had real hard proof, and we wouldn't have known what Kevin was after or if he was working with someone in his company. Now we have incontrovertible evidence against him. It's thanks largely to you that we do."

"Yeah, right. Then why do I feel dirty all over?"

"I'm sorry, Tamara. If it's any consolation, I do, too. Can you forgive me?"

"I don't know, Francie. Probably." She paused, scrubbed her forehead with her fingers. "You're right. I can't lie worth a damn."

She scrubbed some more, then took her hands away from her face and looked at Francie. "Yes, all right, definitely. I can stay mad at everybody but you. I forgive you. We've been friends too long to let someone like Kevin come between us."

She gave Francie a wavery smile, and Francie returned it as relief washed over her. She hadn't lost Tamara. She could weather this storm.

Tamara slumped back in the chair. "I'm just so angry at him right now. I feel betrayed on some deep level I haven't figured out yet. Just the thought of having had Kevin's hands on me is revolting. I know, I know," she said with a rueful shake of her head before Francie could interrupt, "the son of a bitch used both of us." She took a deep breath and let it out in a huge sigh. "I guess I should be happy I broke up with him before he could call me to bail him out of jail."

"See, there *is* a silver lining here."

With a blank look, Tamara stared off into the distance, then started chuckling. The chuckle turned into laughter. "Can you see me bailing the klutz out of jail? Putting up my very hard-earned money for a man like that, who uses me and my best friend in such an idiotic scheme? I can't even imagine traipsing into the jail, or the court, or wherever, money clutched in my hot little hand to bail out my sweetie, like in one of the TV cop and lawyer shows. The picture boggles my mind." She made a little mincing, prissy motion with her hand and her body and started laughing in earnest. "Which of my outfits do you think is suitable for jailhouse visits?"

"Oh, the hot pink with the stripes, certainly." Francie joined in the relieving laughter. If Tamara could joke about the situation, everything between them would be all right. When they both sobered, she said, "I was scared to death for you, Tamara, that he would try to involve you in his scheme. I was so happy when you broke up with him."

"Yes, me, too. What did I ever see in the guy?"

"Well, he *was* a good dancer." That remark set them off again.

When they stopped giggling, Tamara looked Francie up and down, as if she had not paid any attention to her before. "This mess really got to you, didn't it? Are you all right? You look exhausted."

"I'm all right. The strain, the worry, dealing with . . ." She made a motion to wave it all away. "But it's over with now. Brazos will see that Kevin is prosecuted, and neither of us has to see him again, although I may be called to testify."

"What about Clay? You can't tell me your reaction was all playacting on your part, Francie. I know you too well. Are you going to see him again?"

A sharp stab in the solar plexus reminded Francie of the emptiness around her heart, but she covered up her reactive jerk by pulling her legs up and hugging them. "I honestly don't know. We just didn't suit, didn't fit, couldn't agree on some basic levels at the end. It's probably better this way, to find out before getting in too deep." She listened to the facile explanation, the dishonesty in her words and wondered if Tamara heard them.

The redhead gave her a shrewd look that took in her shapeless clothes, the drab colors, the big eyeglasses, and her careless hairdo, and Francie was certain her friend saw right through her.

"He served one good purpose, though," Tamara said. "He got you out of those awful clothes and out of this apartment. Now, you're right back in them. You have to promise me something. Promise me you'll ditch your old wardrobe and start wearing real clothes again." She shook her head at Francie. "Don't give me that mulish look, woman. You know you've been enjoying the new clothes, and I'll bet everybody has been complimenting you, right?"

"Well . . ." Francie fidgeted, but knew Tamara wouldn't let her return to her shell.

"And you have to promise me . . ." she crossed her

heart, ". . . if a nice guy asks you out, you'll go."

"I'll think about that one," Francie replied. Date somebody else? How could she? The pain flared but subsided when she shook her head at the idea.

"If I have to come over here in the morning and dress you for work, I will," Tamara remonstrated.

"Okay, okay." Francie held up her hands in surrender. "I'll wear 'real' clothes, but I reserve judgment on the other."

Tamara looked at her watch. "Oh, my gosh. I have to go. I have to help my saleswomen close the shop." She rose and when Francie did also, gave her a hug. "I'll check on you tomorrow. Remember your promise. Maybe I'll find a couple of guys we can go out with this weekend."

"Oh, no, I'm not ready for that. Not yet." Francie held her friend at arm's length. "Don't tell me you have your eye on a new man already!"

Tamara grinned. "Lieutenant Childress *was* sorta cute. I wonder if he's married. He wasn't wearing a ring."

And he's Clay's friend, Francie thought, but didn't say. She simply turned Tamara toward the door. "Go take care of your shop. I'll see you tomorrow."

After Tamara left, Francie closed the door and leaned against it. Explaining to Tamara had gone better than she expected, better than she had a right to ask for. Her best friend was still that—her best *friend*. She could stop worrying about betraying Tamara. The police had Kevin. The nightmare was almost over.

The doorbell rang, and the sound jerked her upright and around. She looked out the peephole. Good Lord. What were the gamesters doing here? She opened the door, and Jim, Linda, and Rick walked into her apartment.

"Hey, y'all. What's up?" she asked as the trio made themselves at home on the sofa and chairs.

"Are you all right?" was the first thing out of Linda's mouth.

"Of course," Francie answered blithely—or so she hoped—as she sat on a chair. "Why?"

"Because you don't look so good, kind of pale, and your eyes are red."

"No, I'm fine," Francie replied. "It's been a hard week. Can I get any of you something to drink?"

"Nothing for us. We're on our way to dinner," Jim stated after a good long study of Francie. "I've been doing some thinking about marketing Conundrum, and I decided I'd better talk to Clay before going any further. Would it be okay to call him, do you think? Do you have his number?"

At the sound of Clay's name, a sharp pain, much stronger than the one that hit her when Tamara was there, took her breath, but she covered her sudden bending over with a cough.

Rick reached over to pat her back. "Are you sure you're okay?"

Francie nodded and breathed deeply. "Yes, something just went down the wrong way," she said hoarsely.

"I'll get you his number." She rose and walked into the kitchen where she wrote his number on her notepad, tore off the page, and brought it back into the living room.

"Here it is," she said, handing the paper to Jim. "Uh, I need to tell you—Clay and I have broken up."

"Oh, no," Linda groaned.

"What happened?" Jim and Rick said in unison.

"Did he hurt you?" Jim asked angrily. "If he hurt you, Francie . . ."

"Oh, honey," Linda rose and came to give Francie a hug.

The friendship expressed in the hug caused Francie's eyes to well up, and she blinked back tears as she stepped out of Linda's embrace. With sheer willpower, she stopped the sorrow and emptiness cascading through her. Damn. Where was her self-control?

"No, no, y'all. It was a mutual decision." What had she told Tamara? Oh, yes. She repeated her former prevarication. "We just didn't suit, didn't fit, couldn't agree on some basic levels at the end. It's probably better this way, to find out before getting in too deep. You don't need to worry, really, and it's still okay to give him a call. He's a man of his word. If he said he'd help with the financing, he'll follow through. You can trust him, no matter what the situation is between him and me."

Jim looked distinctly skeptical, Rick was confused, and Linda wore a distressed expression, but her friends rallied around her. "Come with us, why don't you?"

Linda asked and the guys agreed.

With some difficulty, Francie managed to turn down the invitation and persuade them to leave without her. She didn't think she had convinced them of anything about the "breakup," but at least she thought Jim would call Clay to discuss the game.

Her own words rang in her head as she slumped—again—against the door after the trio left. She was so exhausted. She pushed herself off the door, walked into the kitchen, and dug a package of chicken-noodle soup out of the cupboard. Hot comfort food was about all she could handle for supper.

As she ate the soup, an idea began to form in her mind. What she needed was some rest, time to come to terms with the situation, preferably away from there. She had plenty of vacation time accrued. She'd go to work tomorrow and ask Herb for the next week off. She could visit her parents, or maybe just go to Galveston and walk Seawall Boulevard. Someplace where she wouldn't run into Clay.

Clay. Her heart gave the tiniest of jumps, and her mind replayed what she had told Tamara and the gamesters.

She hadn't lied. She and Clay didn't suit. They couldn't agree on some very basic levels. Like the existence of magic.

She couldn't figure it out. How could Clay, an honest, trustworthy, intelligent man in every respect, believe in such a thing?

In her bones, she knew he was a man of honor and integrity. That being true, why on earth did the man think he could cast spells and cause machines to do his bidding? That he was, in fact, in actual, provable fact, literally a computer wizard? That this ancient imperative not only existed, but was causing them pain because they weren't together?

He couldn't be telling the truth about all that, could he?

She'd told the others that they could trust him.

Why couldn't she?

In counterpoint to her thoughts, her breastbone began throbbing again.

CHAPTER TWENTY-THREE

Damn it! He'd told Francie the truth—about practitioners, soul mates, and himself. And look at where it got him. Why couldn't she at least trust him enough to give him the benefit of the doubt and the chance to prove it? Now here he was, sitting at his kitchen table on Saturday morning, practically crying in his coffee from sheer frustration at being able to do nothing, *nothing*, to get through to her. And he had to depend on his sisters to rescue him—one of the lowest blows of all. Not even last night's little norther had made him feel better, as the cooler air always did.

Clay looked around his kitchen at the dirty dishes, messy newspapers, piles of junk mail, and general woebegone aspect of the place. If his mother could see it, she'd read him the riot act, even if he was in his thirties. His sisters were supposed to talk to Francie today. Daria told him last night they'd come by afterward. He'd better clean up the place and—he rubbed his unshaven chin—himself. He'd be damned if he showed them the bad shape he was really in. He did, after all, still have *some* pride.

He had just completed the cleaning chores and was on his way upstairs when the doorbell rang. Before he could even take the three steps, someone started pounding on the door. He opened it to find on his threshold the gamesters, all five of them, all with scowls on their faces.

"We want to talk to you, Clay," Jim stated, looking like there was no way in hell he'd allow Clay to refuse him.

"Sure, come on in." The gamesters had evidently spoken to Francie, Clay surmised as he stepped back and waved them into the living room.

For once, his house had no effect on its visitors. The quintet kept their attention totally on him. Nobody sat, they just arranged themselves in an arc with him as the focal point.

Clay shut the door. "What can I do for you?" he asked. He felt his muscles tighten in fight-or-flight anticipation, and he made himself relax. Although he didn't know them well, he didn't think any of them would sucker punch him.

"What did you do to Francie?" Jim demanded.

"Yeah, what?" Gary snapped.

The other three frowned harder.

"I did nothing to Francie." He crossed his arms over his chest and frowned back.

"Well, somebody sure as hell did," Jim stated. "She

looks like she's been crying for days, and she's losing weight."

"That's not all," Linda interjected. "She's wearing her oldest, baggiest clothes, and her eyes are, well, I guess the best description is, full of pain."

"She didn't get that way by herself," Jim said. "The last time she looked like this, it was because a guy hurt her really badly. Now, what did you do to her?" He thrust out his chin and stared Clay in the eye.

Good, just what he needed—interference from her friends. Clay had to struggle to keep his voice down as he held on to his temper, so his words came out slowly between his gritted teeth. "I repeat, I did nothing to Francie."

"Then why did you break up with her?" Linda asked.

"I didn't break up with her." Clay shook his head slowly from side to side to emphasize his statement.

"That's not what she said," Rick put in.

"What *exactly* did she say?" Clay really wanted to hear this.

Jim was the one to answer. "Something about how you two didn't suit each other, disagreed on some fundamental issues, crap that doesn't mean anything. Now, once and for all, why did you dump her?"

The group leaned forward at the question. Clay thought he heard somebody growl. He felt like growling himself. He decided he'd had enough of this interrogation. Time to get his own two cents in.

"I didn't." He leaned toward them, his hands on his

hips, enunciating each word precisely. "I don't want to break up with her. I want to *marry* her." There, he'd said it out loud to somebody at last.

Amazement on their faces, the gamesters stood up straight, then looked at each other and back to Clay.

"Well, hell," Jim said.

"Great!" Linda put in.

"Oh, man." Gary clapped his hands together.

Rick just grinned.

Tom kept frowning. "I don't get it. Why is she implying you did? That's what those 'we don't suit' statements usually mean. So what's going on?"

What indeed? Clay thought, but he replied, "I don't know. I can't persuade her to talk to me. She said something about a guy named 'Walt,' and I couldn't get a straight answer out of her." He watched the group exchange significant looks. "What's the deal here? He's the one who hurt her, right?"

Jim cleared his throat, looked down at the floor, then up at Clay. "Yeah, he . . ."

"It's Francie's story to tell, Jim," Linda interrupted, shaking her head at him. She turned to Clay. "We promised her never to discuss that mess with anybody, Clay. I'm sorry. You'll have to ask her."

"Yeah, I understand," Clay said. He understood loyalty and trust also, and these friends of Francie's had both in abundance.

"Come on, guys," Rick said. "Let's leave the man in

peace since we're not going to beat him up. Sorry for the intrusion, Clay."

"It's okay."

"We hope you work things out with her, Clay," Linda said with an earnest expression. "We're rooting for you. Do you want us to talk to her?"

"Thanks, but no. It's something we have to resolve ourselves." They couldn't really help anyway, not with the fundamental problem.

"Look, when the dust settles and Francie comes to her senses," Jim said, offering his hand, "I'd like to get together with you about the game."

"Fine with me." Clay shook Jim's hand and ushered the group out the door. As he closed it and started upstairs, he couldn't help smiling. What good friends that bunch was to Francie. He had no doubt they would have willingly done all they could to punish him for hurting her.

His statement about wanting to marry her had stopped them cold. They had fortunately not noticed the reaction the declaration had given him: a red-hot flash had radiated out from his center to suffuse every cell in his body. He had barely managed to remain still. The good old SMI was certainly alive and kicking him right in the solar plexus.

He walked into his bathroom and took his razor and shaving cream out of the cabinet. As he started the water running, he took a deep breath and let it out slowly. The gamesters were on his side. Tamara would probably be there, too—if he could talk to her and if she knew the true situation. But none of it did him any good.

The primal problem remained. If Francie did not believe in magic, could not be convinced magic existed, then ... No, he refused to consider such an outcome. His sisters would make her see the light. They were probably doing so right about now. Once they started a project, whether to bedevil him or help him, those two witches never gave up. They'd truly work magic on Francie.

Damn right, they would.

CHAPTER TWENTY-FOUR

Francie stared at the two women standing at her door at ten o'clock Saturday morning. She recognized Daria. Her companion must be the other sister. Same green eyes; same dark, curly hair; same beauty. The only differences were the sister was a couple of inches taller and her hair was longer. They both smiled up at her in a friendly manner. Whatever Clay may have told them about her didn't seem to have made them angry.

"Hi, Francie," Daria said. "This is my sister, Gloriana. May we come in and talk to you? Please?"

Francie peered at them suspiciously. They could only want to talk about Clay and this "magic" business. Damn. If she'd stuck to her original plan, she wouldn't even be here to have to deal with this. She'd have been on the road already, but she had too many tasks, too many errands, and she simply hadn't been able to get herself together, packed, and out the door. Even the little cold front that had blown in during the night didn't invigorate her. Something—a lethargy, a premonition, an anticipation—was not letting her move with her usual efficiency and dispatch.

She wasn't going to be deterred now, however, so she stood up to her full height, frowned down at the smaller women, and answered, "No, I'm sorry, but I don't want to talk to anyone right now. I'm sorry, too, that Clay is trying to use you in this mess."

"What we have to tell you is critical to your life," Gloriana said, frowning back. "You really need to listen to us."

"No, I don't," Francie replied and shut the door in their faces.

They immediately began to ring the bell and pound on the door. "Francie! Yes, you do!" one of them shouted. "Open the door!" the other yelled.

When they didn't stop pounding or ringing or shouting, Francie threw open the door and put one hand on it and the other on the jamb to bar them physically. She scowled down at them. "Look, don't interfere in my business. Get out of here, or I'll call the cops. I don't and won't listen to anything you have to say."

She didn't really think it would come to the police, and she didn't anticipate not being able to get rid of them, by force if necessary. After all, she had at least five inches on both of them and much better muscle tone. The two of them together didn't look like they could lift a chair.

The two sisters exchanged a sneaky glance and a nod

with each other, then turned back to her. They said in unison, "Oh, yes, you will."

"No, I won't." She began to shut the door.

Flash! A brilliant blaze of light burst in front of her, and all she could see were multicolored lights whirling about her.

The next thing she knew, she was flat on the floor with a sister leaning on each arm, holding her down.

"Oh, yes, you will," Daria said, and used her foot to kick the door closed.

"Let me go!" Francie tried to sit up, but the sisters' grips were tight. She tried to struggle, but she couldn't budge them. They were just pip-squeaks. She should have been able to throw them across the room. How could they feel like two tons of lead on each of her arms?

She tried kicking, but each sister simply moved a hand to Francie's nearest leg and held that down also. If that weren't enough, a feeling of total weakness flooded her body, and her breastbone ached like a mule had kicked it.

"Now, listen, you two—" she began with a wheeze.

Flash!

When she blinked back to sight again, she almost screamed. Now, instead of two sisters, a dragon sat on one of her arms and a panther on the other. Both were black with big green eyes and sharp-looking teeth.

"No, you listen," the dragon said in Daria's voice.

"Oh, for pity's sake," the panther said, sounding like

Gloriana, and rolled its eyes at the dragon. "I told you it would come to this, Daria. She's just like Clay, as a proper soul mate should be, and we always had to resort to trickery to get to him. Now, aren't you glad we planned ahead?"

"I prefer to think we're forthright and persistent," the dragon replied. "And truthful. And, yes, you were right, she left us no alternative but to use our spells."

Francie lay on her back and watched the beasts bicker above her while she tried to get her mind going again. What in the hell had just happened? How had the two women become . . . animals? Werebeasts? Were they shape-shifters? Were they going to drink her blood?

No, that happened only in fantasy novels. Didn't it? This was the real world. Wasn't it? She opened her mouth to let them have it verbally—her only recourse—but all that came out was, "Uh."

That brought the attention of the two sisters back to her.

"Are you ready to listen, Francie?" Daria asked. "We'll let you up if you agree to calm down and hear us out."

"No tricks, now, Francie," Gloriana admonished, waving a claw-tipped paw in front of her nose.

"O-o-okay," Francie pushed the word out of her mouth by sheer willpower.

"Okay," the sisters said together and let her go.

Francie sat up and rubbed her eyes. When she opened

them again, Daria and Gloriana were back to their normal selves—whatever "normal" meant to these two.

The sisters hauled her to her feet as though she was full of feathers, pulled her into her living room, and plopped her down in her overstuffed chair.

Daria took a seat on the couch, but Gloriana marched over to the window and picked up one of her potted plants. She placed the dark green ivy on the table next to Francie.

"Just in case you need more convincing..." Gloriana said, as she looked intently at the plant, "... watch."

Francie could not stop from turning her face toward the ivy. As she watched, one new leaf emerged, then another, both the clear light green of new growth. The ivy tendril grew by at least two inches.

Her mind whirling, she stared at the plant. She blinked. The new leaves were still there. The ivy had truly grown.

"And there's the old standby..." Gloriana waved her hand, and a six-inch glowing ball of swirling indigo and violet light burst into being, zipped around the room like a firefly on steroids, and finally came to rest, floating serenely, one foot in front of Francie, who drew in her chin as she contemplated the object.

A bright blue globe had appeared before her in the midst of the argument with Clay, she recalled. She had ignored it and accused him of a magician's trickery. She couldn't repeat those actions now.

The sphere floated up and almost bonked her on the nose. She reached out and touched it lightly with a fingertip. The surface was hard and cold, and she felt a slight tingle travel up her hand to her arm. She quickly pulled her hand away from it.

"Don't worry," Gloriana said. "It won't hurt you."

Francie looked at the ball, then at the two sisters, then off into space. A thundering headache suddenly formed behind her forehead. She had just seen proof of something—*several* somethings that could not have been staged, not here in her own apartment. Was it magic? Could it have been anything else?

No, she told herself. It couldn't have been magic. Magic didn't exist. But her protest seemed automatic to her; she felt helpless in the face of the evidence before her.

She closed her eyes and rubbed her forehead as the headache throbbed with increasing intensity. The pain in her middle returned, accompanied by an enormous sense of loss. Loss of Clay, loss of happiness, loss of a bright future. What was she going to do now? What would she do without him? The headache formed itself into cannonballs that ricocheted around in her skull, thudding dully each time they hit bone. She moaned to herself and rubbed harder.

Francie felt a hand on her shoulder and looked up to find Gloriana kneeling by her side. The ball of light had disappeared.

"Headache?" Gloriana asked. When Francie nodded affirmatively, Gloriana offered, "Can I help? I can cast a healing spell, but if you'd rather not . . ."

"No," Francie croaked, and a particularly large cannonball hit her cranium directly over her right eye. Maybe she'd reconsider. After all, what would it hurt to indulge her guests' fantasies? "Well, I mean, go ahead. I don't think you can do anything, but, what the heck? Pills certainly don't help."

"Close your eyes and try to relax," Gloriana said.

Francie leaned back in the chair and rested her head on its high back. She put her hands in her lap and shut her eyes. She felt Gloriana's hand rest lightly on her forehead, and a healing warmth spread slowly through her entire skull. She had the distinct sensation her blood vessels were relaxing, the blood itself slowing, nerve endings ceasing to fire, her thought processes returning to their normal operation.

After a period of time—she had no notion how long—Francie opened her eyes. The headache had vanished, and in its place a sense of calm well-being permeated her entire body.

Gloriana had moved back to the couch. "How do you feel?" she asked.

"Fine. Just fine," Francie answered as she mentally checked over her body. Gloriana's spell seemed to have had another effect besides curing her headache. For the first time in days, she had absolutely no pain in her middle. "I really do," she said, hearing the wonder in her own voice. "Did you hypnotize me?"

"No," Glori said with a smile. "I just cast a garden-variety healing spell."

"Let me make us some tea," Daria said. "Then we can talk."

"I owe you an apology," Francie said. "When I can think again. I feel like I'm floating without a care in the world."

Gloriana laughed. "That's one of the side effects. You just sit. We'll find what we need."

"You don't want to show her your microwave imitation? Double bubble, toil and boil?" Daria asked with a playful smirk.

"I can heat water, that's all," Gloriana said to Francie after she shot a glare at her sister.

Francie sat there in her mild state of bliss and let the sisters have their way. Within minutes, the three had cups of tea in their hands.

"Now, about our idiot brother," Gloriana stated. "We can't believe he sandbagged you like he did, telling you *everything* without at least one of us there to help him. You poor thing, you must have been flabbergasted."

"Well . . ." Francie hesitated. Their "idiot brother"? They were on her side? What could she say to that?

"As he probably told you," Daria interjected, speaking quickly, "I'm not great at casting visible, incontrovertible spells, but mine do affect the way people perceive me. Except for defensive spells, of course, but we'll get to those. Clay can cast *lux*, the light ball spell, but he can't spell anyone else, either, only those computers and such. How he ever expected to convince you about magic solely by manipulating a computer is beyond both of us. At least *I* knew I couldn't do it by myself when it came time to tell Bent. He's a nonpractitioner like you. Did Clay mention that?"

"Clay can be so dense at times," Gloriana agreed. "As we understand it, he didn't give you a chance to get a word in edgewise, just laid it all out about practitioners, how the talents are hereditary but varied, how we use them to make our livings, how we're basically . . ."

"Wait, stop," Daria held up a hand to her sister. "We're getting ahead of our audience here. Not only that, but we're acting just like Clay, not allowing her to get a word in edgewise."

"Oh. You're right," Gloriana said.

"Let's be clear where we stand before we get into any details," Daria continued. "Francie, what's the whole picture here? Do you believe us, that we can work magic, that Clay can, too, and that he wasn't stringing you a line? Were our demonstrations convincing? Those were some strength and illusion spells we used to knock you down and become beasties, and Glori really can make plants grow. Do you want to see some more?"

Francie looked from one sister to the other. It did appear that they were on her side. But how would she answer their questions?

Did she believe in magic? Did she, who'd always prided herself on her grasp of reality, believe that there were people who could do *magic*? That was the question, wasn't it? But what was reality, after all? What you perceived, the way you thought?

If you had not personally perceived, had not actually experienced an event, that did not mean it didn't exist, hadn't happened. People had not believed the earth revolved around the sun until Copernicus, and he had certainly had problems convincing them of it. Was she like those ancient, ignorant people, refusing to accept a new reality because it ran counter to her own, to what she wanted to believe?

Or was she like those people who didn't believe human beings had gone to the moon, that it was all just movie special effects? Two little women had knocked her down and sat on her, and that had been real. The dragon and the panther may have been special effects of another sort, but they certainly appeared real to her, from her position on the floor.

What did the sisters' demonstration mean? She could think of only one answer: she had just experienced magic, *real magic*.

Clay had been telling the truth, and she . . . she, who'd always considered herself open-minded, had refused to listen to what he had to say or look at what he wanted to show her. She hadn't given him the chance to offer his proof.

Now, here were his sisters, who'd left her no other alternative than to accept the *idea*, the *fact* of magic. Oh, they'd shown her in the simplest and probably kindest way possible, she supposed. She couldn't deny the actuality of what she had just seen, right here in her own apartment. They couldn't have held her down, created those animals or the light ball without the help of some sort of power. Her ivy plant had not grown by itself. Her headache definitely had not cured itself.

What else could it be but magic? Real, honest-to-gosh enchantment, spells, sorcery. As her acceptance of the idea permeated her mind, she felt her view of reality, her understanding of the universe, spin, tilt, and come to rest in a totally new place. And her solar plexus radiated warmth.

She had to admit to herself she was convinced now. She should have listened to Clay in the first place. She had been such a coward. So afraid of being hurt, not realizing that, by not opening herself up to new possibilities, she was, in truth, hurting not only herself, but also Clay.

Clay . . . What must he think of her? Would he even speak to her?

Francie looked from one woman to the other. Though she might feel embarrassed by her former actions, she had to tell them the truth, the conclusion she had come to. "I don't see that I have any choice. Even if I denied seeing the dragon and the panther, I can't dispute you made my plant grow or your touch cured my headache." She couldn't help sighing or stop her shoulders from sagging. "I hope I haven't made too big a fool of myself."

"No, not at all," Gloriana said. "We were a little anxious about this, so we planned on overwhelming you with spells if we had to. When you wouldn't let us in, we resorted to them to, let's say, get your attention. I hope we didn't bulldoze you too much."

"I think you displayed a great deal of composure and common sense," Daria said. "If I had been in your place, had all this dropped in my lap, I would have come completely unglued. Clay was foolish to think he could simply talk to you, use a puny light ball as proof, and then conjure those computer spells of his and expect you to believe him."

"Probably if I had given him the chance to show me how he worked with a computer, I might have believed him." Francie heard the words come out of her mouth and realized she was defending Clay, a point evidently not lost on his sisters, who gave each other one of those did-you-catch-that looks. "As long as it wasn't his own computer," she amended, in the interest of being perfectly clear.

Daria gave her a big grin and shrugged at Gloriana. "Well, what did we expect? She was bound to be as much into computers as he is." She turned back to Francie. "Okay. What do you remember from Clay's explanation?"

"Well," Francie said after she took a couple of sips of tea, "he said you all are magic practitioners, you use spells to do your work, and you're just ordinary folks otherwise."

"Basically, that's correct," Daria answered. "Practitioners use internal energy to cast spells and cause things to happen. The kind of magic you can make, the type of talent you have, seems to be random, although the ability to do magic is inherited. Most practitioners can cast spells on objects or people, but I'm a little different, being able to cast spells only on myself."

"Clay said you had used one to make sure I was telling the truth the first time we met."

"Yes, you responded to my I-will-hear-only-the-truth spell," Daria said. "You evidently are sensitive to magic, because you blinked when I enhanced the power. You reacted today also."

"I saw big flashes of light today. It was just little ones before."

"Hmmm, more than just a little sensitive, then. Clay told you more than simply about practitioners and our ability to use magic, didn't he? Glori and I had a twofold mission today, Francie. First, we were going to do everything we could to convince you of the existence of magic and our ability to practice it. You say we've accomplished that goal. The second part is to explain the phenomenon of practitioner life called the soul-mate imperative."

"You mean that's true? It's all true? It wasn't just a line?" Francie jerked back in her chair, and her hand shot up to her throat. "But I thought he just wanted to . . . And I jumped to the conclusion . . . And I accused him of . . ." Every scornful word she had said to Clay ran through her mind like a plundering horde intent on reducing her inner fortress to rubble. She felt her walls crumble. "Oh, God, what must he think of me? What have I said to him?"

"No more than he deserved," Gloriana remarked dryly.

"Take it easy, Glori," Daria warned. "I agree Clay brought most of his misery on himself. You haven't been through this yet, and I know you like to give Clay a hard time. But I learned the imperative has its own methods for enforcement, and speaking from experience, the situation couldn't have been easy on either of them."

She turned to Francie. "I had a similar reaction to yours when I heard about the imperative—disbelief. At first when Mother reminded me I should be meeting my soul mate soon, I was, to put it mildly, outraged and horrified. The whole situation sounded so medieval, something arranged without my approval, and I had no say in the matter. *No free will.* Some man would come into my life, and I'd be hit with the soul mate thunderbolt and stuck with him, no matter who or what he was. I felt *trapped.* All of a sudden, I had *no control* of my life. Then I met Bent, and before I knew it, the imperative had me in its clutches." She demonstrated by clasping her hands together and shaking them sharply.

"The SMI, as Clay calls it, does make itself known. For example, do you have an itch, a pain right under your breastbone? Right here?" Daria pointed to the spot on herself.

"Yes, more than an itch, a real pain, and it's been driving me crazy." Francie rubbed the end of her sternum, which, mercifully, for once only itched slightly. "First I thought it was a bug bite. When it started hurting, I decided it was heartburn, and finally an ulcer—or something worse. Why right here?" Francie rubbed the area, which seemed to be vibrating, in a happy sort of way.

"A practitioner's 'magic center' is right in that spot, next to the heart," Gloriana said. "It's where we gather our energy to do magic."

"But . . ."

"Soul mates, even when one is not a practitioner, have centers that resonate with each other," Daria said. "It's a kind of sympathetic vibration, I guess. Bent and I both itched like crazy. He also thought he was developing an ulcer because the spot hurt so much until he gave in to the imperative. The itch goes away after the First Mating."

"The *what*?" Daria's words brought Francie upright in her chair again.

The two sisters exchanged one of their looks. Gloriana rolled her eyes and mouthed the word "idiot," while Daria put up her hands in a calm-down gesture.

Gloriana said, "I guess Clay didn't get that far, did he?" When Francie shook her head, Gloriana turned to her sister and said, "This one's yours, Daria."

"Let's back up a minute," Daria said. "What did

Clay say about soul mates?"

"They get along well, have similar likes," Francie answered, frowning as she tried to reconstruct what Clay had actually said, not what she might have heard in his tone, not what conclusions she had been jumping to. "They're attracted to each other. Something about a bond between them, a lifetime commitment. Some deal about the first time they make love. Is that what you mean?"

"Exactly, but there's more to it," Daria said. "I cannot begin to tell you how powerful the imperative is. It kept Bent from marrying anybody else, although he tried a couple of times before he met me. It causes pain, as you know, but it also brings euphoria."

"I can attest to both of those," Francie said, with a rueful smile. Then several incidents came to mind. "Oh, so that's why . . . I couldn't understand how my mind would shut down when he kissed me. I had no control at all. I actually considered the possibility of being possessed by an alien."

Daria laughed. "I hadn't thought of it like that, but you're right. Bent will agree also. The imperative does take over your mind."

"But I'm not a practitioner. How could this force affect me?"

"It doesn't matter if one of the pair is not a practitioner," Daria said. "The imperative applies just as it would if both were. In the practitioner concept, the two soul mates are bound together. Emotions are heightened, and the attraction is irresistible, as I can attest. They are as in love with each other as it is possible for two people to be. The feeling grows that one is not 'complete,' not 'whole' without the other, and the bond grows stronger over time."

Daria took a sip of tea, then continued. "You don't have to worry that your feelings aren't real. The imperative doesn't bring together people who wouldn't be mates. It just hurries the process some. Also, Clay has not cast any 'love spell' or such nonsense on you. Soul mates can't spell each other, except for healing and defensive purposes. That's one of the ways two people know they are, in fact, soul mates and not under somebody else's enchantment. And in a practitioner family, the members can't spell each other, except for healing and defense. It's just how magic works for us." She paused, then smiled. "And now we have reached the subject of the 'First Mating.'"

Francie had a sudden premonition that what Daria was going to say next would have a profound effect on her life. Her center began to tingle like crazy, and she clasped her hands over the spot.

"It's the first time you make love with your soul mate, and it holds a special place in the concept, not just because it seals the bond between the two of you. The First Mating often enhances practitioner powers and talents." Daria shrugged. "But there's no guarantee."

"What happened to you?" Francie asked. What would happen to *her*, she wondered. The tingle grew stronger.

"Bent gained the ability to see the aura around me when I have cast a spell on myself. I can now spell him for healing and defense. That was the extent of our enhancement. No one has any idea what the First Mating will do, what talents it might increase, or by what magnitude. In some cases, the practitioner gains nothing, and in others, completely new abilities. Therefore we don't know what will happen to you. According to my mother's sources, however, as far as we know, the SMI has *never* granted spell-casting abilities to a nonpractitioner in the First Mating."

"Oh." Francie immediately felt deflated and disappointed. She laughed at herself as she realized the cause. When both sisters raised their eyebrows in question, she explained, "I had a sudden vision of being able to cast a spell. Paradoxical, isn't it? One minute I deny the existence of magic, and the next I want to use it. What a turnaround."

"One thing we all have to get used to," Gloriana said, "is that each and every one of us has his or her own brand of magic, his or her individual talents. This is no different from nonpractitioners and their non-magic talents. All we can do is be true to our own natures and abilities." She grinned. "Thus endeth the lesson for today."

"What else do I need to know?" Francie asked.

"Well," Daria answered, "we witches are always virgins at our First Matings, mostly because the imperative turns us off to any man except our soul mates, but the situation doesn't apply to nonpractitioners, from what we've been able to find out. Warlocks are seldom virgins—because of all their testosterone, according to Mother."

Francie forced herself to keep her mouth closed at the implications of Daria's statement, but she felt herself turning red. No way was she going to tell these two anything about her lack of virginity, especially anything about Walt. It was bad enough that she remembered what she had said to Clay about the bastard, how she had compared the two men. She shut off her memories to concentrate on what Daria said next.

"There's one more thing, and it's very important," Daria said. "The First Mating must be totally without physical or artificial barriers. No condom, no diaphragm, no pills."

"But . . ." Francie sputtered. Not in this day and age did one consider such a thing.

"It has to do with making the bond a secure one," Daria said with an earnest look.

"Don't worry, Clay's healthy," Gloriana interjected. "Mother makes sure we all have thorough physicals by practitioner doctors, and I know Daddy preached condoms to Clay even before his first girlfriend." She gazed intently at Francie for a moment. "The subject of the First Mating brings us to the birth-control issue. Practitioners don't have children unless both of them want to. We witches have our own spells to ensure it, and they don't count as a barrier. You can't conjure your own, but I can cast a contraceptive spell on you. They last about a year, and we usually renew them every six months to be certain. Would you like me to conjure the enchantment?"

Here it was, Francie said to herself. Decision time.

She had accepted the existence of magic. By agreeing to Gloriana's spell, she would be agreeing Clay was her soul mate, agreeing the two of them belonged together, agreeing they would make love.

Daria leaned across the space between the couch and Francie's chair and put a hand on Francie's arm. "We're not asking you to make a decision about Clay right this moment," she said, "or even to tell us what it is, although I think you know how we would like you to decide. But the spell can't hurt you, and it does protect you. We can always remove it later or simply let it wear off, whatever you like."

If she took the spell, she couldn't use the fear of pregnancy as a reason to reject him, Francie thought. She dithered for a moment, then took the leap. "Oh, what the heck," she said with a sigh. "I might as well have it. Just in case. Not that I know what I'm going to do yet." Her qualifications sounded hollow, even to her own ears. Her center gave a little lurch, and she could almost hear it say, "*Liar.*"

"Let me cast the spell, and then we'll get out and you can think about all this without our influence," Gloriana said as she rose and came over to stand beside Francie's chair.

"What do I do?" Francie's center was tingling again, and she could feel excitement beginning to bubble in her veins. She might be procrastinating, but the good old SMI seemed to have made up *its* mind about her decision.

"Just relax," Gloriana said. She concentrated for a moment and reached over to lay her left hand on Francie's abdomen. She made a complicated gesture with her right hand and then covered the left with it. Francie sensed a warmth settling in her core, and she blinked as a shimmer of light came and went on the periphery of her vision.

Gloriana stepped back. "There. That should take care of things for a while."

"What did you feel?" Daria asked.

"Like I had a heating pad on my stomach for a moment," Francie answered. "And there was a flicker like far-off lightning at the edge of my sight."

"Good," Gloriana said. "It means the spell took."

"I want to try something," Daria said. "I'm going to put one of my spells on myself. Tell me what you see, Francie."

"Okay," Francie agreed. She watched Daria closely. At first nothing at all happened; Daria didn't even wiggle a finger. Then . . . "Oh."

"What happened?" Daria asked.

"First a tiny, dim flash of blue light surrounded you, and then suddenly I had the absolute feeling I could trust you and should tell you the truth. What does that mean?"

"I think it means you're extremely sensitive to magic," Daria replied. "I put only a minuscule amount of power into the spell. Even the vast majority of practitioners would have been unaffected. As a nonpractitioner, you shouldn't have seen the light or had any 'sudden,' or definable feeling at all."

"You're almost as sensitive as I am," Gloriana put in. "I could barely see the aura. But wait a minute." She turned to Daria. "The spell affected Francie. If this were one of your interviews, she would have told you the truth without any questions. But if Francie and Clay are soul mates, and the members of a practitioner family are not affected by each other's spells, how can she be feeling the enchantment?"

"Probably because they haven't mated yet," Daria answered and rose. "Come on, Glori, let's get out of here and leave Francie in peace."

"But I still have more questions," Francie protested. "How does this all work in practice, and what happens . . ."

"I'm sure you do, but we're not the ones to answer them," Daria said with a kind smile. "Clay is."

The sisters had their things together and were heading for the door before Francie could think of anything to say except a weak, "Thanks for all your help."

Daria and Gloriana both gave Francie a hug. "We'll get together later," Daria promised.

"Don't let him off the hook too easily," Glori counseled.

"Don't mind her, her mission in life has always been

to give Clay a hard time," was Daria's rejoinder. "You'll know what to do." And then they were gone.

Francie shut the door and looked blankly around her apartment. "Magic. Soul mates," she said aloud. "What am I going to do now?"

Her answer came in a stab of pain in the solar plexus so sharp, it robbed her of breath and almost bent her double.

"All right, I get the message," she grumbled toward her middle. "Go to him."

She staggered toward the bedroom to find her shoes, and the pain subsided. Should she call him first? What if he wasn't home?

A needlelike twinge told her the SMI obviously wanted her moving, not on the phone.

"Okay, okay," she told it as she sat down to put on her socks and sneakers. "That's enough out of you."

The spot subsided to its normal itchy condition.

Francie put her elbows on her knees and leaned her head on her hands. She had to be going crazy. First she was seeing dragons and panthers and balls of light in her own living room. Then she was agreeing she believed in magic. Now she was talking *out loud* to some implausible, invisible "concept," an "imperative," that had teeth and didn't hesitate to bite. Next she would probably be trying to cast spells herself. She shook her head at the unreality of the situation.

Well, unreal or not, a significant transformation was

happening to her, and she had to come to terms with it.

"It" had a name: *soul mate.* Clay's soul mate. The concept did explain the intense, immediate attraction they felt for each other, the reaction each drew from the other. And the result, the culmination of all this confusion and craving and frustration and lust was a lifelong commitment to each other.

What had Daria said? Soul mates were "bound together."

"Not complete without the other."

And the clincher: "They are as in love with each other as it is possible for two people to be."

Yes, she was in love with Clay Morgan. She might as well admit it. She lusted after his body, she craved his attention, she enjoyed his conversation, she longed for his companionship. She wanted his children.

She needed to be with him, no matter what, forever.

She felt a great calm settle over her as these last conclusions filtered through her mind, permeated her body, and settled in her bones. All her anxieties vanished, and the spot under her sternum hummed. Exhilarating excitement, fiery desire, and almost overwhelming joy mixed into a frothy brew that bubbled in her veins more than the most expensive champagne ever could. She realized she was hugging herself, holding on as if to stop from blasting off into space from sheer delirium.

She had to see Clay. He had said he wouldn't come to her, so she had to go to him. She had to explain how she felt. She had to . . .

Forget her pride.

Apologize.

Beg his forgiveness.

Oh, God, this was going to be painful.

But he was her soul mate, wasn't he? It meant he had to forgive her, didn't it?

She took a deep breath to gird herself for battle. She could do nothing except go find out.

She looked at herself in the mirror as she rose to grab her purse. All she had on were old jeans and a ragged sweatshirt. Her hair was a tangled mess, and she had on no makeup. His sisters must have thought she looked like a bag lady.

She ran a brush through her hair, but when she contemplated taking the time to make up her face, the damn spot in the middle of her chest started itching like crazy.

"All right! I'm going!" She gave it a rap with her knuckles as she walked out the door.

CHAPTER TWENTY-FIVE

It seemed like only seconds before she was pulling up in front of Clay's home. Wherever her mind had been during the drive, she would probably never know. She looked around before climbing out of her car. The house, the yard, the block, the neighborhood, all looked quiet and serene in the noonday sun. The little norther had left the sky a bright blue and given the air a crispness not usually found in humid Houston.

Francie shivered as she approached the front door. "You can do it," she muttered to bolster her courage, but she rang the doorbell with a not-quite-steady finger.

Nothing happened. No sounds emanated from within, no shadow appeared at the front window, no click signaled the locks disengaging.

Disappointment close to despair speared through her, but she refused to give up. *He had to be there.*

As she reached for the button again, the door abruptly opened. The man who was her soul mate stood in the door frame.

He didn't say a word. His face betrayed no emotion. He just looked at her with eyes of molten silver.

Francie's mouth went dry. He was so gorgeous, standing there barefoot in jeans worn white with use, an old Renaissance Festival T-shirt stretched tightly over his muscular chest, and his black hair all mussed up. It was all she could do not to hurl herself into his arms, but the stiffness in his posture, the wariness rolling off him in waves, told her they had to talk first. Wasn't that what the basketball game had been all about—his wanting to talk to her?

Her SMI spot was totally quiet, no help at all in indicating her best approach.

She drew herself together, a little surprised to find her pride had returned. They'd meet as equals. She'd apologize, but she wasn't going to grovel. "Can I come in?" she asked, thankful when her voice remained steady.

Clay stared at her. He'd been fidgeting all morning, expecting his sisters. Daria had told him they'd be over after seeing Francie. Neither sister had called, and he'd been unable to concentrate on anything beyond conjuring up scenarios about how their mission was going. He'd pictured every possibility from Francie throwing them out to all three becoming such buddies they tried to teach Francie how to cast spells. As if a nonpractitioner who didn't believe in magic could enchant so much as a match to burst into flame.

Now here she was on his doorstep. She looked wonderful, with those tight jeans and the thin sweatshirt hugging her luscious curves, her blond hair loose on her shoulders and shining in the sun. He wanted to haul her into his arms and hold her until they fused together.

But they had to talk first. Up to and including that damned basketball game, he'd been assuming too much, been overconfident. No more. She was here. It had to mean she had decided something, but what? At least she had the guts to tell him face to face.

She didn't look angry. She didn't look sad. Her brown eyes were smokier than usual, and there was a sense of anticipation about her. A spark of hope flared in his chest. Everything would be all right. She was his soul mate, wasn't she?

Hold on, Morgan, he told himself. You can't jump to any conclusions with this woman. Look where it's gotten you in the past. After all you've been through, you need to hear her say the words clearly, unambiguously, unprompted. He stepped back from the door and waved her in.

She seemed nervous as she walked stiffly into the living room. She put her purse on the couch and moved to stand in the open area before the fireplace—where he had stood when he tried to explain magic to her. She turned to face him.

Clay stopped at the end of the couch. His hands itched with the need to touch her, so he slid them into his back pockets to anchor them. His magic center, which had been quiet all morning, vibrated for a few seconds, then fell still. The only part of his body that was aching was his heart. It would just have to wait. He'd humbled himself the last time she was here; he wouldn't do it again. He waited for her to speak.

Francie licked her lips, noticing how his gaze followed the motion before returning to look into her eyes. Why wasn't he saying anything? He didn't look angry, thank goodness, just intent. He certainly wasn't making it easy for her, but then she couldn't exactly blame him, not after all she'd put them through. She clasped her hands—in back of her so he couldn't see how tightly she was holding on to herself—and took the plunge.

"Clay," she started, then had to stop to clear her throat. "Daria and Gloriana came to see me this morning. They showed me some . . . spells . . . some magic." There, she'd said the word. Maybe it would get easier if she just kept talking. "They turned themselves into a panther and a dragon, and Gloriana made one of my plants grow. I think I was finally convinced when Glori cured my headache."

She stopped. She felt like she was babbling. She started again. "What I'm trying to say is . . . I do believe now you all can do magic, you are magic practitioners."

Clay didn't say a word, didn't change expression, just looked at her.

"I'm sorry I didn't give you the chance to show me

how you cast spells on the computer. I've always prided myself on my open mind, my willingness to investigate new ideas, and my caution not to jump to a conclusion. I did that with you—jumped, I mean—and I apologize for it. Some ancient mental baggage and fears clogged my thought processes and got in the way of what you were trying to tell me. I listened to those old liars instead of you. I know deep in my heart you would never do the things I accused you of. Can you forgive me?"

Clay nodded, a quick jerk of his head up and down. His mouth remained shut.

Francie could feel her hands twisting each other behind her back. Stay calm, she ordered herself. He hasn't thrown you out. He's just waiting for you to say the words. The SMI spot tingled—an encouraging stimulation, she hoped.

"Daria and Glori also explained about soul mates," she continued. "About how Daria and Bent are mates, about what it really means, how some of it works. They wouldn't answer all of my questions, however. They said I had to talk to you." She paused, but he still said nothing, although she thought she could see a distinct gleam in his eyes, a hot flame burning in the silver. The SMI gave another flutter, and she knew exactly what she had to say.

"I've done some thinking, Clay, even before your sisters came to visit. I've been 'helped' by what I understand now is our mutual tormentor, the imperative," she said with what she hoped was a smile, but felt more like a grimace of pain. She tried to keep her voice steady, but she could hear the anguish, the pleading in it. "A lot of thinking and a lot of feeling. I've been miserable since we've been apart, and not just because of the imperative. I miss you. I want you. I won't fight it or you any longer. I don't want to be without you ever again."

He didn't say a word.

She took a deep breath. Now or nothing. "To answer your question from the last time we were in this room, yes, I will be your soul mate. Will you be mine?"

A tidal wave of relief flowed over Clay as he growled, "It's about damned time." He closed the distance between them in a nanosecond, hauled Francie into his arms, and took her mouth, delving deep, demanding, devouring. When she wrapped her arms around him and kissed him back, it felt like coming home, Christmas morning, his birthday, and his first successful spell-casting on a computer—altogether, only infinitely better.

How long they stood like that, Clay never knew. He didn't notice she was crying until they had to loosen their grip enough to breathe and his lips slid to her cheek. "Francie?" he whispered. "Did I hurt you?"

"No, no," she answered, shaking her head but she hiccupped with tiny sobs. "Of course not. Just the opposite. It's relief. I was so scared you'd say no, and . . ."

"Oh, darlin'," he chuckled. "There was no chance of that." He gave her a comforting kiss, ran his hands up and down her back, and felt her catch her breath and relax against him. He gave her a moment, then pushed her away enough to see her face. "Are you okay?"

"I'm fine," she answered with a smile. Then she frowned slightly. "So we're soul mates, right?"

"Yes, we are." He couldn't help grinning at the thought.

"What happens next?"

He grinned wider at her innocent question. "Now, Francie, we mate."

CHAPTER TWENTY-SIX

Clay kissed her again, softly, tenderly, before she could respond. He didn't care what she might be about to say. She'd said the most important things, the exact words he needed to hear. They'd done enough talking.

He wooed her with light kisses first. His little butterfly kisses wandered over her face, landed lightly around her jaw, nibbled at her ear, sipped the nectar of her skin. Every time she tried to say something, he kissed her lips until she quit trying.

He let his hands lightly wander here and there over her body, never lingering long. Later he'd touch, or kiss, or taste every inch of her, but for now, it was enough to explore, to luxuriate in the feel of her in his arms. He felt her tremble wherever he touched her. When she spread her hands over his back and pressed those magnificent breasts to his chest, he couldn't suppress his own shiver.

A faint humming, a low melody seemed to fill the room, and he began to move from side to side in a slow dance—rubbing the most important parts of their two bodies together.

Too much, it was almost too much. Too little, it was definitely not enough. He grasped her hips and pulled her into the cradle of his thighs, into the rock-hard rigidity of his erection. Ah, that was better. She sighed and tilted her hips just right to match his movement. They hadn't danced together until now, but it was all right. Now was when it counted.

She followed his lead, swayed with him, reciprocated when he kissed her mouth, did some of her own nibbling when he bent to taste the creamy surface of her neck.

Clay slow-danced her across the living room and didn't stop kissing her even as they climbed up the stairs to his bedroom. Once next to his bed, he abandoned his slow approach to concentrate on serious kissing, his tongue plunging deep, thrusting, claiming, possessing. His, she was his at last. She moaned, twined her arms around his neck, and he felt his blood heat to the boiling point.

Kissing was no longer enough. He needed to feel her skin against his, and he tugged at her sweatshirt. Francie whimpered when he released her mouth to pull the garment over her head, but when she realized what he wanted, she breathed, "yes," and pulled his T-shirt out of his jeans. Arms tangled as each tried to undress the other, and finally they succeeded to the point where Clay was bare-chested and above her waist Francie was wearing only her bra.

Her pale pink, lace-and-silk, almost-transparent bra.

"Oh, Francie," Clay whispered, his fingers lightly tracing the edge of the material. "If I'd known what you wore under those awful clothes, I'd have had you out of them earlier." His fingers met on the front clasp and released it, then slowly lifted the sides apart to let her breasts spill into his hands. She filled his hands to overflowing.

He froze, transfixed by the sight of her loveliness—full pale globes topped with peach-colored nipples, already taut, calling to him. He bent and kissed each tip, took one, then the other, in a more thorough caress. She tasted like peaches, too, and he suckled and flicked until each peak curled tight and she threw her head back and moaned. He smiled in rampant satisfaction as he weighed her now-swollen breasts in his hands.

It was almost too much, Francie managed to think as she arched her back and held his head to her, seeking a stronger touch. It wasn't enough. Her breasts had been aching, and his hands soothed the ache, but his lips caused lightning bolts through her body and produced another, almost excruciating, ache between her legs. She needed soothing there, too.

Clay's lips and hands worked their way down to the belt at her waist. Unbuckling the belt, he unzipped her jeans. His lips never left her body as he knelt to pull off her shoes, socks, jeans, and panties. She tried to cooperate, but her movements were sluggish. The sensations he was calling forth stole her energy and diminished her ability to respond. All she was capable of was *feeling*— the slightly raspy slide of his fingers, the soft suction of his lips, the smooth glide of his tongue.

Francie ran her hands through his dark hair, holding him to her, using him as an anchor in a world of sensation. Then his mouth reached the dark golden curls at the apex of her thighs. The shock that zinged through her trembling body when his exploring tongue stroked first her feminine folds and then the hidden little bud arched her back and thrust her hips forward.

"Clay . . . ."

"Yes, darlin'," Clay murmured as her legs buckled and he caught her with one arm. "I've got you." Rising, he stripped the bedcovers back with his free hand and then lifted her as though she weighed nothing—again the sensation Francie had not felt since she was a small child.

He laid her down and leaned over her stiff-armed, taking his time looking, running his gaze from the top of her head to the tip of her toes. No man had ever looked at her like this before, a potent mixture of lust, need, want, desire, and possession. She could see silver flames in his eyes, and she knew hers returned every nuance of the same expressions.

She liked him to look at her, she realized as she made no attempt to cover herself. She couldn't help blushing, however, and it drew forth a chuckle from Clay.

"You're just perfect, Francie," he said as his gaze

traveled again up and down her body. And she was. Her luminous skin beckoned him, her pouting nipples called for his lips and tongue, the flare of her hips attracted his hands, and her thighs . . . and the blond thatch of curls between her legs . . .

His cock, hard almost to pain before, now began to throb, and he fought the urge to simply spread her legs and thrust himself into her warm depths. But he couldn't act like a rutting bull. She was his soul mate. Control, he told himself, control. Remember, she hasn't done this in a while.

He gave her a light kiss and stood straight to remove the remainder of his clothing.

Francie just lay there and watched. She'd known he was strong; his arms around her had been steel bands and he had lifted her easily. She'd known he had a rangy build; she'd felt it under his clothes and seen it in the way he wore his basketball uniform. But she hadn't known how his unclothed body exuded masculinity, a gorgeous maleness of long bones and lean muscles, a contoured chest lightly sprinkled with curly dark hair that drew the eye downward to a flat stomach and farther to his manhood rising from its own nest of curls. Her fingers itched to explore him, and she held out her arms to him. "Come here."

He slid onto the bed and she turned so they faced each other, lying on their sides. When he took her in his arms and pulled her close with no barriers between them, it felt so unabashedly *right*, so excruciatingly *good*. She groaned with pleasure.

"Oh, yeah," Clay purred, "we fit together perfectly." He lowered his head to hers.

Their lips met, tongues played, legs intertwined, and hands explored. Her fingers speared through his chest hair, felt his abdomen quiver, noted the play of his back and shoulder muscles, and kneaded his buttocks. His stroked her breasts, traced the line of her rib cage to the flare of her hips, drew her top leg over his hip, and stroked all the way to the bottom of her foot and back up. He kissed her so tenderly she thought she would cry.

Smiling. She could feel him smiling against her lips, and she smiled in response. He drew back, and their gazes locked for a long moment. His silver eyes shone, bright with desire.

Her brown eyes were no longer smoky, but burning with a golden flame far in their depths. Just for me, Clay thought, and he murmured, "Francie . . . "

"Clay . . . "

He caressed her breasts, molding, teasing the nipples with his thumb, and the resulting sensations caused her to thrust her hips forward, sliding her soft, damp folds along his rigid shaft nestled between her legs.

Her movement made him catch his breath. Oh, God, it was almost too much. He had never had such an explosive reaction to a woman or her touch before. On the contrary, he'd always been able to draw out his lovemaking for the better part of an hour until it was the woman who trembled, not he. Not so with Francie, it appeared. Not so with his soul mate.

Shaking with the effort, he clamped down on his control. He had meant to take this slowly, to entice, to linger, to savor, but his hunger and need demanded release, and every movement of her body, every soft moan from her throat, every urging clasp of her hands told him she felt the same. "Not too fast, Francie," he cautioned, his voice raspy with the effort to speak through his lust.

Kissing her fiercely, he turned her onto her back. He let his mouth travel down her throat, he paid homage to her breasts with his lips, and he teased her navel with his tongue as he moved between her legs. He settled himself and turned his attention to her silken inner thighs, then to the nest of curls with their hidden secrets. Kissing her intimately, he worked the small bud of nerve endings with his tongue.

Sensations spilling through her, Francie arched her back, began writhing, then panting, as tension spiraled tighter and tighter within her. She was on fire, and her body urged her on. She had no experience with these tumultuous feelings, this sharp edge of desire, this ruthless demanding need, but her body knew there was *more*.

She didn't want him *down there*; she wanted him *up here*, she wanted him *inside her*, and she wanted him *now*. Fisting her hands in his dark hair, she hauled his head up. "Clay," she gritted, *"come here. Now!"* And she tugged on his hair.

A hard, primitive look on his face, he surged up her body, braced himself straight-armed above her, and locked eyes. Slowly, inexorably, he thrust himself into her.

He was thick and long, and she could feel herself stretching to accommodate him, her unused muscles protesting, then accepting. She placed her hands on his arms to hold on and lifted her legs to grasp him around the hips, arching to take him deeper.

"That's right, darlin'. Take all of me," he groaned. He pulled back a little, pushed forward, then repeated the motion until he was seated to the hilt.

At the moment of complete joining, they both froze, suspended in the moment, as a rush of electricity rippled through their bodies.

"You're mine now," he stated fiercely, his expression savage.

"Yes," she agreed in a whisper, "and you're mine." He stretched her, filled her, completed her. She felt his possession in her bones.

He began to move in long, powerful thrusts.

Around them, Francie thought the air seemed to shimmer, turn all the colors of the rainbow, as they gazed at each other, intent on their rhythm, their uniting. The rest of the world receded from her senses until only the two of them existed. They and their need to complete this act, to become one, to fuse together, to merge, to mate.

She met him, her hips rising to bring him closer, her body straining as tension mounted within her. Each time, at the moment of his maximum penetration, she tightened around him, and a raw cry forced itself from her throat, echoed by a corresponding low growl from his. He increased the pace until it took her breath, the strain became an exquisite torture, the intensity almost too much to bear. She seemed to be standing on a cliff's edge, hanging right over the unknown abyss below, hanging . . . hanging . . .

A burst of colors blinding her eyes, she suddenly convulsed, waves of pleasure racking her body as it clenched around him. She heard herself cry his name. Then all she could do was hold on to him.

With a harsh, guttural groan and the word, "Francie," he went over the sharp edge with her, pounding with quick, hard thrusts as he emptied into her.

Clay collapsed into her arms and lay there stunned, laboring to breathe, multicolored fireworks still going off on the backs of his closed eyelids. He thought he'd been prepared, certain he could bring her pleasure and satisfy himself.

Little did he know.

Their First Mating had gone far beyond his expectations. First it had been those fiery kisses, then the stupendous feeling of bare skin on bare skin. But transcendent could be the only description when he had finally thrust into her silky depths, the first time in his life he hadn't used a condom. Now he knew why the imperative demanded no barriers; the feeling of binding, of merging, of uniting into one being, was incomparable.

He felt euphoric and exhausted. Never had the act of making love meant so much, been so powerful, so intense, so compelling, so perfect. Never had he felt so much at peace.

Eventually he raised his head, lifted himself slightly to lessen his weight on her chest, and looked into her eyes. She gazed back, wonder and contentment on her face. He knew his expression mirrored hers.

He smiled, and she returned it. He kissed her, and she kissed him back.

"Soul mates," he murmured.

"Soul mates," she repeated.

He shifted one leg to the outside of hers and rolled until she was sprawled on top, but still joined with him. She lay her head half on his shoulder and half on the pillow while he rubbed his hands slowly up and down her back. He felt her breathing slow, her body relax and slide into sleep. He soon followed.

≈✳✷✲≈

He was floating, he became aware at some point, holding on to a smooth, warm, peach-scented, undulating body straddling his own, a body in whom he was still buried. He moved his hands, first down, then up.

Thighs, butt, hips, he identified and sighed with pleasure as he reached higher and found glorious breasts. He would like to see them swaying above him, but his eyelids were too heavy to open. Instead he concentrated on his tactile sense while his mind continued to hover in a blissful doze.

Smooth, soft hands glided over his chest, splayed through his chest hair, teased his flat nipples. A warm mouth kissed his shoulders, drifted across his collarbone and up one side of his neck. A teasing tongue tweaked his earlobe, and he would have squirmed but he was too filled with contentment to move. Except for the part of him that was thickening, growing longer and harder.

"Hmmmm," was all he could say. He felt rather than heard a chuckle from the body he was holding.

Alluring lips continued their journey along his jawbone, met his mouth for an instant, lifted off, then returned for a longer stay. A flirtatious tongue skimmed his lips, coaxed him to open his.

When he did, it thrust into his mouth and immediately engaged his own in play, advancing, retreating, tangling. Clay was suddenly, irrevocably awake, thoroughly aroused, and . . . completely inside Francie. She was kissing him like she had in his dreams. No, better. She was doing things to him even his heated imagination had not conjured up. When her inner muscles tightened, he felt himself harden and swell even more.

Francie tightened her fingers in his hair and broke the

kiss to lean back enough so their eyes could focus. She laughed in triumph at the success of her machinations.

She had awakened, still on top of Clay, still holding him inside her. She felt so happy, so glorious, so . . . *mated*. There was no other word for it. She lay there for a while, her head on his shoulder. She could feel him breathing, a steady in-and-out, in-and-out that seemed not to notice her weight. She could inhale his scent, a combination of cool shaving lotion, himself, and pure sex. She could hear his heart beat—it seemed to be beating in unison with her own.

Carefully, she had sat up and given his body the same sort of inspection he had given hers earlier. He was powerful even in repose with those silver eyes closed behind lids with spiky black lashes. She wished she were a sculptor, able to capture the strength lurking in his relaxed body, the anticipation of smooth movement one witnessed in large cats, the hardness of his muscles.

The beauty of his hands. Long fingers, blunt-cut nails, slightly callused, totally male. She knew she must have noticed his hands before, playing on the keyboard, playing with her. If she doubted he was a warlock, his hands would have convinced her as they magically drew trembling, fiery responses she hadn't known existed within her. It had to be magic.

Their mating had been glorious, beyond any of her expectations, certainly beyond her past experience. She'd never had an orgasm with Walt. He had never given, only taken. Now she knew what had been missing. Well, in truth, a lot more than an orgasm had been missing in that so-called relationship.

Nothing was missing from this one, she was certain. Not caring, not commitment, not trust, not passion. The passion in herself surprised her; she thought Walt had killed it. If so, Clay had resurrected it like a phoenix from the ashes, and the fire bursting forth shocked her.

Then there was love. What was it again, what Daria had said? "They are as in love with each other as it is possible for two people to be." She had yet to hear him say it, but then they hadn't done much talking after her apology.

No, she decided, nothing was missing.

Except . . . A tiny vibration in her soul-mate center gave her an idea: he had claimed her in their mating; now it was her turn to claim him.

Careful not to waken him, she had proceeded to have some fun. Now he was awake. She laughed again as she gazed into his rapidly heating eyes. "Hi," she purred and squeezed slightly with inner muscles.

"Hi to you, too," he answered, although his voice sounded strained.

"I'm not hurting you, am I?" Another little squeeze.

"Oh, no, not at all," he gritted, and his eyes darkened to black with just a sliver of silver showing at their rims. His hands flexed on her breasts, and lightning shot through her to her womb.

Still smiling, she leaned straight-armed on her hands and rose and fell slowly along his rigid length. Once. Twice.

The air shimmered in rainbow colors. His silver gaze fiercely bored into hers, and he arched his body into her.

She lost her smile as she repeated her motions, increasing the speed. The rhythm captured them both until breath was short and a sheen of perspiration covered their bodies.

"You're mine. My soul mate," she told him, her tone fierce.

"And you're mine," he agreed, then pulled her mouth to his, as they both shattered in a bright flash of multi-colored lights.

CHAPTER TWENTY-SEVEN

Recovery came faster this time, Clay reflected as Francie slid off his body and he turned her to spoon himself around her back. His top arm hugged her to him, and she grasped his hand in hers and kissed it after he tried to use it to play with her breast. In retaliation, he kissed the nape of her neck and along her shoulder until she squirmed and nipped his finger.

"Ouch."

"See what happens when you mess with me?" She kissed the small hurt.

"Yes, ma'am."

Growl. Rumble.

"Was that me or you?" he asked.

"Both of us, I think. What time is it?"

"I don't know." He raised up enough to see his alarm clock on the chest by the bed. "Eight o'clock in the evening."

"What day?"

"Still Saturday, I think. When did you eat last?"

"Last night, I guess. I wasn't very hungry this morning."

"Well, come on, woman. We've got to eat something if we're going to keep this up!" He paused to give her a smacking kiss on the shoulder and a little pat on the behind. When she turned onto her back to give him a teasing glare, he leered, grinned, and promised, "And we are going to keep 'this' up."

He kissed her quick on the lips and levered himself out of bed. Disappearing into the walk-in closet, he called, "Don't put your jeans back on. I've got a robe you can wear."

"Okay." She headed for the bathroom. As she washed her hands and splashed water on her face, she inspected herself in the mirror. She didn't look any different than usual—or maybe she did. Her hair was all over the place, her skin looked flushed, her eyes sparkled. She looked well loved, she decided, and she was, she decided that, too. Funny, she felt no embarrassment or modesty about being naked in front of him. Must be all those years spent in locker rooms, she shrugged. Or maybe with soul mates, you just didn't care, just enjoyed looking at each other. She smiled in remembrance.

She grew sober as she dried her hands. She and Clay had to talk about being soul mates, discuss seriously what it meant, where they were going. She had to analyze what was happening to her, come to terms with her own reactions to him, with her newfound self-confidence where this particular man was concerned, with the idea of him in her life and her future.

But not this minute. Right now she was going to enjoy the situation and him—especially him.

She finger combed her hair, restored some order, and simply gave up on the rest. He was right, they needed food. When she came out of the bathroom, he was waiting with a dark red, silk robe held open and ready for her. He wore a tattered terry-cloth robe of an indeterminate color that might once have been blue.

She raised her eyebrows in speculation about the robe, then turned her back to him and slipped her arms into the sleeves.

He closed the robe around her, giving her a hug in the process. "A present from Daria," he clarified.

"I need a shower," Francie said, wondering if he could read her mind.

"We'll bathe after we eat," Clay said. "I've heard several times from my stomach, and I'd just as soon appease that first. Come on, let's see what we can find in the kitchen."

Francie's stomach gave a growl, and she laughed. "I agree with you."

They went down to the kitchen and turned on the lights. "How does some pasta with my mother's sauce sound? I have some in the freezer she gave me the last time I visited. It would be quick," Clay suggested.

"Sounds wonderful. Do you have anything for a salad?"

"Check the fridge." He pulled a large pot out of one of the cabinets.

She opened the refrigerator door and stood back in amazement. "My goodness."

"What?"

"There's so much food in here."

"What did you expect? Cold pizza and beer?"

"Well . . ."

He laughed. "My mother's training was thorough. I prefer my own cooking to eating out or buying takeout all the time."

They prepared the meal as if they had been doing it together for years, Francie thought as she sliced tomatoes and sprinkled them with olive oil, basil, and a bit of pepper. Clay opened a bottle of red wine, and in a short time they were spooning Parmesan cheese over linguini with a rich red tomato-and-mushroom sauce.

Neither spoke until they each had three forkfuls in their stomachs.

"I feel like I'm just shoveling it in," Francie said before she took the next bite.

"Me, too," Clay nodded, then took a swig of the wine. "I've never been this hungry after . . . uh . . . before . . . uh . . ." He flushed and took a bigger gulp.

She couldn't help but smile inwardly at his discomfort. Of course, he'd been with other women; she recalled what Daria had told her about male practitioners. All their testosterone, indeed. But he was hers now, so she'd let him off the hook—for the moment—by ignoring the statement.

Then he looked even more uncomfortable and swallowed his bite in a big gulp. "Oh, Lord, I forgot," he said, with an almost-stricken look on his face.

"Hmm?" was all she could say around a bite of tomato.

"In all this talk about soul mates, did Daria mention the bit about barriers, or did Glori cast any spells on *you*?"

"Yes, both. *That's* been taken care of."

"Oh, good." He applied himself to the pasta again.

"This hunger we have?" she said between bites. "Do you think it's a result of our First Mating?"

"I don't know. We did expend an awful lot of energy there," he said, waggling his eyebrows at her.

Francie could feel herself blushing and decided a diversion was in order. "Speaking of energy, I could have sworn different-colored lights, or fireworks, or lightning, or something was in the air. Now don't get your ego inflated," she warned in the face of his distinctly smug grin, "I'm serious. Glori and Daria ran a couple of experiments on me, and I could see a little flash of light when Daria cast a spell. It was like that, only much more intense."

Clay stared at her a moment, then chewed and swallowed. "You know, I did see them. The lights were stronger the second time."

"I agree. Could it be another manifestation of the imperative?"

"We'll have to ask my parents. Mother has been doing quite a bit of research into the phenomenon. Daria and Bent haven't mentioned anything like it." He took another bite of tomato, then another swallow of wine. "We're forgetting something else—the notion that the First Mating might increase powers."

"Daria said something about that. How do you know if it did?"

"The surest indicator is to cast *lux*. That's the light-ball spell. Its color will give you an idea. Let's see." Clay snapped his fingers.

A six-inch globe of swirling blue with a few streaks of indigo light hovered over the table.

"Wasn't it just bright blue before?" Francie asked. "What do the different colors mean?"

"Yeah, it was." He stared at it for a moment. "I guess my potential maximum level has gone up. The colors indicate levels, and levels indicate how much power a practitioner has or can aspire to. The colors match the spectrum and after that go up through silver and gold to white. Someone who can only cast a red ball is level one or two. Blue, where I was, is level nine to ten. These designations aren't exact because there are so many variables, like the type of talent you have and how much you study. If you don't study, then you may never reach the potential your color designates."

"That's right, you mentioned the 'practice' part of practitioner. Glori's ball was indigo and violet, as I remember."

"Yeah, she's up around level twelve to thirteen. The top is twenty. She's the highest in the family, even higher than Mother. Mother tops out about ten, and Dad about nine. Anything above ten is rare and very difficult to attain. After ten, the requirements go up exponentially with each level."

"What about Daria?"

"Because she can't cast *lux*, nobody knows for sure. She's worked with some of the masters, however, and they think she's a five or six." He looked at Francie with a speculative glint in his eye. "Then there's you. I wonder what the mating brought you, Francie. How do you feel?"

She blinked, then ran a quick mental inventory of her parts. "Fine. I feel fine. A few muscles are sore, but I don't feel like anything changed . . . outside of the obvious, I mean," she hastily added in reaction to Clay's raised eyebrows and "Oh, really?" look. "Daria and Glori decided I was sensitive to spells. Maybe the mating enhanced that."

"I have a hunch those lights indicate more than sensitivity, but I don't know what. Now that I think of it, I felt like we were in the middle of a fireworks display the second time." He paused, then grinned. "Wouldn't it be something if you did become a practitioner, though?" An intrigued look crossed his face. "Let's try something."

He rose, rummaged around in a drawer, pulled out some candles, and said, "Come on," as he went out the kitchen door.

Totally puzzled, Francie followed Clay to his bar-beque grill outside on the patio.

He pulled the top off the globular grill and wedged a candle into the rungs of the grill rack. "Let's see if you can light a candle. That's *flamma*, the simple spell every practitioner starts with. Here, stand back here with me." He moved them about six feet from the grill.

"I don't know about this, Clay," Francie said. "I feel really foolish, if you want to know the truth, standing here barefoot in a robe, thinking I'm going to cast a spell. Besides, I don't know how to go about it. What if I start a fire? Assuming, of course, I can make anything happen at all."

But he wasn't going to let her off the hook. "You won't know if you don't try," he coaxed. "Don't worry, novices don't have much power, and you can't hurt the grill. Okay, here's what you do. Spell-casting uses energy, your personal energy. To light the candle, what I do is visualize a small, hot bit of energy, a spark, right here," he touched his magic center, "and I mentally move it to a spot right on the end of the candle wick. Like this." He snapped his fingers.

The candle wick glowed, then lit as though a match had been applied.

"You reverse the process to put it out."

The candle went out at his snap.

"Now, take a deep breath, but don't hold it, keep breathing, and try it. Concentrate right on the spot where you want the flame. You don't have to snap your fingers. Mother waves her hand and Dad just frowns at the wick. Just do whatever you feel like doing."

Francie shot him an extremely dubious glance, but his excitement was inciting hers, so she focused on the candle. She thought about her SMI center, which had begun to itch slightly, and visualized a tiny little flame in there. She tried moving the flame from inside her chest to the outside air.

The flame, the energy bit, the spark, whatever it was, didn't seem to want to move, however. It just sat there in her center. She did feel slightly warmer there, but she told herself it was just her imagination.

She closed her eyes and tried to play it out like a movie on the back of her forehead. She could see the spark move from herself to the candle and the wick start to glow, but when she opened her eyes, the picture vanished, and nothing happened. Except the itch got stronger.

She sighed. "I don't think this is working, Clay."

"No feeling of warmth? No little zap? It's what happens to me."

"Nothing. Not really. Except I'm itching again." She rubbed the spot. "I thought Daria said the itching went away with the First Mating."

"God, I hope so, because I'm itching, too." He scratched his chest. "Look, it doesn't matter, your not being able to cast *flamma*, I mean. I might not be teaching you correctly."

"Or, more likely, I simply can't cast any spell at all. I'll admit, it would be intriguing to be able to do that, and it's fun to think about, like daydreaming what you would do with the money if you won the lottery. I do believe you and your family and other practitioners can work magic, but the idea I can, well, that's pretty far-fetched to me."

"Yeah, Mother did say she hasn't been able to find any evidence a nonpractitioner gained the power from mating. I just sorta hoped, I guess." He gave her a quick kiss. "But enough of this. Let's shove the dishes into the dishwasher and go take our own shower. We have a First Mating to enjoy."

Enjoy was the operative word, Francie discovered in Clay's oversized shower stall. Shampooing, soaping, and rinsing became opportunities to explore each other's bodies: slide here, rub there, be sure to remember to rinse before tasting. She had never received such a thorough shampoo or had such an attentive shampooer. His large, long-fingered hands massaged her scalp and the back of her neck until she felt like purring. She had never known the delight of running her hands over slick hard muscles and hair-roughened skin. Her own fingers traced the line of his shoulders, measured the width of his chest, and almost satisfied her craving to touch and explore his wonderful body.

But when he bent her backward over his arm to suckle at her breasts, her pleasure turned to hunger and she rubbed her mound against him. When that wasn't enough, she twisted one leg around his and ground herself against his rigid erection.

Clay needed no further invitation. He had been hard and ready since they entered the shower. He slid his hands from her back to her buttocks, gripped, lifted, braced her against the wall, and with an exultant "Ahhhh!" drove into her. Just where he wanted, was meant, to be.

She wrapped her arms around his neck and her legs around his hips. His thrusts forced from her little grunts that soon became words: "Yes, yes, yes."

He took the words from her mouth, sealed them in with his lips, and answered them with his tongue. As he thrust, each time reaching deeper into her hot depths, lights appeared again on the backs of his eyelids. He raised his head and opened his eyes. The lights were still there, around them, intermixed with the water falling from the shower. It was like being inside a rainbow in a rainstorm.

Her eyes shut, Francie moaned, tugged at him to return to the kiss.

"Look, Francie," he murmured, pumping his hips again.

Her eyes slitted open, but her gaze was groggy.

"Look at the lights," he said.

"Yes," she whispered, "yes, yes, yes," and she brought her ravenous mouth up to his.

To hell with the lights, Clay thought—his last bit of consciousness for a while. He thrust again, certain this one had to touch her womb, and felt her go over the edge. He followed into oblivious ecstasy.

His senses finally returned as her legs loosened from around him and they disengaged. She slid limply down his body. He held her until he was sure she could stand on her own, then stepped back. "Francie?"

"Hmmmm?" she said. She blinked at him sleepily.

He laughed. "Come on, let's get ourselves dry and go back to bed."

"All right," she agreed dreamily, pleasantly, as though he had suggested a walk in the park.

Not until he was rubbing the towel over her did she wake up. "Wow," she said. "What train was that?"

"I don't know, the SMI Express, I guess."

"Is this the way it usually is, the First Mating, I mean?"

"I have no idea. Nothing anybody told me prepared me for this, this . . ."

"Explosiveness?"

"That's as good a word as any." He gave her hair a final rub. "There. Enough."

He gave her a little push out the bathroom door and followed her to the bed. She flopped down and burrowed into the mattress. He thought she was probably asleep before he could get around to his side. Once his head hit the pillow, he was gone, too.

CHAPTER TWENTY-EIGHT

Pain!

Francie jerked upright in the bed, almost doubled over, her hands pressing into her center. Spasms of agony radiated from it to all parts of her body. She could barely get her breath. The distress diminished as she rubbed, and she realized Clay was sitting up also. Even in the not-quite dark, she could see he was massaging *his* breastbone.

"What happened?" she panted. "Where did that come from?"

"I don't know," he answered with a hoarse, shaky rasp. "I was dreaming of you . . ."

"I was dreaming about you . . ."

"And I felt this horrible need . . ."

"And I wanted you so badly . . ."

He turned toward her and flipped the covering sheet down to the end of the bed. He reached out his hand toward her chest. "Does it hurt?"

She reached toward his chest. "Not so much now.

Does yours?"

Their fingers touched each other's center at the same time. Energy surged between them, as if a circuit had been completed, and they both gasped.

Her gaze leaped to his. Rainbow lights began to play around them, and in the brightness she could see his gaze turn hot, his expression become fierce. He moved between her legs with the speed of a panther, pushed her down flat, mounted her, then entered her with a powerful, passionate thrust that forced a cry from her throat. The raw energy raging in their centers roared down their bodies and through this new link, completing the final circuit.

Both cried out again as lightning coursed through them, but their eyes remained locked on each other's and their hands maintained the initial contact on their centers. For a long moment, neither stirred. Then the spectrum burst around them, and Clay began to move with great driving thrusts that raised her off the bed. She wrapped her legs around his thighs and, curving like a bow, rose to meet him.

She was drowning in his molten silver eyes, coming apart under the force of his savage possession. And she reveled in it. *More*, her body screamed. *More!*

Tightening every muscle she owned when he was fully inside her, she bore up on him, trying to take more, to get closer, to make herself such a part of him and him such a part of her they could never come apart.

The energy rushing between them raced faster, threw

off sparks, doubled and redoubled in power.

It was agonizingly painful.

It was excruciatingly exquisite.

They seemed to be melting, flowing together, reaching for something, reaching . . .

Until . . .

There it was, there, there, there.

Fusion.

The light around them changed, became only red, then rippled through the spectrum. Red, orange, yellow, green, blue, indigo, violet.

Silver. Gold. Pure, dazzling white.

Blinded, she screamed, her body arching to his as ecstasy rolled through her like a huge tidal wave and hammered her hips against his.

Her convulsion triggered his own.

The brilliant white light rendered him sightless, but he didn't need vision to pour himself into her, empty himself, in contractions that went on and on and on. Exhilaration, exaltation, and absolute joy speared through his body, increased with every tight hug in her embrace, and exploded into sheer rapture.

He was certain he was dying. No one could stand this much pleasure and live. When they had touched each other's center, he had been suddenly filled with a lust that turned his cock into granite and produced an overwhelming need to bury himself in her. His only remedy for the wild desire, his only solace from the potent pain, would be with her, in her.

As they joined and he felt the soft, hot clasp of her body, saw the golden flames in her smoky brown eyes, and shook from the intensity of the energy surge, he knew they would never be completely apart again. The link had been melded in a white-hot crucible and forged into permanence with hammer blows of enormous power.

When sight and sanity returned, he found himself lying on her, his face buried half in the pillow and half in her neck. Her arms lay limp around him, as did her legs. He didn't want to move. He wasn't sure he could. He could reach her neck with his lips, so he kissed her, felt her pulse beating with his tongue. Her hands flexed and so did her inner muscles.

The little jolt of electricity resulting from the small squeeze gave him the energy to rise to his elbows. He looked down into her eyes, all smoky again. "Are you all right?"

Francie nodded, although it was difficult to move. She had to clear her throat to speak. "I . . . I think so. What was that?" The knowledge came to her unbidden, but certain, with such a depth and rightness, it could not be denied. "That was power, magical power, wasn't it?"

"Had to be. When I've cast a really powerful spell, I've gotten a buzz, but I've never felt anything like it. We could have lit up Houston." He gave her a little kiss, then frowned. "Where did it come from? We woke up hurting, and I remember reaching for you. It started when

I touched your center and you touched mine, didn't it? An energy surge?"

"I think so. It was like we were connected." She broke their eye contact and looked around, running her gaze over his body. "Clay, I can still see some lights around us. They're faint, but they're there."

He turned his head to the side. "You're right. Hold on, let me slide off you." He maneuvered himself and her so they were lying on their sides, facing each other, legs intertwined. He was still inside her, but their chests did not touch.

"Let's try it again. You touch my center and I'll touch yours."

They touched. Both jumped at the slight zap, but they didn't break contact.

"That was like an electric shock," Francie said. "And I feel the tingle all over inside. I think the lights are brighter."

Clay glanced down their bodies. "Yeah, they are." He studied the lights for a few seconds. "What this looks like to me is a magical aura. I've seen one on Daria when she has spelled herself. The lights form sort of a frame, shaped like your body, but standing off it a little. Do you see it?"

Francie raised her head to peer around. "Yes. Take your hand away." They cut the contact. "That dimmed the lights quite a bit, but not entirely. I still feel, oh, I don't know, 'current' running inside me."

"So do I. But we're still connected." He looked down their bodies to the place where they joined. He withdrew from her slowly. Both caught their breath at the moment of separation. "No current."

"Me, either. The lights are dimming, but still there. Scoot over until we're not touching at all." When they split completely, Francie said, "They just went off entirely."

"For me, too." He flopped over on his back and rubbed his chest. "Well, that was the damnedest thing I ever saw or experienced. I know Dad says being soul mates just gets better all the time, but if we go through this every time, it's going to kill us both."

She propped herself up on an elbow. "If the imperative's causing this, it didn't hurt us, did it? I mean, I feel fine now—exhausted, but fine." She yawned, a big jaw-breaking yawn that she felt to her toes.

"Yeah." He copied her yawn, then stretched up and looked at his bedside clock. "Two in the morning. Let's get some sleep—if the damn SMI will let us." He lay back down and pulled her into his arms. "Do you see any lights?"

"No. Everything is dark again," she answered.

"Good." He snuggled her closer.

Francie felt him fall into sleep. She yawned again, as she considered the previous minutes. What had happened? Except for absolutely stupendous lovemaking, *what*? The two of them, when literally together, created some sort of "aura" around themselves. Would this continue, or would the lights fade over time? What did the surge of power mean?

Had the SMI done something to her? She didn't feel any different. Well, no, that wasn't a correct statement. She did feel different, in a state of absolute well-being. Well loved and in love. As if she was complete, had found her other half. A little hum in her center seemed to confirm these notions.

As for the magic? The lights, the lightning between them? It must have been the SMI sealing the bond between the two of them. Daria had said the First Mating did that very thing. She, Francie, had assumed the process was just one act of lovemaking, but Clay was treating it like it was a series of acts, like a honeymoon. What had he said? "We have a First Mating to enjoy."

His reasoning made more sense. The First Mating wasn't one event, but a series. The last event, with the lights and the power, was the culmination of the bonding. Clay had received more power. She had received her soul mate. It was all magic.

As for herself being able to cast spells? She almost snorted in self-ridicule. Such a notion was too fantastic.

She yawned again and felt his arm tighten around her in response to her movement. She couldn't help smiling even as sleep overcame her.

CHAPTER TWENTY-NINE

While Francie slept Sunday morning, Clay ran to the store in the West University Village and brought back bagels and cream cheese. They were lingering over breakfast and the newspaper in his sunny kitchen when he put down his section and regarded his soul mate. He couldn't help feeling content, appreciative, and, to be truthful, smug. She was his, she was gorgeous, and they mated perfectly, if he did say so himself.

Francie glanced up and raised her eyebrows in interrogation at his look.

"I'm just enjoying having you here," he said. "And I'm happy we can make love without electrocuting ourselves." They had woken up to sunlight and had made slow, absolutely glorious love—without the fireworks of the previous time.

"Me, too," Francie said. "Although I did see some colored lights."

"So did I. But they were much dimmer than before.

Maybe the SMI is finally settling down." He took a gulp of coffee. "I've been thinking about those lights. I wonder if anybody else could see them."

"Clay Morgan, I am not letting anyone watch us when we make love, just to see if they can see lights. I am not an exhibitionist."

"Calm down, darlin'. We'll just have to note when they appear. If they show up when all we do is kiss, then it would be all right to show someone, wouldn't it?"

"I guess," she answered grudgingly. "Maybe." She went back to the story she was reading about the Houston Rockets.

Clay grinned to himself. She was so cute when she was disgruntled. He also turned to the paper and began reading a story in the business section about a startup high-tech firm. The name of one of the founders caught his eye. Walter Somebody. Walter. *Walt*. The guy in the paper was only twenty-four, so he couldn't be Francie's Walt. Clay suddenly burned with the need to know about Walt the Asshole. Would she tell him? He'd never know until he asked.

Clay put down his paper. "Francie, I have to ask you something."

She looked at him over the top of the sports section and seemed a little startled, a little apprehensive, probably by his tone, but she put down the paper. "What about?"

"Now, I'll only ask this once," he said, "and if you don't want to tell me anything, it's okay. I don't particularly want to talk about it, either, but curiosity is eating me up, and after all you've said to me, I'd really like to know."

The expressions on her face ran from apprehension to concern to puzzlement. "What is it, Clay?"

"Who's Walt?"

"Walt?"

"Yeah, Walt."

She grimaced. "I was hoping you'd forget I ever mentioned him."

"I can't. Not after being compared to him. I assume he's part of the 'old mental baggage' you referred to yesterday."

She fiddled with her spoon, then her knife, and took a sip of coffee. She was clearly not happy with the subject.

"I swear, I'll never bring up the name again," he said, holding up his right hand, palm out.

She put down the paper, then took a deep breath and exhaled. "All right. I'll tell you. But like you did with me, ask no questions till I'm done. Okay?"

Now he was the apprehensive one, but he nodded. "Okay."

"You have to understand something," she began with a soft voice. "I 'developed' late." She waved her hand at her body. "When I was growing up, I was often, usually, taller than the boys, and I was a skinny, scrawny smart kid. I was also basketball crazy. I caught the computer bug early, too.

"In high school, boys became my buddies, either

because I could beat them in basketball or because I could help them with their computers." She shrugged in a self-deprecating motion. "I had no real dates in high school. By the time I entered college, I figured I was destined not to have any boyfriends, ever."

Clay watched her closely, a little sorry he had asked the question he could now see—despite her feigned nonchalance—how painful it was for her to discuss this, but he had to know. He nodded to indicate he understood her situation.

"So," she continued, "I decided to make the most of my intellectual abilities. My parents always stressed using my mind over my body. Daddy used to tell me my brain would certainly last longer than my speed on a court. They supported me in basketball, and if I had wanted to go out for the varsity team, they would have been just as proud as they were I was the high-school valedictorian. But I was more excited about and fascinated with computers, and I turned down athletic scholarships for academic ones."

She flashed him a happy grin. "I met Tamara the very first day at UT, and it was friendship at first sight for both of us. She already knew she wanted to open a fashion boutique and was going after a marketing degree. She was also already a clotheshorse, dressed in the latest fashions. She claimed to be envious of my tall, skinny body, and she helped me learn how to dress for my height. Then . . ."

Clay could picture Francie skinny, but it took *all* his powers of imagination. Or maybe, he simply liked her as she was now—curvy and definitely not skinny. Liked? Lusted. He confined his response to one word. "Then?"

"Somewhere late during my freshman year, I started developing a female figure. By the beginning of my sophomore year, I had, uh, 'bloomed.' Tamara called me a 'guy magnet' and claimed when men's eyes traveled down my long legs and back up to my, uh, top, they almost popped out of the guys' heads. I felt like I was instantly 'popular,' and Tamara talked about beating men off me with a stick. But all my dates turned out to be, at best, back in the buddy category or, at worst, wrestling matches."

She stopped to take another sip of coffee, and Clay knew the worst part of her tale was coming. Francie wasn't looking into his eyes, but off into the distance while her fingers fidgeted with her napkin.

"Anyway, by the new year, I had just about given up on finding any man who would see my brain as well as my body. That's when I met Walt."

Clay had to restrain himself from growling at the sound of the name. He forced himself to remain calm. She'd never tell him all of it if he acted like a possessive lunatic.

"Walt Gibbons was a tall, blond, good-looking engineering major and a senior. He seemed truly interested in me, my mind, not just its housing. He was kind, considerate, attentive. I guess the correct phrase is the old cliché, 'he swept me off my feet.' I was in love, I thought. We became lovers."

This time Clay couldn't quite hold in his feelings. Francie jumped, and he disguised the snarl with a cough. He motioned for her to continue.

"One day late in the school year, Tamara and I were in a restaurant on Sixth Street. We were sitting in a high-backed booth, you know, the kind where the back goes up about five or six feet. You can't see your neighbors, but if they're talking loudly enough, you can hear them."

Clay nodded.

"We heard these guys talking in the booth next to us, and we recognized Walt's voice. I was going to pop my head around the booth and say hello, when one of the others mentioned my name, said something about losing some bet that included me."

Clay groaned. He had a pretty good idea what was coming. "Francie, you don't have to tell me any more," he said, reaching a hand to her across the table.

"No, I started it, I'll finish it," she responded and went on in a flat tone, but Clay could hear the anger behind it. "Walt proceeded to brag about how easy I'd been, how much of a disappointment I was in bed, how relieved he was he could drop me now he'd won the bet, and then he talked about his next target. Tamara and I just sat there and listened to it all. After they left, she took me back to the dorm and listened while I cried and raged until I got Walt out of my system."

The smile on her face told him the memories were bitter ones. He could easily imagine her anger—it was the same outrage gripping him now.

"He called the next day," she continued, "and I told him I wanted nothing more to do with him and hung up on him. He came up to me between classes, made some cutting remarks while we were standing in front of the student union. I told him off, right there in front of God and everybody, and he left me alone after that.

"During the summer at home, I decided I didn't need men, especially handsome, charming ones, to whom I didn't matter as a person. All that type of man wanted to do was use me. I was sufficient unto myself. That's the story of Walt."

She took a deep breath, then let it out. "When you and I first met, I'm afraid I automatically put you in the same category as Walt, afraid you'd be like him and I'd end up alone. My fears got the better of me. So I was fighting you and the imperative to avoid going through the pain again. I'm sorry for hurting you and for comparing you to someone who's not fit to be in the same room with you." She looked at him with a face full of contrition.

Clay stood and pulled her out of the chair and into his arms. "Thank you, Francie. That's all I wanted to know. I'll never ask again." He kissed her lightly and then just held her, rubbing her back. Her muscles were tight, and he could feel the strain in them brought on by her tale.

He didn't need to hear any more; he knew what had happened. After what Walt did to her, she had started wearing clothes to hide her body. She had barricaded herself behind those big glasses, too, hoping to force men to acknowledge her mind. She probably thought men couldn't see past them, but he knew differently. The only ones who had been able to get past her defenses, however, had also been smart enough not to let her know it—the gamesters, for example. He wasn't worried about Walt any longer, but he had to be sure she understood one very important thing.

He lifted her chin with a finger so he could see her eyes. "Francie," he murmured, "you are definitely *not* a disappointment in bed to me."

She smiled, then the smile grew into a grin, and a sparkle came into her eyes. "Well, I should think not. Not after all those fireworks!" she said with mock indignation.

"Would you like me to go after Walt? Beat him up or something?"

"No, of course not. I have no idea what happened to him, and I don't care."

"Okay, but if we ever meet him, just say the word and I will make his life miserable. All it takes is a few spells and every computer he owns, desktop, laptop, handheld gadget, cell phone, watch, car, microwave, hell, I don't know, his cable connection, all of them will fry completely."

Francie started laughing and gave him a big hug.

"No, let's just forget him."

"Okay with me." He gave her another kiss. "How about if we go to the grocery store? We're running out of provisions."

"Fine, but I need to go home and change clothes. I can't run around like this all the time." She waved at the robe she was wearing.

"But I like you so . . . accessible." He gave her immediate frown a friendly leer. "But all right. We'll go by your place. I'll clear the breakfast dishes. You get dressed."

Francie climbed the stairs, walked into the bedroom, and realized this was the first time they had been apart, if you didn't count trips to the bathroom and his excursion for bagels. But she had slept so hard, she hadn't even known he was gone until he returned and waved a cup of coffee under her nose, so she didn't count it.

She needed the break, she decided, as what she had told him about Walt came back to her. Talking about the scumbag hadn't been as hard as she thought it might. Clay had given her just the right amount of support when she had finished. She almost had to laugh at what he considered the most important part of his support—that she wasn't disappointing in bed. All that testosterone, indeed.

Remembering his offer to wreak vengeance on Walt did make her laugh out loud. His method had been the exact one she had thought of way back then, but she'd had no means to bring it about. Revenge on Walt didn't matter now. She had Clay.

They still hadn't talked seriously about the future, and she had thought he was going to bring it up at the table. She had felt abruptly unprepared for such a talk. She knew she wanted to be with him forever, so that wasn't the cause of her qualms. It was more like she was waiting for something else to happen.

At that thought, her center tingled slightly. "Is that a yes?" she asked it as she hunted for her sneakers.

No answer, of course.

CHAPTER THIRTY

"By the way, what's your schedule for this week?" Clay asked as they pulled into the parking area at her apartment.

Francie winced. She'd forgotten all about her previous plans. She might as well tell him all of it, she decided. "As a matter of fact, I intended to take this week off. I was going to leave town."

"What? Why?" He looked first outraged, then a little hurt.

"Because I thought getting away from you would give me time to rest, to come to terms with the situation. I was originally going yesterday morning, but something kept holding me back, I couldn't get organized, and then your sisters came over . . . and we know how that turned out."

"Thank God for the 'something.' Must have been the good ol' SMI at work." He flashed a cocky grin at her. "I knew it was on my side all along."

She gave him an oh-for-Pete's-sake look and rolled

her eyes. Soul mate or not, the man's confidence could be downright annoying.

Walking up to the apartment after collecting the mail, they ran into Tamara carrying a load of laundry. The redhead's eyes grew large when she saw the two of them together.

"Hi, Tamara," Clay called out cheerfully.

Tamara marched right up to them. "Does this mean you two are back together? You've made up?" she asked, looking pointedly at their clasped hands and Francie's wrinkled clothes.

Trust Tamara to come right to the point, Francie thought as she opened her mouth to answer.

Clay beat her to it. "Yep, we're definitely together," he announced with a big, broad smile.

"Great! I am so happy you worked things out," Tamara said, with a big grin of her own.

"I'm sorry the situation with Brenner didn't end better," Clay said.

"He's such a rat," Tamara replied. "I'm just glad I don't have to see him anymore."

"Did you talk to Childress?" Clay asked.

"Oh, that's right," Francie interjected. "I didn't tell you about it." Or, she thought, about how their friendship had withstood the storm. She'd relate the story later.

"Yes, I did," Tamara answered, then winked. "And I wouldn't mind seeing more of him. That is one nice man. You wouldn't happen to know if he's married, would you?"

Clay laughed. "No, he's not married. So, good luck."

"Great. Look, I have to get this laundry done and then check in some inventory at the shop," Tamara said. "Will you be around later?"

"Come over about five and we'll go get some dinner," Francie said.

"Sounds good to me," Clay agreed.

"I'd like to hear how you took the sleazeball down. See you then." Tamara headed for the laundry room, and Clay and Francie climbed the stairs and entered Francie's apartment.

"I just can't keep my hands off you." Clay closed the front door and immediately took her in his arms and kissed her. By the end of the kiss, Clay's hands were under her shirt, and they were standing in a rainbow again. They held onto each other for a while.

"You know," Clay murmured, "we have to get control of this thing or we'll never get anything done. All I want to do is take you to bed."

"I've noticed," Francie said, giving her hips just a little push into his.

"Have some pity, darlin'," he groaned, "walking around with a permanent hard-on can be painful, not to mention embarrassing."

Now, there was a picture, Francie thought, stifling a giggle, but she suggested, "Let's try doing something to occupy our minds. You never did show me your computer spells.

Turn on my computer while I change into clean clothes."

"Sounds like a plan to me." He gave her a quick kiss and walked into her office.

By the time she joined him, Clay was playing Spider Solitaire, the hardest level with four suits. He was winning, of course.

"Do you have a spell active?" Francie asked as she pulled up the other chair. "I can never win this one."

"Madam, are you implying I'm cheating?" he asked in a snooty tone.

"No, of course not," she said hastily. She knew he wouldn't do that.

"Good. We computer wizards are touchy fellows, you know."

"Touchy-feely is more like it," she scoffed.

"You're right about that." He gave her thigh a squeeze. "But no, no spell." He won the game and closed the screen. "Now, let's see what we can do."

"Call up the program you loaded here when Kevin tried to hack."

"Good idea." He displayed the program.

Francie couldn't help but jump when the code came on the screen. "Oh, my goodness."

"What happened?"

She leaned toward the monitor, then sat straight up. What she was seeing didn't change. "I can see . . . a sort of bluish glow around the text. It's not strong, but it's there. And it wasn't when you showed me the program the first time."

"Hmmm. I wonder if we have found your soul-mate enhancement," Clay said. "Let's try this." He closed the program and returned the display to her regular desktop. He took his hands off the keyboard and reached down to lay one hand on the tower holding the computer's processing unit. He concentrated for a moment, then snapped the fingers of his free hand.

"Oh, my goodness," Francie said again as various windows opened and closed, programs began and ended on her monitor. Her word-processing application opened and displayed the last letter she had written, a spreadsheet showed a budget she and Tamara had created for the shop, and the project-management software exhibited the progress made on a task at work. Finally her e-mail in-box opened with the list of her most recent messages. She looked from the screen to Clay and back again.

"What do you see now?" Clay asked.

"The programs aren't glowing, but *you* are! There's a luminosity, sort of a flickering, around you *and* the tower. It's a solid color, sort of a dark blue. This must be the spell aura you were talking about."

"Okay. Now for something more complicated." Without touching the keyboard, he closed all the open windows except for the Internet connection. "My computer is turned on at home, and I'm always connected to the Internet. First, we'll access my machine . . . Here's my desktop. . . And here's the code for a little application

I've been working on."

Francie's jaw dropped as the displays changed to match his descriptions. "You can get in anywhere, into any computer you want to, can't you?"

"Probably. Hacking as a pastime or for the hell of it has never appealed to me. I have much more fun doing it for money, testing my clients' firewalls, or, conversely, catching people trying to hack them."

She sat back in her chair and looked from the screen to Clay. What a talent to possess. No hacker, especially not an inept one like Kevin, would stand a chance against Clay's abilities. His computing skills had impressed her before. Now . . .

She sighed in surrender. "After this demonstration, I have to admit, Clay, if I *had* given you the chance to show me what you could do with a computer, I probably *would* have believed you can work magic."

A huge grin broke out on his face, and he punched both fists in the air. "*I knew it!* I knew that's all I had to do. Daria and Glori tried to tell me differently, but I felt it, right here." He poked his finger at his magic center, then leaned over and gave her a big, smacking kiss. "You're definitely my soul mate, Francie."

"Wait a minute," she told him. If she let him get away with this, he'd be insufferably overconfident, not to mention arrogant, just like he was when they met. "What do you mean *all* you had to do? You could have broken it to me a little more gently, you know. Led me into it? Showed me the computer *before* you started talking about practitioners. I told you how I felt about the idea of real magic."

He had a distinctly worried look on his face, but she wasn't going to stop now. She was on a roll. "You might also have brought in Daria and Glori earlier. Their dragon and panther business definitely caught my attention, but the clincher was when Glori cured my headache."

"I know, darlin', I apologize. I'm just impatient, especially when it comes to you." He said the last with a big grin. "Besides, it doesn't matter now. We're together."

She shook her head. It was clearly going to be impossible to crack his rock-hard confidence. That was okay. He'd soon learn, if he didn't know it already, he couldn't run over her. "All right," she responded, "then what else can you do, oh great computer wizard?"

"Just watch this."

They stayed on the computer for the rest of the afternoon, jumping around the Internet, playing games, showing each other their favorite Web sites, and discussing the merits and demerits of various computer gadgets.

Finally Clay leaned back and stretched. "Wait until we get back to my place where we can play some of these games together on my network. I want to try out Conundrum on my machine."

"The gamesters are going to explode from ecstasy when they see your office," Francie grinned. They'd probably adopt him into the group on the spot.

The doorbell rang.

"Oh, my goodness, Clay, look at the time," she said. "It's almost five. I'll bet that's Tamara. You turn off the machine, and I'll let her in."

"Okay," he replied.

Francie rose and walked to her front door. She spied Tamara's red hair through the peephole and threw the door open wide. "Hi!"

Kevin and Tamara stood in the doorway. He held a gun to her head. "Hi to you, too," he snarled.

Francie, feeling like a bucket of ice water had just been poured down her back, looked from Tamara to the man behind her.

Kevin pointed the gun at Francie. "Back up, away from the door."

Francie backed up into the apartment until she was stopped by the couch. "Tamara?" she asked.

Tamara, her face deathly pale, whispered, "I'm sorry, Francie."

"Shut up and get in there, bitch!" Kevin ordered Tamara and pushed her over the threshold. Standing slightly behind her, he kept one hand on her shoulder and used the other to point the gun at the back of her head.

Francie kept her eyes on the twosome. Maybe she could maneuver them deeper into the living room, and Clay could attack Kevin from the rear. She had to alert Clay somehow, but nothing came to mind.

She didn't get the chance to do anything because Clay

came around the corner from the hall at that moment.

"What's going on?" The question died on his lips when he saw Brenner.

Kevin kicked the door shut behind him. "Oh, good, the big, bad computer hacker is here," he said in a snide falsetto, then dropped into his normal range. "Just the man I wanted to see next. I should have known all of you were in it together."

"What do you want, Brenner?" Clay asked in a low, lethal tone.

"Want? I want payback. You cost me my job and five thousand dollars."

"Why aren't you in jail, Kevin?" Francie asked, trying to keep her voice from shaking. Think, woman, think. Distraction, that was it. She had to distract him somehow so Clay might be able to jump him.

She moved slightly to the left to increase the distance between herself and Clay. As she would in basketball, she assumed a guarding posture, a slight crouch, hands spread and out in front, weight distributed, but ready to move in any direction. She glanced at Clay, who moved forward, then stood in the deceptively relaxed posture he had used just before he exploded in a drive to the basket in their game.

"You two don't move," Brenner said, pressing the gun harder to Tamara's head as he turned to face Clay.

Tamara moaned and squirmed at the pressure of the gun.

Kevin gave her a shake. "Damn it, hold still!" He looked from Clay to Francie and back again. "I'm out on bail. I'm getting out of here, and I need money. You're going to get it for me."

"Why should we do that?" Clay asked.

"Because I'm going to hurt someone if you don't," Brenner said. "I was going to shoot Tamara, but I think Francie's a better target since you're here. Bigger, too."

"You won't get any money for sure if you do that," Clay told him.

"Oh, yes, I will, and it will give me a great deal of satisfaction to put a bullet in Miss High-and-Mighty." He shot a glance at Francie. "Oh, yeah, I know how much you don't like me, how you don't think I'm good enough for Tamara, how you tried to sabotage what we had going. The fact that you worked for Brazos made my idea perfect."

He turned back to Clay. "And if you'd helped me like you were supposed to, I'd have taken over my idiot boss's job in a flash."

"Brenner, you're a stupid son of a bitch," Clay said, shaking his head, an expression of absolute disgust on his face. "You're such a lousy hacker, Brazos caught you in the act before they ever called me in. And if you're as bad a salesman as you are with computers, then NatChem was just looking for an excuse to fire you."

"Bullshit," Kevin retorted. "NatChem loves me. I've been their top salesman for years. The new manager they brought in—he hates me, the jealous bastard. He's the one who gave me that bunch of losers for a sales team and no help with our competitors. I had great plans for kicking him out—plans you and this blond bitch here ruined. Now I want some money, a lot of money."

"Just how do you expect us to get it?" Clay asked. "It's Sunday, the banks are closed."

"We'll hit every ATM we can find. That's how."

"You're crazy, Brenner," Clay replied. "I'm not giving you a cent, and neither are Tamara or Francie."

The two men glared at each other and traded more threats and refusals, but Francie paid little attention. They had to get the gun away from Kevin, but he was practically screwing it into the back of Tamara's head. If she jumped him, it would probably go off. What could she do to distract him?

Damn the man! What a slimebucket! What an idiot! To think he could come in here and order them around, gun or no gun. The more she thought about it, the angrier she became. As she stared at Kevin, she could feel the heat of her anger rising.

Heat. Fire. That's what she would like to do to Kevin—burn him good. What she wouldn't give to be able to cast the *flamma* spell Clay had been trying to teach her. She'd charbroil the scumbag to a crisp.

Or maybe just a small piece of him. How nice, how satisfying it would be, to set Kevin's nose on fire. To place a little spark of red-hot energy right on the end of its rounded tip.

Her SMI center began to tingle slightly, then turn warm.

How dare Kevin pull a gun and hurt Tamara! How dare he threaten Clay! There was no way on God's green earth she was going to let the bastard get away with it. She wished she could literally send him to hell. Let the damn man rot in all the devil's flames till he roasted.

Her center grew warmer still as Kevin's next words brought her attention back to what he was saying.

"Cut the crap, Morgan. You're going to do what I tell you or else . . ." He grabbed Tamara's hair and jerked her head back. Tamara cried out. "Or else, I'm going to hurt somebody," Kevin snarled.

She had to do something, Francie decided. Where was all this magic when she needed it? What had Clay told her? To focus on the spot where she wanted the flame? She squinted her eyes and concentrated her gaze and her mind as hard as she could on the end of Kevin's nose. She could feel heat building inside her, right under her breastbone. The tingling transformed itself into a feeling of excitement, then exultation. The joy and the heat grew exponentially into a rapturous conflagration inside her. She was on fire!

"*Flamma!*" she cried and flung out her right hand, its finger pointed directly at Kevin's nose.

A tiny white-hot flash of flame appeared exactly where she was pointing.

"Aaaahhh! Shit!" Kevin yelled. He pushed Tamara away to bat at his nose with his free hand.

Clay jumped forward, knocked the gun out of Brenner's hand, and punched him in the mouth.

Francie couldn't see if the blood that spurted put out her flame, but she wasn't going to take any chances on Kevin. She cocked her arm and waded in.

Clay's blow threw Brenner backward. He hit the door, rebounded, and ran right into Francie's fist, which she buried in his stomach. He bent over with an "Oof."

"You jerk!" Screaming with rage, Tamara jumped on Kevin's back and started pummeling him about the head and shoulders.

"Turn him this way, Tamara!" Francie yelled and wound up for another go.

"Holy hell!" Clay swore with disgust as he watched the women attack Brenner. Now he had to rescue the asshole. He plucked Tamara off Kevin and held her back with one arm. He used the other to pull Francie from the man, who crumpled to the floor groaning and bleeding.

Tamara kicked and screamed, "Let me go! I'll kill him!"

Francie drew back her foot and shouted, "Rot in hell, you bastard!"

Just what he needed, a redheaded berserker in one hand and a blond amazon in the other. "*Ladies!*" he bellowed at the top of his lungs.

Panting, the two women subsided.

"Francie, call the cops," he ordered and gave her a

little shake. "And tell them to alert Bill Childress." He let her go.

Francie took a deep breath, shook herself, nodded at him, and went for the phone in the kitchen.

"Tamara, don't move, just stand here," Clay said. "Are you all right?"

"Almost." She made a move toward Brenner, but Clay pulled her back.

"He's not going to get up. Now, stay put, okay?"

"Okay," she agreed grudgingly and, glaring at Brenner, crossed her arms over her chest. Her body remained stiff with anger.

Clay let her go and bent to pick up the gun. Brenner for once had the good sense to say nothing; all he did was turn over on his back and groan again.

Francie came back in with some paper towels in her hand. "The police are on the way. Here, Kevin, use these." She dropped the towels by his head.

"Go on and sit up, Brenner," Clay said, "but don't do more than that."

Kevin gingerly sat up and pressed the towels against his nose. Clay was pleased to see the moron didn't try anything else. He himself was still angry enough to let Tamara finish the job of beating the jackass to a pulp— and he wouldn't mind getting in a few licks of his own.

"I hear sirens," Clay said. "What did you say to get them here so fast?"

"A man with a gun forced his way into the place and

was threatening to kill us."

"What did you do to Kevin that he started yelling and pushed me away?" Tamara asked. "I was looking at Clay because I was thinking I should faint or something and give him an opening to attack Kevin."

"I don't know," Francie said. An expression of wonder spread across her face, and she said again, "I don't know."

CHAPTER THIRTY-ONE

The police arrived in a cacophony of sirens that brought out the neighbors, and a pool of spectators formed at the bottom of the stairs. The officers took charge of Brenner, who demanded to be taken to a hospital. He claimed his nose was both broken and burned. They sat him in a squad car instead and told him to shut up.

Clay, Francie, and Tamara were sitting in Francie's living room when Bill Childress walked in. As the police lieutenant went straight to Tamara, Francie exchanged an eyebrows-lifted glance with Clay.

"Is everybody all right?" Bill asked, his eyes on Tamara.

Tamara nodded, and Clay said, "Everybody but Brenner."

"Good. What happened?"

"Before we start again, I'm thirsty," Francie announced. "Would anyone like some coffee or a soft drink?"

"Coffee for me," Clay said. Several officers nodded.

"Tamara?" Francie asked and couldn't help grinning

when she had to ask again. Tamara's attention had been totally on Bill.

Francie excused herself to make the coffee as the redhead said, "I had just come home from the shop, and Kevin came up behind me as I opened the door." She then launched into her tale.

Clay followed Francie into the kitchen and took some cups from the cabinet while she fixed the coffee. "So what did you do to Brenner?" he asked in a low voice. "I was thinking about popping a light ball in his face, but then his nose seemed to catch fire. I know that wasn't my spell."

"I'm not sure what happened," Francie replied in a whisper. "I was so furious with him, and my anger made me feel hot. Then I started thinking about the spell you tried to teach me, and my center began to tingle, and then it got hot, really hot, and it felt like something inside me was trying to get out. So I said, '*Flamma!*' and pointed at his nose. And this flame appeared! I don't think I've ever been so shocked in my life." Her center itched, and she rubbed it. "Now it's bothering me again."

Clay stared at her with a speculative look. "Darlin', we have to get you tested. I think you may just have become a practitioner."

"What? From the First Mating? But I thought it was impossible."

"No, it's probably just never been recorded as happening before. We'll talk to Daria and my mother.

They'll know what to do."

Francie looked at him helplessly. She was flabbergasted. One minute she didn't believe in magic, the
next, she could make it happen. As if to punctuate that
thought, her center vibrated, and happiness seemed to
spread throughout her body. All she could do was shake
her head.

"Come on, the coffee's done," Clay prompted her.
"We'll talk it through later."

Francie nodded and busied herself with the mugs.

The police finally took Brenner off to the hospital,
and Bill walked Tamara back to her apartment. The
neighbors who had come out to investigate the hullaba-
loo also departed.

Francie shut the door and turned into Clay's arms.
They hugged for a long moment, until Francie took a
deep breath and leaned away from him. "Thank you,"
she said.

"For what?"

"For being here when we needed you."

"Francie, you and Tamara didn't need me." He
started laughing. "I thought she was going to kill the
son of a bitch, and that was a mean body blow you gave
him, not to mention setting his nose on fire. He's lucky
I was here to save him."

Francie had to join in his laughter at that last claim.

"Now," Clay said, "let's get this place cleaned up and
decide what we're going to do about dinner. I'm starved,

and it looks like Tamara has other plans."

Francie mopped the entryway tiles, washing away the smears left by Kevin's bloody nose, while Clay put the coffee cups in the dishwasher and rinsed out the pot. When she had replaced the cleaning utensils in the closet, she turned to him. "Let's get out of here."

"I agree. Throw what you need for tonight in a bag. We'll go to my place and order pizza."

Within ten minutes, they were on their way.

*   *   *

At Clay's they ate and then called Daria and Bent. Both couples switched on their speakerphones. Clay explained what had happened, including the multicolored light show, his attempt to teach Francie the spell, and her successful casting of it against Brenner.

"Lights?" Daria said.

"A rainbow?" Bent asked.

"Yeah," Clay replied. "Around us when we kiss."

"I don't remember lights, do you, Bent?"

"Neither do I," Bent said, "but I do remember 'internal fireworks,' so to speak. Remember the first time we touched each other's magic center?"

"Oh, that's right," Daria said. "Have you two tried it yet?"

"Yeah, but it was internal *and* external fireworks for us." Clay grinned at a blushing Francie.

"This is embarrassing," Francie whispered to him. She hoped he wouldn't go into any more details.

"It'll be okay," he whispered back and kissed the back of her hand he was holding. "You know," he continued in a normal voice, "that particular instance may be the moment when Francie actually became a practitioner, when she received the true enhancement from the First Mating. She couldn't cast *flamma* before it. I know because I tried to teach her the spell. Her ability to see my spell aura—like you, Bent, can see Daria's—could be just a secondary enhancement."

"Man," Bent said with a wistful note in his voice, "I'd really have liked to have seen Brenner's nose go up in flames."

"Clay," Daria interjected in a worried tone, "you tried to teach her the spell *by yourself*?"

"Yeah, well, I thought we'd see if she had gained the ability. Wishful thinking at that point, but it paid off later." He shrugged at Francie.

She thought he looked very smug and sure of himself, but she had nothing to add to his statement. He was correct.

"Whatever else, Francie, you must be tested and quickly," Daria said. "When I was undergoing all my magic studies, and the master teachers were trying to help me cast *flamma*, the one thing they all impressed on me was that an untrained practitioner is dangerous, both to herself and others. Don't try to cast it again by yourself, or even with Clay. I saw novices with the power to burn down a building."

Remembering Clay's nonchalance about her attempt on his deck, Francie looked at him with consternation. "A building? Clay, we could have set fire to your house."

He just shrugged. "I have a fire extinguisher."

"So, what should I do next?" Francie asked after rolling her eyes at him. "I'm not even sure I can cast it again. And the thought I have become a practitioner is throwing me for a loop."

"I'm going to take her to the HeatherRidge here," Clay told Daria and Bent. "Francie, that's a center for practitioners where we study and there are master teachers who can test and train you. We have them all over the country."

"Clay, we've got to tell Mother and Daddy," Daria said. "You both are going to need them. Think of what will happen when you march into the HeatherRidge and announce that a nonpractitioner has become one of us with a First Mating."

"What?" Francie asked. "What will happen?"

"Oh, holy hell," Clay said. "It will be a three-ring circus."

"*What?*" Francie said, her voice climbing.

"Don't worry, Francie," Daria said. "Practitioners all demand privacy. Mother will run interference with anybody who tries to invade yours. But I'd tell our parents soon."

"Francie has the week off, so we'll probably go see them in a couple of days."

Francie opened her mouth to protest all these plans being decided for her, but Clay stopped her words with a kiss.

"It will be all right," he murmured. Turning to the phone, he spoke into the microphone. "Listen, you two, thanks for the help. We'll keep you apprised of events."

"You'd better, big brother," Daria said. "And Francie? We're glad you're Clay's soul mate."

"Thanks," Francie said faintly. "I am, too."

"Bye," Clay said and punched the button to hang up the phone. He rose and held out his hand. "Let's go to bed, darlin'. We can worry about all this in the morning."

CHAPTER THIRTY-TWO

Francie was probably exhausted, Clay thought as they walked into the bedroom. She looked a little shell-shocked, and he certainly couldn't blame her. He wasn't in the greatest shape himself.

He wondered if she accepted the fact that she had become a practitioner. Probably not, given her resistance to the whole idea of magic at first. She had, however, evidently accepted that they were soul mates. Thank God.

He took her into his arms. He wanted nothing more right this minute than to make love with her, renew their bond, cement their seal. He looked into her eyes and saw the smoke turn to flame. "Ah, Francie," he murmured, "let's set off some fireworks." And he kissed her.

They undressed each other slowly, taking the time to linger with a touch, a rub, a slide of the hand or body. She lay down on the bed, and he joined her, propping himself up on an elbow and running his hand over her shoulder, around to cup a breast briefly, then down over her hip and thigh and back up to her breast again. "You are so beautiful," he whispered as he flicked the nipple with his thumb and slid his top leg between hers.

"So are you." She pressed one hand to his center and used the other to pull his head down for a kiss.

Lights began to play around them as he deepened the kiss and pressed into her magic center with his thumb while the rest of his hand held her breast. He could feel himself hardening, his muscles heating, his cock reaching for her. The desire, the need, the all-encompassing satisfaction running through him when she was in his arms made him want to shout with joy. His, she was his.

They still had to talk, settle some issues, like when she was going to move in, but it could wait. He knew his self-confidence drove her crazy, and he vowed to try to be a little more humble. How could he not in the face of their overwhelming feelings and need for each other? But that could wait also. He had another task at the moment: making love to his soul mate. He turned her to face him, pulled her top leg over his, and slid into her hot, wet, tight sheath—right where he was meant to be.

Francie let out the breath she had been holding when he thrust all the way in. Everything, the mess with Kevin, her own transformation into a practitioner, the need to talk with Clay about their future, every serious subject floated away as she filled with a rainbow of lights, overarching delight, a distinct easing in her heart—was it possible to have peace of heart as well as mind?—and him. He possessed her, all of her, as she possessed him. It was glorious, utterly glorious, and she gave herself over to him.

With arms wrapped tightly around each other and their centers touching, chest to chest, they made slow, enthralling love to each other.

She felt her body tightening as his thrusts reached her womb and he pressed tightly, further stimulating the nub of nerve endings at the entrance to her core. He wouldn't be hurried, though, and he grasped her hips when she tried, holding her to an excruciatingly deliberate pace.

"Easy, darlin'," he said against her lips, his voice deep and low. "We'll get there." And he resumed their kiss and his thrusts.

Just as Francie thought she'd burst from the internal pressure, her center seemed to catch fire. A corresponding blaze emanated from Clay's chest, and it spread through their bodies, finally engulfing them in a dazzling incandescence echoed in the sparkling rainbow around them.

Minutes passed as they held each other afterward, waiting for their hearts and lungs to return to a normal pace. Eventually they were able to pull back enough to see each other's eyes.

Francie couldn't hold it in any longer. She looked in his eyes and said, "I love you, Clay."

He grinned and gave her a small kiss. "Of course, you do. We're soul mates."

"Well?" she raised her eyebrows at him. He was still an overconfident, arrogant male, but she wasn't going to let him get away with it this time.

"Well, what?" He was still grinning.

"Do *you* love *me*?" She poked him in the ribs with a finger to emphasize the *you*.

"Of course, I love you. We're soul mates." He kept grinning. "We just proved it. I know," he said in the face of her frown, "I need to say it more often. Daria gave me hell for not saying the words when I told you about practitioners."

"At least one of the Morgans has good sense," she stated, punctuating the comment with another poke to his rib cage.

He started laughing and captured her hand before she could do any more damage. "Francie, I promise I'll say it to you every day of our lives. At least once. Probably more. I love you." He kissed her tenderly.

"I love you, too," she responded and kissed him back. "And if you don't fulfill your promise, I'll set your nose on fire."

"Oh, darlin', didn't I tell you? Soul mates can't affect each other with spells, except for healing and defense."

"Your sisters said something about that, but I'd forgotten. How disappointing," she pouted, then slitted her eyes at him in warning. "But I'll think of something."

"I'm sure you will. That you can cast *flamma* reminds me of something else. What do you think about being a practitioner?"

She looked at him blankly for a moment as she tried to force her mind around the concept. "I don't know. It's not real to me yet. I don't know how I put a spark on the end of Kevin's nose. I don't know if I can do it again. Whatever I did could have been caused by the stress of the moment. I do feel different from the way I felt before I came over here yesterday, but my being somewhat 'unsettled' could all be caused by our being soul mates."

"That's my Francie, still needing to experience the proof with your own eyes. We'll have you tested. I think you did become one of us, and I'm really looking forward to telling my parents. They'd love you anyway, but this will be the star on the top of the wizard's hat." He gave her a big grin and a hug.

Then he grew serious. "Now, the way I see it, we have some decisions to make. First, when you're moving in here with me. Second, when we're getting married. And third . . ." He was silent for a few seconds, " . . . I can't think of a third."

She contemplated the earnest expression on his face. He'd made statements, not asked questions. He was going to have to realize she'd only put up with so much of that, and now was a good time to convince him of it. "Wait just a minute, Clay. First, I haven't been *asked* to do either. Second, you shouldn't assume you can always have your way."

His face had fallen with her words, but he rallied quickly. "Francie, will you marry me?"

"Yes, I will."

"When?"

"After I meet your parents and you meet mine and I take these tests you mentioned."

"But that'll take several weeks," he complained.

"It will also give us time to plan the wedding. I know Tamara will want to help with my gown, and she'll be my maid of honor, and we have to find a place, and send out invitations, and . . ."

"Enough! I give in! We'll do all of it, and I'll be patient—somehow—and stop making assumptions. Just do one thing for me, will you? Move in with me now. Or I'll move in with you. Whatever, as long as we're not apart."

"I want us together, too," she agreed.

He relaxed with a sigh. "Answer just one more question for me. Do you believe in magic?"

"Oh, yes," she breathed. "And love is the best kind."

❧✦✱✦❧

Also available by Ann Macela:

THE OLDEST KIND OF MAGIC

PROLOGUE

Black. Windless. Soundless. Odorless. Empty.

Not cold, not hot. Not hard, not soft.

Definitely not "just right."

Where was she?

In a cave? A huge building without any windows? Another plane of existence?

Apprehension stiffened her backbone as a wave of malevolence swept over her.

Someone or something threatened. Was she in danger? Was someone else?

Who threatened? Where was it?

She'd cast *lux*, that's what she'd do. A ball of light would be of great benefit in this situation.

"*Lux!*" she said, clapping her hands.

Nothing happened.

"*Lux!*" This time she snapped her fingers.

Same result.

What was the matter with her? Why couldn't she cast a simple spell?

Oh, that's right. She had never been able to spell anything except herself.

What was she going to do? The threat grew stronger.

The blackness around her faded to a pale monochromatic hue.

She could see! She could see . . .

Nothing—just a dim grayness.

She brought her hands up in front of her eyes. At least she could see her fingers wiggling.

She looked forward, then back. The expanse yawned in all directions. She still couldn't make out any walls, any edges to the space.

She revolved in a slow arc.

As she reached the three-quarter point in her revolution, a long elevated stage materialized in the middle distance, and she walked toward it over a gray stone floor. She knew she was walking, she could feel her muscles moving and her feet striking the surface, but her footsteps were silent.

As she got closer to the structure, some human figures appeared on the stage. A ramp grew out of the raised platform and the people walked down it toward her.

She felt the menace intensify as the figures came closer. Cold fear washed through her body, tried to overcome her. She refused to give into it. She could defend herself.

Someone appeared at her side. A man. Tall with blue eyes, he looked down at her and smiled. He was not there to hurt her, she knew, she felt it in her bones. He was there to help.

The intimidating figures changed from human to monsters and were almost upon them. She could see their gleaming fangs and scent their noxious, dead-fish odor.

She had to do something. Who did these creatures think they were, fooling around with her? Hot anger drove out the fear; she gathered every little bit of magic in her and cast the most powerful spells she could devise.

Lightning cracked, thunder rolled, fire flashed. A roar vibrated the air, and the ground shook.

Nothing changed.

The creatures still advanced, clawed hands now reaching for her and her companion.

She cast again and again, until she was exhausted.

It did no good.

The blue-eyed man beside her did nothing. Evidently, he was having the same problems she was.

The beasts were upon them. She could see their crazed yellow eyes, smell their foul breath, sense their vile hatred.

She could feel their sharp claws, and she jerked away from them, frantically fighting the amorphous shroud they had thrown over her.

"No, no!" she screamed, but her voice sounded only like a whimper.

She opened her eyes and stared straight into a yellow-eyed face with long sharp fangs.

"Mrrrow?" her male cat asked as he pushed at her arm with his paw. His claw was caught in her nightshirt.

"Yaahh?" asked the female from her other side.

"Oh, for heaven's sake," Daria groaned as the tension drained from her body and her muscles went limp with relief. After a long moment to let her heartbeat return to normal, she stirred. "Okay, I'm awake," she told the cats, disentangling herself from the sheet and the claw.

She reclined on her pillow for a moment. What a dream. Threatening monsters, a black cave, a man, and she couldn't cast a spell to save them. She ran her hands through her hair and rubbed her scalp.

Where had all that come from? What was going on in her subconscious to cause such a dream?

The job, probably. Something about this last client was bothering her and appearing in her dreams. Only a few more days and it would be over. Thank God. Did she ever need a vacation.

"Come on," she told the cats as she climbed out of bed. "Let's get some breakfast."

By the time she reached the kitchen, she was in control of herself again and couldn't for the life of her remember what the dream had been about. But the memory of the blue, blue eyes of the man who had stood beside her lingered for a much longer time.

THE OLDEST KIND OF MAGIC
ANN MACELA
ISBN#9781932815436
US $6.99 / CDN $9.99
Mass Market Paperback / Paranormal
Available Now
www.annmacela.com

For more information
about other great titles from
Medallion Press, visit

www.medallionpress.com